T0385357

HOLLOW GRAVE

Also by Kate Webb

HOLLOW GRAVE

KATE WEBB

QUERCUS

First published in Great Britain in 2025 by

QUERCUS

Quercus Editions Ltd
Carmelite House
50 Victoria Embankment
London EC4Y 0DZ

An Hachette UK company

The authorised representative in the EEA is Hachette Ireland,
8 Castlecourt Centre, Dublin 15, D15 XTP3, Ireland (email: info@hbgi.ie)

A CIP catalogue record for this book is available
from the British Library

HB ISBN 978 1 5294 3 353 1
EB ISBN 978 1 5294 3 354 8

2

Typeset by CC Book Production
Printed and bound in Great Britain by Clays Ltd, Elcograf S.p.A.

Papers used by Quercus are from well-managed forests and other responsible sources.

1

Day 1, Monday

DI Matt Lockyer rang the bell of a neat, terraced house in Keynsham, near Bristol. DC Gemma Broad was at his side, and he could tell she was tense. They both knew this wasn't going to be easy.

The door was opened by a woman in her sixties, with faded auburn hair and a polite smile.

'Hello,' she said, peering to see their faces behind the visors they were required to wear.

'Mrs Kirmani?'

'Yes?'

They showed their ID, and her smile vanished.

'I'm Detective Inspector Lockyer, and this is Detective Constable Broad,' Lockyer said.

She swallowed. 'Have you found her?'

'No. I understood a colleague of ours had called to—'

'Yes, of course,' she said. 'I just thought— Sorry. Come in. I'll fetch my husband.'

She led them through to a sitting room, the decor dated but comfortable. A shelf above the gas fire held photographs of grinning kids and wedding anniversaries, the framed portrait of a girl with flawless skin and beautiful dark brown eyes, wearing a graduation cap and clutching a scroll. Lockyer had seen it before: one of many the Kirmanis had provided when their daughter disappeared. As though more photos made it more likely she'd be found. In every one, a silver necklace hung around the girl's neck. A locket, engraved with tiny stars. Lockyer stared at it.

When Mrs Kirmani returned she kept her distance, judiciously opening a window to let the cold, damp air pour in. The November sky was flat grey, and drizzle blurred the view of identical houses outside.

'Do sit down,' she said, as her husband followed her into the room.

He looked a little older than her, and of Asian heritage. A small man, taking short steps. The stoop of his shoulders spoke of a burden he'd carried for a very long time. His eyes were sunken, tinged with grey; there were deep brackets in his cheeks either side of his mouth. If he'd ever had any hope of seeing his daughter again, Lockyer suspected it had died some time ago.

'How may we help you?' he said, in a solemn, courteous way.

'Mr Kirmani, thank you for seeing us,' Lockyer said. 'As you know, a bag we believe may have belonged to your daughter has recently been found in the River Kennet, a few miles east of Marlborough.'

The older man nodded, but said: 'I do not think it belonged to Nazma.'

'Some children found it, we were told?' Mrs Kirmani said.

'That's right. They realized it could be important and showed it to their parents.'

'They shouldn't have been playing by a river,' she murmured. 'It must be deep at this time of year.'

Mr Kirmani patted her clasped hands, though whether to comfort or forestall her, Lockyer couldn't tell.

'I agree, but in this instance, I'm glad they were,' Lockyer said. 'Mr Kirmani, what makes you think the bag didn't belong to your daughter?'

'I never saw Nazma with this bag. It looks like a man's bag. The clothes could have belonged to any person – it's impossible to say what they looked like, originally.'

He was right. Twenty-one years in the muddy bank of the River Kennet had rotted the garments to shreds. But four half-moons of rusty wire remained, proving that at least two bras had been inside. Lockyer chose not to mention them just then.

'And the money,' Mr Kirmani went on, 'why should she have money like that? Cash, rolled up, like a . . . *criminal*?'

'Her passport and rail card could have been stolen,' Mrs Kirmani added. 'That's more likely, isn't it? That somebody stole them – and the money – then tried to get rid of it all. Or lost it.'

No one would deliberately ditch a hundred and seventy pounds in cash, least of all a thief, but Lockyer understood why the Kirmanis didn't want the Nike duffel bag to have been their daughter's. Clothes, cash, railcard, passport: it was obviously an escape bag.

Lockyer gave Broad a slight nod, and she cleared her throat quietly. 'We found something else in the bag, and were hoping you might be able to identify it for us?'

She brought out a small plastic evidence bag. Inside it, metal gleamed dully through a layer of tarnish. A locket, engraved with tiny stars, on a silver chain. Broad set it on the coffee-table and retreated, and Mrs Kirmani reached for it.

'Oh . . .' she whispered, grasping her husband's arm.

Mr Kirmani took it, his brows drawing down. He sagged a little more as he fumbled the plastic in his fingers.

'Please don't open the bag,' Broad said. 'I'm sorry. It's unlikely that we'll retrieve any forensic evidence after so long in the water, but we can try.'

Mr Kirmani nodded. 'But you have opened the necklace? You have looked inside?'

'We have,' Lockyer said.

The older man shut his eyes for a moment, taking a deep breath.

'A small plait of hair, and a photograph?'

'Yes.'

Just a few rotted strands of hair in fact, and the photograph had all but vanished. Only a tiny, colourless scrap remained. The passport, cash and student rail card had been in a plastic Ziploc wallet, which had accidentally preserved them, but the necklace had been found in the side pocket of the duffel bag. Not packed away carefully, just dropped in, like an afterthought. Or as though someone had been in a hurry.

There was a hung moment. The evidence bag trembled in Mr Kirmani's fingers, and tears welled in his wife's eyes.

'Is this your daughter's necklace?' Broad asked them quietly.

'Yes,' Mrs Kirmani said, when her husband didn't speak. 'It's Nazma's and her mother's hair plaited together ... Hari's first wife, Amrit. She died when Nazma was only little. They made the locket together so that Nazma would always have her mother near. The photograph was of her – of Amrit.'

Lockyer heard no trace of bitterness in Mrs Kirmani's voice. Only sadness.

'So this necklace was dear to Nazma?' he said.

'She never took it off. Well – only to go swimming or to shower. She wouldn't have lost it. Or left it anywhere.'

'It seems unlikely to me that three items we know belonged to Nazma would be in a bag if that bag hadn't belonged to her,' Lockyer said carefully.

'But . . . I *said*,' Mr Kirmani began, after a sudden snatched breath. 'I said from the very start, she did not run away! My Nazma would not do such a thing to us, to her family!'

'You were close?'

'Of *course* we were close!'

'Hari,' Mrs Kirmani said softly, 'they have to ask.'

'They ask, but they do not *listen*! Twenty-one years ago they asked, "Why would she run away? What reason would she have? Were you a close family?" And I said, "She would not!" I said, "She had no reason! There was no bad blood between us." But they did not *listen*.'

'We're very sorry,' Broad said. 'There seemed to be good reasons to believe that Nazma had simply . . . started over, somewhere new.'

'But this is nonsense,' Mr Kirmani said. He held up the locket. 'This *shows* it is nonsense. She packed this bag, you say. She ran away, you say. Why then was it in the river, all these years? And her most precious possession. Why would she throw it away?'

'She wouldn't,' Lockyer agreed quietly.

There was fury as well as grief in the old man's eyes. 'Had she disappointed me, they asked. Had she offended our *religion*? I said, would they ask that of a white family? Hm? Or only of a Pakistani family?'

Lockyer didn't reply. But he felt the shame of it.

'I told them: "We are just a normal family. She was happy and cared for. Always smiling . . ."' His voice broke. 'She loved her job, and she came at the weekends to see us, and her brother. She did not "resent her stepmother", and she loved Andrew. That she should just *go*, and never tell us . . .' He shook his head emphatically. 'She would never do that. She *would not*.' He jabbed one index finger into the palm of his other hand for emphasis.

'Mr Kirmani—'

'And where was her face in the papers? Where was her name on the *Crimewatch* programme on the telly? It was not there. Because she is a Pakistani girl with brown skin, not a white girl with pretty blonde hair. No "reconstructions of last movements" for Nazma, no rewards, no appeals.' Mr Kirmani's face was ravaged. 'My daughter was taken, and it was simply . . . *allowed* to happen.'

In the chasm after these words, his uneven breathing was the only sound.

Lockyer tried to imagine all those years of pain, of not knowing, of believing the worst and not being heard. Of having so little information that you were forced to speculate on the final moments of the missing – and there being no limit to the horrors the mind might suggest to fill that void. He could barely comprehend how hard it must be to endure.

He also felt the terrible significance of a potential police failure of that scale.

He glanced at Broad. Time to go. They got to their feet.

Nazma's father looked up. 'So, what will you do?'

'We will review every last piece of evidence into Nazma's disappearance,' Lockyer said evenly. 'And we will do *whatever* we can to discover what happened to her.'

'Thank you,' Mrs Kirmani said.

Her husband managed only to nod, turning his face away. Men of his generation were often ashamed to show their feelings, but not this man. Pain had pushed him past any such pride.

'Can we keep her necklace?'

'I'm sorry, Mrs Kirmani. It will be returned to you, but not while the investigation is ongoing. Thank you for talking to us. We'll see ourselves out.'

*

They hurried out to Lockyer's solid old Volvo, heads bowed against the rain. Sat for a moment listening to it patter on the roof. *My daughter was taken.* It happened all too often: women and girls vanished on their way home from work, or from the shops or the pub. While they were out jogging or walking the dog. Grainy CCTV images of them appeared in the press. Eyewitness statements gave conflicting accounts of their movements, their demeanour, who they were with. Then nothing. Silence. The case going cold, sometimes permanently. The failure – of the victim, of their family – was a heavy load to carry, and this one had just been handed to Lockyer and Broad. Wiltshire Police's two-person Major Crime Review team. But along with it, just maybe, came the chance to catch a hidden killer.

'Do you think he's right?' Broad asked. 'Do you think her disappearance wasn't given as much attention because she wasn't white?'

'It still happens now, Gem. You can bet your life it happened back then.'

'And less of an effort made to investigate? Because of her race?'

Lockyer considered it. 'However much I hate it, it's likely. But there *were* good reasons for the investigation to conclude she'd run away. And we need to scrutinize every one of those reasons.'

'So you believe the Kirmanis – that she wouldn't have left without a word?'

'She was planning on going *somewhere*, the escape bag tells us that. But even if she made good on that plan, how the hell did that bag – containing her passport *and* her most treasured possession – end up dumped in the river just a few miles from where she was last seen?' He squinted out at the drizzle as he started the car. 'And, yes, I did believe them.'

'Yeah. Me too.'

They spoke little on the drive back to Devizes. Broad had been quieter of late, generally, and definitely since the announcement of another impending lockdown. Lockyer had asked before, but he asked again now: 'Everything okay, Gem?'

She looked across with a tiny start, as though he'd pulled her from deep thought. 'Yep, course,' she said.

She was a useless liar, but Lockyer didn't push her. He'd always firmly believed that if someone wanted to talk about something they'd do so of their own accord. Still, he wished he knew a way to reach out that wouldn't just embarrass them both.

'How's Hedy? And the bump?' Broad asked, changing the subject to one Lockyer absolutely did not wish to discuss.

'Fine,' he said.

It was the second of November. In three days' time, the whole country was going back into lockdown, as Covid-19 infection rates surged, and hospitals teetered on the edge of overwhelm. Lockyer knew that the final few weeks of Hedy's pregnancy were going to be fractious. Her blood pressure was high and she'd been told to rest when, increasingly, all he sensed in her was restlessness. An impatience that went beyond simply having to stay at home. It made him think he was kidding himself about their future together.

Broad knew him well enough not to push on this topic, either.

'Mr Kirmani was actually brought in for questioning,' she said, reading from the file.

'As a suspect?'

'Person of interest. They didn't go that hard on him but, clearly, the theory was that it could've been some kind of honour killing, or that they'd been planning to ship her back to Pakistan for an arranged marriage, and Nazma had run away instead.'

'An arranged marriage? When Mr Kirmani chose a white British woman as his own second wife?'

'Yeah. The theory fell apart when Mr Kirmani pointed out that he isn't even Muslim.' Broad looked across at him. 'He's Anglican. Been going to Sunday services at St John's in Keynsham for decades – as the vicar was more than happy to confirm.'

'Christ's sake,' Lockyer muttered, staring out at the road. 'So he can hardly be blamed for claiming that the police saw a Pakistani first and a worried father second.'

'Seems that way,' Broad said gravely. 'I mean, they ditched the honour-killing theory pretty quickly, but still. Damage done, I imagine.'

'How long has Kirmani been in the UK?'

Broad turned back a few pages. 'Hari and Amrit moved here as newlyweds in 1973, from Lahore. Nazma was born in 1975. Then there was another little girl, who died shortly after she was born. Amrit died from a congenital heart condition in 1982, when Nazma was seven years old. Two years later Hari Kirmani married Liz, née Stokes, and their son Andrew – Nazma's half-brother – was born in 1985. Apparently Andrew and Nazma were very close, in spite of the age gap. Nazma had just turned twenty-four when she disappeared. Same age as me. Andrew was fourteen.'

'Was the brother ever brought in? Questioned?'

'No. Nor Liz,' Broad said. 'They were checked, but there was nothing to suggest any of the family was involved. But, then, it wasn't long before Nazma came off the misper list altogether.'

'Right.'

If Nazma *had* been taken against her will, Lockyer wondered at what point the perpetrator had started to relax. How long had it been before they'd realized the police weren't coming for them?

'We're coming for you now,' he muttered under his breath.

Back in their poky third-floor office at Wiltshire Police HQ, in Devizes, Broad had stuck detailed photographs of the contents of the Nike bag on their white board. Lockyer studied the stained remnants of the clothing. The natural fibres had rotted away, leaving only bits and pieces behind: the nylon care labels; the wire from the bras; five brass buttons from a pair of Levi's jeans. One T-shirt, with a high polyester content, had fared slightly better than the rest. A section of the neckline and back had survived. Careful cleaning showed it had been yellow, originally, a size L, with a section of printed text that appeared to be a list of dates. Perhaps band tour merchandize. Nazma had been five foot two and under eight stone, but women often wore oversized T-shirts to relax in.

Broad selected Nazma's graduation photo from the file and pinned it to the board alongside the others. She had a lovely smile. There was nothing cynical about it. She had a slight dimple in each cheek; long, lustrous black hair. She'd been graduating with a degree in archaeology and anthropology from Exeter University. Afterwards, she'd stayed on to do a master's, and had just started a PhD when she vanished.

'So,' Lockyer said, and, again, Broad gave that little start, 'let's go through the basics. As part of her PhD, Nazma had been working on an excavation at Avebury, with a group of archaeologists from . . . What was it?'

'Brittonic Archaeological Services,' Broad said, checking it in the paperwork.

'Right. And it was quite a big deal – it was being filmed for the *Dig Britain* show, which aired on Channel 4. The excavation wound up at the end of September. On the evening of Saturday the second of October, Nazma went to the Marlborough Mop, with a group of colleagues, to celebrate. She left the others to find a toilet and never came back. Sent a text to one of the group saying she'd had enough and was getting a taxi home. Which was unexpected, apparently.'

'Police tried to trace the taxi driver?'

'Yep. Spoke to all the licensed cabbies in Marlborough. No joy. But it could have been unlicensed. Traffic-camera coverage wasn't great back then.'

In silence, they stared at the smiling young woman in

the photograph. Police Headquarters was quiet, half empty. Covid had forced the workforce to spread out as much as possible, into their own homes or reopened old police buildings, so the sprawling brick building they were in had an eerie hush.

'I've been to the Mop a couple of times,' Broad said. 'A group of us from the sixth form used to go, until my parents realized what it was like. I mean, it's basically a massive drunken riot. There's all the funfair rides and candy-floss and whatever, but the pubs stay open all along the high street. I remember lot of pissed people – a lot of *underage* pissed people. And probably a lot of drugs changing hands – not that I had a clue about that at the time.' She gave him a sideways glance. 'I'm surprised you've never been, guv. Growing up nearby, and being such a party animal.'

'Ha-ha.' Lockyer pulled a face. He'd always hated crowds, especially drunken ones. 'That was more my brother's line,' he murmured. His younger brother, Chris, had been to the Mop a few times and always come back the worse for wear. Even though he'd died the night it had actually become legal for him to drink.

Broad nodded awkwardly, pulled up by any mention of Chris. One more unsolved murder case. One that Lockyer carried with him, each and every day.

'Which brings us to the single verified sighting of Nazma *after* that evening,' Lockyer said. 'The sighting that made the police stop looking for her.'

Broad went back to her desk, found another photograph and put it up on the board. It was a grainy capture from security-camera footage, taken at the front desk of Islington police station and faxed to the SIO in Wiltshire at the time. The camera was angled to give a good view of whoever was standing at the desk, but the young woman in the footage was wearing a cap, and kept her chin down. There was the long dark hair, the slight build. The angle of the jaw looked right, as did the gently rounded cheekbone, but the shadow of the cap hid her eyes and nose.

'That's the best shot they could get?' Lockyer said.

'Yeah. But the desk sergeant was satisfied that this *was* Nazma Kirmani. She presented a wallet containing her bank cards and driving licence as proof of ID. Said she'd come in because she'd heard the police were concerned for her well-being. She said she was fine, and not in any trouble,' Broad said.

'When was that?'

'Friday, the eighth of October. Six days after she was last seen in Marlborough.'

'So that, coupled with the text messages, shut the investigation down.'

'Understandable, I suppose,' Broad said.

It was. The precipitous way in which Nazma had left meant she'd been categorized as high risk to begin with, but it was pure luck – and most likely an oversight – that the scanty file hadn't been binned since then. It contained the original form-nine missing-person report, which had been compiled by a DS Brodzki, giving details of where Nazma was last seen, what she'd been wearing, the places they'd checked, and who'd been spoken to regarding her whereabouts. There was a phoned-in witness statement from a street vendor, who thought he'd seen her in Marlborough that night and, tantalizingly, an entry regarding a sample of soil from a shoe print collected from the barn at Trusloe Hall. No further details, so Lockyer supposed they hadn't got as far as actually analysing it. Forensic work like that would have been done in-house back then. Lockyer didn't like their chances of ever finding the sample now.

'No record of the contents of her text messages,' Lockyer murmured. 'Or what she might have been running from.'

'No. Or *to*,' Broad pointed out. 'I mean, she might have been running *towards* something, as much as away. Something she didn't think her family would approve of. Or understand.'

'True.'

He reflected on Hari Kirmani's terrible certainty that harm had come to his child, and that the police had given up far too easily. He was determined not to do the same thing.

'Then again,' Broad said, 'if she ran, why didn't she take her emergency bag? And if she was fine and texting a friend, then why not text her parents? Or her brother?'

'Well, perhaps they were the problem. But it's entirely possible that they just didn't have mobiles in 1999,' Lockyer said.

Broad blinked – the mental gear-shifting of someone her age imagining a time before mobile phones. 'I'm guessing no tracking info was gathered from Nazma's phone?' she said.

'That was in its infancy, Gem. And, besides, why would they bother, after she'd texted a mate and presented herself at a police station?'

'If that *is* her in the picture.'

'It looks like her. And she had her wallet, her driving licence,' Lockyer said.

'Is that what you think, then?' The question was almost an accusation.

Lockyer took his time to answer. *No reconstructions of final movements. No appeals or rewards.* 'I don't think anything yet.' He tapped the photo from the CCTV. 'But if that *is* her, and she did just leave, we can assume she's still alive. She'd be in her mid-forties now. Probably using an assumed name, if she really did want to disappear. So, let's find her. We can start with the friend she texted in the days *after* she left Marlborough. Her flatmate. What's her name?'

Broad checked. 'Emma Billingham.'

'See if you can track her down. I'm going to try to find out who was on the desk at Islington nick the day Nazma supposedly walked in.'

He stared at the grainy picture – the woman in the cap, keeping her face down. Looked back and forth between that image and the smiling graduation portrait. The photos *could* be of the same person but it wasn't conclusive. And if they weren't, then the woman who'd gone to Islington police station was an unknown player. Someone who, for some reason, had wanted the police to stop looking for Nazma. And it had worked.

2

The track leading to the pair of isolated cottages where Lockyer lived was already pocked with muddy puddles, before winter had even started. A light was on in the front room of the left-hand cottage, home to Iris Musprat, his elderly neighbour. Lockyer waited until he caught a glimpse of movement inside. At some point he couldn't recall, he had begun to keep watch – that her lights were switched off and on, her curtains opened and closed, her goat let out of its rickety stall in the morning and put in again at night. If the TV didn't come blaring through the party wall in the evening, he caught himself listening for other sounds of life.

Iris was as much of a loner as Lockyer, and far more prickly. It had taken a long time for her to decide to trust him, so it'd come as a surprise how readily she'd taken to Hedy.

'Yours, is it?' she'd said to him, when she first noticed the bump.

'Yes, mine,' he'd replied. She'd given a single ambiguous nod, possibly of understanding and acceptance, possibly of disgruntlement. Since then, she'd called around more often, bringing strange mixtures and gifts for Hedy, or for the baby. And she told Lockyer, regularly, what he should and shouldn't be doing.

Yes, mine. It still jarred him every time he remembered. Every time he saw Hedy. Maybe it was fright. Disbelief, joy, anger. Hard to say. Neither Lockyer nor Hedy liked to raise their voice. Their fights were so quietly intense that they charged the air, like an incoming storm. These days, he opened the front door with a palpable tightening inside. Sometimes he missed the solitude of before.

'Hedy?' he called. From somewhere inside came the chatter of a radio.

'Up here.'

He found her in the spare room, kneeling on the floor, halfway through assembling a chest of drawers. Screwdriver in one hand, sheet of instructions in the other, a look of pure fury on her face.

'Don't say a word,' she warned him.

The baby seemed to be stealing from her: as it grew, she got thinner. There were hollows beneath her cheekbones and collarbones; her arms were stick-like, her eyes huge.

She glared up at him. 'I *refuse* for this to be beyond me.'

Lockyer felt a stab of helpless love. 'Hedy, flatpack furniture is designed to raise your blood pressure.'

He held out his hands, and after a moment's hesitation, she let him pull her to her feet, where she swayed, adjusting her balance. Her hands went to the bump as soon as she was steady, with the small frown he so often saw.

'Bastard thing,' she muttered, chucking the instructions onto a pile of slats and bags of washers and bolts.

'I'll finish it later,' he said. 'You're supposed to be resting.'

'If I do much more resting, I'll go completely mental,' she said. 'Can we please get a TV?'

'As soon as there's a TV all you'll want to do is watch it. I don't even miss it any more.'

'You want to watch it because it's *entertaining*. Seriously. This is worse than prison.'

'Won't be too much longer,' he said.

'You said that about my last sentence, too. But it feels like years.'

With a sigh, she went to the window and peered out at the darkening evening, the sodden trees in their autumn brown. Again, he sensed her powerful need to escape. The one that made him nervous. The baby had about five weeks to go.

'Mrs Musprat came round earlier, with the most revolting concoction,' she said. 'Wouldn't go until I'd drunk it.'

'Please tell me you didn't?'

She shrugged. 'I think it was mostly castor oil. And we still don't have a cot, by the way.'

'I told you I was taking care of that,' he said.

'So *mysterious*.'

'Pot, kettle.'

She'd always been hard to read; possessed of admirable self-control, and a kind of stillness that often left him at a loss, unable to guess her thoughts. But he also remembered visiting her in prison before he'd managed to clear her name. How desperate she'd been to be free, to rebuild some kind of a life. To have a family of her own. He guessed an accidental pregnancy with the detective who'd put her away in the first place wasn't exactly what she'd dreamt of. She wanted the baby: that much was completely clear. He just wasn't sure she wanted *him*.

'You know this lockdown means you won't be able to come in with me when I go in to labour?' she said.

'Yes. I'd supposed as much.'

'I called the maternity unit this morning. You'll be allowed into the delivery room while I'm actually pushing, but that's it. You won't be allowed onto the ward at all.' She said it blandly. 'I'd be grateful, if I were you. If I hear one more person call this kid "Baby" in a gooey voice, like it's their name, I'll scream.'

She'd had her twenty-week scan in France, just before returning to the UK; Lockyer had seen the grainy picture of the baby, sex still unknown. Hedy hadn't wanted to know. She'd been assigned a midwife, whom Lockyer hadn't met, and had been doing NCT classes online. Lockyer had played no part in her plans for the birth. No part in her decision to have the child in the first place. If she hadn't chosen to come back, he wouldn't even have known she was pregnant. His child might have been born and raised and gone out into the world without him knowing they existed. How could he not be angry about that?

But she *had* come back.

'Still okay for dinner at the farm this evening?' he said.

Hedy glanced back over her shoulder, showing little enthusiasm for the idea.

She nodded. 'I suppose it'll be our last chance for a while. Until Christmas.'

'By which time there'll be three of us.'

Hedy smiled faintly. They were heading into uncharted territory, and they both knew it.

The farmhouse where Lockyer had grown up was as windswept as ever, though it'd been a relatively dry month and their low-lying fields weren't yet underwater. Inside was the warm, familiar fug he knew and loved: the smell of sheep and dogs, cooking and old carpet. In spite of the absence of Lockyer's younger brother, which haunted the house and the family alike, it still felt like home. Jody Upton, who'd arrived as a temporary farmhand in the summer and still hadn't left, did a good job of banishing the shadows, as well as being a tireless worker. Lockyer was profoundly grateful to her for both.

Trudy opened the door, wreathed in smiles, and Lockyer noted the careful way she steadied herself before letting go of her wooden crutch to hug Hedy. A serious reaction to the Covid virus, resulting in a long stay in hospital, had left her depleted; she tired easily, struggled with manual dexterity, and walked unsteadily. Her years of being able to help with the farm work were behind her.

'How are you, dear?' Trudy asked Hedy.

'I feel like a tanker. And my back's killing me.'

'You poor thing,' Trudy said. 'I remember it well. People kept telling me I looked "blooming" . . . blooming miserable was more like it. Come and sit by the fire, and I'll get you a hot water bottle.'

She grabbed her stick and turned gingerly, wary of her balance. Patted Lockyer's shoulder as she passed him, and he bent to kiss her cheek.

'Where's Jody?' he asked.

'Finishing up on the yard,' she said. 'You could go and tell her to come in. Dinner will be on the table in about half an hour.'

He found her forking haylage along the feeding racks in the barn, where their small herd of beef cattle had just come in to overwinter. Wearing overalls, a woolly hat, and her perennial rigger boots, Jody had her AirPods in and didn't hear him approach. The stink of slurry was strong. He put himself in her eye line, raising one hand.

'All right?' she said, rubbing her nose on her cuff.

'Yep. You?'

She gave a shrug, and gestured around at the drizzle and muck. 'Living my best life.'

'Mum says dinner in half an hour.'

'I'm almost done. I wish she'd let me cook. It'd take me a tenth of the time it takes her.'

'It's something she can still do.'

'I get it,' Jody said. 'I just don't know how much more shepherd's pie I can take.'

'Hedy's here,' Lockyer said neutrally.

'I saw.'

'Think you can be nice?'

'Doubt it,' Jody said cheerfully.

They were like oil and water, so it was no surprise they hadn't taken to one another. But in Lockyer's experience women usually found a way to rub along, if they had to. Not these two, not yet.

'She's having a shit time,' he said. 'She's uncomfortable, and . . . with everything so uncertain—'

'She's having a *baby*, not a trial by fire. Women have been doing it since the dawn of time. I've been pregnant, don't forget. It's not half as hard as she's making out.' Jody jabbed a finger at the bullocks. 'One of these buggers just stood on my foot, and I'm pretty sure it's broken two of my toes. *That*'s uncomfortable.'

'Come on, Jody . . . Can't you cut her some slack?'

Jody rolled her eyes. 'Fine. I'll make an extra special effort to be nice to Lady Hedy, the Duchess of Hedyshire.'

Lockyer grinned. 'Can you hear yourself right now?'

'Sod off.'

'Do we need to go and get your foot looked at?'

'So I can sit for hours in Minor Injuries, waiting for them to wrap some tape around it? No, thanks.'

'Right, well, then, stop complaining. You've got time for a shower, and if you don't mind me saying so, you need one.'

'I do mind, actually, office boy,' she said, as he walked away.

She came to the table smelling fresh, with her cropped blue and black hair still damp. The meal was fish pie rather than shepherd's, and began in the usual fashion, with Trudy chatting easily, and Lockyer's father, John, murmuring the odd reply, Lockyer endeavouring to fill the gaps, and the two younger women pointedly ignoring one another.

'You ought to eat a bit more,' Jody said, when Hedy didn't finish her first helping. 'You're getting skinny as a scarecrow.'

Jody's robust, athletic physique highlighted how much weight Hedy had lost.

Hedy levelled a cool gaze at her. 'I'm fine, thanks.'

'I reckon it's a boy, the way it's sucking you dry,' Jody went on.

Hedy didn't look away, and she didn't blink. Jody smiled, unperturbed.

'Have the two of you thought of any names?' Trudy asked.

Lockyer and Hedy exchanged a glance. He supposed most couples probably would have done by now. But, then, he wasn't sure they *were* a couple.

'Well,' Hedy said, 'my mum's name is Pauline, but I've never been keen on that. And I'm not in touch with my dad, so no great inspiration there. My grandma's name was Elise, which is lovely . . . Maybe Daniel, for a boy. I've always liked Danny.'

Lockyer winced inwardly, and even Trudy studied her cutlery for a moment. That Hedy should choose *that* name for a boy, of all the thousands available, and that she should make no reference whatsoever to naming the baby after its other grandparents, the ones with whom she was currently sitting. She seemed to forget that the baby was going to be part of their family, too.

Lockyer glanced at Hedy, and she flushed, as though

realizing what she'd done. On the other side of the table, Jody took a sip of water and eyed Hedy appraisingly. Hedy couldn't have had any idea that Danny had been the name of Jody's son, who'd died at the age of three, but, with a sinking feeling, Lockyer braced himself for the fallout.

'Will your mother be able to come over again when the baby's born?' Trudy asked, with a hint of stiffness.

'I – I don't think so,' Hedy stammered. 'Not without spending another fortnight in a quarantine hotel, which she *hated* the last time. And there are hardly any flights.'

'Ah. That's a pity.'

Jody cleared her throat. 'Hedy, you know Matt's been getting his knickers in a twist about us not getting along, right? Well, I've thought of something we have in common.'

'Jody—' Lockyer tried to forestall her, but she brushed him off.

'No, it's good – it's pretty funny, actually. You and me were in the clink together. Eastwood Park, 2012. Course, I only did eighteen months, not fourteen years. But we were there at the same time.'

The moment hung. Nobody spoke. Then John started to laugh – something Lockyer hadn't heard for so long he'd all but forgotten the sound. It was unexpectedly boyish for such a sombre man, with a pronounced wheeze. 'Jody!' he gasped. 'You're a devil!'

Jody grinned at him. 'What? I'm just . . . finding common ground, that's all.'

'John, *really*,' Trudy said, when he had to stop laughing to cough and catch his breath.

'Hedy, pay her no mind, girl – she's mischief, this one,' John said, to which Hedy replied with a thin smile.

'Eighteen months barely even counts,' she said calmly.

'Yeah, I was just passing through.' Jody turned her lupine grin on Hedy. 'I'm pretty sure I remember you, though. Tracey Grant used to pick on you, right? She was such a bitch. She always picked on the ones who wouldn't fight back.'

Hedy said nothing.

'She went for you in the canteen one day, but someone stuck a foot out and sent *her* flying instead. Rolling about on the floor, covered in oxtail soup, roaring like a moose . . . It was bloody *hilarious*. She thought it was Gwen, and all hell broke loose.'

Hedy twitched. 'I remember that.'

Jody leant forwards. 'It wasn't Gwen.'

The moment hung. Lockyer and his parents could only watch, and wait.

'Thanks,' Hedy said eventually.

'Don't mention it.' Jody reached for the pie dish and shovelled an extra portion onto her own plate. 'And my little boy was called Danny, in case you're wondering why everyone went so weird a minute ago. He died when he was little. Don't let that stop you choosing the name, though. It's no skin off my nose.'

Hedy made a tiny sound of distress, though her gaze never wavered. Soon afterwards, she said she was tired, and asked to go home.

'I don't know why she has to be like that,' she muttered, once they were in the car.

'She wasn't— Look, I know she's tactless, but, honestly, I think she was trying to make friends with you just then.'

'Oh, really? You think so?' Hedy said scathingly.

'Hedy—'

'Why didn't you tell me she'd lost a child?'

'It just . . . it's not the sort of thing that drops into a conversation. Least of all with—' He broke off.

'With me?'

'With an expectant mother.'

'But you talk to Jody about me? Why do you need us to get along, Matt?'

'I don't. But it would make life a lot easier of you could. Jody's been great for the farm. If she left now we'd struggle to replace her, and my parents couldn't cope on their own.'

'That's not it,' Hedy murmured. 'She's . . . territorial. Doesn't want me anywhere near your parents – especially your dad. And she definitely doesn't want me anywhere near *you*.'

'Hedy, that's nonsense.'

'Is it? Have you slept with her?'

Lockyer's startled silence said it all. Hedy looked away. 'I thought so.'

'Just once. We weren't ever . . . together, or anything like that. It was just . . .'

'What?'

'I don't know. One of those things,' he said. 'Look, you'd left. I had no idea if you were ever coming back. I certainly had no idea you were pregnant.'

'Just forget it, Matt.'

'Forget what?'

He drove up the rutted track as gently as he could, so as not to jar her back, and pulled to a halt.

'Forget what, Hedy?'

'Trying to reassure me. You don't need to.' She shot a glance at him as she levered herself out of the car. 'I don't care.'

They walked to the front door in silence.

'I might go for a walk,' Lockyer said, before they went in.

'You do that.'

She was used to his habit of walking after dark. It was his way of clearing his head, ordering his thoughts, making it more likely he'd manage to sleep. But it didn't always work, and he didn't think it was going to that night. They just weren't ready to have a baby together. Hedy had been out of prison less than a year, and even though they'd known each other for a long time, they'd hardly had any contact during that time. He loved her, but he'd also got used to the idea that she'd left him, for good. Like he'd got used to the fact that fatherhood – a family life – was going to pass him by. He hadn't necessarily been happy about it, but he'd accepted it.

And now here they were. Reunited, but wholly untested, about to do the most stressful thing a couple could do, when they'd barely found ways to communicate to one another how they felt about any of it. *Doesn't really matter, though, does it?* his old friend Kevin had said, when Lockyer had told him all of this. *The kid's coming, ready or not.*

He breathed in the damp night smells of Salisbury Plain,

the slick, chalky mud and collapsed brown grasses, the clammy air that promised more rain. He tried to think about Nazma Kirmani instead. Whether she was alive somewhere or whether she was dead. Hari Kirmani's certainty of foul play had got under his skin: he was already thinking of the woman in the Islington CCTV footage as a suspect, not as Nazma herself.

But it was no good. His thoughts circled back, irresistibly, to his own situation. Could Hedy be right about Jody's resentment? Or was she just a little bit jealous of Jody? He took some comfort from the thought, since it would indicate that she *did* care for him. Because there was an alternative to the rocky road ahead: the possibility that Hedy would take their child, once he or she was born, and disappear again. Try as he might, Lockyer couldn't decide how that might make him feel. Because, though he'd silently denied it a thousand times, the truth was he felt trapped.

3

Day 2, Tuesday

Emma Billingham, Nazma Kirmani's former flatmate, was a teacher currently signed off work with stress. She lived in the top-floor apartment of a grand Georgian building on one of the main roads into Bath. Her face was pinched and anxious. Her dark brown hair had a broad stripe of grey along the roots – a now common pandemic hairstyle. Her gaze roamed constantly, never holding eye contact for more than a second at a time. She took them through to a sitting room with a sloping ceiling, where Lockyer – at six foot two – had to duck slightly, then fetched a face mask and put it on.

'We can talk outside, if you'd be more comfortable?' Broad said.

Emma shook her head. 'It's fine. You said you wanted to talk about, um, Nazma?'

Lockyer noticed the slight hesitation over her old flatmate's name.

'Yes. We understand you were living with her at the time she disappeared. Was that here, in Bath?'

'Yeah – well, in Weston. A long way out, but that was all we could afford, back then.'

'How did the two of you meet?'

'At uni. Exeter. We were in halls together.'

'Were you close?'

'She was my best friend,' Emma said, with a slight twitch of her face. Her hands were shaking visibly – Lockyer wondered if it was baseline anxiety, or having to talk to the police. 'Have you found her?' she said.

Beside him, Lockyer felt Broad's attention intensify. He shook his head. 'No.'

He hated the necessity of face masks: they made it so much harder to read people's expressions. Emma dropped her head, brows drawing together.

'I thought . . . maybe you had. After all this time. I mean, there are ways to identify people, aren't there? Even if there's nothing but bones left. Or . . . teeth.' She looked up, eyes wide. 'Sorry. I didn't mean—' A shake of her head. 'Go on.'

'We're looking into Nazma's disappearance in light of some new evidence,' Lockyer said. 'The original investigation concluded that she'd left of her own accord, so there isn't much information on file. We'd like to ask you about her, particularly in the weeks and months leading up to her disappearance. And about the text messages you received from Nazma shortly after she disappeared on October second, 1999.'

'Okay.'

'Over what period did you continue to get messages from her?'

'A few days. Not long at all.'

'I don't suppose you kept the phone, or recorded the texts somehow?' Lockyer asked.

'No. Sorry. That phone went out with the Ark.'

'Do you remember what they said?'

Emma didn't answer at once. Lockyer felt his suspicion growing: something wasn't right.

'Miss Billingham?' Broad prompted her gently.

'Just what you'd expect. That she had to go away for a bit, and I probably knew the reason why. That she was fine, she'd see me soon, that sort of thing. But she said not to contact her, and not to tell anyone where she'd gone.'

Tears shone in Emma's eyes.

'It's okay,' Broad said. 'Take your time.'

'I'm sorry. I can't believe I'm getting upset after all this time.'

'She clearly meant a lot to you?'

'Yes. She was the best. You know those people you sometimes meet, who just . . . make you feel better about yourself? About life? That was Naz. And . . . I was really hurt when she just left like that.'

Lockyer leant towards her a fraction. 'Miss Billingham, please, be honest with us. *Did* you know why she'd gone?'

'Not exactly. I said at the time – she'd told me at some point that she might go up to London when the dig was over. Just for a couple of weeks, for a change of scene. That was it. It was just a vague plan. She had some cousins in London, I think, but—' She broke off, tugging her mask down to blow her nose. 'Sorry. I'm a mess. It's just stress. All of it.' She made a vague gesture with one hand.

'It's all right. You told the police about this at the time, and about her texts to you. Is that correct?'

'Yes. I got the first one the evening after she'd gone missing, and another the next day. Then there was a gap, and I think it was, like, three or four days later that I got the last one. I mean, I'd sent lots more to her, and tried to call her – especially after Liz rang me.'

'Liz Kirmani?'

'Yeah. They were going out of their minds with worry. I told Naz to ring them, and when she didn't, I asked why not. Several times.'

'Did she give any explanation for that?'

'No. She just said there were things I didn't know about, or something like that. Which was news to me. We used to tell each other everything. At least, I thought we did.' She took a deep breath. 'We'd seen less of each other that summer. She spent so much time at Trusloe.'

'That was the dig she was working on?'

'Right. She was on a team excavating in the grounds of Trusloe Hall, which is this big old house over there. The woman who owned it let them camp in a barn – they turned it into a kind of dormitory. Naz stayed there all week, and came back to our place at the weekends. Well, some weekends.'

'Was she having a good time?'

'Time of her life.' A shrug. 'It was a really warm summer, she got on well with her team and she was basically being paid to do what she loved.'

'Sounds idyllic,' Broad said.

'Yeah. But . . .'

Emma looked from Broad to Lockyer then away, and suddenly Lockyer saw guilt. Guilt that would explain how upset about it she still was, two decades on.

'Something wasn't right,' she said.

'What makes you say that?' Lockyer asked.

'I could just tell. She . . . she was in a relationship with one of the guys from Brittonic.'

'The archaeology company?'

'Right.'

'Can you tell us who?'

'The boss. Edward Chapman. Only she hadn't told her parents, because he was much older than her, and he was married. With kids. Unhappily married, or so he told her.' A cynical lift of her eyebrows. 'We were so young back then. Naz really fell for him – she took everything he said as gospel.'

'Did you tell the police about this at the time?'

'No, but I knew they'd be talking to her colleagues, and I knew *they* all knew, and one of them was bound to say something. I just . . . I knew the Kirmanis really well – I didn't want them to know I knew.'

'The relationship was common knowledge? You're sure about that?'

'Naz said they all knew at work. She and Edward were

really careful not to rub it in people's faces – no public dis-
plays of affection, or whatever, especially since they were
being filmed for that TV thing. Cameras everywhere. He was
adamant his wife couldn't find out until the time was right,
because she was seriously ill or something, and Naz didn't
want to rock the boat.'

Broad was scribbling intently in her notebook.

'How long had they been seeing each other?' she asked.

'I think it started when Naz first went on placement with
Brittonic. So, about a year.'

'And what made you think something wasn't right with
her?' Lockyer said.

'Well . . . she'd stopped raving about him. Edward. She
talked about him less, and smiled less when she did. I mean,
she'd always defended him to the hilt with me, whenever
I suggested she should end it, or that he wasn't going to
leave his wife, or whatever. She'd had boyfriends at uni, but
he was her first serious relationship. When I asked if she'd
gone off him she denied it, but . . . that was the impression
I got. Plus she was distant. I'd be chatting away to her, then
realize she was miles away. Not listening.'

'And she never said what was bothering her?'

'No. I mean, I started to think it was *me*, that I was getting on her nerves, and she was going to move out. When
I pushed her on it she said it wasn't that, just some stuff
that'd been going on at work.'

'What sort of "stuff"?'

'She wouldn't go into it, just said she was probably wrong,
or being paranoid. I can't remember exactly . . . She talked a

lot about the woman who lived in the big house, and how amazing she was, what an amazing life she'd led, and all that. She reckoned her dad was Picasso, I remember that. I can't think of her name, something European. So maybe they fell out? But I don't know.'

'Were things all right between her and her family?'

'Yeah. I mean, as far as I know. Mr and Mrs Kirmani are lovely. Her brother Andy, too.'

'Yet Nazma didn't tell them about an important relation-ship she was in?' Broad said.

'Well, no. But that wasn't because they weren't close, or anything. We were in our early twenties. At that age your parents want to hear about nice young men you might go on to marry. Not married lovers twenty years older than you who already have a family. Not your *boss*.'

'Right. I see what you mean,' Broad said.

'When we arrived today, you thought we might have found Nazma's body,' Lockyer said. 'Was that because of the way she'd been behaving?'

'That, and I just . . . I could never completely believe she'd run away like that, and cut me off. And her family. I know people *do* just walk out on their lives, and it usually comes as a massive shock to the people they leave behind, and everyone says it's so out of character . . . But with her, it really *was*. Utterly.'

'But she had texted you.'

'Yeah.' Emma lingered over the word. 'Except . . . did she, though? The texts were from Naz's phone, but . . .'

'You're not convinced she sent them?'

Tears welled in Emma's eyes again. 'I'm not. I never was.'

'Why not?'

'Because I *didn't* know why she'd gone away, really. And why wouldn't she want anyone to know? And she called me Emma. In the texts.' She registered their incomprehension. 'Naz *never* called me that. She'd given me this stupid nickname in the first year of uni – Moonie – and it just stuck. She always, *always* called me Moonie.'

'So you think someone else had her phone, and used it to send those messages?'

Emma nodded. 'No facial recognition back then, no fingerprint ID; just a four-digit code, and you were considered pretty paranoid if you bothered with that. I never locked my phone, and neither did Naz.'

'Did you tell this to the police at the time?' Broad sounded tense.

That guilt again, the self-recrimination. 'I didn't notice right away. I thought it was weird that she wasn't calling me back, and hadn't called her family, but by the time I noticed the Moonie thing the police had told her parents she'd gone into a police station and was fine. Didn't want to be contacted.'

'And you were reassured by that?'

'Well, I tried to accept it. It was hurtful. I thought she'd just ditched me, so I dropped it. Tried not to care. Her direct debit for the rent carried on for another three months, until the lease was up. I rang her one more time then, and she still didn't answer. So I had to find a new flatmate. *Shit.*'

She dropped her face into her hands.

'I went into the police station, the one here in Bath. I told them I was worried about her, she wasn't answering her phone, emails, or anything. The woman wrote it down and said she'd make some enquiries, but I never heard anything else. And I've searched for her online, over and over. There's never been anything and, honestly, I never expected there to be.'

'You thought something had happened to her?'

A nod. Then Emma looked up with hollow eyes. 'Strange, the way you can know something without ever really admitting it to yourself. But now you're here, looking for her at last, and . . . She would *never* have walked out like that. Not willingly. Something happened to her.'

Lockyer and Broad exchanged a long look.

'Thank you, Miss Billingham. You've been very helpful,' Lockyer said.

Emma shook her head. 'I should've done something. Made more noise.'

'Could we contact you again, if we have more questions?'

'Yes, of course.'

'And there's nothing else you can think of that might have had anything to do with her disappearance?'

'No.'

The denial was equivocal. Lockyer and Broad both heard it, and halted in the act of turning for the door. Emma took a big breath then sighed it out.

'I don't *know*, not for certain. So, I've never said anything to anyone, but . . . Naz had stopped drinking. The last month or so, I don't remember when exactly. She'd always loved a big glass of wine, or several, on a Saturday night. Suddenly I noticed she kept saying she'd just have water because she was thirsty, or had a touch of cystitis and was sticking to cranberry juice. At some point, I twigged. She was off the booze, and that was out of character, too.'

'You think she was pregnant?' Broad said, getting there faster than Lockyer.

'But I don't *know*,' Emma stressed. Her face fell. 'That's the kind of thing I'd have expected her to confide in me about.'

Broad's phone pinged as they got into the car, and twice more as they started the drive back. She glanced at the screen, but ignored it.

'A married older man with no intention of leaving his family might have had a real problem with his girlfriend falling pregnant,' she said instead. 'I can't imagine he'd have wanted her to keep it.'

Lockyer didn't reply at once. He couldn't help thinking of Hedy. Whether, if she'd come back sooner, they'd have talked about terminating the pregnancy. He had no idea if he would have wanted that. But was that why she'd stayed away as long as she had – to take that possibility off the table altogether?

He became aware of Broad's expectant look.

'Yes. It could've caused trouble between them.'

'Shall we talk to him next?'

'We'll talk to him, yes.' Lockyer took a moment. 'There are three possibilities here, as I see it. The first is that the original investigation got it right. For whatever reason, Nazma walked out on her old life, changed her name and started anew. She'd packed a bag, so *something* was going on. If she was pregnant, that could've been the trigger. She might be alive and well somewhere. Proving that, and finding her, will be very difficult.'

'Don't you have to have a deed poll, or something, to change your name?'

'Only if you want a new passport. Otherwise you can call yourself anything you like.'

'So if that *is* Nazma at Islington nick, and she changed her name afterwards, then . . . she's basically gone. But why would she ditch the escape bag, in that case?' Broad said.

'No idea. Getting rid of ID that would prove who she used to be?'

'And a hundred and seventy quid? And a treasured keep-sake—'

'That could readily be used to identify her.'

'The cash couldn't,' Broad said.

'True. And the only way to prove this scenario will be to find out why an apparently happy young woman with a supportive family, good friends and a job she loved would suddenly need to vanish.'

'Personally, I don't buy scenario one, guv.'

'Me neither.'

Broad's phone pinged. She ignored it again. 'What could she possibly have got caught up in that was *that* bad? And the bag could have been packed for a sneaky weekend in Paris as easily as for an emergency. Except for the cash, I suppose.'

KATE WEBB | 41

'Maybe,' Lockyer conceded. 'The second scenario is that she was snatched from the Marlborough Mop by an opportunist predator, probably for sexual reasons. She could have been taken anywhere, and is probably dead. The strongest supporting evidence for that will be if she had the Nike bag with her in Marlborough that night, and the perp then ditched it.'

'Would a random predator take her phone, and try to pretend she was still alive?'

'It's possible. That kind of sick bastard is sometimes deliberately cruel to both the victim and their family. But it's rare.'

He felt the queasy thrill of this possibility, a mixture of dread and longing. Serial sexual offenders usually lived in deep cover, lurking like the predators they were, surfacing only briefly, now and then, to transgress again. To destroy more lives. That flurry of movement when they struck – the police had only those brief windows in which to catch them, before they slunk back out of sight.

'So, who is the girl at Islington nick, with Nazma's wallet, pretending to be her?' Broad said.

'Right. Which brings us to scenario three.'

'Something along the lines of her packing the escape bag because trouble was coming, and it catching up with her before she could get away?' Broad said sombrely.

'Trying to pretend she was still alive – sending texts to her best mate, and getting a decoy to present themselves at a police station . . . Those are the actions of someone who knew her. Someone close to her, who was keen to avoid suspicion falling on them,' Lockyer said.

Broad was quiet. Her phone starting ringing, and she abruptly switched it to silent.

'Someone clearly wants to talk to you,' Lockyer said.

Her cheeks mottled pink. 'It's just Pete. He knows I'm at work.'

'Could be important?'

A small shake of her head, and she kept her eyes to the front. 'It won't be.'

Lockyer dropped it. But he remembered Pete, Broad's long-term boyfriend, using mobile-phone tracking to find her in a pub garden earlier that year, and basically extracting her. *He's just been a bit . . . twitchy, since the whole Covid thing,* she'd said, in his defence. And they were about to go back into lockdown.

She was fiddling with the kirby grips that kept her frizzy blonde curls in check.

'Gem, is . . .' But Lockyer couldn't think how to frame the question '. . . everything . . .'

'Yep. Everything's fine, guv,' she said, in a way that told him it really wasn't.

'If you want to talk about it?'

She looked at him then. A quick smile and a shake of her head.

He made a stab at levity. 'You know by now that I don't mind bending the rules for a friend. If you ever need anyone kneecapped . . .'

'I'll know where to come,' she said, with a short laugh. 'Honestly. It's nothing.'

'Look, this is cheeky, but do you mind if we take a bit of a detour?'

'Course not. Where are we going?'

'Old Hat Farm. I need to check on something.'

A startled pause. 'Something to do with the case?'

'No.'

They both stared straight ahead, and he sensed her reluctance. It wasn't so much a detour as a fifteen-mile overshoot.

'Okay,' she said eventually.

'Great, thanks. I'll shout you lunch afterwards.'

Back in the summer, they'd worked a difficult case centred on Old Hat Farm, the upshot of which was that just one person lived there now, trying to carry on a life that had been beaten to pieces. The multiple crimes their investigation had uncovered weren't Lockyer's fault, but he'd been left with a lingering, misplaced guilt about the destruction that had followed. It was proving slow to dispel.

The ramshackle farmyard was quiet and looked different. In summer the fields had been golden, drenched in a heat that had felt endless. Now the land had been left to go fallow, the yard mossy with neglect. Lights were on in the large workshop, though, warm and inviting.

'This'll only take a minute,' Lockyer said, as he pulled up. 'Coming?'

'I— No, I'll wait here. Maybe call Pete back,' Broad said.

'Right,' he said, vaguely disappointed.

He knocked softly, and heard Jason McNeil inside – he'd kept the surname of his unofficial adoptive parents, in spite of the charges that had been brought against them.

'Yup,' came the reply.

'Hello, Jase.'

'Thought it was you,' Jason said, cocking his head. 'Recognized the engine.'

He was wearing a baggy jumper, and a woolly hat over his short dreadlocks. The light from the bulkhead lamps made his skin glow across his cheekbones. The workshop was warm, and smelt richly of sap and wood shavings.

'I just thought I'd drop in and see how it's coming along,' Lockyer said. 'Not long to go, now.'

Jason straightened with a smile. 'Check I'm doing what you asked, you mean, and not exacting some weird revenge by making you something hideous.'

'If I thought that I'd hardly have asked you in the first place.'

'Yeah, maybe. Come on, then.'

He ducked through a door in the far wall into another shed, and Lockyer followed. The cot looked finished to Lockyer's eye, and it was as beautiful as he'd hoped. It was made using natural lengths of wood, with waney edges, twists and knots, all waxed and polished to a satin finish. It was rustic without being crude or hokey, and completely unique. Lockyer ran his hand along the top edge. As smooth as bone, nothing that might snag at newborn skin. Whether or not Hedy would like it, he had no idea.

'The joints are all rock solid. This side drops down,' Jason said, stepping forwards. 'See here, where I've hinged it?'

'It's perfect. Thank you.'

'Standard cot size for the mattress, so you can get on and order that.'

'Is it finished?'

'Almost. I want to take a bit more off the top corner posts. And have you decided about your initials?'

When they'd first discussed the commission, Jason had suggested a motif on the headboard, entwining *M* for Matt, *H* for Hedy, and whatever the baby's initial turned out to be.

Lockyer smiled wryly. 'Perhaps leave it plain. Feels a bit like getting a tattoo too soon.'

Jason grinned. 'Have a little faith, man. You'll always be the kid's parents, even if you don't stay together.'

'I know. But still.'

'Give me a couple more days on it, then.'

'Fine. Just text me when it's ready, and I'll come with the cash.'

'Thanks.'

They went back through to the workshop. Lockyer ignored the urge to ask if there was anything he could do to help Jason. He had no idea what that help might look like, and they weren't friends. Not quite.

'DC Broad not with you?' Jason asked.

'She's in the car, had to make a phone call,' Lockyer said. 'You planning on keeping this place going, then?'

A rolling shrug. 'Not mine, is it?' Jason said. 'It'll go out from under me, sooner or later. Thought I'd stick the year out, maybe make a move in the spring. Hard, though.'

'Where will you go?'

'No idea.' That smile again, tinged with sadness. 'That's most of the problem.'

He followed Lockyer out, and gave Broad an oddly formal wave. Still on the phone, she lifted one hand uncertainly in response. Lockyer wasn't sure why he'd wanted to bring her with him. Perhaps because he knew she'd liked Jason. And to remind her that the people they investigated didn't just vanish afterwards. Or, in any case, they didn't *have* to. As he and Hedy proved.

'What was that all about?' Broad asked, once he was back in the car.

Lockyer shrugged. 'Hedy didn't like any of the cots in the shops. She's been scrolling on eBay like a lunatic, trying to find something antique, but everything she likes goes for thousands. So I thought of Jase.'

'Right.' She sounded sceptical. 'Is that not a bit . . . weird, guv?'

'Why?'

He knew full well why, but Broad clearly wasn't prepared to spell it out.

'I don't know,' she said. 'I guess I'm just surprised he's still here, after everything.'

'He won't be for much longer, I think.'

There was a thoughtful silence while he turned the car around.

'So, where's lunch?' Broad said.

Back at the station, Broad wrote *Pregnant?* next to Nazma's photo on the whiteboard. She underlined the question mark twice, then settled at her computer, tasked with getting the names and contact details of people who'd been on the dig at Avebury with Nazma. After some searching, Lockyer discovered that Police Sergeant Keith Wheeler, who'd been on the desk the day Nazma had supposedly walked into Islington police station, had since retired and was living in sheltered accommodation in Kent, suffering from dementia.

'So I doubt he'll be able to help you much,' said the female officer he spoke to. 'I remember *him*, though.'

'What was he like?'

'Old school. I was fresh out of college and he was months from retirement, just watching the clock till he was out of there, really. His views didn't align particularly well with modern policing, if you know what I mean.'

'I think I do, but feel free to elaborate.'

'Well, I'd only just joined back in 'ninety-nine, like I said. Keith wasn't a bad bloke, really, but he made it very clear that I was only there to tick a box and make the tea, as far as he was concerned. Any kind of push back and he'd ask if I was . . . you know, "on the rag", that kind of thing. Don't get me wrong, he was nice enough – as long as you were white, male, and straight, in that order.'

'I think I know the type.'

'Plus, according to the records, Miss Kirmani came in on a Friday afternoon. Is that right?'

'Yes. Friday, the eighth of October. The capture is time-stamped four forty-two.'

'Well, then,' the officer continued, 'lunchtime pints on a Friday, wasn't it?'

'So, what you're telling me is that Sergeant Wheeler's mind might not have been firmly on the job when she came in?' Lockyer said.

'I don't want to badmouth the guy, really. He was just . . . of another era. Not that the Met's a model of inclusivity now. But, yeah, I'm pretty sure he wouldn't have paid too much attention to a young Asian woman.'

'And I suppose there's no chance the CCTV footage was kept anywhere?'

'None at all, sir. You're lucky someone took that still. I expect Keith phoned it through to the SIO, sent the image and promptly forgot all about it.'

Lockyer took a moment. 'It's a working hypothesis that the woman who came in wasn't actually Nazma Kirmani at all. How closely would Keith have checked her face against her ID, do you think?'

The woman scoffed gently. 'Even if he *had* looked closely it probably wouldn't have done much good. "They" all looked the same to him – he told me so on more than one occasion. Always with a shrug and a grin, like he couldn't understand how anyone might be offended by that. As I said, it was high time he retired.'

When he came off the call, Lockyer looked at the image again. He studied the side of the woman's face – smooth jawline and rounded chin, mouth set in a resolute line, no lipstick. Big hoop earrings glinted through the straight lengths of her hair. It *could* be Nazma, but from that angle it was impossible to be sure. Sergeant Wheeler had been satisfied, but Lockyer wasn't at all inclined to take his word for it.

Next he ran a search for Trusloe Hall, where Nazma's team had been digging, back in the summer of 1999. The owner was a woman called Inez de Redvers – the 'European' name Emma Billingham had mentioned. Nazma had got to know her, been impressed by her. He searched nominals on the PNC – the Police National Computer – and came up with a record. Inez de Redvers had been cautioned for possession of cannabis and amphetamines, and had a spent conviction for vandalism. She'd also been arrested and cautioned numerous times after various protest marches, evicted from women's camps and squats, and fined for public indecency.

'That's an impressive CV,' Broad said, when he showed her. 'I've been on to an admin at Brittonic Archaeology, who was very helpful. I've got a list of their staff who were working on the Avebury dig that summer. She stressed that there were plenty of other people there as well – two universities were involved, and had their own teams.'

She presented him with a printed map of Avebury and the surrounding mile or so of countryside. 'The main dig was over here.' She tapped a point to the west of the village. 'They were trying to prove the existence of a second processional avenue into the stone circle from that direction.'

'And did they find it?'

'Oh, yes. She was very keen to tell me all about it. Nazma's team, however, were in this field here.' Again she tapped the map, in a field to the east of Trusloe Hall, west of Avebury again but south of where the main dig had been happening. 'They were looking at some other feature linked to the site.'

'How many of them were with Nazma?'

'A team of six – those are the names I've underlined. Overseen by Edward Chapman, who went back and forth between there and the main dig site. Mr Chapman has since retired and lives with his wife, Antigone, in a place called Kingston Deverill. I've no idea where that is.'

'It's south of here, just this side of the A303,' Lockyer said.

'So I guess he never did leave his wife. I've got a phone number for them here. Shall I see if he's up for talking to us?'

'Yes, do that. I'm going to try to reach Inez de Redvers.'

But when it came to it, there was no phone number listed anywhere for Trusloe Hall. Broad had more luck with the Chapmans' number, but her call went unanswered.

'Shall I start ringing Nazma's teammates from the dig, guv?' she suggested.

He stood up with an impatient shake of his head. 'No. Let's go to Avebury.'

4

Trusloe Hall sat behind a high brick wall in the hamlet of Avebury Trusloe, barely visible behind the tangled mess of what might once have been an orchard. The main gates – tall, wrought iron – were knotted with brambles and long, sagging grass. They clearly hadn't opened in a very long time.

'God. What a mess,' Broad said. She lived with Pete in a new-build house so neat and tidy it made Lockyer's teeth ache.

'Let's go round the side,' he said. 'There must be another way in.'

They found a track tunnelling through overgrown shrubs that led past a thatched threshing barn to the northern elevation of the house. The barn had collapsed altogether at one end. Its rotten roof beams stuck up like broken bones against the sky, and pieces of tarpaulin had been strung over it here and there. They flapped in the breeze, doing nothing whatsoever to keep out the rain.

'Do you think that's the barn where the archaeologists set up camp?' Broad said.

'Could be,' Lockyer said. 'I hope no one was in it when it went.'

Trusloe Hall was a grand seventeenth-century farmhouse, the kind once occupied by the type of farmer who made the money but never actually got his hands dirty: three storeys of Flemish bond brickwork with tall, symmetrical windows; a mansard roof with dormer windows to light the rooms where servants would once have slept. The window frames were rotten, and several had missing or broken panes. Swathes of green algae marked the places where the gutters were blocked, or had fallen down. The gardens were so overgrown that only glimpses of what had once been a sweeping rear terrace were now visible, choked with buddleia and thistles.

A cobbled path led to a door where a large hole might have been meant for a cat flap. There were no signs of life whatsoever.

'Looks derelict,' Broad said. 'Maybe she had to go into a home or something?'

'She's only in her sixties,' Lockyer said.

A cast-iron postbox was rusting on the wall, with a wad of junk mail poking out – including a pristine Domino's Pizza flier that hadn't yet been rained on.

'Postman thinks someone still lives here,' he pointed out.

'I'm not sure that proves anything,' Broad said. She took a step closer to peer in at the window, and there was a crunch as she stepped on a snail. 'Oh, *gross* . . .'

Lockyer knocked, shaking the door in its frame. He waited while Broad wiped her shoe on some moss, then knocked again. No reply. He tried the handle, and the rickety door swung open.

'Hello?' he called, 'Mrs de Redvers? Is anybody home?'

'I really don't think—'

Broad was cut off by the thump of a door from further inside the house.

'Darren? Is that you?' The voice was thin, and not overly loud, but instantly, obviously, upper class.

'Mrs de Redvers, we're the police,' Lockyer called. 'May we come in?'

'The police?'

A woman appeared at the end of the dim hallway, wearing a tattered robe of some kind, and a turban with a threadbare peacock feather at the front. She was leaning on an ebony walking cane, and had a surgical boot on one foot.

'The police?' she repeated, then, before they could answer, said: 'Well, come in, do. Try not to let the cats out.'

With some trepidation, they stepped inside.

The interior of the house was as neglected and decrepit as the grounds. There was a hole through the floor just inside the door, and the boards felt spongy with rot.

'Watch your step,' Lockyer said.

Wallpaper was hanging off in shreds, and the plaster underneath was dark with mildew. If there'd ever been a carpet, all that remained of it were brittle shreds of underlay. The ceiling sagged, and was blotched with water-marks. There was litter everywhere, graffiti here and there. The air had the kind of damp, dead cold that came from not having been heated in years, and the smell of the place defied description.

'Come into the parlour,' the woman said, as they approached. 'I've got the fire going in there. Jenny will bring us some tea.'

'Mrs de Redvers?' Lockyer said.

'Do call me Inez, young man. I'm not "Mrs" anybody.'

'I'm DI Lockyer, this is DC Broad.'

'What a pleasure to meet you,' Inez said, thudding along unevenly on her surgical boot.

She led them into a room where there was a bit more light and warmth, and a lot more rubbish. Piles and piles of it, from mangy taxidermy to gilt candelabra, to bulging black sacks and endless carrier bags containing who knew what. The smell was even stronger, and Lockyer spotted several cat-litter trays that hadn't been mucked out in a long time. A sofa with a nest of blankets and stained pillows sat at the eye of a storm of biscuit wrappers, Pot Noodle containers, used tissues and discarded clothes.

Behind it all – barely visible – was an elegant panelled room with a Georgian fireplace. Ivy and bindweed crowded the windows, snaking through in places, and if Lockyer had assumed Inez meant she'd lit a real fire, he was soon disabused of the notion. A two-bar electric heater was glowing feebly, next to a pile of newspapers three feet high. One slip and the whole lot would go up in flames. Inez sat down on the sofa.

'Do sit,' she said, though there was nowhere for them to do so. Lockyer removed a cardboard box of spent lightbulbs from a rococo dining chair, and offered it to Broad. She perched on it cautiously.

'I *am* sorry about the mess,' Inez said. 'I've been sleeping down here since I broke my ankle and the stairs proved too troublesome. And I've been having a bit of a sort-out, you see.' She looked around listlessly. 'Though I don't seem to have got very far.'

'Not to worry,' Broad said amiably, though Lockyer could see she was horrified. 'How did you break your ankle?'

'I— Do you know, I'm not entirely sure?' Inez said. 'It was some time ago now. It does seem to be taking an awfully long time to heal.'

They glanced at her injured foot and quickly away. Her toes were red and angry; the yellowed nails, bedded deeply into swollen skin, still had flecks of pink varnish clinging to them. At close quarters, Inez's own personal smell soon reached them – the prickly reek of the long-term unwashed. If her date of birth was correct she was only sixty-eight, but she looked much older. Deep wrinkles around her eyes and along her top lip; no sign of any hair beneath her grubby turban. Her eyelashes were clotted with black mascara. She'd drawn her eyebrows with wavering pencil lines, and had a stab at some green eye-shadow. Her hands shook continuously.

'Where were we?' she said, then leant towards the closed door and called: 'Jenny? *Jenny?* Tea for three, please, my dear. And one for yourself, of course.'

Lockyer didn't need to listen for movement to know that Jenny had left some time ago, and wouldn't be bringing any tea. Which was a relief.

'Have you come about Pippa?' Inez asked.

'No,' Lockyer said. 'We're reinvestigating the disappearance of Nazma Kirmani, and we'd like to ask you a few questions, if you don't mind?'

'Who? Who is that?'

A quick glance between Lockyer and Broad.

'Nazma Kirmani. She came here in 1999, with some other archaeologists, to dig in your field. Do you remember that?'

Inez's eyes widened. 'Oh, heavens, yes! What a *happy* time it was! I do so *love* to have young people around – they make it seem like summer, don't you think? All of them out in the barn, camp fires and sleeping bags. Oh, it was just like the old days!'

'It sounds lovely,' Broad said.

'It *was*.' Inez's face fell. 'It *was*.' She sounded less sure this time.

'Do you remember Nazma?'

'The little brown girl? Of course, of course. Pretty as a starlit sky.' Inez looked coy. 'She took rather a shine to me, you know.'

There was a rustle from a far corner of the room; it could have been a cat, or something else. Inez didn't seem to notice. Lockyer saw Broad's slight shudder.

'Did police officers come and talk to you at the time of her disappearance?' he asked.

'I think they did.' A faint frown. 'They would have done, I'm sure. There was so much going *on*, you understand. The archaeologists and the TV people, then the police . . . Were they here for Nazma? I think that's right. I showed them the barn, and they wanted to know which was her bunk, which were her things. And they got very excited about some mud on the floor! Ha-ha!' She clapped her hands. 'What nonsense! I had to laugh. Those people spent all day digging in the ground – of *course* they tracked mud behind them wherever they went. I did *try* to get them to take their boots off at the door, but you know how people are.'

Lockyer looked around at the unutterable squalor, and wondered what Inez saw.

'Were you able to tell them anything about Nazma's time here? Anything that might have had a bearing on her disappearance?' Broad asked.

'A bearing upon it? Tell whom, precisely?'

'The police officers, back in 1999.'

Inez looked blank, and then troubled. 'Goodness, I can't remember. Though I rather doubt it. I thought they'd come about *Pippa*, you see. "Why aren't you trying to find *her*?" I asked them. And, do you know, I'm quite sure they were perfectly ignorant of the whole thing? Couldn't have been less helpful.'

Tears glimmered and she blinked at them rapidly.

'Sorry – who is Pippa?' Lockyer said. Inez ignored him.

'I'm an artist,' she said, at length. 'It's in my blood. My father was Pablo Picasso – oh, yes. You won't believe me – people never do. My mother was in Paris in 'fifty-one. They had a torrid affair, and lo! I sallied forth. He was seventy by then, but clearly he still had lead in his pencil.'

'Wow, that's amazing,' Broad said. 'What was he like?'

'Oh, I never knew him.' She placed a trembling hand on her bony chest. 'But I can *feel* him. Deep inside me.'

Broad looked uncomfortable.

'*Jenny!*' Inez called again, with a fraught edge. 'Do shake a leg, girl!' She leant towards Broad conspiratorially. 'She was scared off by the rooks, you know.'

'Who was? Jenny?'

'No, that dear little archaeology girl. They come clattering at the windows sometimes.' Inez stared into the distance. 'Beating themselves bloody – they can't tolerate their own reflections. She said she couldn't stand it for another second. Blood everywhere.'

'Nazma? What couldn't she stand?' Lockyer said.

'No – *Pippa*, you silly man,' Inez said. 'She left me, you know. Not a word of goodbye – is that right after all our years together? Is that *fair* when I loved her so very, very much? Hm?'

'We're very sorry to hear that, Inez,' Broad said carefully. 'It doesn't sound right, no.'

Inez smiled at her. 'You *are* a dear girl to say so.'

'What about Nazma?' Broad said. 'Did she perhaps . . . talk to you, about why she needed to go away?'

Inez looked confused. 'Nazma? No. She was very upset that day, mind you. Not with me, I don't think. Although she did raise her voice – I remember it quite clearly, because she never had before. Such a sweet, placid girl.'

'What was she upset about?' Broad said.

'She said it was *dangerous*. Against the law, she said. So silly. I think Darren had put her nose out of joint somehow – that's more likely. Though she was tangled up with that Chapman fellow, wasn't she? Charming man, terrible cad.'

'What was against the law, Inez?' Lockyer asked.

The coy look returned. 'Ha! You'll not catch me out that easily, Officer. I've always got on *tremendously* well with your lot, you know. They'd cart us off in the back of a wagon, and we'd always have jolly good laugh about it, and a sing-song.' She laughed. 'Tea and custard creams all round, and home in time for bed. Those were the days. Ban the Bomb, Ban the Bill. Ban anything we could think of. Reclaim the streets! Burn your bra! Would you like to see some of my paintings?'

'Er . . .' Broad said. 'Yes, please.'

'Splendid. Come this way.' Inez levered herself to her feet. 'Do forgive me – people should wear exactly what they please, I've always said so – but *must* you keep that riot gear on indoors? It does seem rather *aggressive*.'

'Sorry, but we have to wear these visors,' Broad said. 'To help stop the spread of the virus.'

'Oh, the virus? Gosh. I see. Of course.'

It was obvious that Inez had no idea what Broad was talking about.

They followed her along another corridor, from which more rooms led off, and passed a cramped kitchen that was every bit as filthy and knackered as any Lockyer had seen in a derelict squat. Among the litter on the floor, his feet kept rustling on empty blister packs. They were everywhere. He picked one up and had a quick look before pocketing it: diazepam. They passed a staircase that was impassable both up and down, blocked by bulging bin bags; a toppled long-case clock; a massive stuffed boar's head, half eaten by worms.

'I think Jenny must have gone out, you know,' Inez said to Broad. 'I *do* apologize.'

'That's all right, not to worry.'

'Oh, you *are* sweet. Here we are.'

They'd arrived at the far end of the house, where steps led down into a room with a towering ceiling of cob-webby beams. From the huge, blackened fireplace, Lockyer guessed it had once been the kitchen. Now it was heaped with furniture, boxes and more rubbish. One corner was stacked with large canvases, and a trestle table was covered with paints.

'Gracious, what a mess I've left it in,' Inez murmured. She'd halted at the top of the steps and didn't seem inclined to go any further. 'I must have been having a frantic sort of day.'

'Have you always painted?' Broad asked, and Lockyer was grateful for her ability to chat, since he'd been struck more or less dumb by the desperate state of this woman's life.

'Oh, *yes*,' Inez said. 'I did have a go at sculpture for a while, but they never really came *alive*. Paint is my true *métier*. Well, you shall have to come back when I've finished it – far better to see it then.'

It wasn't clear which painting, if any, she was referring to.

Broad pointed to a circular stone feature in a far corner. 'Is that a well?'

'Oh – yes. Very old. One wouldn't want to fall in – it drops about a hundred feet.'

'*Seriously?*' Broad looked alarmed. The well had no cover of any kind.

Lockyer noticed a stack of boxes against one wall that appeared in better order than the rest. Clean and dry, still sealed, in fact. Labels, logos and QR codes on the sides.

'What are all those, Inez?' he asked.

'Hm? Oh, haven't a clue.' She waved a hand. 'Some of Darren's clobber, I expect. He's forever running out of places to *put* things.'

'And Darren is . . .?'

'My nephew, of course. He's never been much of a *people* person, you understand, but he's a treasure, really. A diamond in the rough. He looks after me.'

'Does he live here with you?' Lockyer asked.

'No, no. Along in the village. Boys always want their independence, don't they? I've been by myself here since Pippa left.'

They went back along the hall, and Inez stopped outside the kitchen.

'I shall have to make the tea myself,' she said, but then looked blankly at the grimed worktops and sagging drawers. There was a plastic kettle, but no sign of any cups or teabags. Her expression was at first puzzled, then tipped towards anxious.

'Shall we go back and sit by the fire?' Broad said, giving Lockyer a significant look.

'What a good idea,' Inez said. 'Gosh, doesn't this winter seem to be dragging on and on? Roll on spring, I say.'

Neither of them had the heart to point out that it was only autumn.

'Would you mind if we had a walk around the field?' Lockyer said, once Inez was back on her rancid settee. 'We'd like to see where the dig took place.'

'Of course. Yes – you came about the dig! Have a look over there, my dear,' she said to Broad. 'Over there – by the telly. That's a video of it. Would you like to see it?'

'We really would, thank you,' Broad said. 'Only we're a bit pressed for time right now. Would it be okay for us to borrow it? And perhaps make a copy? I promise we'll return it.'

'Yes, all right,' Inez said. 'Only you *will* be careful not to lose it? *Such* a happy time.'

'We'll be very careful.'

'Well, have fun,' she said, as though they were heading out for a game of tennis. 'Look out for the marker stone. And do keep away from the barn, won't you? It's become rather unstable. And call again, any time.'

'Inez, would you like us to arrange for somebody to come and visit you?' Broad said. 'We could ask the district nurse to come and check your ankle, if you like. Perhaps someone to do some cooking and cleaning – or a chiropodist, for a bit of a pedicure?'

'Well, honestly, that *does* sound lovely! It's very kind of you, but no, thank you. Darren looks after me, and he gets rather cross if I ask too many people around. He says they'll only steal from me. People can be *wicked*, at times, can't they?'

'I'm afraid so,' Broad said grimly. 'Is Darren a de Redvers, too?'

'Oh, no, dear. He's a Mason.' She laid a wobbling hand on Broad's arm. Her nails were split, black underneath. 'He isn't *really* my nephew, you understand? But don't tell him I said so.'

Outside, they both took lungfuls of fresh air. Lockyer could feel the outrage coming off Broad in waves. She was almost tearful.

'How on *earth* do people end up living like that?' she said. 'They don't ask for help.'

'I want a word with Darren bloody Mason, if he's supposed to be looking after her. I mean, fuck's *sake*, guv!' She very rarely swore. 'There are rats in there! And the *stink* . . .'

'I know, Gem.' He showed her the empty blister pack of diazepam. 'These were everywhere. If she's been taking them for a long time it could explain her shakes, and the confusion.'

'Poor thing,' Broad muttered. 'She didn't even know about the pandemic. It's not safe in there – she could drop through the floor at any moment. Or else have the roof cave in on her.'

'It's awful. But you offered to arrange some help and she declined – and Darren might have tried, too, for all we know. If she wants to stay in her own home, there's not much else we can do.'

Broad fell into a mutinous silence. Lockyer doubted she'd let it go that easily.

'The video was a good find, though.'

'If that's even what's on there,' Broad said.

'Might be worth us contacting the production company, or Channel 4,' he said. 'See if they've got any other footage we could look at. Any outtakes.'

Broad nodded. 'I'll get on it as soon as we get back.'

'I know it's horrendous, Inez living like that,' Lockyer said, 'but we need to focus on Nazma. I'm not sure how much help Inez is going to be, but she did say something useful: there was a row, involving Nazma.'

'Yeah. She thought Darren had upset Nazma. All the more reason to pay him a visit.'

'And that Pippa also disappeared.'

'Do you think Pippa was her girlfriend?'

'It sounded like it,' Lockyer said. 'Could be worth looking at it. Two women vanishing from the same place would be a bit of coincidence. And I *hate* coincidences.'

'She probably got buried under an avalanche of junk and couldn't escape,' Broad said. 'Or fell down the well. Besides, Nazma disappeared from Marlborough, not here.'

They made their way to the barn and peered in through the collapsed end wall. Beyond the piles of rubble and rotting thatch, two sets of bunk beds were visible in the gloom.

'You don't think those were the actual beds they used during the dig?' Broad said.

'Could be. Inez doesn't seem the type to put things away.'

'I've never seen anything like that house. I mean, you see hoarders on TV, trying to get it all sorted out.' She shook her head. 'But a place *that* size, full to the rafters?'

'Whoever eventually tackles it will need a bulldozer,'

Lockyer said. 'Come on. Might as well see where the dig was.'

Nearby, rooks bickered in a twisted yew tree. *She was scared off by the rooks, you know.* Inez might know a lot more than she'd told them, but whether she'd ever be able to retrieve those memories, or link them to the questions they were asking her, was another thing entirely. *Such a happy time.*

The field where Nazma's excavation had taken place was about three acres of choppy grass, grazed by a neighbour's sheep. It had a clear line of sight west, to Avebury, a village that had grown up alongside and partially inside the largest prehistoric stone circle in the world. Lockyer had always found it a strange and resonant place.

The marker Inez had mentioned was a flat slab of stone, inscribed: *Site of Cist Burial,* circa *2000 BC. Excavated in 1999 by Brittonic Archaeology.*

'You mean, they just covered it over again?' Broad was incredulous.

'Best way to protect these things sometimes.'

'What do you think they found in there?'

Lockyer shook the video cassette. 'Hopefully this will tell us.'

He turned to look back at Trusloe Hall, peeking out above the tangled trees. In the other direction, a line of hawthorn and crack willow grew along the south-eastern boundary of the field, and Lockyer realized something.

Broad followed as he set off in that direction, almost jogging to keep up with his longer strides. 'What is it, guv?'

'Just checking something,' he muttered.

Sure enough, it was a river. Sunk down between its banks and not particularly wide, but deep, and flowing with steady conviction. Lockyer opened the OS map on his phone.

'This is the River Kennet,' he said. 'It runs south from here and curves east, into Marlborough, then out through Mildenhall, where the boys found the Nike bag. It gets so slow here in the summer that you'd hardly notice it but, like Liz Kirmani said, around this time of year – the time of year Nazma went missing – it's deep, and fast enough.'

'Fast enough for what?'

'For whoever threw her escape bag into the water to have done it *right here*, not in Marlborough.'

'Okay . . .' Broad said. 'What does that tell us, guv?'

'I don't know yet.' He turned to look at the house again. Its watchful windows. 'We need to speak to someone who was on the original investigation for the five minutes it ran. What was the name?

'DS Brodzki.'

'Right. Let's find Brodzki. I want to know why they bothered with a forensic sample of mud from a boot print in that barn.'

Back in the car, cautiously optimistic, Broad said: 'Inez is a nice name. Good name for a baby girl?'

'Come off it, Gem,' he said. 'We're Wiltshire folk. You can't go calling your kid "Inez", unless you're prepared to spend a lifetime claiming their father was Pablo Picasso.'

She chuckled. 'You think that was just a story?'

'Don't you?'

'Oh, I don't know. Picasso had enough mistresses – enough illegitimate kids – for it to be at least *possible*.'

They headed east, towards Marlborough. The road took them past the foot of Silbury Hill, a vast conical mound, built in prehistoric times by unknown hands.

'So what will you call her, if it's a girl? You must have a shortlist by now,' Broad said.

'No.' Lockyer kept his eyes on the road. 'Not yet.'

'Hedy is an unusual name,' Broad pressed on. 'Is that a tradition, in her family?'

'Her mum's name is Pauline.'

'Oh.'

She let it drop, and Lockyer felt bad. 'Look, sorry. I don't mean to be a grouch about it. It's just . . . all a bit up in the air, still.'

'That's okay, guv. None of my business, anyway. But you must be excited, right?'

There was something off-key in her tone. As though she *needed* him to be excited, to be looking forward to the birth, and to this new life of his. His life as a father. With a sinking sensation, Lockyer recognized that what he actually felt was closer to foreboding.

'It's . . .' he began. It was what? Out of his hands? Utterly unknown? Deeply unsettling? He sighed sharply. 'I've got no idea what it's like, Gem. I've got no idea what Hedy plans to do once the kid's born. I've got no idea what we'll call it, or how I'm going to . . . adjust. It just—'

He broke off, leaving a startled silence. They watched the road for a while.

'It'll be amazing, guv,' Broad said eventually.

Lockyer didn't reply.

They parked on Marlborough's wide, elegant high street, where every year for centuries the Mop Fair had been held in early October. Today there was just the usual array of well-heeled shoppers and lunchers, wrapped up against the cool breeze. Hard to imagine it flooded with a raucous party crowd, lit by whirling rides and smelling of beer and candy-floss.

'This is it,' Lockyer said, at the entrance to Figgins Lane, a cramped alleyway heading south-east off the high street. Broad had the few pages of the original file in her hands.

'Nazma was last seen running off down here to have a pee at about half past ten that night,' she said. 'Weird. There would've been portaloos.'

'Maybe, but there were also probably queues for them,' Lockyer said. 'And they probably stank by that time of the evening.'

'Good point.'

Figgins Lane narrowed and became a footpath, cutting between high brick walls. Lockyer checked the satellite map.

'There's a public park in there,' he said, pointing to the left-hand wall. 'Priory Gardens.'

'That'd be my choice for an *al fresco* wee, rather than out here in the alleyway,' Broad said. She shot him an uncomfortable look. 'It's different when you have to drop your pants completely.'

'I'm sure it is.'

They found a gate and walked down through the tidy

gardens, to where they met the River Kennet, faster and deeper between man-made banks. Some light industrial sheds and a large car park were visible through the trees on the far bank.

'Figgins Lane car park,' Broad said. 'You can't get to it from inside the gardens here. You'd have to go back out into the alleyway, and right to the bottom.'

They did that, crossing a footbridge onto the tarmac.

'And this is where the kebab man thought he saw her?' Lockyer said.

'Yes. Giannis Andino. His van was pitched right there.'

She pointed to a spot directly opposite the end of Figgins Lane.

'What exactly did he see?'

'Well, he called it in, so it's pretty brief. Just a note that Mr Andino reported seeing a woman matching Nazma's description, in the company of a man, being assisted towards the car park. He said she appeared drunk, and the man was supporting her.'

'It would have been dark, of course,' Lockyer said. 'Anybody else see her?'

'It doesn't say.'

'Any description of the man she was with? Or the car they presumably got into?'

'No, guv. Nor of seeing them chuck anything into the river.'

'Course not.'

'Whoever was with her might have been giving her a ride somewhere?' Broad said.

Nazma could have caught a mainline train to London from Swindon or Pewsey, but she'd have needed a lift. It was a good eleven or twelve miles to either station. And her rail card had ended up in the Kennet, with her passport and the rest of her things.

'But if Emma's right, and Nazma wasn't drinking by then . . .' Broad went on.

'Then it might not have been her Andino saw,' Lockyer said. 'Or she wasn't drunk at all.'

'Just . . . incapacitated in some other way,' Broad said quietly. 'Not being helped along but . . . dragged.'

Lockyer glanced around. 'No cameras in Figgins Lane, or the gardens. Not many back here, either. Probably none at all in 1999 – not that the footage would have survived, in any case. But I wonder if anyone checked for it, back then.'

'There's nothing else in the file. It's practically useless,' Broad said.

'Well, they had good grounds to drop it.'

'Not good enough,' Broad muttered. 'I mean, what if that *was* her, guv? And the man *was* dragging her off, and then killed her? What if that was the last sighting of Nazma Kirmani alive, the police dropped it, and the man who took her just . . . carried on with his life, like nothing had happened?'

Lockyer didn't need Broad to point out the raging injustice of that. The crashing failure. And if she *had* been pregnant at the time, then two lives had been taken. 'If that's what happened, Gem, we're going to find out who took her. And where.'

'Right,' she said.

In that moment, his determination felt strong enough to overcome the difficulties involved in picking up a trail left to go *so* cold. Strong enough to crush the possibility that they wouldn't succeed.

'Come on,' he said. 'Let's get back. We need to find DS Brodzki, and Giannis Andino.'

5

Day 3, Wednesday

Lockyer woke early, as he always did. The sun wasn't up, but from the pale glow at the window he guessed it wouldn't be long. He turned, and felt the strangeness of Hedy being there; less of a shock now than at the start but not gone. She was sound asleep on her side, knees drawn up to the bulge of the baby, wearing a tiny frown as though dreaming a serious conundrum. She often had nightmares, and roused him with a kick or a thrown fist, stray syllables called out in fear. He would wake her, see the panic replaced by relief, and then, sometimes, doubt.

Her night terrors never let him forget what she'd been through. Loss, betrayal, imprisonment. The first half of her life had been cruel; he wanted nothing more than for the second half to be happy. As lightly as he could, Lockyer laid his hand on the bump. The baby was awake, wriggling around as though keen to be up and about, out in the world. A child of his, of theirs. He'd got so used to the idea of it not happening to him that he still struggled to grasp this new reality. His solitary life, his late-night walks, the freedom to lose himself in thought, and keep to his own timetable: all that was about to change.

He realized now how easy it was to fall in love from afar – and how different and more precarious it was than falling slowly in love with someone you saw all the time. Someone you'd come to know implicitly. There'd been no entwining of roots, no tempering to strengthen their bond.

When he'd first told his mother about Hedy's return, and about the baby, she'd caught her breath. So thrilled he'd been wrong-footed. He knew she liked Hedy, but he'd expected some note of caution.

'Oh, *Matthew* . . . That's just the most wonderful news!'

'You think so?'

'Of *course* it is, you silly thing!' Tears had sparkled in her eyes.

'We hardly know each other, Mum. Not really.'

'But you care for Hedy, I know you do.'

'Yes. But . . . this is . . .'

'All a bit sudden? Well, yes, I suppose it is. But it's still *wonderful*.' She'd smiled, and clasped his hand, her grip still frail after her illness. 'It's new life, Matt. It's a new start for you. For this family. I'm going to be a *grandma*. Do you have any idea how happy that makes me?'

'I'm getting that impression.'

Her smile had faltered a little. 'You do want this child, don't you?'

'Yes. I just . . . I can't imagine it.'

'Well, don't worry about that. Anything you imagine will be nothing like the reality, in any case. And don't *worry*. It doesn't matter whether you've been together two months or ten years, no relationship ever comes with a guarantee. But the child will be so *loved*, by all of us. This is a *good thing*, Matt. Trust me.'

A new start for this family.

'Chris would have laughed his arse off,' Lockyer said. 'He was always carping on about my lack of spontaneity.'

Sadness crept into Trudy's smile. 'Yes, he would. But he'd have loved it, too.'

'He'd have been the fun uncle, the one the kid runs to when I try to set boundaries and they hate me,' he said, and she laughed. 'He'd have taken them out for McDonald's, and let them get their ears pierced when I'd said no.'

'That's *exactly* how he'd have been. And they'd have *adored* him.'

And even though they'd both fallen quiet, acknowledging the huge gap Chris had left in their lives, Lockyer had felt easier. He tried not to think of the baby as something he was giving back to his parents, some tiny step towards assuaging his own guilt over his brother's death. Tried instead to hold on to the mental image of his brother – older but still irrepressible – horsing about with his niece or nephew on his shoulders.

There was a particularly sharp little jab from the bump, and Hedy's eyes snapped open.

'Good morning,' he said.

'Did you kick me?'

'Not me.'

She smiled slightly, rubbed her eyes, then turned slowly onto her back, shoving herself further up the bed, and leaning forwards. Automatically, Lockyer dropped an extra pillow behind her shoulders. Little things like that gave him hope.

'Thanks,' she said.

'Tea?'

'Yes, please. But in a minute.' She reached across and took his hand.

'What are you going to do with your last day of freedom?' he said.

'Oh, God, I forgot.' She sighed. 'Mind you, I don't think being under lockdown will make much difference to the hectic social whirl of my life.'

'No. Nor mine.'

She poked the bump. 'I can't wait till this one is on the *out*side, so I can at least go for a walk. Then *you* can carry him or her for a while.'

'We really should think of some names. People will keep asking.'

'It's none of their business.'

Privacy was hugely important to her. A hangover from prison, Lockyer thought. 'I know. But they're just trying to be nice,' he said. 'This is my parents' first grandchild, too, not just your mum's.'

'I know.' Hedy shut her eyes. 'I feel rubbish about the other night, when I went on about family names. I just . . . I struggle, sometimes, to . . .'

'To take me into the equation?'

She looked at him, that steady grey gaze. 'I've been by myself for a very long time, Matt.'

'So have I.'

A small shake of her head. 'Not like I have.' She lifted his hand and kissed his knuckles, and he accepted it as a peace-offering.

'Do you want to call her Katie, if it's girl?' he asked, after the sister Hedy had adored, lost to cancer at a young age.

Hedy considered it for a moment, then shook her head.

'No, I don't think so. Do you want to call him Christopher, if it's a boy?'

'No,' Lockyer replied. He'd given it no thought, but knew immediately that it wouldn't feel right. It wasn't necessary. None of them would ever forget Chris, or what had happened to him.

'Okay,' Hedy said. 'So, tell me some names you *do* like.'

'Well . . .' He drew a complete blank. 'I haven't a clue.'

'Come on, you must have *some* idea. Even if it's just a type of name.'

'All right. Something simple. Nothing posh, nothing made up, nothing in another language. Nothing double-barrelled, and nothing with more than two syllables.'

'Right. So . . . Bob, then?' she said.

'Great, that's settled. And if it's a boy?'

Hedy laughed, and pulled him closer.

The fuzzy footage on Inez's video cassette reminded Lockyer how much better picture resolution had got. After a few adverts that looked more than twenty years out of date, and made him feel old, the episode of *Dig Britain* began, with strident title music and sweeping aerial views of various historical landmarks. Then the presenter – a photogenic female archaeologist – introduced Avebury and the excavation in search of the lost Beckhampton Avenue, the existence of which was hinted at by the Longstones, two standing stones remaining to the west of the henge.

Lockyer watched the hour-long episode right through. It focused primarily on the main dig site, several hundred metres from where Nazma had been working at Trusloe Hall. Lockyer paid particular attention when Edward Chapman appeared on screen: the head of Brittonic Archaeology.

'For generations, these two stones have been known locally as the Adam and Eve Stones, and thought to be an isolated feature,' he said, addressing the nodding presenter rather than the camera. 'But we believe they may be part of a far bigger structure, linking the henge at Avebury to Windmill Hill, behind us, which is actually the site of far earlier human habitation . . .'

He spoke clearly, using his hands a lot. A tall, rangy man, with a deep tan and loose waves of light brown hair, swept back and turning fair in the sun. He had an open, handsome face, blue eyes, and an air of affability that worked well on camera. He didn't look the type to be cheating on his wife with a student, but you never could tell. Other footage showed Edward with the top two buttons of his khaki shirt undone, displaying a V of weathered chest as he clambered through trenches, explaining as he went.

Then the presenter introduced the second dig site, with the exciting possibility of a burial.

Nazma appeared on camera. She talked the presenter and viewers through the crop marks that had led them there, and the results of a subsequent geophysical survey.

'What do you think it is?' the presenter asked.

Smiling, Nazma replied: 'We think – we *hope* – it's a cist burial. A stone-lined burial chamber from the Bronze Age.'

'So there could be the remains of one of our prehistoric ancestors in there?'

'It's possible, yes. Quite often this kind of burial was used for cremated remains, so we might find pieces of a burial urn, or other grave goods. We just won't know until we get down there and have a look.'

'Well, you'd better get digging!' the presenter said.

Nazma laughed, agreed. A trace of nervous excitement.

The camera loved her – Lockyer supposed that was why she'd been singled out to talk to the presenter. Her black hair shone in the sun; her figure looked good in a tight Brittonic T-shirt. Slim legs in battered Dr Marten boots. There was no way to know if she was already pregnant at the time of filming. She may not have known herself. Lockyer searched for her in the background of every shot, and spotted her here and there. Footage of her crouching in a trench, carefully scraping the soil from a large flat stone. Then looking on from one side as Edward explained to the presenter that this was the capstone, and that it appeared to be intact and undisturbed.

'Until now,' the presenter said. 'Isn't it *amazing* to think that we'll be the first people to see inside this tomb since it was built *thousands* of years ago?'

'Archaeology is time travel,' Edward said. It sounded like something he'd said many times before.

Later, Nazma made a short speech about the cist still being a fascinating piece of prehistory, despite it being entirely empty, before the programme returned to the main dig site, where enough buried stones had been unearthed to prove the existence of the avenue. A review of finds; a CGI reconstruction of the site; the diggers all gathered together in a marquee, raising plastic cups of beer to toast their success.

A younger, far more with-it Inez appeared on screen beside a tray of muddy flints and pot sherds, wearing a pink Panama hat and enormous chandelier earrings. A caption below her read: *Inez de Redvers, local landowner.*

'Well, I think it's all completely *fascinating*,' she said, fixing a gaze of avid sincerity on someone behind the camera. 'It's been an utter delight having the team here these past few months, and I'm simply *thrilled* that they've had such success with their endeavours.'

At the end, as the presenter summed up, Inez was in the background, posing awkwardly on a folding chair next to a bearded archaeologist twice her size. Nazma stood behind her, resting one hand on her shoulder as though to reassure her. They all cheered; the credits rolled. A blizzard of empty tape filled the screen and then an episode of *Birding with Bill Oddie* resumed, mid-sentence.

Lockyer ejected the tape and asked the technician to

make a digital working copy. He got some tea for himself and coffee for Broad on his way back up to their office.

'Nothing revelatory,' he told her. 'Watch it yourself once the copy comes through. Inez is on there, looking forty years younger, not twenty.'

'And Nazma?'

'Looks happy. Keen.' Lockyer shrugged. 'No hint of an undercurrent. But most of the footage she's in is from the start of the dig, when they still thought they might find something in the cist.'

'Thanks for the plot spoiler, guv – they didn't find any-thing?'

'Sorry. Just an empty, stone-lined hole in the ground, which was still exciting for them, but clearly not for the TV producer.'

'Oh. Shame.'

'Nazma's wearing her locket in every shot,' Lockyer added.

They both glanced at the photo of the locket on the board. Tarnished; its contents rotted by two decades of mud and water.

'How've you got on?' he asked.

'Okay. I've got through to two of the Brittonic lot who were at Trusloe Hall with Nazma. They're happy to talk to us, but neither wants an in-person visit because of Covid. Both are happy with a video call.' She handed him a piece of paper with the details. 'I was about to run a check on the mysterious Pippa, but then I realized we didn't get her surname, so that'll have to wait. I've found Darren Mason, though. Born April twenty-first, 1980. Looks like he's lived in Avebury Trusloe all his life. Arrested more than once for various antisocial offences: drunk and disorderly, possession with intent to supply, breaking and entering. He did a short stretch in juvy for assault, but the rest is just fines and community-service orders. He's gone quiet over the past six or seven years.'

'Perhaps he finally grew out of it,' Lockyer said.

'Or just got better at it.'

Broad was keen to go and talk to him, Lockyer could tell. Probably to grill him about his relationship with Inez, and her shocking living conditions.

'Well,' he said, 'if he's lived there all his life he's not going anywhere. Let's talk to these archaeologists. See if we can get a clearer idea of what was actually going on there that summer.'

They called Ingrid Roach first, a woman in her mid-sixties with a strong jaw and small, very pale eyes. She now lived in Didcot and was no longer working as an archaeologist. Lockyer recognized her from the episode of *Dig Britain*: she'd never spoken to camera but had been in several shots, consulting a map, or pointing out blurred shapes on a computer screen. Her hair had had more blonde in it then, her athletic physique an Amazonian quality that had got bulkier with age.

'Comes a time one has to accept the reality of a situation,' she said baldly. 'I wasn't going to marry a millionaire, and I wasn't going to have much of a retirement if I stayed in archaeology, however much I loved it.'

She had a clipped, efficient way of speaking that gave the

impression of her tolerating their request for help. A busy person, managing to fit them in.

'What do you do now, Ms Roach, if you don't mind my asking?' Lockyer said.

'It's "Miss" Roach. I'm not divorced. I'm an accountant, and I also proofread, mostly for academic textbooks.'

'That must have been quite a gear shift.'

'Not really. My specialism was in geophysical survey – the more data-driven side of things. I have an analytical brain.'

'How long were you with Brittonic?'

'Oh, I came on board with Edward right at the start. 1986? Something like that. I left in 2005.'

'We understand that you worked on the excavation at Avebury Trusloe in 1999, alongside Nazma Kirmani. What can you tell us about her?'

'Not a great deal, really. Not much substance to her, but she was pleasant enough. Competent, when she could keep her mind on the job. I wasn't at all surprised when she took off the way she did.'

Lockyer was taken aback. 'What makes you say that?'

'She was just very ... What's the word? *Flimsy*, I suppose. She seemed very young for her age, to me. Impulsive – just the type to flounce off when things didn't go her way.'

'What wasn't going her way?'

Ingrid waved one hand, as though irritated at being asked to elaborate. 'Well, I don't know exactly. She'd got very chummy with the batty woman in the big house, but then I got the impression it'd gone sour, towards the end of the dig. So perhaps it was that. Or boy trouble of some kind.'

'"Boy trouble"? We understood she'd been in a relationship with Edward Chapman for around a year, prior to her
disappearance?'

'Well, I'd hardly call it that.'

'You're saying they *weren't* in a relationship?' Broad said.

A flash of real annoyance crossed Ingrid's face. 'I suppose I wouldn't know. She had a crush on him, that much
was clear – never mind that he was twice her age, give or
take. He was very gracious about it, for the most part, but
I suppose he wouldn't be the first man to give in to the
temptation of low-hanging fruit. They're all susceptible,
sadly. Even the clever ones.'

Her poorly veiled bitterness spoke volumes.

'What kind of man is Mr Chapman? Lockyer asked.

Ingrid fixed him with a cool gaze. 'A very dear old friend.'

'How did you come to work with him?'

'Oh, we go way back. We were at Oxford together. Not
in the same college, of course – I was at St Hilda's. But we
both read economics.'

'Not archaeology?'

'No, that came a little later. We actually dated for a
while but, really, we were better off as friends. He needed
a shoulder to cry on when he got his heart broken by one
posh dimwit or other.'

'Can't have been too many dimwits at Oxford, surely?'
Lockyer said.

'Don't you believe it. Less so, these days, perhaps, but
back then it was often more about who your parents were
and which school you'd been to than whether you could tell

your arse from your elbow. We handful of state-educated entrants toughed it out together – Edward and I included.'

'I've just watched the episode of *Dig Britain*. Mr Chapman seemed to me like the sort of person who'd fit right in to those circles.'

'Well, by then he was, of course. That tends to be what happens – people change their plumage to fit in. I could never be bothered with any of that, so I was never terribly popular. That was the main reason Edward and I didn't work as a couple. He'd been raised to believe he had "betters". Always far too concerned about cosying up to "the right sort". Seemed a bit desperate, to me, but it was hardly surprising, I suppose.'

'No?'

'Edward's father bolted when he was very small, but I met his mother once or twice. Shirley Ann Chapman. Heartless shell of a woman. Suffice to say, she'd have sold her own soul – and Edward's – to see him rise up the ranks. She had the very *sharpest* of elbows, which at least showed a certain ambition, I suppose, given that they lived in a two-up, two-down in Mile End.'

'Mile End? I didn't hear that in his voice,' Lockyer said.

'No, well, you wouldn't – elocution lessons, you see. I honestly think Shirley expected Edward to be prime minister one day. Or appointed to the peerage. Luckily, she died before having to accept that it wasn't to be.' Ingrid looked away, considering. 'Honestly, the things people do to their offspring. I always *understood* Edward – I knew that he was an exceptional man. But it took decades for *him* to see it. For him to grow comfortable in his own skin.'

Lockyer changed tack. 'Did you get to know Inez de Redvers?'

'The woman at Trusloe Hall? No, not at all. I spoke to her once or twice – and I got the impression she was plastered, on both occasions.'

'What did you speak to her about?'

'Practically nothing. It was her suggestion that we use the barn, if we wanted, and there was some discussion about that. Otherwise, I really can't remember.'

'Did you stay in the barn?'

'I did, for a couple of weeks while the weather was warm, though I wasn't completely convinced of the safety of the structure.'

'Did you ever meet Mrs de Redvers's nephew, Darren?'

'No, I don't think so. Unless . . . Was he the surly young man who did odd jobs for her?'

'Possibly.'

'He assembled the bunk beds in the barn for us. If that *was* him, then he was a complete oaf. When I suggested a different layout, to give us each a bit more privacy, he suggested that I could stick them wherever I wanted – only those weren't his exact words. If he was her nephew, then all I can say is that the noble bloodline had got very diluted.'

'And you never saw anything unusual going on there?'

'What do you mean, "unusual"?'

'We're trying to establish why an apparently happy and secure young woman might have chosen to walk out on her life,' Lockyer said. 'If that is what she did.'

'No, I never saw anything I'd class as unusual. And she

seemed flighty to me, as I said. I mean, you say she was in a relationship with Edward, but what about that other young man?'

'Which other young man might that be?' Lockyer asked, as neutrally as he could.

'Haven't a clue, but I kept on seeing them together, and they were *very* flirty. Lots of *accidental* contact in passing, and lingering eye contact, that sort of thing. I remember thinking that at least he was an appropriate age for her.'

'And it wasn't Darren Mason?'

'Lord, no. I suppose he might've been one of the university students from over on the main site of the dig. Or someone from the television programme. I really don't know, but I'm sure the police must have spoken to him at the time. All I'm saying is that, to me, Nazma seemed the type to enjoy a little *drama*.'

'Did you go to the Marlborough Mop on the night that Nazma disappeared?'

'No. Not really my scene,' she said, with a grating loftiness. Lockyer hoped that Broad was managing not to roll her eyes on screen.

'Well, thank you, Miss Roach,' he said, stopping short of saying she'd been helpful. 'We appreciate you taking the time to talk to us. And if you do think of anything else, however irrelevant it might seem, please don't hesitate to get in touch.'

'Happy to help. Goodbye.'

She cut the call with a nod rather than a smile, and Broad pulled a face. 'Well, isn't *she* just a bundle of fun?' she said. 'Pretty low opinion of Nazma, too.'

'And she didn't seem at all surprised – or even interested – to hear that Nazma hasn't resurfaced in all these years.'

'That's true.' Broad got up and went back to her own desk. 'Do you think Edward Chapman was the millionaire she was hoping to marry?'

'Once she'd finished her stint as his shoulder to cry on? I reckon so. She certainly enjoys talking about him. If so, jealousy might be why she wasn't too keen on Nazma. Emma Billingham didn't seem to know anything about her having a new boyfriend, and isn't that the sort of thing you'd tell your best mate?' he said.

'Definitely,' Broad said. 'At least, I would. Not that I have. Or . . . whatever.' She regrouped. 'But Emma also said that Nazma had always defended Edward, and defended her relationship with him when Emma was down on it. So that might've made it harder for her to talk to Emma about a new bloke, or if she was cooling off.'

Lockyer nodded. 'Have we got a list of everyone who was on site that summer? From the two universities, as well?'

'No,' Broad said, with a hint of disinclination. 'Just the Brittonic lot so far. I could widen the net, but I think we'd be talking in the region of about eighty people at that point.'

'I've dealt with bigger fields than that. But let's talk to the other archaeologist you contacted first. I wish we knew whether the investigation did speak to anyone else Nazma had met that summer, even if Ingrid got the wrong end of the stick about a romance.'

'Has no one got back to you about that yet, guv?'

Lockyer shook his head. The brief investigation into Nazma's disappearance had been handled by Swindon CID. DS Michelle Brodzki, who'd filled out Nazma's misper report, was now a DI on the Oxfordshire force. She hadn't returned his call.

'The other archaeologist is Jonathan Tate,' Broad said. 'He said he'd be at work until four, so he can't talk till after that.'

'Fine. Any luck with the kebab man?'

'Giannis Andino? No. He moved back to Greece after Brexit. I'm still trying to track him down.' She gave him an expectant look.

'All right,' he said.

'Darren Mason?' she said.

'Get your coat.'

6

Darren Mason's address took them to an end-of-terrace house on a small estate in Avebury Trusloe, only a few hundred metres from the ramshackle gates of Trusloe Hall. It was clearly a house that had been built to serve a practical purpose, on a budget that left nothing in reserve for beautification. Its residents hadn't given it any personal touches, and the front lawn hadn't been cut for a long time. A VW Golf was parked on the drive, with tinted windows and an *Isle of Man TT 2019* banner in the rear windscreen.

'I thought that was for motorbikes?' Broad said.

'It is,' Lockyer said. 'Perhaps they're all in the garage.'

'They are,' said a man, appearing around the side of the house. He was mid-height, with burly shoulders, baggy jeans and a savagely short haircut. Eyes puffy beneath sunken brows. He'd have looked younger than his forty years if it hadn't been for his expression: habitual distrust, bordering on hostility. He kept his distance.

'What do you want?'

'To ask a couple of questions,' Lockyer said, as they showed their ID.

'About what?' Darren was wearing a T-shirt; the skin of his arms was mottled with the cold, but he clearly wasn't going to invite them in.

Lockyer suspected that had far more to do with them being police than it did with the pandemic. 'Inez de Redvers,' he said, and to his surprise, Darren's expression changed at once. A flash of concern, bordering on fear.

'What about her? She all right?'

'She's fine, as far as we know,' Lockyer said.

Darren exhaled. He dropped his chin briefly, looking down. 'Always half waiting to hear she's carked it,' he muttered.

'She says you look after her.' Broad couldn't keep the accusation out of her tone.

'I do what I can for her.'

'The house is falling down around her ears.'

From inside came the high, thin wail of a very young baby. Darren glared at Broad, his mouth twisting to one side.

'Right, well, I'll just pop over and fix it up for her, shall I? Only wants a team of thirty or so, I reckon, maybe a budget of a million or two. Inez hasn't got two pennies to rub together, and neither have I.'

Broad managed to stifle whatever reply sprang to her mind.

'Could you tell us about your relationship with Mrs de Redvers?' Lockyer said instead. 'She speaks very highly of you.'

A shrug. 'We're friends, I suppose. I've known her since I was a kid. She never had any of her own. Likes to tell people I'm her nephew. She never had any of those, either.'

'How did you meet?'

'Me and my mates used to go into her garden, daring each other to ring the doorbell, that kind of shite. Then one time she came roaring out with a shotgun and we nearly shat ourselves. After that I had the garden to myself when I needed some space. One day she just came over and talked to me like she knew me. Needed some help moving a sofa or something, and would I mind terribly. So in I went, gave her a hand. She gave me a bottle of champagne, and asked if I was interested in art. I was twelve years old and no one had ever given me anything before, 'cept grief.'

'So she took you in?'

'Sort of.' Darren lit a cigarette. 'I'd go there after school and that. Sometimes instead of school. She never *lectured* me. Never went on about my clothes being dirty or any of that social-worker shit.'

'And these days?' Lockyer said.

'She won't move out of there, if you're on about trying to get involved.'

'When we spoke to her, Mrs de Redvers seemed confused.'

'She's always been batty. Bound to get worse with age, weren't it?'

'We found evidence of a lot of prescription-drug use in the house.'

Darren stared again before answering. 'There's a lot of all sorts of crap in that house. She lost the plot when her friend

Pippa buggered off. Her drinking got worse, and she started popping pills for her *nerves*, and all that posho bullshit. Why are you asking about her? She just wants leaving alone.'

'Actually, she invited us to call again,' Broad said.

'Yeah, well, she says that to everyone,' Darren snapped. 'Look, I've got things to be doing, so—'

'Do you remember Pippa?' Lockyer asked.

'Yeah, course I do.' He hesitated. 'Don't tell me you've *found* 'er?'

'Is she missing?'

'I dunno. Inez always says so, but I reckon she walked out. I don't know how things work with lezzers, but I guess if you've had enough you just hop it, right? Same as any relationship.'

'I imagine so. Can you tell us her full name?'

'Inez'll tell you. If she wants you to know.'

Lockyer smiled briefly. 'We saw a lot of cardboard boxes at the house, Darren. Looked new. Inez told us they were yours.'

'She's wrong. Nothing to do with me.'

'We've seen your record, Darren.'

'That was all years ago, I don't do any of that stuff now. I've got a family to support.'

'What do you do for a living these days?'

'Spannering. Custom motorbike builds, that sort of thing.'

Lockyer looked for signs of shiftiness or nerves in Darren, but saw only minor fluctuations in his hostility towards them.

'Look, we're not here to make trouble for Inez,' he said.

'Or for you, unless we have to. She mentioned Pippa's disappearance, and we tend to prick up our ears at things like that. We're actually looking into another missing person – a woman named Nazma Kirmani, last seen in 1999.'

Darren took his time to answer. He wasn't stupid, Lockyer decided, and he probably had good reason to say nothing whatsoever, to go inside and shut the door in their faces. But he was still standing there, with goosebumps all up his arms. From that, Lockyer took that he cared a great deal about Inez de Redvers.

'Yeah. That girl. One of the history lot,' he said eventually.

'Do you remember her?'

'Not especially. She latched on to Inez, or maybe it was vice versa. Inez was still moaning on about Pippa and her broken heart, and all the rest of it, and that girl was pretty, right? Helped take her mind off it, maybe. She hung around the house a bit, after hours. I saw her there a few times. The place wasn't quite as much of a shithole back then.'

'Inez suggested that you and Nazma might have fallen out about something?'

'Like I said, you don't want to go taking everything she says as gospel.' He tapped the side of his head. 'She gets muddled. Did then, sure as shit does now.'

'Has she ever had a medical diagnosis for her cognitive decline?' Lockyer asked.

'Don't think so. Her artistic brain, she always says. She used to drink a lot.'

'And she was drinking in 1999?'

'Yeah.'

'So you and Nazma never argued about anything?'

'I spoke to her maybe twice. Maybe four words on each of those occasions. If that.'

'Were you surprised to hear she'd disappeared?'

'No.'

'Why not?'

'I wasn't surprised, I wasn't not surprised. None of my business, was it?'

'Right. So there's nothing you can tell us about it? Or about Nazma's time at Trusloe?'

'Only what I just said.'

Lockyer and Broad exchanged a look, and an expression of defensive resentment flickered across Darren's face.

'Why are you asking? She wasn't even missing in the end, right?'

'We have reason to believe that she *was* missing, that she still is, and that her disappearance might somehow be linked to her time at Trusloe Hall.'

At this, Darren's brows lowered even further. 'What reason?'

'A bag of Nazma's possessions has been found in the river, east of here. Things she's unlikely to have discarded herself.'

Darren said nothing.

'Did Inez say anything to you about it at the time?' Lockyer asked. 'Did she and Nazma fall out about something?'

'I've already said, I don't know nothing about it. They all left, didn't they? All the history lot and the TV people – bunch of wankers. They all left and we stayed, and that was the end of it. I 'an't given it another thought in twenty years.'

'I can assure you that Nazma's family have,' Lockyer said quietly.

'Well, we've all got our problems, I guess.'

'Absolutely. Inez de Redvers in particular, I'd say.'

'Look, I'm not her nephew, all right? It's not up to me to look after her. I get her shopping in, and stuff like that. Check in on her. But it'll take a crowbar to get her out of that house – and I've tried. Worth a mint, even with the state it's in. Ninety-odd acres of farmland round here is still hers, an' all. I've told her she could sell it, live somewhere clean and new, and let some other bugger deal with the mess. She just looks at me like I've suggested cutting off her leg and eating it. And it's up to *her*, right?'

Lockyer thought of his own parents, and their reluctance – particularly his father's – to consider selling the family farm, when it was too much for them and had been for some time. Jody's arrival had given them a reprieve, for a while, but she'd made it perfectly clear she wouldn't stay for ever. In this one regard, he completely sympathized with Darren's predicament.

'Yes, it is up to her,' he said.

'There are more proactive things you could do, though, instead of just waiting to hear she's "carked it",' Broad said. 'Like getting the district nurse to—'

'I've fucking *tried*, all right?' Darren snapped. 'She doesn't like interference, let alone from anyone official.'

Lockyer cut in before Broad could tell him to try harder. 'Thank you, Mr Mason. If you think of anything else that might—'

'Yeah,' Darren muttered. 'Whatever.'

He crossed to the front door, but glanced back before going in.

'Philippa Harmon,' he said. 'She buggered off 'round January-February time, 'ninety-nine. Inez was proper cut up about it. She hit the bottle, and went a bit mental. More mental than usual, for a while.'

With that he shut the door, and they were left with the deserted street, and the drizzle spitting at their faces.

In the car, Lockyer sensed Broad's dissatisfaction. 'He's right, you know,' he said. 'He can't force Inez to accept help.'

'There must come a point, though, right, guv? A point where the state could step in for her own safety? That house should be condemned.'

'You really want to do that? Have her sectioned, turf her out of her home?'

Broad sighed. 'No, I think it'd be far better to let her trip over a pile of rubbish, fall badly and be eaten by vermin.'

'Come on, Gem. She's not at that stage. Yet. What did you make of Darren?'

'I suppose it seemed like he *does* care about her,' Broad said grudgingly. 'And I guess him not actually being family makes it harder to action anything on her behalf.'

'Exactly.'

'But I don't believe for a second he's gone straight. I don't know. Something about him just reeked *opportunist*, to me.'

Lockyer made a face. He knew from his friend Kevin's experience how hard it was to cut those connections. The tangled webs of loyalty, debt and threat left after an upbringing in even low-level crime, and how difficult it was to get free of them. 'He *might* have cleaned up his act,' he said. 'People do settle down, especially when they get married and start having kids.' He paused, reminded that he was now just such a person. 'We've no real reason to think otherwise.'

'Unless those cardboard boxes have vanished from Trusloe Hall the next time we go round.'

'Yeah. Maybe then.'

Broad's phone rang another three times as they drove back to the station, and every time it did Lockyer felt her tension increase.

'Maybe just talk to him, Gem,' he said. 'If it'll stop him calling every two minutes.'

'It won't,' she muttered. 'That's the problem.'

He felt a flash of impatience. 'Well, put it on silent, then.'

'Sorry, guv.' She did as she was told, and Lockyer felt the immediate regret he always did whenever he was short with her. He was still trying to think of a way to smooth things over when she added: 'He doesn't think I should be coming in.'

'What – to work?'

A scant nod. 'He's just worried. Scared I'll get the virus and give it to him.'

'Don't tell me he's quarantining you in the spare bedroom again?' Lockyer said, with a smile she didn't return.

'Not quite. Not yet, anyway.'

Lockyer glanced across at her. 'You're a police detective. He understands what that means, right?'

'Yeah. Thing is, I think he'd rather I wasn't.'

'Has he said that?'

'Not in so many words. But . . . I don't know. It seems to stress him out more and more. He says I'm putting myself at risk.'

'Well, we're managing those risks as best we can. And, in any case, it's not up to him.'

'I know.' She shifted, clasping her hands in her lap. 'I think . . . We got together when I was *fifteen*, and Pete was just turning seventeen. I was different then. Maybe that's the problem. He says I've changed, and he thinks it's down to my career.'

'Come off it, Gem. *Everyone* changes from the age of fifteen.'

'Do they?'

'It'd be weird if they *didn't*.' He thought about it. 'The fundamentals might stay the same – unless there's a major upheaval. But you grow, you develop. Lose a few inhibitions, get a few new ones. Your priorities change. At least, they should.'

'I suppose you're right.' She gazed out of the window at the wide sweep of farmland, now mostly ploughed between the Wiltshire tumps – the ancient burial mounds that scattered the county, where beech trees put down roots through the prehistoric dead.

'Pete must have changed, too,' Lockyer said.

'Not so much,' she said. 'He's got a shorter fuse. I think he feels a bit . . . let down. By life, maybe.'

'Don't we all?' Lockyer murmured, then smiled to show

he didn't mean it. Not completely. 'Bit young to be having a midlife crisis, isn't he?'

'Yeah.'

That one quiet word silenced Lockyer for a moment. This was the first time she'd really tried to talk to him about her relationship. The first time she wasn't prepared to make a joke or brush off his concern. And there was precious little he could do. Telling her to shake Pete off wouldn't help one bit.

'Want me to talk to him?' he said.

She shot him an intensely sceptical look.

'No, I mean it,' he said. 'I'd be nice, I promise. Maybe I could reassure him about our Covid-safe measures. And that I'd never put you in harm's way. That kind of thing.'

And absolutely not tell him that, as far as Lockyer was concerned, he was a pathetic bully, frustrated by his own mediocrity and, by the sound of it, threatened by how good his girlfriend was at her job.

'No. Thanks, though, guv,' she said. 'I'm not sure it'd go down too well.'

It was Lockyer's phone that rang as they got back to head-quarters, and, seeing Hedy's number, Lockyer waved Broad inside while he took the call.

'Hedy? Are you all right?'

At once came the small *tsk* she made when she was irritated. 'I wish you wouldn't ask that *every* time we speak. Like you're always waiting for some impending disaster.'

Lockyer steeled himself. Stayed steady. 'Okay. I'm sorry for that. What can I do for you?'

His tone checked her, and when she spoke it was with a kind of chilly calm. 'I need you to tell Mrs Musprat to leave me alone. She's banged on the door three times today already.'

'Iris? Is she okay?'

'She's fine. She brought round a rusty old key, and says I should drop it into everything I cook to give me more iron. It looks like she dug it up out of the garden, for God's sake.'

'She's only trying to help.'

'I've explained to her about iron tablets at least ten times already,' Hedy said.

'I think you're the first female company she's had since the 1960s. And I think she likes you.'

'I think she just likes sticking her nose in.'

'Well . . . perhaps a bit. But she's by herself, too, you know.'

'Maybe so, but I don't need her trying to mother me, or telling me what to do. This is *my* body, *my* baby—'

'*Our* baby.'

'That's what I meant.'

Lockyer wasn't at all sure he believed her.

'There's another thing,' Hedy said. 'A cot mattress with bedding and buffers has just arrived.'

Lockyer cursed inwardly. He'd hoped to intercept them somehow. 'Yes. I ordered them.'

'Well, you needn't have. We can get it all as a bundle when we buy the cot, it'll be much better value. I guess we could send these ones back.'

She had money – a huge compensation payout from her fourteen years of wrongful imprisonment. But she hadn't yet got used to thinking like someone with money.

'I've got the cot,' Lockyer said.

'What? Where from?'

'It was supposed to be a surprise. It's a one-off. I think you're going to l—'

'A one-off? What does that mean? Really, Matt, it needs to be—'

'For Christ's sake, Hedy.' Lockyer pinched the brow of his nose. 'Trust me to buy a bed for our child.'

He heard her sharp intake of breath, right before she rang off.

Women were supposed to be difficult when they were pregnant, he knew that. Hormones galore, and a whole new set of fears. The trouble was that he didn't know Hedy well enough to say whether her waspishness was due to the pregnancy, or whether living with her was always going to be like this.

Broad ran some preliminary searches for Philippa Harmon – Pippa – that turned up nothing. She'd never been reported missing. Lockyer was reluctant to give it too much of their time, but he would've been far happier if they'd found her alive and well somewhere, with no link to Nazma's disappearance.

'She had a joint British-Dutch passport that expired in 2002 and wasn't renewed,' Broad said. 'She's not on the electoral roll, and I can't find her anywhere else, either. There are about three million Philippa Harmons on social media. If we can get a photo and a date of birth from Inez, I could—'

'No,' Lockyer interrupted her. 'We need to focus on Nazma.'

'Yeah. Course, guv.'

'No harm in trying to get more information about Pippa from Inez, if we go back there, though. Which I somehow think we will.'

As arranged, they waited until the end of the afternoon to call Jonathan Tate, and a man of around forty-five appeared on screen. Lockyer recognized the large, bearded figure who'd sat next to Inez in the final frame of *Dig Britain*. There were touches of grey in his hair now; he wore his beard in a plait, and a diamond stud sparkled in one ear. Jonathan was still an archaeologist, though he'd left Brittonic some years back and now taught at Warwick University.

'Officers,' he said amiably. 'Sorry to make you wait all day, but I'm all yours.'

'We appreciate you taking the time to talk to us,' Lockyer said.

'Are you joking? Most exciting thing that's happened to me all year. And that includes fighting for the last loo roll in Asda.'

'We were hoping to ask you some questions about the 1999 dig at Trusloe Hall, and more specifically about Nazma Kirmani.'

'Ah, Snazzy Nazzy! God, I remember her – seems like aeons ago. She went *totally* off the radar after that summer. Lovely girl, though.'

'You got to know her quite well?'

'Yeah. It was a summer friendship sort of thing, you

know – our lives overlapped for that brief time, and then we went our separate ways. But, yeah, we had a right laugh. Well, mostly.'

Lockyer remembered the young man Ingrid claimed to have seen Nazma flirting with. 'Was your relationship ever more than just a friendship, Mr Tate?' he asked.

'Just Jon is fine. And no – I'm gay.'

'Oh, right. Well, could you tell us what Nazma was like?'

'Bright, friendly, a bit conventional, perhaps, but not at all in a bigoted way. She just . . . came across as quite young for her age. I was forever teasing her about it. Her idea of flying off the rails was, like, doing a vodka melon or something.'

'We understand she got along well with Inez de Redvers?'

'Inez – oh my God, I'd forgotten all about her! Mad as a box of frogs, that one. Very sweet with it, but completely batty. I mean, I've met all sorts, but I don't think Naz had ever encountered anyone quite like Inez before. And she had this undercurrent of . . . vulnerability, I suppose. Naz was such a kind person – she was like a moth to a flame. Wanting to help her, cheer her up.'

'Was Inez depressed?'

'Depressed, anxious, alcoholic, lonely – take your pick.'

'Did they ever fall out that you know of? Or have an argument?'

'No, I don't think so.' He thought back. 'I know she was worried about Inez. She asked me about it a couple of times.'

'What did she ask?'

'Whether she should tell social services, or Inez's GP,

that kind of thing. I told her to keep out of it. There's a fine line between helping and meddling, right? Inez was clearly rolling in dosh. If she'd wanted help – or company – she could've got it easily enough.'

It sounded cynical to Lockyer's ears. Perhaps it would have sounded almost callous to Nazma, if she'd been as kind and impressionable as everyone seemed to think.

'So maybe she stuck her oar in a bit too far, and got it slapped back,' Jonathan said. 'But I'm just speculating there.'

'Were you aware of Nazma's relationship with Edward Chapman?' Lockyer asked.

'Oh, yeah – everyone was. Even though they did this comedy act of being "just colleagues", which was frankly ridiculous.'

'Did they seem happy together?'

'I think so, yeah. But I did wonder.'

'What did you wonder?'

'Don't get me wrong, Edward was a real stunner back then. He had the whole Peter O'Toole in *Lawrence of Arabia* thing going on. *Very* charismatic. But he was just so much older than Naz. Plus, there was the whole married-with-kids thing. It was obviously going to run its course eventually, and maybe Naz was starting to realize that. I'd just get these little hints of it, now and then. But I don't think she was ready to admit it to herself, let alone to anyone else.'

'We've spoken to another of your colleagues from back then, Ingrid Roach. She'd formed the impression that Nazma had met someone else that summer. Somebody more her own age.'

'Ingrid? Ha! That miserable old boot. More like wishful thinking on her part, I'd say.'

'How so?'

'Because she was in love with Edward, of course. Had been for *years*, I reckon. There she was with her biological clock tick-tocking away, hoping to entice him into an affair, and along comes Nazma and bewitches him. Ingrid couldn't *stand* Naz.'

'Did you ever speak to Ingrid about any of this?'

'Speak to Ingrid? Lord, no. She wouldn't dream of talking about anything personal, let alone to the likes of me. No, I'm just telling you what was plain to see. If Naz so much as sneezed, Ingrid would give notes on her delivery, you know what I mean? Picked her up on everything. Unless Edward was around, then she was just "one of the girls".' He gave a little shudder. 'Ugh. Now you're reminding me how *awkward* it could be at times.'

'So you weren't aware of Nazma meeting anyone new while you were all at Trusloe Hall?'

'No. And I bet Ingrid wasn't either. More likely just trying to manifest the end of Naz's relationship with Edward – as though Naz was the only barrier to him being with *her* instead.' He rolled his eyes. 'Mind you, if Naz *had* met someone, she'd have kept it on the down-low, what with Edward here, there and everywhere. But I doubt it, to be honest. She was the loyal type.'

'Was Nazma pregnant, do you know?' Lockyer asked it casually, but Jonathan's eyes widened.

'Was she? I never heard about it, if so.'

'We don't know.'

'Inspector, I'm starting to wonder why you're not asking Nazma any of this.'

That gave Lockyer a little kick of adrenalin. 'Have you heard from her lately?'

'Oh, no. Not for ages.'

'When was the last time that you recall?'

'Well, that year, I suppose. 1999. Off she dashed, and there was a bit of drama with the police taking it all very seriously, but she'd just gone up to London. Ducked out on Edward, I suppose. Or else he'd ducked out on her, and she needed a fresh start.'

'Were you with her on the night of October second? At the Marlborough Mop?'

'I was, yeah. Heaps of fun – not that I remember a *great* deal about it. I was fairly well sloshed, I'm afraid. Didn't have a very effective off-switch back then. But, then, we were all at it.'

'You were all drinking? Including Nazma?'

'Yeah. That is . . . I think so. Oh – you mean the pregnancy thing? Well, I couldn't *swear* to it, to be honest. I was too far gone myself.'

'Did Nazma have a bag with her?'

'That's a weird one. I expect so. Women always have bags.'

'Do you remember it?'

'Her handbag? Now you're asking, Inspector.' Jonathan pulled a face but, a second later, snapped his fingers. 'Actually, I do! And don't go pinning the fashionista tag on me for this because that's never been my scene, but she hung it round my neck early in the evening when she went on one of the rides. It was a little denim thing, with a long strap, across the body. Like a small messenger bag. I've probably got a photo of it somewhere.'

'Really?'

'I always used to take a disposable camera with me on a night out.'

'Would you mind sending us any pictures you can find? Any from that night, or of that summer at Trusloe Hall?'

'Yeah, sure. Might take me a while to find them in the heaps of junk I lug around from place to place.'

'And that was the only bag she had with her?' Broad asked.

'The *only* bag? I suppose so. Why would she have another one?'

'You don't remember her bringing any others? Maybe a bigger one?'

'Nope. Not that I recall.'

'And she went off down Figgins Lane to relieve herself,' Lockyer said. 'How was she, as she left the group?'

Jonathan shrugged. 'Fine. Having a great time. I think.' He'd started to sound less certain.

'Were you worried when she didn't come back?' Lockyer asked.

'Not at first. We hung around waiting for a while. Then she texted to say she was heading home.' He shrugged.

'Who reported her missing?'

'I did. When I sobered up in the morning and realized her

stuff was still in the barn, but she wasn't. I felt stupid when she texted the next day.'

'Saying what, do you remember?'

'That she was fine. Staying with her cousins, or something. I said let's keep in touch, but I guess it wasn't to be. Just one of those things, I suppose – like when you meet people on holiday.'

How easily people had believed Nazma had chosen to cut them off, Lockyer thought. How readily they'd moved on. But Jonathan was right – people came and went. Drifted apart, caught in the currents of their busy lives.

'If you speak to her, tell her I said hi,' Jonathan added.

'We would very much like to speak to her,' Broad said.

The archaeologist hesitated, and Lockyer saw him jump to the right conclusion.

'Shit. She's missing, isn't she? You don't mean . . . Has she been missing *all this time*?'

'It's a possibility we're looking into.'

'Holy hell. I had no idea.'

Jonathan stared off to one side, and Lockyer saw real shock on his face.

'You really need to talk to Edward Chapman,' he said. 'Even if Nazma was cooling off, she was still with him, one hundred per cent.'

'You're certain of that?'

'That's the type of person she was, Inspector. Brad Pitt could've walked in and offered to buy her a coffee, and she'd have politely declined in case the great Edward was hurt. You need to talk to him.'

'Thank you. Can we call you back if we have further questions?'

'Of course. Any time. And I'll dredge the memory banks, see if I can come up with anything useful.' He gave a slow shake of his head. 'I can't believe it ... I mean, *someone* must have seen her since then? Unless—' He broke off, face falling.

It had taken him longer than Lockyer might have expected.

'You don't think she's *dead*?'

'We don't know,' Lockyer said. 'But we're doing everything we can to find out.'

7

Day 4, Thursday

Lockyer's desk phone was ringing when he reached it. He snatched up the receiver.

'DI Lockyer?' said a voice he didn't recognize. 'This is DS Michelle Brodzki, Oxford CID. I got a message you were taking another look at Nazma Kirmani?'

Lockyer sat down, grabbed a pen. 'That's right. Thanks for getting back to me. You remember the case?'

'Oh, yes. First time I'd taken the lead on a high-risk misper. But we were only on it for a few days. Worked the scene in Marlborough as best we could, found a couple of potential witnesses, but there was nothing on the ground. No physical evidence of the girl or of a violent incident.'

'We're trying to track down Giannis Andino.'

'The kebab-van man? I'm impressed.'

'Well, we haven't found him yet.'

'I was quite struck by his testimony at the time, but my DI thought the lack of physical evidence spoke louder. Nobody heard a scream, or saw an actual struggle – and the place was heaving that night, with the funfair.'

'Which meant nobody would've given a scream a second thought,' Lockyer said.

'True. After Marlborough we moved to Trusloe Hall, where she'd been staying. The misper's personal items were as she'd left them, as far as we could tell. Nothing looked disturbed.'

'Was the barn secure?'

'The opposite. Wide open. Anyone could've got in.'

'Still, you took a forensic sample?'

'Yeah, that's right. It just seemed off to me – the floor was swept, but there was this trail of mud from a boot tread, leading from the side door over to her bunk. To me, that implied it was very recent. There wasn't enough to establish what make of boot it was, and everyone there basically lived in hiking boots or DMs. Anyone could have left it *except* the girl – she was wearing trainers when she disappeared.'

'So you figured it could have been the perp's?'

'Yeah. Maybe. If they'd looked for her there first, then gone to Marlborough when they didn't find her.'

'So, a planned abduction? Not an opportunist?'

'It was a theory. If the boot print *was* anything to do with it, then that said planned to me. Someone who knew exactly where she'd been sleeping.'

'Was the mud analysed?' Lockyer asked.

'No. We were stood down. We'd spoken to the friends who were with her that night, and to her boss, the one she was shagging. Nobody could tell us why she might have wanted to pull off a vanishing act like that. But she was sending text messages, and then the call came through from London, and we were taken off it without a backward glance.'

'Her turning up in London reassured you?'

'Course. She ran off – people do. She was fit and well, in her twenties. Not vulnerable in any of the ways we might use that term.'

Lockyer thought for a moment. 'Do you recall *anyone* you spoke to suggesting that Nazma might've been pregnant?'

'Pregnant? No. Why – was she?'

'We believe so, yes.'

'Well, that's kind of telling, isn't it? Young woman, sleeping with her boss. She probably skipped town to have a termination.'

'And never went home or contacted her family ever again.'

'What?'

'You didn't know that?'

'No. I – I left Swindon not that long afterwards, transferred to Oxford. But there wouldn't have been much we could've done, in any case. Nazma had made herself known to us, and asked to be left alone. Completely within her rights.'

'Yeah.' Lockyer sighed. 'I know.'

He told Brodzki about the escape bag and its precious contents, lodged in the bank of the River Kennet these past twenty years.

'Well. Shit,' Brodzki said. '*Shit.*'

'My thoughts exactly. Look, you must still have mates in Swindon – is there any chance you could try to track down that mud sample for me? I know it's a long shot, but if there's even an outside chance it could be in storage somewhere . . .'

'Leave it with me, DI Lockyer. I know the very man for the job.'

Edward and Antigone Chapman lived in a large, L-shaped house, with a thatched roof and leaded windows, and an immaculate garden of box hedging, staddle stones and espaliered fruit trees. An ornamental pond lay dormant in the centre of a perfect lawn. Twin Range Rovers, one silver, one black, were parked in the coachhouse, and the sun had put in an appearance, as if to show the place in its very best light.

'Very *Homes & Gardens*,' Broad murmured, as they pulled onto the gravelled driveway.

'Isn't it just?' Lockyer said.

'Fiver says the wife brings us tea on a tray, with a milk jug.'

'Only an idiot would take that bet, Gem.'

Broad smiled as she lifted the lion's-head door knocker.

Edward Chapman was instantly recognizable from the episode of *Dig Britain*, in spite of him verging on scrawny now. His face was almost gaunt, and there was more grey than brown in hair that was now receding somewhat. He was in his mid-sixties but still vigorous, and tall enough to look Lockyer in the eye.

'How do you do?' he said, in a cultured, accentless voice. Lockyer remembered what Ingrid had said about his elocution lessons. 'Do come in. No need for that,' he said, waving away their ID. 'I trust you are who you claim to be. Would you mind very much if we sat in the conservatory? We can open the big doors that way. It'll still be warm enough, on a day like today.'

'Wherever you feel most comfortable, Mr Chapman,' Broad said.

'Excellent. It's this way.'

The inside of the house was as immaculate as the gardens, each room graced with large floral arrangements. Lockyer didn't know much about decor, but the coordination of colours and fabrics, and the consistency of the finish, made him wonder if they'd used an interior designer. It was not at all the sort of house he'd expected a field archaeologist to live in.

'You have a beautiful home,' Broad said, as they reached a kitchen with a vaulted ceiling and a marble-topped island the size of Lockyer's bathroom.

Chapman smiled off-handedly. 'How kind of you to say so. Tiggy does it all – my wife. She has such a talent for all that.'

The conservatory led off the kitchen. It was a large, oak-framed room with an enormous chandelier dangling from the apex of the roof. Not at all the white uPVC lean-to Lockyer usually pictured when someone said 'conservatory'.

'If you'd like to sit over there at that table? We've got it all set up for Covid quite nicely, you see.'

Two tables and chairs had been arranged at either side of the room, with the double doors between them open to the garden, and windows open to create a through-draught. With the sun shining, it was still perfectly warm.

'I'll just give Tiggy a prod, and I'm sure she'll rustle up some tea for us,' he said.

'Thank you,' Lockyer said.

Shortly afterwards, Antigone Chapman came in and introduced herself, wearing a flawless smile that somehow managed to be profoundly unfriendly. Her hair was bobbed, artfully dyed a natural-looking ash-blonde, and her face was handsome rather than beautiful – a little on the wide side. Cheeks and lips with the suspicious smoothness of subtle surgical intervention.

'Tea? Or perhaps you'd prefer coffee?' she said.

'One of each would be lovely, thank you,' Lockyer said, and watched a flicker of irritation cross her face.

'Of course,' she said dispassionately.

'Now, how can I be of assistance?' Chapman said, seating himself at the table opposite them. He crossed one leg over the other, resting his clasped hands on his knee.

'We're looking into the disappearance of Nazma Kirmani,' Lockyer told him.

'Yes, your colleague mentioned that on the phone. But I must say, I'm a bit confused as to why you think I might be able to help. I haven't heard from Nazma in *years*. I really wouldn't be able to tell you anything about her life these days.'

'It seems that nobody can tell us anything about her life these days,' Lockyer said. 'As far as we're aware, nobody has seen or heard from Nazma since she disappeared from Marlborough on the night of the second of October 1999.'

Chapman looked bewildered, then shocked. 'Good God . . . Are you *sure*?'

'The investigation is ongoing. She's had no contact with her family since that date, and there's no trace of her in any of the online records we've been able to search.'

'But that can't be right – the police found her up in London. Do you think something *happened* to her there?'

Lockyer didn't want to give away too much. He was also watching the man's reactions closely. 'No,' he said. 'That's not what we think.'

Chapman's forehead furrowed in consternation. He drew breath to speak but his wife returned before he could. She was carrying a tray covered with a cloth, a milk jug *and* cream alongside a small cafetière and a pot of tea. Lockyer carefully didn't meet Broad's eye.

'Here you go,' Antigone said, setting it on the table, then retreating to sit next to her husband.

'Thank you,' Lockyer said, reaching for the coffee.

Antigone raised a hand at once. 'It will need to brew for a little longer, Inspector,' she said, in a mildly reproving way. 'Did I hear you say you're here about Nazma Kirmani?' She turned a steady look on her husband. 'Isn't that the girl who was on your dig at Avebury?'

'Yes, that's right,' Chapman said. He brushed a piece of imaginary fluff from his cords. Antigone could have been gazing out of the window at a horse in a field. Her expression gave away nothing whatsoever.

'Did you ever meet her, Mrs Chapman?' Broad asked.

She swept her cool scrutiny back towards them. 'I suppose I might have done, but I don't recall. I certainly visited Trusloe Hall on a number of occasions that summer, to see how it was all going, and drop in on poor Inez.'

'You know Inez de Redvers?' Broad said.

'Oh, yes. We were at Cheltenham Ladies' together.'

'The . . . racecourse?' Broad said tentatively.

'No, Constable.' A faintly patronizing smile. 'The school.'

Broad coloured. 'Oh. Right.'

'It was my friendship with Inez that convinced her to let Edward dig in her grounds that summer. Just one of those happy coincidences.'

'Are you still friends now?' Lockyer asked.

'Well, I wouldn't say *friends*. We were rather close as girls, but she was a fey creature even then, and became increasingly unstable with each year that passed. It's mostly just Christmas cards, these days. Perhaps I ought to drop by sometime, and see how she is.'

'She's not at all well, actually,' Broad said. Lockyer shot her a warning look.

'No? That's a pity, though I can't say I'm surprised. She inherited that simply splendid house, and was given every opportunity in life, but some people simply aren't equipped to help themselves, are they?'

It was a rhetorical question, and Lockyer cut in before Broad could say anything else.

'But you don't remember Nazma Kirmani at all? What about you, Mr Chapman?'

'Well, I remember her, of course, but as I said, I've had no contact with Ms Kirmani for many years.'

'*Ms* Kirmani?' Antigone scoffed. 'Really, Edward. Don't be so coy.' Her expressionless eyes landed on Lockyer again. 'I know all about his little dalliance with the girl, in case you're worried about sticking your foot in it,' she said.

'I see,' Lockyer said, caught off-guard by this cool admission.

She gave a short sigh. 'Next you'll ask if you might talk to my husband alone, since he's clearly too embarrassed to speak freely in my presence.' She directed a withering look at her husband. 'Don't *squirm*, Edward. You're a grown man, not a schoolboy. Though you haven't always behaved like one.' She got to her feet.

'It's much appreciated, Mrs Chapman,' Lockyer said.

'I dare say.' She left without another word.

Chapman shot them a rueful smile. 'It wasn't a mere woman I married so much as a force of nature,' he said. 'Thank heavens she's never quite managed to shake off her affection for me.'

'She forgave you?'

'Forgave, perhaps, but certainly didn't forget. We've weathered worse storms, though, during our forty years together.'

'Worse than an affair with a girl half your age that lasted over a year?' Lockyer said.

'We all make mistakes, Inspector. And I'm not sure Tiggy appreciates exactly how long it went on for . . . so please keep your voice down, if you wouldn't mind.'

'All right. Will you tell us about the relationship, please, Mr Chapman?'

'It was just a . . . a . . . *coup de foudre*. I was at a dangerous age, you could say. One starts waking up with the first creak of old age in the bones, bringing intimations of all the roads not travelled. Our daughters were far less dependent on us than they had been, but Tiggy was always a very devoted mother, and when she wasn't mothering, she was busy with this committee or that.' He smiled in a self-deprecating way. 'There's no fool like an old fool, as they say. Nazma was a very lovely girl, and when she took a shine to me . . . I confess, I didn't try very hard to resist her.'

'So, she was your midlife crisis?' Broad said baldly.

Chapman winced slightly. 'What a way with words you have, Constable. But perhaps that *is* what it boils down to, at its basest level. I was very fond of Naz, and I thought she was fond of me, too.'

'Thought?' Lockyer said.

'Well, in the end she upped and left. So, I can't be sure.'

'We're no longer certain she left of her own accord.'

Chapman's face fell at this reminder. He swallowed. 'I do so hope you're wrong about that.'

'Didn't you think it was strange when she just vanished the way she did?'

'Yes and no. Young people can be so impulsive, and head-strong.'

'Had your relationship ended?'

'No, not exactly. But I suppose she'd grown impatient with me. I'd always been very honest with her about being a married man. I'd told her, many times, that I had no wish to leave Tiggy or the girls. But perhaps we only hear the things we want to hear.'

'Nazma's flatmate told us a different version, Mr Chapman. She told us you had in fact promised to leave your wife, but that you always found some reason to delay.'

'No. That's simply not correct,' he said. 'I was very clear about where my duties lay.'

'Had you talked about ending the relationship?'

'Not in so many words, no.'

'Not even when your wife found out?'

'She didn't. Not until afterwards.'

Having spent about a minute in Antigone's company, Lockyer doubted that very much. 'How did she find out?'

'I confessed – thought it best to make a clean breast of it, especially since Nazma had ended things.'

'How did she take it?'

'Not well. But I can't imagine how that's relevant.'

'Did you go to Marlborough on the night of October the second, 1999?'

'To the Mop? No. Nazma tried to persuade me – she wanted us to ride the big wheel together.' He smiled again, wistfully. 'But fairs have never been my thing, really. I had a terrible experience on a tilt-a-whirl when I was a boy. And, besides, Tiggy had a fundraiser that night, and it was the au pair's night off, so I was watching the girls. I came straight back here when we'd finished packing up at Avebury.'

'What time was that?'

Chapman looked faintly perturbed again. 'It was twenty

years ago. I honestly haven't a clue. But I seem to remember that it was still light, and that I gave the girls their supper, so it would have been before six, I suppose.'

'How old were your daughters back then?' Broad asked.

'Lexie was about eight, I suppose, Bella nearly ten.'

'Did you try to contact Nazma after her disappearance?'

'Once or twice. She wouldn't answer my calls, but a day or two later she emailed to say it was over and to leave her alone to get on with her life. I could hardly argue with that. Part of me was even *pleased*. Happy for her. I pictured her emerging from our association . . . fully fledged, in a way.'

'You're certain she emailed? It wasn't a text message?' Lockyer said.

'I— Well, I'm not *completely* sure. It could've been a text – I'm afraid I really can't remember. Only the gist of it.' He sighed, looking away across the manicured lawn as his face sank into lines of something close to sorrow. 'For anything to have happened to that charming girl,' he murmured, 'for her to have been *harmed*, if that's what happened . . . would be simply atrocious.'

'Mr Chapman, was Nazma pregnant?' Locker asked.

He jerked back to attention. '*Pregnant?*'

'Had she told you?'

'No! Was she?'

'We think it's a possibility,' Broad said. 'How would you have felt about that?'

Chapman looked completely stunned. 'Well, I – I really have no idea.'

'No?' Lockyer said. 'I imagine it would have made things

quite a bit more complicated. Particularly where your wife was concerned.'

'Well, yes. It would. But a child is *always* a blessing.' He shook his head, leaning towards them. 'I don't think she *can* have been, though.'

'Why's that?'

'Firstly, I believe she would have told me. We were very open with one another. And, secondly, it . . . it couldn't have been mine.'

'Why not?'

'I love children, and I *adore* being a father. I always wanted more than two. I wanted four, five, six little ones, a whole gaggle, to chatter around the table at breakfast time . . . My own father ducked out when I was only six, and left such wreckage in his wake. My mother and I had a very grim time of it. I wanted to do better – and I *have* done better. But pregnancy was such a terrible trial for Tiggy. The morning sickness put her in hospital a couple of times. Then she went back in again with pre-eclampsia. So much worry. And with Lexie, she was in labour for close to thirty hours. After that, we agreed: no more.' He glanced at Broad, then back to Lockyer. 'I had a vasectomy. In 1990. Almost a decade before Nazma and I met.'

He turned to look out of the window again. 'So I think you must be mistaken. Because if Nazma was expecting a child, I *cannot* have been the father.'

Lockyer let the implications of that sink in, for all concerned.

'I see,' he said at last.

Chapman gave a sad smile. 'Perhaps she wasn't quite as fond of me as I thought, then, or as open. But if it's all the same to you, I'll go back to believing she *wasn't* expecting.'

They asked him questions about Nazma's friendship with Inez, about Darren Mason and Trusloe Hall, but he couldn't tell them anything more than they'd already heard.

'I do think poor old Inez was pretty pissed, most of that summer,' he said, in a hushed voice. 'I know Tiggy has a kind of nostalgic fondness for her but, really, I've never been able to make head or tail of the woman. On another planet, for the most part. And have you ever seen any of her paintings?'

'No.'

'Be glad.' He made a face. 'Stuff of nightmares, for the most part.'

When they took their leave Chapman stayed in his seat, seeming to forget proper form. 'Will you let me know, please? If you find out anything more about Nazma?' he said.

'If you like,' Lockyer said. 'Once we've concluded our investigation. Can we contact you again, if we have further questions?'

'Yes, by all means. But, really, there's nothing more I can tell you. In my memory she's like a summer's day from long ago. Something lovely that couldn't last.'

'That's very poetic, Mr Chapman,' Broad said neutrally.

Lockyer looked for Antigone on the way out, hoping to ask her more about Inez, but she was nowhere to be seen. He sensed that Broad was keeping something in. Once they were back in the car it burst out.

'Ugh! *Men!*' she said. 'Present company excepted, guv.'

He smiled. 'You didn't warm to him?'

'Let's just say I know who *I* believe, when it comes to how honest he was about planning to leave his wife. And that thing about him sending her off "fully fledged". I mean, seriously. Like being with him was a valuable *education* for her. Arrogant git.'

'Okay. I take your point. And I'm sure the affair did wonders for his ego.'

'He basically justified it by saying his wife was too busy working and raising the kids to pay him enough attention.'

Lockyer thought back. 'He did. But I guess Nazma got tired of it in the end. Seems like Ingrid might have been right about her meeting somebody new that summer.'

'That's if she *was* pregnant,' Broad said. 'I wish there was a way to find out for sure.'

'Well, we can apply for her medical records.'

'If it was very early days she might not have been to see anyone about it,' Broad said.

'But it's worth a try.' He looked out at the beautiful old house again. A pair of running hares decorated the ridge of the thatch. 'Who knew archaeology was so lucrative?'

'It's not,' Broad said. 'No way did archaeology pay for all that. Did you clock the greenhouse? Probably cost more than Pete's and my house. I reckon it's *her* money. You don't meet many Antigones down at Morrisons.'

'And Cheltenham Ladies' College isn't cheap. Maybe it's family wealth.'

'I sort of believed him about the babies thing, though,' Broad said. 'That he'd have been okay with it if Nazma *had* been pregnant.'

'Well, maybe in theory. But no child of Nazma's was ever going to sit at *their* breakfast table, was it?'

'No. Did you see the way Antigone looked at him when we started talking about Nazma? Like she wanted to turn him to stone.'

'Exactly. It would have been problematic.'

'But if the baby couldn't have been his, that would explain why Nazma never told him about it, if there *was* a kid on the way,' Broad said. 'Maybe the escape bag, the money . . . maybe she just wanted to get away for some time to think.'

Lockyer nodded. Something about the situation was making him uneasy. 'What if he hadn't told her about the vasectomy?' he said.

'You mean, what if Nazma thought the baby *was* his, and told him about it?'

'I can't imagine *that* would have done his ego much good.'

'No,' Broad said. 'Definitely not.'

Lockyer thought a lot about pregnancy as he made his way home. The balance of power that so often caused a clash – and left a woman holding the baby. Unless she was able and prepared to have a termination, she could be forced into unplanned motherhood, effectively. The course of her life changed for ever. But women could force men into fatherhood, too – by simply not telling them about it, if the pregnancy was unexpected and unplanned, or by ignoring their wishes if they didn't want the child. In the most manipulative of cases, people of both sexes lied about birth control. Men could and did walk away from situations like that, but without doubt there were emotional – and financial – implications, regardless of whether they agreed to take any custody of their offspring.

It was so delicate, so serious, so nuanced a situation. Men so often declared that they would stand by the woman's decision and *take responsibility*. But Lockyer wondered if it oughtn't to be equal in all parts. Equal responsibility, equal discussion, equal decision? Equal say in what should be done? But, in the end, it was perfectly polarized: have the baby; don't have the baby. There was no grey area, and if an agreement couldn't be reached, Lockyer understood why it fell to the person who would carry and give birth to the child to choose. The woman had the casting vote.

It was what Hedy had done, after all; and as far as society was concerned, it was completely acceptable. Forcing him into fatherhood. She'd given him no voice in the discussion, no seat at the table. Whatever he would have said, whatever he would have chosen, was irrelevant. He'd asked her to stay, now, and to have the baby with him at her side. But, really, had that even been his choice? Or had he simply been trying to make the best of the *fait accompli* she'd presented him with?

'What is it, Matt? You're miles away,' Hedy said, sitting opposite him at the kitchen table with the remains of a

Chinese takeaway spread out between them. In the low light her grey eyes were huge and shining. She was wearing one of his old sweatshirts, and it hung loosely from her bony shoulders.

The words were out before Lockyer could stop them. 'Hedy, why did you come back?'

She put down her fork and took a sip of water. He saw the subtle closing of her expression, eyes glassing over into the flawless neutrality he remembered of old. It told him she was aware that she'd made decisions he should have been party to. And that she was fully prepared to defend that position in a fight.

'To see you,' she said.

'Why?'

A shrug. 'I wanted to see how you felt about this. About us.'

'"Us" as in you and me, or "us" as in you and the baby?'

She blinked, and said: 'Both.'

Lockyer knew it was really the latter. She and the baby were 'us'. He was simply somebody else.

As if reading the quality of his silence, she said: 'We've been over this. You can be as involved or uninvolved as you want. I'm not going to ask you for money; I don't need it. I just—' She broke off, and reached for her glass again.

'When did you realize you were pregnant? Before you went to France?'

'No, of course not. I went to France about a week after I left Westdene.'

'So when did you realize?'

'About two months later. Around the time most women do. And it was a shock, given my age and how careful we were – or *thought* we were.'

'Did you ever think about a termination?'

'Matt, you do know we're at home, right? Not in one of your interview rooms?' she said.

'I think I have a right to ask.'

'Maybe. But I don't want to talk about it over the dinner table.'

'When would you like to talk about it?'

Silence.

'We agreed, as soon as you got back, that we'd be open and honest with each other,' he said.

'Fine. Well, why don't *you* be honest, and say what you really want to say? Because it's a bit late now for you to mind about this baby.'

'But it was always going to be too late for me to mind, wasn't it? You kept it secret and you stayed away so that there couldn't be any discussion about not keeping it. Right?'

She looked at him steadily. 'Yes.'

'You've given me no choice about any of this.'

'I can go, if you want. You needn't see either of us again. You can forget all about it, if that's what you choose.'

'No, I can't "forget all about it" because I *am* going to be a father. Do you seriously think I could carry on as though nothing had changed, knowing that my child was out there in the world, knowing nothing about me?'

'If it's fame you want, I can tell them you were a hero who

died saving us from an axe-wielding madman, or something like that.' Her tone was coolly mocking.

Lockyer shut his eyes for a moment. 'I don't want to get into a fight about this,' he said.

'It really seems as though you do.'

'I don't. I just want . . .'

'What?'

'I want you to admit what you've *done*. Because I think you know. You've changed *everything*. And don't give me the line about it taking two to make a baby. I know that. But it should also take two people to decide what to do about it. And you cut me out of that. Deliberately.'

'What would you have said if I'd rung you up and told you, as soon as I knew?' she asked.

'I—' Lockyer shook his head. 'I have no idea.'

He looked up and met her gaze. Saw conflict there, but also a bulletproof resolution. 'I'd have asked you to come back and talk,' he said. 'I'd have asked to see you. I never wanted you to go.'

She took a deep breath. 'I know what I did. And I'm sorry. I can see why you feel like I've . . . forced it on you. Made you powerless in it all. I do know.'

'So why did you do it?'

'Because . . .' She leant away, pushing at the table like she wanted to escape. A shake of her head. 'You don't know – you *can't* know – what it's like to spend that long locked up. Or what it's like *not* being locked up any more. I'm doing better now, but at first it . . . it felt like . . . falling. That's the only way I can describe it. No structure. No timetable. No goals. No end point. There was this kind of mad . . . *decompression*. I thought I was losing my mind. So I thought it'd be better to be by myself for a while.'

'I understand that—'

'I know you understand the words I'm saying, Matt, but you don't know what it was like. You *can't*.'

'Okay.'

'Then I was pregnant. Just like that. Believe me, it wasn't my idea, and for a heartbeat I was *terrified*. But then I wasn't. I was calm. Happy.' She gave him a look that was almost pitying. 'I *couldn't* risk telling you. Not when I knew, one hundred per cent, that I was keeping this child. If you hadn't wanted it, we'd have fallen out. Perhaps permanently.'

Lockyer released a slow breath. It made sense. Of course it did. But it still wrote him out of the script. 'So why come back at all?' he said.

Hedy almost smiled. She reached for his hand, gripped it hard. 'Why do you think?' she said.

'I've no idea.'

'Because this is your baby, and I don't *want* us to fall out. Because we could be a family. Because it's *you*.'

8

Day 5, Friday

Broad came into the station with dark circles around her red-rimmed eyes. It was such a contrast to her normally fresh-faced appearance that she caught Lockyer's worried glance.

'Think I must have eaten something dodgy yesterday, guv,' she said. 'Believe me, you don't want the details.'

'You should go home, Gem. Rest up.'

'Oh, no – I'm fine. Honestly. It was just a rough night.'

'Well. If you're sure.' Lockyer suspected she was lying, but there was no kind way to challenge her on it. She nodded, and started filling out a data-protection form for access to Nazma's medical records. 'Ask for Inez's, too,' he said. 'Let's find out what she's taking, and how long she's been taking it. And then get on to Financial – ask them to go back as far as they can on the Chapmans, Inez, and Darren Mason.'

'On it, guv.'

Lockyer rang the Kirmanis and asked for contact details for Nazma's cousins.

'What for?' Hari Kirmani asked. 'They would have told us if they knew anything. They're good people.'

'I'm sure they are,' Lockyer said. 'But people sometimes don't realize that what they do know could be important.'

There was a heavy pause. 'Very well,' the old man said. He gave Lockyer two phone numbers, two addresses. 'Adam lives in Reading now, but he was living in Wales at the time Nazma was taken. Alina is still at the same address. She and her husband purchased their flat from their former landlord.'

'Thank you, Mr Kirmani.'

Lockyer pulled up a map of the London address. Alina lived in a flat on Bryan Street, on the Barnsbury Estate. On foot, it was ten minutes, if that, from Islington police station. He dialled her number.

After several rings a woman answered, sounding hurried but not bad-tempered. In the background, other, younger, voices competed to be heard.

'Hello?'

'Hello, could I please speak to Alina Shah?'

'Yep, you are. Who's this?'

'Hello, Mrs Shah. This is Detective Inspector Lockyer from Wiltshire Police. I'd like to ask you a few questions about your cousin Nazma Kirmani, if I may.'

There was a rustle as she adjusted the handset, then the click of a door closing, and the background noise got quieter. Lockyer waited, expecting Alina to ask if they'd found her. But she didn't.

'Why?' she said, at length.

'We've recently uncovered new evidence that may shed some light on your cousin's disappearance, so we're looking again to see if we can progress the investigation at all.'

'Yeah, I heard. Family grapevine,' Alina said. 'You found a bag of her stuff.'

'Can I ask what your thoughts were, when you heard about it?' Lockyer said.

'Not much.' Her tone stiffened. 'I mean, it was so long ago. We were basically still kids.'

'Nazma was twenty-four, and you were twenty-six. Hardly kids.'

'Well.' He heard her swallow. 'It seems like a long time ago.'

'Were you close?'

'When we were growing up, yeah, we were. We saw less of each other as we got older, and she went off to university and whatever, but she was nice.'

'When did you last see her, or speak to her?'

'I don't know. I can't remember.'

Lockyer left a gap, because she was clearly lying, but all she added was a quiet 'Sorry.'

'We think Nazma had packed the bag we've found as a going-away bag, and was planning to travel somewhere. Spend some time away from home. Do you have any idea where she might have intended to go? Or why?'

'No.'

'Mrs Shah, I can't help feeling you're not telling me everything.'

'I don't *know* anything.'

'I'm sure you must remember when you last talked to Nazma. Roughly.'

'Look, I just told you I don't. It would have been earlier that summer, I expect. We usually called to catch up every couple of months.'

'And you weren't aware of anything troubling her? Any problems she was having?'

'No. None.'

Lockyer was sure he heard a slight tremor in Alina's voice. The grip of nervous tension.

'She'd got a placement on some big project,' she went on. 'An important dig. She was really excited about it. Look, I'm sorry, but I really need to go and—'

'Mrs Shah, anything you can tell us about what Nazma was doing that summer might be crucial to—'

'I have to go. I'm sorry. There's really nothing I can tell you. I've got no idea where she went, or where she is now. I really haven't.'

With that she rang off, and Lockyer chucked his phone down in frustration.

'No joy, guv?' Broad said.

'I wouldn't say that,' he said. 'She's lying. She knows *something*, I'd bet my life on it. Whether we can get her to tell us is another matter. But she lives a stone's throw from Islington nick.'

'Seriously? Want me to call her back?'

'No. I think I need to get up there and speak to her face to face. Get a better feel for her.'

'Do you think we should speak to Nazma's brother, guv? Andrew Kirmani?'

'Yes, do.'

'Don't you want in on the call, guv?'

'No, you can handle it. I'm going to get up to London. One good thing about lockdown is that you know people will be at home when you bang on the door.'

He was about to leave when an email from Jonathan Tate landed in his inbox, with six pictures attached. *My photos of Naz from 1999, as requested*, it read. *Not great quality and not that many – sorry. But I hope they're useful.* Lockyer downloaded them all, and opened the first.

In it, Nazma was standing in a group of four, wearing a guarded smile. In the background were strings of lights and brightly coloured stands, all hazed by movement. The Marlborough Mop. This was the last night Nazma was seen by friends or family – possibly her last night on earth. She was wearing bootcut jeans and a cropped T-shirt under a denim jacket, showing off a narrow strip of flat midriff. Gold platform trainers on her feet, and the small cotton bag Jonathan had described, its thin strap going across her body. She looked small between her companions – two other girls and a guy, all grinning and posing for the camera. Nazma's body language was more reserved, her smile not as wide and her eyes not as bleary.

Lockyer stared at her flawless young face for a long time, feeling the same pang he often did when looking into the faces of the lost.

Nobody in the picture was carrying anything like a

holdall or duffel bag. Nazma's little denim handbag was familiar, though. He checked the image on the whiteboard: the woman in Islington had it.

There were two other shots from that night, but they told Lockyer nothing new: Nazma from behind, walking along, her face turned sideways to laugh with one of the others. Nazma, even more blurred, posting a hotdog into her mouth. The other three photos were of the dig at Trusloe Hall. One was a selfie of Jonathan and Nazma, both squinting in bright sunshine. In the next, Nazma was in the background, standing beside a trench and holding out some muddy artefact in the palm of her hand. She was showing it to a man who was much taller than her. Smiling up at him. At first glance Lockyer thought it was Edward Chapman – same build, same khaki shorts and Caterpillar boots – but then he changed his mind. This man was broader across the shoulders, and had longer, slightly darker hair. He was three-quarters turned away from the camera, so it hadn't caught his face.

The final photo was a group shot: eleven archaeologists, standing in front of the fully excavated cist burial in various poses of pride or amusement or forbearance. Ingrid had her feet set square and her hands held awkwardly behind her back, not quite smiling. Her haircut might have been in homage to Lady Diana, but on her it looked masculine. Edward Chapman had one hand on Nazma's shoulder, smiling directly into the lens. Her gaze, though, had drifted off to one side. Lockyer stared at the posture, trying to decipher it. Hard not to read it as proof of Nazma's thoughts being elsewhere, her mind on escape, Chapman's hand proprietorial, perhaps even territorial. He parked the idea. You could look at any moment caught on camera and read into it whatever happened to be at the forefront of your mind.

'Gem, take a look at these,' he said, forwarding her the pictures and waiting while she clicked through them.

'Ingrid does not photograph well,' she said, a few minutes later. 'No sign of the escape bag at the Mop.'

'No. I think we can go with the assumption that she didn't take it with her that night.'

'So, it was either taken and discarded at some point *before* she went there that night, or afterwards.'

Lockyer shook his head. 'After. Look at her neck, at the Mop.'

Broad peered closely at her screen. 'She's wearing her locket.'

'Right. The locket that ended up in the holdall, in the river.'

'So . . .' Broad rubbed at her eyes, as though struggling to focus, '. . . if she went back to get it, why would she then chuck it?'

'She wouldn't. She didn't.' Lockyer's gut instinct hardened into certainty. 'She was *wearing* the locket that night, her most treasured possession. Even if she'd left and travelled back to Trusloe Hall to collect the bag, why would she take the necklace off, and drop it into a side pocket? It's late, she's hurrying – she's making her escape. Why would she take the time to do that?'

'Maybe the clasp broke, or something?' Broad said.

Lockyer got up and went closer to the photo of the tarnished necklace. The chain was undone, but the lobster clasp and all the extender rings were perfect, unbroken.

'No. It was *taken* off, not torn off,' he said.

Broad squinted at the picture of Nazma at the dig, showing the tall man whatever it was she'd found. 'I've seen that bloke before, I'm sure of it,' she said.

'That guy? Where? Who is he?'

'I don't know – must have been in the TV show. Hang on, let me check.'

She opened the video file, and ran it forwards at double speed until she found what she was looking for.

'Here, guv.' She froze the footage and tapped the screen. 'That's the same guy, right?'

Lockyer leant down to see. It was a shot of the whole cist burial site, possibly filmed from the back terrace of Trusloe Hall. Figures were in and around the various trenches and the small finds tent that had been erected to one side. And there was Nazma, at the edge of the shot, talking to the same broad-shouldered, tousle-haired man. His arms were folded but the posture was easy, relaxed.

'How did I not spot this when I watched it? I looked everywhere for Nazma,' he said.

'It's really brief,' Broad said.

She hit play, and the footage came to life. A panning shot that didn't linger on the diggers, turning a slow one-eighty to finish on the presenter, coming down the steps from Inez's terrace. Broad wound it back. Nazma and the man exchanged a few words, then laughed. She laid the fingers of one hand on his forearm, just briefly, then snatched them back. Smiling, the man turned towards the camera, and Broad froze it again, catching that split second. It was tiny, and pixellated, but gave them a rough idea of his face. As he'd turned he'd unfolded his arms, and the breeze had flapped open his shirt.

'Guv . . .' Broad said.

'I see it.'

Lockyer grabbed another photo from the whiteboard and held it beside the screen. Beneath the shirt, the man was wearing a yellow T-shirt, the exact colour of the tattered remains found in Nazma's escape bag. Lockyer squinted, trying to find the best distance from which to make it out. The artwork on the front was instantly familiar: the band's name in black bold type, and a circular motif in a brighter yellow than the background.

'That's a Stone Roses T-shirt,' he said.

Broad shot him a sceptical look. 'How can you possibly tell?'

'The slice-of-lemon logo. Pretty much *everyone* had that T-shirt when I was at uni.'

'So this could be the man's T-shirt Nazma had in her bag? Which would make this the guy Ingrid saw her getting friendly with? Maybe the man who got her pregnant?'

'Slow down. We *think* we've got the remnants of a band merchandize T-shirt in Nazma's bag, in a large size. And we have a witness saying she made a new friend that summer. This guy is wearing a similar T-shirt. Those are the only facts we have right now,' Lockyer said.

'I know, but we want to find him, right?'

'Definitely. Ask Tech to print out that screenshot, would you? As clear an image of his face as they can get – they might be able to clean it up a bit. Then let's get it out to everyone we've got hold of who was on the dig that summer. I want to know who he is, and who he was to Nazma.'

'On it, guv.'

Maybe the man was nobody of importance. Maybe he was a new boyfriend, and gave Nazma his T-shirt as a keepsake. But there was another possibility, too: that he'd needed to dispose of the T-shirt, along with Nazma's escape bag. That there'd been evidence on both he hadn't wanted found.

Lockyer drove to Swindon, took a train to Paddington and the tube to Angel. The Underground was quieter than he'd ever known it, for which he was grateful. Its choking crowds and thick, smutty air had always given him the first flutters of claustrophobia.

In Islington he showed his ID to a pair of uniformed Met officers, patrolling with an eye to the lockdown measures, as he made his way to Bryan Street. The flats were in squat blocks, three storeys high. Alina Shah's was on the top floor, overlooking a tidy communal lawn and more flats opposite. When Lockyer pushed the bell he heard voices inside, and the yap of a small dog. The door was opened by a teenage girl with immaculate skin, wearing enormous hoop earrings and her raven hair in a messy bun. She flicked her eyes over Lockyer in his suit and PPE visor.

'Feds, I'm gonna guess?' she said, leaning insolently against the jamb. 'My brother's not here.'

'I'm looking for Alina Shah.' Lockyer showed his ID. 'She's not in any trouble. I'd just like to ask her a few questions.'

A broad grin broke out on the girl's face. 'Shit, you really *are* the police! That's *sick*, man.' She giggled. 'I don't even have a brother, by the way. I was just messing.'

'Right,' Lockyer said. 'Is Mrs Shah at home?'

'Course she's at home. All we ever *are* is at home, yeah?' She called over her shoulder: '*Mum!* So what do you want to talk to her about?'

'I'd rather speak to—' Lockyer broke off as a woman closer to his own age appeared behind the girl, frowning.

'Marnie, you're supposed to be in class.'

'I *am* in class. Then the doorbell rang, which was probably about the most exciting thing that's going to happen today. And you were in the loo.'

'Well, get back on screen. Go *on*.'

Marnie rolled her eyes and sloped off down the hallway, leaving Alina Shah to look him up and down. 'Yes?' she said.

Lockyer showed his ID again. 'We spoke on the phone earlier, Mrs Shah,' he said. 'About your cousin, Nazma Kirmani.'

Alina's mouth pulled into a taut, flat line. 'I told you I had nothing to say about it. You've come all the way up from wherever it was to hear it for a *second* time?'

'Mrs Shah, please. I can tell there's more to it than you've said. Right now we're working on the hypothesis that somebody snatched Nazma against her will on the last night she was seen. We think she might've died that night, and I suspect she may have known her attacker. I'm sorry to be blunt, but I need to hear whatever you can tell me, however trivial it might seem.'

Alina's eyes widened, hearing these words. 'You think she's dead?'

'Yes. So do her father and stepmother. But they don't *know*, and it's torturing them – I don't use that word lightly.'

Her eyes turned fierce. 'You think I don't know that? This is *my* family you're on about.'

'If I could just ask you a few questions about her life that summer? Please.'

Alina hesitated. She drew breath, perhaps to tell him to leave, then changed her mind. 'Wait there. Let me make sure both the kids are back online.'

She shut the door. Lockyer wondered if she was going to come back or simply wait for him to leave, but she reappeared a couple of minutes later with her coat on and a chubby Border terrier on a leash. 'I don't want the girls hearing about this,' she said. 'As soon as they know something they shouldn't, they broadcast it to the entire universe. Come on – we can go to the park just round the corner.' She led him back down the stairs and across the street, stopping frequently for the dog to sniff and cock its leg.

The park had more muddy patches than grass, and the horse-chestnut trees were already bare.

'Is Marnie your eldest?' Lockyer asked.

'No. She's the eldest still at home. She's fifteen, Sara's thirteen. Rayan is the eldest – he's left home. Their brother.'

Lockyer noticed the slight emphasis on the final statement.

'Marnie told me she didn't have a brother.'

Alina made a face. 'So, in the thirty seconds she spoke to you, she managed to tell a lie? Sorry. Cheeking authority figures is basically her only hobby.'

'Are you working from home?'

'Yeah. I'm a PA. It's fine – when the broadband can cope. My husband is a theatre nurse, so he's right in the thick of it.'

'Well, the vaccine is coming. Might not be too much longer before we can go back to normal.'

'I'm not sure what normal's going to look like after all this,' Alina said. She took a deep breath. 'Naz asked to come and stay with me.'

Lockyer's pulse picked up. 'When was this, Mrs Shah?'

'She rang me in September. I can't remember the date, but around the middle of the month, I think. Not that long before she disappeared.' She sighed, clearly distressed. 'Sorry – can we sit down?'

They found a damp, empty bench. Alina stared away across the deserted park, and Lockyer caught himself studying her features for echoes of Nazma. There was definitely a resemblance in the shape of her face and jaw, and the polished mahogany shade of her eyes. Lockyer looked harder, this time trying to match Alina's face to that of the woman who'd gone into the police station just down the road, in 1999, claiming to be Nazma. It *could* have been her, he decided, after checking carefully that his conclusion wasn't based solely on Alina being the right age and ethnicity.

'What did Nazma say when she rang you?' he asked.

'She said she needed somewhere to stay for a while. She sounded . . . not scared, but *almost* scared. Kind of stressed out, which wasn't like her. She said she'd found out about something, or – no, that wasn't it. She said things weren't what she'd thought. Something like that. But the main thing—'

She cut herself off, glancing at him, and he sensed her indecision. 'Mrs Shah, we've spoken to a friend of Nazma's who thought she might have been pregnant at the time she disappeared.'

'Right. So you know.'

'We didn't know for sure. But Nazma told you?'

A nod. 'She said she didn't know what to do. She didn't want her parents finding out.'

'Why was that?'

'Because of who the father was, I guess. You know she was seeing an older man? A married man?'

'We do.'

'Well, there you go. Uncle Hari's pretty old-fashioned. He wouldn't have liked it.'

'What would he have done if he'd found out?'

'God, nothing *bad*, if that's what you're thinking. He'd just have been sad. Maybe disappointed. And Naz would have walked on hot coals rather than disappoint him.'

'What about Liz Kirmani?'

'Auntie Liz wouldn't have batted an eyelid. She'd probably have gone out and started buying baby bootees. But, look, Naz wasn't trying to *hide* from them, exactly. She just said she needed time to think.'

'Was that why you never said anything to the police when she disappeared? To preserve Nazma's privacy?'

A nod.

'Did she say anything to you about the baby's father? Whether or not she'd told him?'

Alina sniffed, the cold air making her nose run. 'All she said was that it was a mess, and she needed time to decide what to do.'

'When were you expecting her to get here?'

'That's the thing.' Alina looked down, a spasm of anguish on her face. 'I told her she couldn't stay with us. My husband and I were going through a bit of a rough patch, working all hours. We were sharing the flat with another couple then. There was hardly any space, but—'

'But that wasn't the main reason?'

A small shake of her head. 'I was pissed off with her. She was sort of the golden child . . . you know? Everything had always just fallen into place for her.'

'She lost her mother.'

'Well, yeah, but she got the world's nicest stepmum. And she *loved* her job. I was strung out, working three crappy jobs while Zain was still in training, and I . . . As I saw it, the situation was entirely of her own making. There *is* such a thing as birth control, you know.'

'Accidents can happen,' Lockyer murmured.

'Well, she didn't *have* to get involved with a married man.'

'And was that what you told Nazma?'

'Not in so many words, but I said she couldn't stay. We

didn't have room. She had a flat of her own, after all. She didn't have to go home to Hari and Liz.'

'Maybe she wanted to be somewhere she couldn't be found. At least, not right away.'

'Maybe,' Alina said tersely. 'But I didn't know that at the time.'

'What did you think when she walked into *your* local police station six days after she was last seen in Wiltshire?'

Alina looked shocked. 'She what?'

'A woman claiming to be your cousin identified herself at Islington police station. That's about a ten-minute walk from here.'

'I don't – I don't understand. She didn't come here. I never saw her!'

'Was it *you*? Are you the woman who went into the police station?'

'Me?' She stared at him. '*No!* Absolutely not. Why the hell would I do that?'

'Maybe to help Nazma make a clean break of it, and hide out while she decided what to do?'

Alina stared at him, open-mouthed. 'I wish that *was* what happened,' she said eventually. 'But it's not. And even if it was, no way would I have let it go on all this time, with Hari and Liz not knowing. No *way*.'

Lockyer had been watching her closely. His instinct was that she was telling the truth, but the location of the police station was one hell of a coincidence. Like all detectives, he had a profound distrust of coincidence.

'We heard she'd come forwards somewhere in London,'

Alina went on. 'But that's all. I just assumed she was staying with someone else. A friend, or whatever.'

'Did she know anyone else in the Islington area that you're aware of?'

'No. I don't know.'

'Why do you think she never got in touch with any of her friends or family after that?'

'I don't know.' Alina swallowed. 'Because something happened to her, like you said. Something bad. I didn't think so straight away; I knew she'd been planning to come up to London. It was only later, after a few months, that I started thinking it was strange. But . . . I don't know. Maybe she did just go off somewhere.'

'Is that what you believe?'

Alina sniffed again, this time because tears were welling in her eyes. 'No. That's not what I believe. Not after all this time. And I'll never forgive myself, in case you're wondering. I'll never forgive myself for not helping her when she asked me. Because maybe if I had . . . maybe if she'd come to my place, then whatever happened to her might not have had the chance.'

'Did you hear from her after October the second? Any texts, or calls?'

Alina shook her head sombrely.

Lockyer handed her his card. 'Okay. Thank you, Mrs Shah. If you think of anything—'

'You won't tell Hari and Liz, will you?' Alina cut in anxiously. 'You won't tell them I knew she was pregnant? Or that she asked to come and stay with me?'

'If I can avoid it, I will.'

He left her sitting on the bench, hunched sadly, her little dog by her feet.

Lockyer called Broad from a westbound train.

'Nazma was definitely pregnant,' he said.

'Alina Shah confirmed it?'

'Yeah.' Briefly, he filled her in on his conversation with Nazma's cousin.

'Did you believe her, guv?'

'On balance, yes. But I don't know. Of all the police stations in the country, someone pretending to be Nazma chooses *that* one to go into?'

'You think it could have been her? The cousin?'

'It's *possible*. She's clearly got a lot of guilt. Maybe what she really feels guilty about is her part in the deception – whether it was Nazma she was helping or someone else.'

'You mean, whoever attacked Nazma?'

'The person at Islington nick effectively called off the search. So, they were either helping Nazma, or they were helping the person who took her. Don't forget they had the denim handbag Nazma took to the Mop, with her wallet inside, so they must have had contact either with her, or with someone who had.'

'So, what next with Alina Shah?' Broad asked.

'She has a son, Rayan, who's older and has already left home. But Alina is about the same age as Nazma, so she must have had Rayan pretty young. Let's find out when, exactly.'

'Okay,' Broad said. 'You don't think Rayan is actually *Nazma*'s kid?'

'Alina made a point of telling me that Rayan was her daughters' brother, as though there was a chance I might've thought otherwise. And one of the girls – Marnie – told me she didn't have a brother. Alina said she was fibbing, and maybe she was. But still. It's something to check.'

'On it, guv.'

It was something that happened, Lockyer thought, as the train passed through Reading and into the rolling hills towards Wiltshire. Unexpected or inconvenient babies, babies who would be awkward for their true parents, were nevertheless kept in the family, raised by a sister or a grandmother as their own. Less common in the present day, perhaps, when far less stigma was attached to young or unmarried motherhood, but Lockyer suspected it still went on. Perhaps the plan had been for Nazma to go up to London to hide her pregnancy from friends and family, and for Alina and her husband to raise the baby as their own. Or for it to be given up for adoption elsewhere, maybe without the father ever finding out, leaving Nazma to rejoin her normal life, free of the complication.

But if that had been the idea it had gone very wrong some-where along the way. Lockyer circled back to the dumped emergency bag, the late-night vanishing from Marlborough. That hadn't been Nazma's plan, he was sure of it. So had she tried to alter it? Had she backed out, for some reason? Had someone else – perhaps someone who desperately wanted her baby – taken matters into their own hands? He tipped back his head, shut his eyes, and tried to lay such heinous acts at the feet of Nazma's family: the seemingly gentle Kirmanis, the hardworking Shahs.

It was a poor fit, whichever way he looked at it. But the person in Islington was key to it all, and if it hadn't been Nazma or a member of her family, Lockyer had no idea who on earth it could have been. Or how they'd ever find her.

Liz Kirmani answered the phone, immediately saying she'd go and fetch her husband.

'It was actually you I wanted to talk to, Mrs Kirmani, if you've got a few minutes?' Lockyer said.

'Oh, right,' she said. 'What about?'

'I just have a few questions about Nazma.'

He needed to tread carefully. Emma Billingham hadn't wanted the Kirmanis to find out she'd known about Nazma's relationship with Chapman; now Alina Shah didn't want them to hear that she'd known about the pregnancy. And Nazma would have *walked on hot coals* rather than disappoint her father. Lockyer had started to wonder just how onerous that disappointment might have been. To what lengths Nazma might have gone to avoid it. Because, as he'd said before, there was a chance that her family had been the problem.

'Well, ask away,' Liz said. 'I'll help if I can.'

'As I understand it, Nazma kept her relationship with Edward Chapman hidden from you and her father?'

'Yes, she did.'

'Why do you think that was?'

'Come now, Inspector. I know it's different for boys, but if you'd started dating your boss, who was twenty years your senior and married, would you have rushed home to tell your mum and dad about it?'

'No. But I wondered ... how did your husband take the news, when the police told you? How would he have taken it if Nazma *had* told him, do you think?'

There was a hung moment, and Liz's next words had harder edges: 'If you think for a second that Hari would've harmed a hair on that girl's head, then—'

'I promise you, I don't think that. I'm just trying to understand what might have been going on in Nazma's mind. What pressures she might have been feeling.'

'You mean, why she might have wanted to run away?'

Lockyer said nothing.

Liz sighed. 'If only you knew how many times we've asked ourselves that same question. In the early days – regardless of what Hari said to the police – he'd turn to me at two a.m., when neither of us could sleep, and ask whether he'd done anything to upset her. Whether he'd been a poor father. Whether he'd pushed her away. And it broke my heart because I knew he *hadn't*. But when we were told about Edward Chapman, and when we were told she was up in London, and just choosing not to contact us ... I can hardly describe it. It was like little bombs going off, you know? Making you wonder if you actually knew a damn thing about a person you loved to the bones.'

'I understand,' Lockyer said.

And he did. There were things he'd found out about his

brother since his death. Things that had made him doubt everything about their relationship. *Little bombs going off* was the perfect description of the feeling.

'Can you tell me about Nazma's personality?' he said. 'Most people speak highly of her.'

'Course they do. She was lovely,' Liz said. 'Don't get me wrong – she was no saint. She had her moments, especially in her teens. She could be impatient, and very emotional. But she was always kind. Even in the middle of a teenage strop, the second she realized she'd gone too far and said something hurtful, she'd just crumble. Couldn't bear it. She was *kind*, you know? And it wasn't just a costume – she really cared about other people, and she had the guts to step up and help them, if she could.'

'How do you mean?'

'Oh, I don't know . . . Like at school, for example – she ran this whole anti-bullying campaign. Nobody asked her to, she just saw there was a problem. And it wasn't about ousting or shaming the bullies; it was about talking to them, and finding out why they were behaving that way. You know, including them. It worked wonders.'

'She sounds like a really good person.'

'She was. And, yes, of *course* she was the apple of Hari's eye but, honestly, she could've taken advantage of that far more than she actually did.'

'You got on well with her?'

'Oh, yes. Straight away. You'd expect a bereaved child to struggle to accept the new woman in their father's life but, if anything, she was worried about me not accepting *her*.

She—' Liz's voice broke. 'The first time I went round for dinner, she'd made me paper flowers. A little posy of them. I've still got it.'

Lockyer chose his words carefully. 'If she'd done something . . . If Nazma had got involved in something she was ashamed of, do you think she'd have hidden it from you?'

'Wouldn't we all hide something we were ashamed of, Inspector?'

'Possibly. In the short term.'

'Well, that's *exactly* it, and— I did sometimes worry about Naz being too much of a people-pleaser, you see. Happens a lot, especially to young women. Hari was so very sad when I first knew him. He was still grieving for Amrit, and there was little Naz trying to cheer him up, being about as sweet as she could possibly be . . . That's the kind of thing that gets embedded in the psyche. You get settled into that role – being amenable. Cheering people up. Making yourself responsible for their happiness.'

'You think that could have got her into trouble?'

'I think the wrong kind of person might sniff that out in an instant, and take advantage of it.'

'You're talking about Edward Chapman?'

'I— No, not necessarily. I don't know the man from Adam. I'd just . . . I'd see Nazma with her friends, or her teachers, or whoever, and I could tell how hard she found it to say no to things.'

Young for her age: both Ingrid Roach and Jonathan Tate had described Nazma as such – with varying degrees of affection.

'But the idea of her going away and never contacting us

again? No. Just . . . no,' Liz said. 'It's one thing not to tell your parents about an unwise love affair. But to cut them off without a word? For ever? She wouldn't do that to us, Inspector. What*ever* she'd got mixed up in.'

Lockyer braced himself. 'It seems that Nazma might have been pregnant at the time she disappeared.' He heard Liz's sharp intake of breath. 'Had she spoken to you about that, at all?'

'No.' Liz's voice shook. 'That . . . Chapman fellow?'

'We don't know.'

'Who told you she was pregnant?'

'I'm sorry, but I can't say.'

'Well . . . I mean, it wouldn't have been what she'd planned, I can tell you that. Naz wanted kids, but only once she was married, she always said. And once she'd had a chance to enjoy just being married for at least a couple of years first.'

'We're wondering if the pregnancy was what made her plan to go away for a while.'

Liz Kirmani read between the lines. 'You mean you think she might have been going away to get rid of it, and never tell us?'

Lockyer heard the flutter of her breathing against the receiver.

'I'm sorry to ask about things like this,' he said. 'I know it must be painful.'

'No. Painful is not seeing her for twenty-one years, Inspector. Painful is having no idea what happened to her. Her being pregnant – if she was – that's not painful.'

'How do you think Hari would have reacted to the news?'

'Well, I expect there'd have been some bluster, to begin with. A bit of woe-is-me. It would've been a shock, given that we didn't even know she was seeing anyone. But he'd have got over it. Yes, Hari's a churchgoer. Yes, he's from an older generation, but he isn't a relic. He knows these things happen.'

'How far do you think Nazma would have gone to keep it a secret?'

'I don't know, Inspector. But she wouldn't have walked out on her life because of it. I just don't believe it.' She took a breath. 'Can I . . . should I tell Hari? About the baby?'

'It's up to you, Mrs Kirmani. Perhaps it might be better, coming from you.'

'Okay.'

'Thank you for—'

'Inspector,' she interrupted. 'I can't imagine *anything* that could have kept Naz away from home for this long. Not unless the love we all felt was somehow not *real*. Not unless we failed her utterly. Do you see? Do you see how we can't let ourselves believe that?'

'Yes.' Lockyer couldn't think of anything else to say.

9

Day 6, Saturday

The day dawned with the kind of bright yellow sunshine that seems like a miracle in November. As Lockyer came out of the shower he saw, through the window, Hedy standing by the collapsed fence between the two back gardens, talking to Mrs Musprat. He hoped she wasn't telling the old woman to get lost. It had taken a long time for Iris to get used to the idea of Lockyer moving into her old friend Bill's cottage, and even longer for her to trust him with her darkest secret. But since that revelation there'd been a subtle shift in their relationship. Iris was never going to be chatty, never going to be warm, but she looked at him differently now. And he felt in his gut that her fussing over Hedy and the baby was her way of caring for *him*.

He put on jeans and a jumper, and went down to join them. Both women were wearing stubborn expressions, and Lockyer hesitated, half wishing he'd stayed inside. The morning sun picked out flashes of amber in Hedy's long hair, and lit her eyes keenly. But when she turned to him, Lockyer was relieved to see as much grudging amusement on her face as exasperation.

'I was just telling Mrs Musprat about multivitamins and B12 injections,' she said.

'The old ways are usually the best,' Iris retorted.

'Sometimes, perhaps,' Lockyer said, 'but maybe not when it comes to medical care.'

'She's not *ill*,' Iris snapped. 'Having a baby isn't about *medicine*. And what do men know about it?'

'They have women doctors now, too,' Lockyer pointed out.

'Ha! Taught by men, I suppose.'

'Okay.' Hedy sighed. 'On that note, I'm going in to do some stretches – stretches *I* devised myself,' she said, as Iris drew breath to argue. In a previous life, Hedy had been a physiotherapist. She walked back to the house, slowly and carefully.

'You have to let her do it her way, Iris,' Lockyer said.

'She's too thin.'

'So are you.'

'I'm *old*. I'm supposed to be thin.' She eyed him beadily. 'Bit grim, that one. Can't help thinking damage has been done to her.'

'Yes. But it's in the past.'

'Was it a man?'

'It was . . . several men,' Lockyer said. Including himself – the young police detective who'd helped put Hedy away for a murder she hadn't committed. 'Ask her about it, if you want to know.'

Iris recoiled. 'Not my business, is it? But I know what she did.' She tsked. 'You never knew a thing about that kid until she drove up to your door. Did you?'

Lockyer looked away into the woods behind the cottages. 'No, I didn't know. But I'm happy about it.'

Iris lifted one eyebrow. 'Makes no difference if you're happy or not, does it?'

'No,' he said, with a sigh. 'Thanks for pointing that out.'

'Big thing she's asking, for you to forgive her for that.'

'But I have to forgive her. Don't I?'

A tiny shrug. 'You either will or you won't. Forgiving someone's like loving them. It's not something you can *try* to do.'

With that the old lady turned and made her way to the goat's stall, where she reached for a shovel. A little more crooked every day, Lockyer noticed, a little frailer, but never less sharp.

He finished tiling the shower cubicle. Hedy did her stretches, called her mother in Spain, made chicken soup for their lunch, then lit the log burner in the living room and settled down in front of it with a book. The way they didn't speak to one another gave Lockyer hope. There was an ease to it: nothing stilted or held back, for those few hours. Just time spent in synchronicity. He knew it wouldn't last – possibly not even beyond whenever he next opened his mouth. So he enjoyed it while it did.

As the sun was failing at the end of the afternoon they heard an engine on the track from the village.

Hedy put down her book. 'Are you expecting someone?'

'Yes.' Lockyer got up and closed the curtains. 'Stay in here for a bit, would you?'

'Why? Who is it?'

'All will be revealed. Stay put, please, and no peeking.'

She rolled her eyes at him but obeyed, and he closed the door behind him, realizing he was actually nervous. He had no idea how Hedy felt about surprises, one of the many things they still didn't know about each other.

'All right,' Jason said, when Lockyer opened the door. He seemed tense, and Lockyer remembered his synaesthesia: visiting a new place for the first time must be a challenge to someone who often tasted sounds, and experienced people's voices as scents and colours. He knew Jason to be a warm, gentle person, but also one who fought against overwhelm, and liked things quiet.

'Thanks for this,' he said, and Jason nodded.

'Upstairs?'

'Yeah. Sorry.'

'Not a problem.'

Jason had offered to deliver the crib, and Lockyer got the feeling he'd wanted a legitimate reason to get off the farm for a while. Any excuse, in a lockdown. Between them, they manoeuvred it carefully up the narrow stairs, and when the blankets were pulled away Lockyer was relieved to find it every bit as beautiful as he remembered. He just had to hope Hedy would, too.

'Want me to clear off, in case she hates it?' Jason said, with a grin that lit up his face. 'Could be awkward.'

'No, stay and have a beer. Or coffee, tea maybe,' he said, remembering that Jason didn't drink.

'Yeah? You're sure your lady won't mind?'

'Course not,' he said, realizing, yet again, that he didn't know.

'All right. Thanks.'

Lockyer went downstairs to fetch Hedy.

'Matt, what is this?' she said, as he led her by the hand.

He sensed how much she wanted to pull free of his grasp. 'Just trust me,' he said.

Jason had positioned himself in the far corner of the room, with his hands clasped behind his back and his chest high, as though *he* were about to be inspected. Lockyer supposed that, to an artist, any appraisal of their work might feel exactly like that.

Hedy gave Jason a startled look and said, 'Oh,' before her eyes settled on the cot.

She ran her fingers along the silky-smooth top rails, and down the side bars. Nothing was straight – they all twisted and curved wherever the branch they'd been cut from had done. The finials weren't simple knobs, they were polished knots of wood, each unique, the grain glowing and lustrous. Hedy curled her hands around the end rail, and looked up at Jason.

'You made this?' she said. Jason flinched almost imperceptibly, then nodded.

'Hedy, this is Jason McNeil. Jase, this is Hedy.'

'Hi,' Jason said.

'Jason, this is . . .' Hedy's voice trailed off. She shot Lockyer a serious, unreadable glance, then stared down at her hands. She clamped her mouth shut, and for a second Lockyer actually believed she hated it. 'It's the most beautiful thing,' she said eventually.

Both men exhaled. Jason smiled shyly.

'You like it?' Lockyer asked.

She looked at him quizzically. 'Of *course* I do. How could I not?'

'Well.' He stopped himself saying he hadn't known. From pointing out the myriad uncertainties between them. 'I've seen Jason's work before. I knew he'd do an amazing job.'

'He has.' Hedy smiled at Jason. 'You absolutely have. Is this what you do for a living?'

'I wouldn't call it a living yet,' Jason said, 'but I'm trying.'

'You'll get there,' she said, with an emphatic nod. She pressed the back of one hand to her mouth, and Lockyer was shocked to see tears in her eyes.

'Ignore me,' she said. 'Hormones all over the place.'

'Fancy that brew?' Lockyer said to Jason.

'Yeah, thanks,' he said.

The failing light made the kitchen a warm and inviting place. Lockyer fed the ancient Rayburn some coal and kindling while the kettle boiled. Thanks to Hedy, there was more food in the house to offer a guest. Biscuits had appeared – and disappeared just as fast. There were crisps, jars of olives, and what Lockyer's dad would have called *fancy nuts*. Lockyer found a fruit cake and put it on the table, making three mugs of tea while Hedy chatted to Jason about Old Hat Farm, his work, and where he might take it.

'How do you two know each other?' Hedy asked.

Jason and Lockyer exchanged a quick look, and Lockyer tried to gauge how much Jason would be happy for him to say.

'We met during an investigation,' he said carefully.

'Oh, right.' She flicked her eyes at Lockyer. 'Like we did,' she said stiffly.

'Yeah?' Jason looked back and forth between them.

'It was a long time ago,' Lockyer said.

'Not that long,' Hedy murmured.

Jason spread his hands. 'But you've sorted it out, whatever it was. You're making a *baby* together. That gives me hope, actually.'

Hedy smiled. 'How do you mean?'

'Things fell apart, thanks to this bloke.' He nodded at Lockyer, who felt his shoulders tighten. 'I suppose I've been ... treading water, since then. Not sure what to do next. Where to go.'

Hedy nodded. 'I know what you mean,' she murmured. 'I might still be doing that now, if it wasn't for this.' She indicated the bump.

'Yeah, I can see how that might change things.'

'It has,' Hedy said. She looked at Lockyer, but he was drawing a blank. He barely knew how to frame their situation to himself, let alone to anyone else.

'The way we meet people – that ... *history*. That's not what matters, is it?' he said.

'Course not,' Jason said. 'But it can be hard to see past. I mean ... I fell in love with my stepsister, and then she got killed. Life goes where it goes, and it doesn't think twice about kicking you while you're down. Still, how does that old song go? You've got to look on the bright side, right?' An ironical roll of his head.

'Yes, you do.' Hesitantly, Hedy reached out and touched Jason's hand. That tiny flinch again, but he didn't pull away. 'I'm so sorry,' she said.

'Thanks.'

'I . . . lost someone, too. My sister. Years and years ago, but I still think about her. Matt does, too.'

Jason looked confused. 'You think about her sister?'

'No. She means I lost my brother. Twenty years ago. There was a brawl outside a pub in Chippenham, and someone had a knife.'

Jason stared at him without blinking.

'But you can't keep focusing on the loss, right?' Hedy said. 'You should focus on the person you loved.'

Lockyer gave half a smile, and looked away. Gently, quietly, she'd been trying to encourage him to talk about Christopher without immediately talking about his unidentified killer. But he still did it, inevitably. The injustice of it was like an open sore.

'Shit, man,' Jason said. 'I didn't know.'

'How could you? It was a random attack. He was out celebrating his birthday, so I guess he was drunk, and . . . I don't know. Maybe a bit high, too. They never caught the person responsible. And I know you know what that's like.'

'Yeah, I do,' Jason said. 'But you—' He looked down at the table. His body language had changed completely: he clearly no longer wanted to be there. 'You helped. The years of not knowing . . . they were the worst.'

Lockyer nodded. 'That's why I do this job,' he said quietly, wishing he knew a way to change the subject.

The Rayburn popped and hissed as it warmed up. Outside in the distance came the crackle and bang of people letting off fireworks in their gardens, since public bonfire parties had been curtailed by the pandemic.

'But you guys'll be fine,' Jason said, after the hiatus.

'Oh? How do you know?' Hedy said.

Jason nodded in Lockyer's direction. 'Back in the summer, when he came looking for answers about Holly, I could hardly stand him talking to me. Gave me all sorts of bitter tastes – I have this thing, synaesthesia. Maybe you've heard of it?'

'Yes, I have.'

'Okay. So, he was pretty hard to be around. Not like his colleague DC Broad, who was just delicious. He was more like car tyres on a bonfire. But now he's like water.' Jason looked at Lockyer again, not smiling, in spite of his words. He gave a rolling shrug. 'Just kind of . . . clean. And the only thing that's changed is you, I guess,' he said to Hedy.

She looked at Jason for a long time, then at Lockyer, before turning away with the trace of a smile. If Jason was trying to be kind, and to help, he'd succeeded. But he still seemed tense, and a second later he stood up, his tea barely touched.

'Sorry. I'd better go.'

'Are you okay?' Lockyer asked.

'Yeah. Thanks. Sorry.'

He left abruptly, hardly acknowledging Hedy's repeated thanks for the baby's new bed.

'Should I not have mentioned my sister?' she asked Lockyer. 'Or Chris?'

'No, don't worry,' he said. 'I'm sure he's fine. He's just . . . I don't know him that well, but he's not someone who hides things. Or pretends to be okay if he's not. I don't think you should take it personally.'

'I'm trying not to hide things any more, too.'

'So am I.'

'Hard to break the habit. Perhaps we'll get there in the end,' Hedy said. 'And thank you.'

'What for?'

'For the cot, of course. It's so beautiful.'

'You're welcome,' he said. 'Thank you, too.'

'For what?'

'Turning me to water.'

Hedy levered herself to her feet and reached for him, kissing him hard.

Later, in the black of night, Lockyer crept out and went for a walk. He'd been lying awake for hours, pointlessly trying to sleep. Something about Jason's visit had left him unsettled. He went down the track into Orcheston, then north on a path that cut across the Plain. After the rain the chalky earth was slimed and slippery; it was heavy going, and he was soon breathing deeply. His thoughts spun, building to a roar of injustice that wouldn't leave him alone. It was often what he felt most keenly on a case – the outrage of a life stolen, of relatives left with the wreckage, of a killer going free.

But he couldn't say whether it was the injustice that had been done to Nazma Kirmani and her family that was bothering him, or something far closer to home. Perhaps Hedy deciding without him on the biggest thing that had ever happened to him, but he wasn't sure. He kept coming back to Jason's hunched unhappiness earlier in the day. But why shouldn't he be unhappy? They'd all inadvertently stirred up painful memories. Jason had lost a brother, too – albeit one he'd been hiding from for years. Then Lockyer remembered that Benjamin, Jason's older brother, had also died of knife wounds. He'd been involved in gang crime in Swindon, mixed up with dangerous people. So maybe that was why Jason had suddenly wanted to leave.

Lockyer walked, and he thought in circles. And by the time he got back to the house, still hours before dawn, he felt no more settled.

10

Day 8, Monday

Bright sunshine lit the dilapidation at Trusloe Hall and managed to make it look even worse. The lurid algae growing on the walls, the rotting window frames and crumbling brickwork. Inez appeared at the end of the hallway again, leaning on her stick.

'How simply *lovely* to see you,' she called. 'Come in, come in! Spring is in the air,' she said. The dank chill inside was unchanged, the smell no less feral.

'How are you, Inez?' Broad asked.

Inez beamed at her. 'All the better for seeing you again, my dear. Come into the drawing room. You'll take a coffee?'

Broad held up the cardboard tray of cups they'd bought en route. 'We've brought you coffee this time. And Danish pastries.'

'Well, how very kind you are! I must admit, I am a little peckish. When it came to breakfast this morning, it turned out I'd finished the last of the bread and not even realized.

I'm so forgetful at times. Jenny really ought to take care of all that sort of thing. I spend far too much time chasing her.'

Broad shot Lockyer a look as they turned to follow Inez back to her squalid burrow of a room.

'What did you have for supper last night, Inez?' she asked.

'Supper? Gosh. It was . . . Or— No.' Inez settled herself on her nest of blankets, shuffling her surgically booted foot into a more comfortable position. 'There we are,' she murmured.

Lockyer cleared his throat. A particularly noxious odour was coming from an NHS commode by the door. He brought out the best image they'd been able to print from the *Dig Britain* footage, of the man in the yellow T-shirt. It had already been sent to Ingrid Roach and Jonathan Tate, neither of whom had been able to identify him. The programme's production company had been similarly unforthcoming, pointing out that the staff had probably turned over at least five times since 1999.

'Inez, would you mind taking a look at this picture, and telling us if you recognize this man at all?' Lockyer said.

Inez peered closely at it. 'I don't think I do. Who is he?'

'That's what we're trying to establish. He was here during the dig in 1999. We think he might have made friends with Nazma.'

The older woman nodded, and looked again. 'I suppose he *is* vaguely familiar. It's not a terribly clear picture, is it?'

'No. But please look as carefully as you can.'

'I'm afraid I shan't be able to help you, Inspector. I do apologize. Is this man in some kind of trouble?'

'No,' Lockyer said. 'We'd just like to talk to him in case he's able to assist the inquiry.'

'The inquiry, yes, of course.' Inez looked blank. She sipped her takeaway cappuccino and shut her eyes beatifically. 'Gosh, that *is* good. Even if it is in a cardboard cup.'

'Have a Danish,' Broad said. 'There's lemon and sultana, or cinnamon.'

'What a *treat* . . . Well, perhaps one. It doesn't do to neglect one's waistline.'

'No, but you're allowed to be a bit naughty now and then.'

Beneath her loose clothing, Inez's body had the wasted look of long-term malnutrition. It only served to compound Lockyer's suspicion that she was addicted to the prescription medication scattered around the house. Not only unable to look after herself, but barely aware of it.

'Have you seen Darren lately?' he asked.

'Oh, yes. He's such a dear boy, you know, always ready to help, however he can. But you've met him, of course, so you know. Salt of the earth.'

Inez blinked, then looked away, two points of colour appearing on each cheek. Darren must have told her they'd been to see him. Lockyer wondered if she hadn't meant to let that slip.

'Inez, we were wondering if you might have a photograph of Pippa that we could take a copy of?' Broad said. 'And also whether you could tell us her date of birth? It might help us track her down for you.'

'Oh, *would* you? Really? I should be so very happy to hear from her, or merely to hear that she is safe.'

'Well, we can't promise anything,' Broad said. 'But with a bit more information, we can at least run a few checks.'

Lockyer had been firm on the amount of time they'd spend on Pippa, but he understood Broad's professional curiosity. After all, Pippa had 'left' just six months or so before Nazma's disappearance. Two women closely associated with the depleted figure in the leopard-print wrap sitting in front of them.

'Well, let me think,' Inez said. 'Her birthday is easy. It was April Fool's Day. As for the *year*, I'm afraid that's rather more tricky. Let me think . . . Was she forty-two, or forty-three, that last year she was with me? Or a little older?' She blinked owlishly at Broad. 'What year are we in, now?'

'2020,' Broad said.

'Yes – of *course*, 2020. Goodness! However did that happen?'

'So, shall we say she was between forty and fifty years old when she left?'

Inez nodded. 'Yes, that ought to cover it. Will that be enough?'

'It should be,' Broad said. 'How about a photo?'

'Yes.' Inez got up and shuffled a few steps towards a bookcase that stood against one wall, heaving with books, papers and old Christmas cards. Her way was blocked by the tide of junk, and she squinted fruitlessly at the shelves. 'There ought to be one . . .'

Broad shot Lockyer a defeated look.

'Ah! I've an idea,' Inez said, turning with an air of triumph. 'I painted her, of course – come and see. It's quite a good likeness, if it's not terribly immodest of me to say so.'

Lockyer gave a nod, primarily because he wanted to see whether Darren had been back to collect his 'clobber' since he'd been alerted to their visit to Trusloe Hall. Sure enough, once they'd followed Inez to the vaulted room at the far end, the stack of brand new cardboard boxes had vanished, leaving a suspiciously bare section of floor.

'Darren must have found somewhere new to store his things,' Lockyer said to Inez, who gave him a look of incomprehension. If she wasn't as ignorant as she was making out to be, then she was a very accomplished actress. He wondered about that.

'I'm sure you're right,' she said. 'Now, let me see . . .'

She made her way over to a stack of mould-spangled canvases that were leaning, facing away, against the wall.

'Why don't you have them out on display, Inez?' Broad asked.

'Well, there are one or two about the place, but I've always thought it terribly vulgar to turn one's home into a gallery of one's own work. And, for the most part, all I see when I look at them are the many ways in which they *fail*. It's terribly dispiriting. Which is very typical of artists in general, I believe.'

'Well, I'm looking forward to seeing some,' Broad said.

Inez's seamed mouth twitched up at the corners. She seemed genuinely flattered by the attention. 'How kind of you, dear girl.'

'Let me help you with that.'

Broad began to lift the canvases out, setting them where they could be viewed. *Stuff of nightmares*, Edward Chapman had said of them, and Lockyer could see what he'd been getting at. Inez's style was somewhere between abstract and impressionistic, with fleetingly familiar shapes emerging from chaotic backgrounds. She worked with thick impasto and bold colours, using a lot of black. In one, steps spiralled down and down into a terrifyingly distant blank spot. One had the vague familiarity of a face, but where the eyes should have been were more black, bottomless depths. Several were filled with wings, feathers and gaping beaks; mad, lidless eyes and ugly splashes of red. Pictures that spoke of a wild violence of some kind.

'Ah, yes,' Inez murmured. 'The rooks. Poor Pippa did hate them! Blood all over the place.'

Another look passed between Lockyer and Broad.

Broad turned canvas after canvas. 'What's this one?' she asked, at one point. The picture was monochrome in blacks and greys; solid shapes – perhaps trees – reared up into the sky and, at the viewer's feet, the ground yawned into a pit. Into darkness, with nothing inside to suggest a bottom. Inez's eyes widened fearfully when she looked at it.

'I— It's called *The Hollow Grave*. It's the cist burial, once they'd dug it all out. It was perfectly empty, you see. Whoever had been buried there was quite gone, and it . . . struck me. Such a cold place. That *absence*, you understand. I suppose, with Pippa having left, and my being so *frightened* . . .'

'I thought that summer was a happy time?' Broad said.

'Well, yes. It was.' Inez frowned, muddled. 'I . . . I was just glad when they filled it back in. It seemed so *ghastly* suddenly, to look out of the window and see an open grave.'

She attempted to smile. 'I haven't been near the thing since. Silly of me, but we artists will have our foibles.'

Broad's face betrayed how perturbed she was. 'I suppose so,' she said.

Inez found the canvas she was after, and greeted it with a small gasp, putting her shaking fingers to her lips.

'There,' she said. '*Darling* Pippa.'

The painting was as close to a formal portrait as they'd seen so far. It showed a woman with a long, angular face and dark red hair. Her eyes had a startling amber intensity, like those of a bird of prey, with flecks of light in the depths of the pupils. But it was very far from being a straightforward enough likeness to use for identification. Pippa's face was described by overlapping triangles of colour, and Lockyer couldn't pick out anything resembling a mouth.

'Such a beauty,' Inez murmured. 'But fierce, good gracious. When she blew up, it was like a hurricane had been through the house.'

'Did you have a row before she left?' Broad asked.

'I think . . .' Inez trailed off, looking dismayed. 'I was very upset, you understand.' And very drunk, Lockyer thought, if others were to be believed. 'It's difficult to remember. And she'd gone off before, you know. A few days here and there, two months once – to a collective in Firenze. Came back because she couldn't stand the wretched bells tolling any more, or so she said.' A sad smile. 'But she always *did* come back, you see. Until . . .'

'Until she didn't?' Broad said.

'Not a word of goodbye. And she wouldn't have done that to me. She *wouldn't*.'

'Would it be okay to take a picture of this portrait, Inez?' Lockyer said.

'Yes, do. Whatever will help you to find her.'

As they turned to leave, Broad said: 'Mind if I peer down your well?'

'What on earth for, my dear?'

'Just curiosity, I suppose. I've never seen one *inside* a house before.'

'Feel free – but, for Heaven's sake, don't lean too far over. We'd never fish you out if you toppled. It would have been *outside* originally, of course. This part of the house only went up in about 1740.'

Shivering in the cold, Inez waited with Lockyer while Broad picked her way over to the well. She put her hands on the circular dwarf wall and leant over to look in. Lockyer's stomach clenched, but he managed not to shout a warning.

'Echo!' Broad called. Over a second later, her voice rebounded back up to her. She took out her phone and shone the torch beam into the depths.

'What can you see?' Inez called.

Broad looked over with a smile. 'That it goes down a very long way.'

'Do come away, dear – you're making my knees quiver.'

Broad stood back, brushing off her hands. Lockyer took a final look at the portrait of Pippa before they left the room, and then at *The Hollow Grave*. Something about the picture dragged at his attention. Perhaps it was the lack of colour, or the claustrophobic way everything seemed to rear above the viewer, as though to force the reluctant gaze down into the pit. The picture exuded a kind of dread, a terrible fear of entrapment and death, provoking echoes of those same feelings in him. Which made it a successful piece of art, he supposed, even if it wasn't something he'd ever want to hang on his wall.

As they went back along the corridor Lockyer peered through a door that had been shut before. The room beyond had a greenish gloom – ivy had grown right across the window – and the ubiquitous heaps of rubbish and mildewed furniture. From the rusting metal stands and stringless cello in one corner, he took it to have been a music room, once upon a time. There was a hole in the ceiling, through which drooped stalactites of cobweb and plaster dust.

'What happened to the ceiling, Inez?' he asked.

She stared up at the hole as though she'd never seen it before. 'Oh, yes – terrible mess. Some of the floorboards upstairs have become a touch fragile. I put my foot clean through one day! Best not to go up there until it's fixed.'

Lockyer looked up through the hole. Caught a glimpse of an elaborate plaster frieze, a gilt gesso mirror, and the corner of a tester bed.

'Best to come away, Inspector.' Inez sounded anxious. 'Just in case any more of it comes down.'

'Lucky you didn't fall right through,' Broad said.

Inez flapped away the concern with one hand. 'You're quite right, but not to worry. I never go up there.'

'When did it happen?'

'Heavens, quite a while back,' she said vaguely.

She shut the door behind them and they carried on, shuffling through her empty diazepam packets. Broad picked one up.

'Does the doctor prescribe these for you, Inez?' she asked.

Inez looked taken aback. 'Yes, that's right. For my anxiety.'

'I'm sorry to hear that. Do you mind me asking how long you've suffered from it?'

Inez peered at Broad through the dim light, her eyes huge, mouth slightly open. Like a woman who'd been given a life-or-death dilemma. 'Well ... sometimes I think I was simply *born* this way,' she whispered. 'My parents were ... well. And then dear Pippa ...' She trailed off.

Broad took hold of her filthy hand for a moment. 'It's all right,' she said. 'You don't have to tell me about it, if you don't want to. Is your doctor's surgery quite local? And the pharmacy? Not too far to travel?'

'Yes, no,' Inez said, turning and walking on, back towards her hidey-hole.

In the car afterwards, Broad squirted sanitizer onto her hands, and offered the bottle to Lockyer.

'I noticed the quantity of pill packets this time,' she said.

'And I don't think she's getting them for herself. Do you?' Lockyer said.

'Course not. Some pharmacies do deliver, but I'm willing to bet that Darren gets them for her. And I don't mean with a prescription.'

'We're not investigating Inez de Redvers's drug habit,' Lockyer said.

'But it *could* be relevant – if it was going on back in 1999. And, anyway, we can't just ignore it, can we, guv?'

'We can flag it with CID.'

Broad gave a barely perceptible sigh. 'If we agree that no legitimate doctor would keep prescribing her a benzo-diazepine when she's clearly an addict, she's getting them through one of two possible means. Either prescription fraud, which Darren operates for her, or the pills are being bought illegally, and are probably bootleg. And, again, I'm willing to bet Darren's the supplier. Though he hasn't managed to buy her any bread this week, for God's *sake*.' She shook her head.

'You're letting it get to you, Gem,' Lockyer said.

'Because it's just . . . it's *horrible*! All the things he could be doing for her – getting her some home help, a health visitor, whatever. And what is he actually doing? Keeping her hooked on benzos, and using her place to stash stolen goods. She's basically his prisoner.'

'You think Inez is completely innocent in it all?' It was a genuine question.

'Yes!' Broad burst out, then moderated her tone. 'I do, guv. She didn't even know what *year* it was.'

'No. And I think the confusion is genuine. But that doesn't mean she's forgotten right from wrong.' He looked out at the sun-drenched ruin of Inez's ancestral home. 'I think you're feeling *exactly* what Nazma felt as she began to understand Inez's situation a bit better.'

Broad paused, thinking back. 'Inez said she thought Darren had upset Nazma. That they'd argued.'

'If Nazma had found out what was going on – the set-up you've just described – then don't you think that could've been what they argued about? The thing she told Inez "wasn't safe"?'

'Well, yes. Very possibly.'

'Question is, would Darren have killed to keep her quiet?'

'He does have that conviction for assault . . . juvenile, but still.'

'Things could've got out of hand.' Lockyer looked across at Broad. 'What were you looking for in the well? Nazma?'

She made a face. 'No, Pippa. But there was nothing to see. It was like that awful painting of hers – the spiral going down into nothing.'

'What about the other one? *The Hollow Grave*?'

Broad shrugged. 'Just a picture of the cist burial, right? Bit gloomy. Why? What did you see?'

'Nothing, probably,' he said. But maybe something more. He started the engine. 'Talk to someone in CID, if you want, Gem. Find out if Darren is on anyone's radar – drugs or stolen goods.'

'We'll know more once Inez's medical records come in, too.'

Lockyer pulled out of Avebury Trusloe onto the main road back to Devizes.

'Did you speak to Andrew Kirmani the other day?' he asked.

'Yes. Seems a nice enough bloke. Works in logistics for a

large brewery. He got pretty emotional talking about Nazma, said he'd had no idea she might've been pregnant, but that he was her grotty teenage brother back then – his words, not mine. They were close, but she wouldn't have talked to him about anything like that.'

'Right.'

'I also found Rayan Shah, Alina and Zain's son. Born at University College Hospital on the second of December 2001.'

'So, he's not Nazma's baby.'

'No, guv,' Broad said. 'I bet Inez started taking the benzos when Pippa left,' she went on, unable to leave it alone. 'But if Nazma found out Darren was up to no good, and if she was worried about Inez, why wouldn't she just call the police? She could have waited till the end of the dig, if she didn't want to face Darren. I can't quite square it with her needing to pack an escape bag and head up to London.'

'The two things could be unconnected. Or maybe the situation was complicated for her by feelings of affection, or loyalty, towards Inez.'

Broad cast him an uncomfortable look. 'Yeah, I can see how that might happen.'

She'd forgiven Lockyer for getting her involved in Mrs Musprat's difficult situation, back in the summer, but it hadn't been forgotten. And he definitely hadn't forgiven himself.

He left a beat. 'Or maybe Nazma discovered something worse at Trusloe Hall? Something more serious than whatever Darren was up to.'

'Like what?'

'Maybe she found out what had happened to Pippa.'

Nazma's medical records came in at midday.

'She hadn't seen her GP in months, and there's nothing about a pregnancy,' Broad reported. 'The only prescription she had was for the pill, and it had lapsed.'

'Lapsed?'

'Yeah. She didn't go in for review, so it wasn't reissued. She would've run out about five months prior to her disappearance.' There was a certain stiffness in the way Broad said this, which Lockyer couldn't decipher.

'Well, that would tie in with her finding out about Chapman's vasectomy, and not bothering with contraception any more,' he said. 'Which explains how she got pregnant, if not who with.'

'Yeah. I guess so.'

The phone rang. 'Lockyer, it's Michelle Brodzki. And I'm about to make your day.'

Lockyer sat up. 'Don't tell me you've found the soil sample?'

'I set my mate PC Tony Copes on to it. He's an old sweat at Swindon, loves nothing more than a low-octane task that means he won't have to engage with the public. He spent a happy afternoon truffling around in the old skittle alley at the nick – have you ever been down there? It's like the land that time forgot. Anyway, he's only gone and found it.'

'You're kidding?'

'I wouldn't do that to you. It's all there – my photos of

the scene, the evidence form and the sample. Want me to courier it over to you?'

Lockyer made a split-second decision. 'The photos, yes, please. But send the sample straight to the lab for a full analysis.'

'Yeah? You don't want to clear it first?'

'I'll clear it after. Thank you, Michelle. This is bloody brilliant.'

After lunch, Lockyer set up a video call with Edward Chapman. The retired archaeologist came on screen sitting at a large desk in a burgundy leather captain's chair.

'Inspector,' he said. 'I hadn't expected to hear from you again so soon. Have you any news about Nazma?'

'Not yet,' Lockyer said. 'Did you get the photograph I sent to you?'

'Yes, I did.' Chapman reached for an A4 printout, and studied it. 'This was the best image you were able to get? Is this man a suspect?'

'Just someone we'd like to talk to. Do you recognize him?'

'Well.' Chapman looked again, sighing gently through his nose. 'I'm usually very good with faces. This one *does* ring a bell – not that I can make him out especially well. Was the image taken from the *Dig Britain* footage, by any chance?'

'It was, yes.'

'I'm very curious as to what might have caused you to single him out. I wonder if he might be someone who befriended Nazma? But, then, I don't suppose you're at liberty to tell me, are you?'

'I'm afraid not. Have you any idea who this man is, Mr Chapman?'

'I used to have a copy of the *Dig Britain* episode kicking around here somewhere,' Chapman said, half to himself. 'But I think Tiggy did away with it. Not a question I'd like to ask her, really.'

Lockyer waited.

'Well, Inspector, as I said, I'm good with faces, and I'm fairly sure this chap wasn't anyone on the dig. Not an archaeologist or a student, I mean. So if he isn't in any way connected to Trusloe Hall, I'd suggest he's TV crew – maybe a cameraman or somebody like that. It would explain his vague familiarity. But that's not much use, I suppose.'

'It might help us narrow things down.'

'Well, I'm happy to help.'

'Could I ask you a personal question, Mr Chapman?'

'Yes, though I might choose not to answer it.'

'Had you told Nazma about your vasectomy?'

'Oh, yes. Why wouldn't I? I knew she'd find it reassuring. Now, if there's nothing further, I really ought to—'

'Would it be possible to talk to your wife, Mr Chapman?'

'To Tiggy? What for?'

'I would just like to put a couple of questions to her, if she's at home. If not, I can arrange to call again another time.'

A look of irritation flew across Chapman's face. 'I really wish you wouldn't. You can hardly imagine she'll have anything positive to say about Nazma, or my conduct that year.

Frankly, I'd far rather you didn't rake it all up. I'm already in the doghouse over something else entirely—'

'I would just like some background on Inez de Redvers,' Lockyer cut in.

'Oh.' Chapman subsided. 'Well, I'll see if she's available. Stay on the line.'

He got up and went off screen. Lockyer waited. A full two minutes later, Antigone Chapman appeared in her husband's place. Silk blouse, subtle makeup, freshwater pearls. Her broad face was calmly impassive, her movements unhurried. 'Inspector. I haven't got long,' she said.

'Thank you for taking the time, Mrs Chapman. You mentioned before that Inez de Redvers had always been an unusual person, even at school. Can you tell me a bit more about her?'

'Is she under some kind of suspicion?'

'Not at this point.'

'By which you mean she may become so, at some point in the near future?'

'We are concerned for her welfare.'

'Are you indeed?' Tiggy considered him, while Lockyer tried – and failed – to read her. 'Well. What do you want to know?'

'Has she had any issues with her mental health, going back, that you know of?'

'Oh, yes. Absolutely. She made a fair stab of just getting on with it at school, but you could always see how hard she had to work to cope. She was always very on edge.'

'Did you ever meet her parents?'

'Yes. I went to stay at Trusloe Hall once or twice, during the summer holidays. They were the reason I didn't go a third time.'

'Oh? What were they like?'

'Mad as hatters. Her father veered between spells of exuberant generosity and bursts of violent temper. He routinely beat seven bells out of her mother, who was a perennial drunk – and who could blame her? She used to rave on about an affair she'd supposedly had with Picasso, which everyone knew was nonsense.'

'Was her father violent towards Inez, too?'

'I never saw it, but given the way she shrank from him, it's likely. I don't think either of them ever forgave her for being gay, her father in particular. He was profoundly *contemptuous* of it. Inez had an older brother, you know. *Adored* him – everybody did. Rupert de Redvers. He even *sounded* like a romantic hero. But he died when he was nineteen, swept overboard, sailing out of Dartmouth. Inez and I were sixteen at the time, and I was utterly in love with him. It was quite heartbreaking. Her mother killed herself shortly afterwards.'

'That's very sad.'

'Weak, I've always thought. She had a daughter who still needed her.'

'When did her father die?'

'I'm not sure, precisely. They rattled around together in there for a number of years, when Inez finished at art school and failed to marry. Perhaps it was some time in the mid-eighties. Inez found him in his bath – drowned. Perhaps as the result of some kind of cardiac episode was the verdict, I believe.'

'That must have been awful for her. And yet she didn't leave Trusloe Hall?'

'One doesn't simply *leave* a family home like that, Inspector.'

'Better to let it fall down around your ears?'

'Well, no. But I can understand why she stayed. Inez has always craved *stability*, above all else.'

'Did you ever meet Pippa Harmon?'

'Yes, several times. They were at the Slade together. It went on and off for years until Pippa finally walked out.'

'What was she like?'

'Volatile. A more talented artist than Inez, as far as I could tell. Intelligent, but very changeable. A strong personality – far stronger than Inez. But, then, couples do seem to run along those lines, quite often. One makes the messes, the other attempts to clear them up.'

Lockyer wondered if she was thinking of her own marriage. The way she'd been able to skewer her husband with a few carefully chosen words. 'Any substance abuse?'

'Well, one of the things they fought about was Inez's drinking. Pippa even got her to enrol in AA at one point, but it didn't last. Pippa would go off and have other love affairs, and poor old Inez would be left holding the metaphorical baby, desperately hoping for her to come back.'

'She never had any other relationships?'

'Well, she barely went out, Inspector. Very hidebound.'

'Is she agoraphobic?'

'Just ... phobic, I think. Scared of the world, and what it can do. It's really very sad,' Tiggy said, though her tone implied more scorn than pity.

Lockyer pictured the way Inez had welcomed them like old friends, smiling, inviting them back. The way she staunchly defended Darren Mason, her 'nephew'. Suddenly he saw her terrible loneliness with complete clarity, and felt a stab of the genuine sympathy that Tiggy apparently lacked.

'So it's hardly surprising that she's happy to make a new friend, when one comes along,' he said. 'Like Nazma Kirmani.'

'I suppose so,' Tiggy said.

'You said you might have met Nazma in the summer of 1999, Mrs Chapman. Did you? Are you sure you don't remember her at all?'

A short sigh. 'I do, actually. You jogged my memory. She was at Trusloe Hall one day when I went to visit. She was having tea with Inez when I arrived. Quiet as a mouse – she soon excused herself once Inez had introduced me, and she worked out who I was.' Tiggy's eyes went curiously flat. 'Which is how I knew, of course.'

'About the affair between Nazma and your husband?'

'People give away *so much* with their body language and facial expressions, Inspector,' she said. 'I've always noticed it, and endeavoured to keep my own thoughts to myself, until such time as I choose to share them.'

She was very good at it, Lockyer thought, though the very fact that she'd chosen to hone that skill spoke volumes about her.

'Your husband seems to be under the impression that you didn't know about the affair until he confessed it to you, some time after the fact.'

A cool lift of her brows. 'It does no harm to let him think so. I'd already known for some months that he was having another of his *petites folies*. There are very clear signs that he seems genuinely unaware of. I just didn't know who the girl was, until I met her.'

'Did you speak to Nazma at all?'

'Other than to say hello, no. There was no need.'

'Do you think Nazma realized that you knew?'

'Haven't a clue. I didn't care then, and I don't care now.'

'You seem to have taken it very well. Better than most wives would, I'd say.'

'Really, Inspector?' She sounded amused. Or perhaps merely cynical. 'What can one say? Or do? Men will philander, and foolish girls will convince themselves that *they*'re going to be the one to reform them. I gave up believing any such thing a long time ago, but Edward has always had a knack for finding the credulous ones. At least this Nazma girl simply left when she saw her mistake, instead of doing anything so stupid as to throw herself down a staircase.'

The comment struck Lockyer as particularly cold.

'Had that happened in the past, Mrs Chapman?'

'Mimi Draper – I'd have thought you'd have dug all that up, given that the girl you're looking for has a similar link to Edward. He's guilty of misleading them, perhaps, but I've always thought it a sign of a very flawed character to be unable to take a knock-back on the chin. To end one's own life because of a failed love affair – can you imagine anything so *wasteful*?'

'Some people – especially young people – are rather more sensitive, Mrs Chapman.'

'Oh, I'm not insensitive, I assure you. Merely undaunted.'

'You must love your husband very much.'

Her face gave a peculiar flicker, and Lockyer wondered what emotion she was hiding so carefully.

'Yes. I suppose I must,' she said. 'He's weak, but so are most people. But one doesn't have to look far to find the source of it. His mother always blamed him for his father walking out. She used to threaten to have him adopted, if he didn't behave. He grew up in the shadow of her bitterness, and caught beneath the weight of her ambition. Small wonder that when female affection is offered, he grabs at it. And, in spite of it all, he's been an excellent father to our girls. They adore him. And he has his own unique sort of steadfastness, I suppose. There's never been any question of him leaving us – or ever wanting to.'

'Still, you've had to put up with a lot, by the sound of it,' Lockyer said.

'How very presumptuous of you to say so, Inspector.' She paused. 'I could have divorced him, it's true. But to what end? I'd have made our girls very unhappy, I'd have made Edward very unhappy, and I'd have deprived myself of his company. We rub along very well, for the most part. And, unlike a lot of women, I'm able to comprehend that sexual infidelity doesn't necessarily indicate a lack of feeling. He cares a great deal for me, Inspector. A very great deal.'

11

Day 9, Tuesday

During the night, while Hedy fidgeted and muttered in her sleep, Lockyer walked up onto Salisbury Plain. The brighter days were turning into frosty nights, and the cold air bit his face as he climbed. He supposed his persistent insomnia might stand him in good stead once the baby was born. He was used to functioning on very little sleep, and had a sudden image of himself carrying the child in one of those backpacks as he walked at night. Lulling it to sleep. It was the first imagined scene of his impending fatherhood that actually felt good.

The perfect stillness of the night was interrupted by the buzz of Jody FaceTiming him, and the brightness of the screen obliterated his night vision, plunging the world beyond his phone into abject blackness.

'Jody,' he said, as her face came into focus – big brown eyes, black hair with a shock of blue at the front. 'What's happened?'

'Chill out, nothing's happened,' she said. Her face was also lit by her phone; otherwise she, too, was in darkness. 'That's the problem.'

'How do you mean?'

'I'm bored shitless.'

'Right,' he said, exhaling.

'You're such an old woman,' she said, 'always waiting for the next disaster to befall.'

'You're bored, so you've rung me in the middle of the night to call me names?'

'Pretty much.' She gave a grin. 'Figured you might be awake. Out on one of your midnight forays.'

'You figured right. Where are you? Why aren't you asleep?'

'I'm out in the barn, didn't want to disturb your folks. And I can't believe this is as close as I'll get to going out for *weeks*. Fucking lockdown.'

'It won't be for ever.'

'As to why I'm awake, no bloody clue. Brain-churn,' she said. 'How's the Duchess?'

'Hedy's fine. She thinks you hate her.'

'I don't hate her. I just haven't found anything much to like yet.'

Lockyer thought about what Hedy had said after their last visit to the farm. That Jody was jealous of their relationship and wanted him to herself. Him and his family. He wondered if she could be right. If, as Antigone Chapman had said, there were signals he was missing. He decided not to ask Jody outright, even though that was what she would have done.

'She guessed we'd slept together,' he said.

'Seriously? Ha! Bet that went down like a cup of cold sick.'

'Pretty much.'

'Well, better to have these things out in the open.'

'I told her there was never anything between us. Just mates. Right?'

Jody rolled her eyes. 'Barely that, most of the time.'

Lockyer smiled. 'Right. Thanks. How's Mum doing?'

'Yeah, pretty good. Taking it steady. Hard to see an improvement when it's so slow, but I think she *is* improving.' Jody shrugged. 'I guess what's more important is that *she* thinks she is.'

'You're probably right.'

'I usually am.'

'Want me to make you a badge?'

'Yeah. Might help you remember.'

He saw her breath clouding in the frigid air of the barn. Noticed the frayed neckline of her jumper. 'Aren't you cold?'

'Nope. Aren't you?'

'Only since you rang and stopped me walking.'

'A *thousand* apologies, Matt.' She made a face. 'How's the bump?'

'Good, I think.' He paused, then asked, on impulse, 'Jody, when you got pregnant with Danny, was it a shock?'

The tiny stutter her grief caused her, at any mention of her infant son. But she didn't blink. 'Hell, yeah. But . . . you know.' She shrugged.

'What?'

'What are you asking me, Matt?'

'I'm asking . . . how did you *feel* about it, to begin with?'

'Well, I dunno. A moment or two of sheer terror, definitely. I mean – me? A mum? Not what I'd had in mind. I felt this ridiculous urge to run away, like I could escape my own sodding womb. I wanted it not to be happening, I guess. But only for a week or two.'

'Then what?'

'Then something kicked in. Hard to describe it, exactly – something a bit primordial. Some bit of lizard back-brain said, "Yep, this is what we're doing. All good." And that was that. *Big* rush of love for a blob of cells growing somewhere in my innards. Ridiculous, really. I guess the whole survival-of-the-species thing had me firmly in its grip.'

'So you decided to keep him.'

'It didn't even feel like a choice by then. I *had* to keep him.'

'Had you . . . Was his father involved at all?'

'Beyond using an out-of-date condom? No, not much.'

'But did you ask him at all? About keeping the baby, or . . . not?'

Jody stared at him for a moment, no doubt trying to unpick the meaning behind the question. 'No,' she said. 'We weren't even a couple, it was just a hook-up at a party, and, like I said, I decided to keep him pretty quickly.'

'Right.'

'What?'

'It's just . . . ' Lockyer chose his next words carefully. 'It would be wrong for a man to force you into motherhood, wouldn't it?'

Now she blinked. 'I didn't *force* him, Matt. He should've shelled out for better contraception.'

'But if he hadn't wanted you to have the baby, you'd have carried on anyway. If *you* hadn't wanted it, and he *had*, would you have carried on?'

'No. Those days are over, thank fuck.'

'I just . . . I'm trying to understand—'

'Do you not want this baby? Christ – is that what you're saying?'

'That's not what I'm saying. I'm saying I was given no choice.'

'Well, you could've chosen not to have unprotected sex.'

'We didn't have—'

'And I bet the Duchess has said you don't have to be involved, right? She seems pretty self-reliant. And she has her own money.'

'But I'll still be a father, whether I'm "involved" or not.'

Jody took a deep breath. 'What I'm hearing is you stamping your foot because you're in a situation over which you have no control.'

'It's not about control, it's—'

'It *is*, Matt. And maybe it *is* a bit unfair. Maybe, finally – in this country – the having or not having of children has been put more into women's hands than men's. But you know what? It's because *our* bodies do the hard part, and are never the same again – and our brains even more so. It's *our* careers that get put on hold. And, most of the time, it's still us that end up doing most of the work once the kid's out in the world.'

'Is that true?'

'Who made your packed lunches, Matt? Who cleaned up your puke? Who made sure your gym kit was washed?'

'That was forty-two years ago.'

'Yep. And, believe me, not that much has changed. So, look, try and let it go, would you? It's just the way it is.'

'"Just the way it is"? Isn't that what women have *hated* being told for the past thousand years?'

Jody grinned. 'All right, you've got me there. But I'm serious, Matt. You want to make a go of things with the Duchess. Right?'

'Right.'

'Do you wish she wasn't pregnant?'

'In . . . some ways. I wish we'd had more time to get to know each other, and decide whether—'

'Blah-blah-blah,' Jody interrupted. 'Yes, of course. That would have been the more *controlled* way to do things. But this is what's happening, and the choice is pretty basic. Get on board, or don't.'

For a moment they watched one another in silence. He saw his own face reflected in her eyes. Her pupils were huge in the low light, which made her look vulnerable, somehow. As if hearing the thought, she blinked and looked away.

'And you've got about two years, I reckon,' she said.

'How do you mean?'

'The first two years of raising a baby together will tell you if you and Lady Hedy are going to stay together. If not, you can get the break-up out of the way and settle the custody dispute before the kid'll have any memory of it. Might save you a bit in child counselling down the line.'

'That's comforting. Thanks, Jody.'

'Hey – you're welcome, Matt. Just be grateful you didn't accidentally knock me up too. Mind you . . .' she tipped her head to one side, musingly '. . . now I come to think of it, I have skipped my last couple of periods.'

Lockyer went cold, until she grinned wolfishly. 'Gotcha.'

He thought about this conversation the following morning at the station. How hard – how potentially infuriating – it was to be told *that's just the way it is,* when things weren't what or how you wanted them. What damage might be done by that feeling of oppression, and impotence. He tried to put himself in Nazma's shoes: finding out she was pregnant, with someone other than the man with whom she was in a long-term relationship. She hadn't said anything to Edward Chapman about it, but had she told the father? Had there been any kind of discussion about what to do? Or an argument? *Things weren't what she'd thought they were,* she'd told her cousin, Alina.

'Gem, what was it Emma Billingham said when we spoke to her last week?' Lockyer asked. 'That Chapman had always said his wife was ill, and that was why he couldn't leave her for Nazma?'

'I think that's right.' Broad flipped through her notebook. 'Yep. "Unhappily married, wife seriously ill." Which was a big fat lie.'

Her distaste for Edward Chapman was in every syllable.

'Perhaps,' Lockyer said. 'Their marriage seems stable, from what I've seen, but I'm not sure I'd call it *happy*. And Antigone *might* have been ill back then. Though when I spoke to her yesterday she talked about visiting Inez that summer – and meeting Nazma – with no mention of it.'

'So, what are you thinking, guv?'

'Alina Shah told me that when Nazma called her to ask to stay with them, she said "things weren't what she'd thought". I wonder if she meant the Chapmans' marriage? Meeting Antigone, seeing she was fighting fit, and realizing Edward had been lying to her? Couldn't that be why she started seeing someone else – and why Emma had sensed her going cool on Chapman?'

'It definitely could've been,' Broad said. 'Hard to know for certain.'

'But a fair assumption, yes? If she *was* seeing someone else.'

'Well, she didn't get pregnant on her own.'

Lockyer borrowed some of Jody's words: 'Could have been a hook-up at a party. A one-off. I'm just wondering whether she told him at all. If he knew about it.'

'Is it important? He's hardly likely to have wanted to keep it, if they'd only just met.'

'I don't think you can jump to a conclusion like that where a child's concerned, Gem.'

She frowned down at her notebook. 'No. I know,' she said, so heavily that Lockyer remembered something they'd spoken about back in the summer: that Pete wanted her to quit her job and start making babies. At the age of twenty-four. Though it was no business of his, the idea made him grind his teeth. She was a good detective, and getting better all the time. And, selfishly, the thought of having to get to know a new partner was exhausting.

With a nasty little jolt, the thought occurred that she might be pregnant already. That could explain the recent changes in her demeanour. It was another way in which women had a little more control, after all – that for the first five months or so nobody even needed to know they were expecting.

'Is that what you're thinking, then, guv?' Broad asked, breaking into his thoughts. 'That this was all just to do with Nazma being pregnant?'

'No. I don't know.' Lockyer leant back in his chair, pushing his hands through his hair. He'd slept for about an hour, in the end, and his head had the familiar too-light feeling of such a restless night. 'We're finding out what she might have been up against that summer. The people she was mixing with. But I can't see anything resembling a bigger picture. I can't see how it all adds up to her disappearing off the face of the earth, with her escape bag dumped in the river.'

'Me neither,' Broad said. 'But it's *got* to be about more than maybe needing to have an abortion, or telling her folks they were going to be grandparents sooner than billed. Unless . . .'

'Go on?'

'Unless her having the baby was a serious threat to someone.'

Lockyer guessed whom she was talking about. 'Where have you got to with the crew of *Dig Britain*?' he said.

'I managed to speak to a head of production at the channel – who sounded about twelve. He said a documentary show of that scale wouldn't necessarily have needed a lot of crew on location. Most likely two units, the first doing pieces to camera with the presenter and participants, the second doing contextual background shots, overviews of the sites, crowd scenes, et cetera. So, in this case, that'd be general footage of Avebury, Trusloe Hall, and people getting on with excavating. That sort of thing.'

'How many people in a unit?'

'Not that many. A couple of cameras, a sound engineer, a director, an assistant. I've checked the credits of the episode, and according to the list of roles the producer told me to look out for, we could be looking at eleven people in total. Though there was a catering unit too, an outside provider called Field Eats.'

'Right. Well, let's hope Mr Stone Roses is a cameraman, and not a chef.'

'Want me to start looking up names, guv?'

'Give me the list. I'll start. You see if the catering company is still operating, and if anyone recognizes our guy. Still no word on the kebab-van man from the Mop – Giannis Andino?'

'No. But I've been in touch with the Greek police, who are running some checks for us.'

Lockyer turned back to his own computer. He'd been about to start on the list of names from the credits of *Dig Britain*, but curiosity made him search for Mimi Draper instead. The ex-girlfriend of Edward Chapman's that Antigone had mentioned. All he could find was an article in the newspaper archive, showing a smiling girl with bottle-blonde curls, wearing an elaborate green cravat and silver jewellery. Potted palms in the background made Lockyer think it must be a corporate portrait of some kind. *Meet the Team.*

Mimi had died in 1993, after falling fifty feet down the central stairwell at her block of flats, in Bristol. The inquest into her death had ruled it a suicide. Mimi had been drinking heavily at the time, and had recently seen her GP to ask for help with depression and anxiety following a break-up. There was no evidence of anyone else having been involved. Mimi had been twenty-two years old. She'd been taking evening classes to sit A levels in history and English literature, while working as a receptionist at a leisure club by day.

Lockyer stared at her smiling face for a while, wondering what had triggered the end of her affair with Chapman. Had it been the slow realization that he had no intention of leaving his wife, as Lockyer suspected had been the case with Nazma? Or had it been something more sudden – like Antigone finding out and putting a stop to it? Perhaps Mimi had issued Chapman with an ultimatum he'd ignored. Or perhaps Antigone had given him one that he hadn't. From the little he knew of the man, Lockyer suspected the archaeologist would take the path of least resistance, if at all possible. And he was clearly in awe of his wife – Lockyer could easily imagine that Antigone Chapman was not an easy woman to be married to. *I'm already in the doghouse over something else entirely . . .*

On impulse, he requested a copy of the transcript of Mimi's inquest.

Seven of the eleven names on the list of *Dig Britain* on-location crew were male. None of the names turned up anything in the PNC, so he resorted to the DVLA, which gave him four hits, only one of which listed a date of birth putting the man at about the right age – under forty – in the summer of 1999. Lockyer squinted at the licence photo of Paul Copeland, who, at a stretch *could* have been Stone Roses Man. Next he put each of the seven through an image search, with a reference to TV work, and pulled up any social-media hits. Paul Copeland's Facebook page ruled him out. Beyond having dark hair, there was no real similarity: he was short and wiry, with sloping shoulders. But the fourth name Lockyer ran brought up the LinkedIn page of Rhys Birch, who described himself as an independent filmmaker. He'd been the second unit director on *Dig Britain*.

'Got him, Gem,' Lockyer said.

'Really?' She got up for a closer look. 'Great. Want me to contact him?'

'Get an address, and let's just pay him a visit if we can. I'd far rather he had no time to polish his reactions.'

'Right, guv.'

Rhys Birch lived in a village on the very edge of Slough, in Berkshire. The kind of place that city people think of as the countryside but farmers call the town. Pretty beamed cottages surrounded a village green blighted by the constant rumble of traffic. Rhys Birch's address took them to a smart new-build, with mock-Georgian pillars, on a street backing onto the railway.

The door was opened by a curvaceous woman in her thirties. 'Hello! Can I help you?'

They showed their ID. 'I'm Detective Inspector Lockyer, this is Detective Constable Broad. We'd like to speak to Rhys Birch, if possible.'

'Rhys?' Her face clouded. 'What's this about? Has something happened?

'Can I ask who you are, madam?' Lockyer asked.

'I'm Louisa. Rhys is my husband.'

'Is Mr Birch at home?'

'Yes,' she said, still seeming to feel she needed to hear more before she'd let them in. 'He's in his studio, out the back. If you don't mind going around the side? One of our daughters suffers from asthma, so we're trying to have as few people inside the house as possible.'

'That's fine. We're happy to stay outside,' Broad said.

'He's not in any trouble, is he?'

Broad was perfectly noncommittal. 'We'd just like to speak to him.'

'Well, the gate's open,' Louisa told them, and Lockyer saw curiosity begin to trump her concern.

Against the back fence of their featureless garden was a modern timber outbuilding, the kind of outdoor office a lot of people had invested in since the first lockdown. The lights were on inside. Lockyer glimpsed movement through the bamboo blinds as they approached, and Rhys was at the glass door before they'd even reached it.

'Sorry, who the hell are you?' he said testily, leaning out.

Now in his early fifties, his hair was shorter than it had been, and salted with grey to match a neatly trimmed beard. His face was regular – handsome – but the crease of a too-common frown sat between his eyebrows, and he'd softened around the middle.

Lockyer and Broad showed their ID again.

'We'd like to ask you a few questions, if you don't mind,' Lockyer said.

'I'm actually right in the middle of something.'

'It shouldn't take too long.'

'What's this about?' he said. 'And isn't it against the rules for you to be here? Aren't we under lockdown?'

'We are. But criminal investigations continue, of course,' Lockyer said evenly. 'We're happy to stand out here and ask our questions about the disappearance of Nazma Kirmani, but it might be more private inside.'

Birch's face froze at the mention of her name. Then he sent a vaguely nervous glance towards the house. Lockyer looked back and saw Louisa at the kitchen sink, washing up very slowly.

'You'd better come in,' he said grudgingly, avoiding eye contact.

They followed him into his studio. A background smell of pine was overlaid with that of hot plastic and static charge. A wide desk was surrounded by an array of mixing desks and other equipment; the desk itself held three huge computer screens arranged in a triptych, each showing the same image of a woman's face pulled into a rictus of fear. As if noticing that fact, Birch hit a single key, and all three screens went dark.

'I'm working on a little indie horror film.' He folded his arms with a frown.

'Can you tell us about Nazma Kirmani, please, Mr Birch?'

He shrugged stiffly. 'What do you want to know?'

'How did you meet her? How well did you get to know her?'

'Well, we met in, er, 1999, I think it was. She was one of the junior archaeologists on an episode of *Dig Britain* I worked on. Did you ever watch that show?'

'Bit before my time,' Broad said.

Birch barely looked at her. 'Right, well. It was popular, at the time. Six point four million regular viewers.'

'Wow,' Broad said neutrally.

Birch left it there, as though that were explanation enough.

'And?' Lockyer prompted.

'And what? Nazma came and said hello one day. Introduced herself. Some girls – well, *people* – find TV work pretty glamorous.'

'You mean it's a good chat-up line?' Lockyer said.

'Used to be. But I was married by then, and we were expecting our first child. My eldest son, Freddie.'

'So you weren't interested in Nazma in that way?'

'Exactly. I mean, she seemed like a nice girl, and whatever.'

'Attractive?' Broad said.

Birch glowered at her. 'Yes. I suppose so.'

'We've just met your wife, Louisa. She seems quite young for you to have been together in 1999.'

'Louisa is my second wife. We have three daughters, and I have two children from my first marriage.'

'Quite the brood,' Lockyer said. 'When did you separate from your first wife?'

'How is that any of your business?'

'It might be relevant. If you wouldn't mind telling us.'

'Well, it isn't relevant, but it was in 2002. Not long after the birth of our second child.' He pulled a face. 'We thought another baby would help. It didn't.'

'I see.' Lockyer jotted down *Baby didn't help relationship* in his notebook, more to wind Birch up than for any professional reason. 'Your relationship with Miss Kirmani never went beyond the professional?'

'No. Well, I mean, I was friendly. But that was all.'

'When did you last see her?'

'Haven't a clue. It was bloody years ago. We wrapped filming in . . . maybe early September, I think. Or middle. So, some time before that.'

'And you didn't stay in touch with her at all?'

'No.'

'What did you think when you heard she'd gone missing?'

He gave a stiff, unconvincing shrug. 'I didn't hear about it.'

'But you know she went missing in the autumn of 1999? And, as far as anyone knows, remains missing to this day?'

'No, I . . .' He appeared to marshal his thoughts. Giving

himself time to assess what they must already know, Lockyer thought. 'I mean, of course I'd *heard* about it.'

'How did you hear about it?'

'I can't remember. Somebody at work must have seen it on the news, or something. I was back in London by then, busy with work and about to become a father – I wasn't exactly keeping up with current events. Anyway, she wasn't missing in the end. Was she?'

Lockyer ignored the question. 'Whereabouts in London were you living at the time?'

'Barbican. Not far from St Bart's.'

'That's quite close to Islington, isn't it?'

He made a face. 'Not especially.'

Lockyer gave Broad a small nod. She took out the picture of Birch captured from the TV footage, and handed it to him.

'This is you, isn't it, Mr Birch?' she said.

'Yes. That's . . . Where did you get that?'

'From the episode of *Dig Britain*. Do you remember that T-shirt, Mr Birch?'

'Er . . .' He made a show of peering closer. He was no better at hiding a lie than he was at hiding his vanity. Lockyer had no idea how he'd managed to keep an extramarital affair secret – if indeed he had. 'I'm not sure. Why?'

'It's a Stone Roses T-shirt,' Lockyer said. 'Do you still have it?'

'Do I still have an old band T-shirt from twenty-one years ago? No. I very much doubt it.'

'Did you give it to Nazma?'

The tiniest flicker before he answered. 'No. Why on earth would I?'

'As a gift to a woman you were involved with.'

'I've already told you, there was nothing like that between Naz and me.'

'The trouble is, Mr Birch, I don't believe you.'

'Well, it's hardly my problem if—'

'I think you *were* involved with her. I don't know how far the relationship went, but I suspect you *did* give her the T-shirt.'

'You're wrong.'

Lockyer was certain Birch was lying. He went out on a limb, hoping the man was no better at spotting a lie than he was at telling one. 'We found the remains of a T-shirt similar to this one in a bag belonging to Nazma Kirmani, which was dumped in the River Kennet, most likely at around the same time she went missing.'

'Well, it isn't my T-shirt.'

'We're having it tested for DNA. Sampling and analysis techniques have improved significantly in recent years. DNA can be lifted from hair, skin cells, saliva, sweat, even after many years. We're confident we'll be able to raise a profile of the shirt's former owner.' He locked eyes with Rhys Birch. 'Would you care to provide us with a DNA sample in order to exclude you, Mr Birch?'

Birch looked away, his nostrils flaring, neck mottling red. Whether it was anger or simply embarrassment, Lockyer didn't care.

'Fine. I gave her the sodding T-shirt, okay?'

'Okay. Why?'

Birch gave a cynical little huff. 'Look, she had a crush on me, all right? She was a sweet girl, but it got a bit awkward at times. I'd be somewhere on site and then there she'd be, just come to say hi, or see what we were up to, or to ask if I wanted to come and film her scraping at some interesting bit of soil she'd just uncovered. She asked me out for a drink a few times. And I went, once or twice, but only as part of a group. They weren't *dates* or anything. She saw me wearing that T-shirt and I guess she went off and bought the album because the next day she's suddenly a fan of the Stone Roses and wants to know if I've seen them live, *yada yada yada*. She was just . . . she was very *young*.'

'How tiresome for you,' Broad said.

'No, she was nice. And I was flattered, I suppose. But that's as far as it went.'

'So why did you give her the T-shirt?' she asked.

'Because she asked if she could have it on the last day of filming. I didn't see the harm.'

'Were you sleeping together?'

'*No.* I was a happily married man.'

'Who got divorced a couple of years later,' Lockyer reminded him. 'Were you aware that Nazma was pregnant, at the time she went missing?'

Another flicker of his eyelids. 'What? No.'

'Were you the father of her baby?'

'*No.*' He ran a hand through his hair. 'Look, she was shagging her boss, right? I can't remember his name. You should ask him about it, not me.'

'We have. Now we're asking you.'

'Well, I don't know anything about it. I gave her that T-shirt to be nice, then went home and didn't hear anything about her until she was missing and then she wasn't. After that, I hadn't given her another thought until you came in just now.'

'Is that so?' Lockyer said. 'Did Nazma ever talk to you about her relationship with Edward Chapman? Or about anything she'd seen or heard at Trusloe Hall?'

This time Birch looked genuinely blank. 'No. Why? What was going on?'

'Didn't you think it was strange of her to ask you out repeatedly when she was already in a relationship?' Broad said.

The mottling on Birch's neck deepened. 'Not really. People do cheat on their partners, you know. And, like I said, she was young. Look, I really need to get back to work. Are we done? I've told you everything I can.'

'It doesn't bother you that Nazma is still missing? That something might have happened to her back then?' Lockyer said.

'Well, I hope you're wrong, of course, but I hardly knew her. The world is full of terrible things happening, every damn day. I've got five kids to stress about without having to worry about a girl I was half friends with for a few months twenty-one years ago.'

'Maybe six,' Broad said, as they turned to leave.

'What?'

'Maybe six kids, if you *were* the father of Nazma's child, and she went on to have it.'

In answer to that, Rhys Birch shut the door behind them.

Back in the car, Broad let out a loud breath. 'What a complete *knob*,' she burst out. 'I mean – *another* one! Poor Nazma.'

'How do you mean?'

'What are the chances of one young woman getting tangled up with two such narcissistic, cheating twats in the same year? Both of them claiming she basically threw herself at them, and that it had nothing whatsoever to do with *them*.'

'They could be telling the truth,' Lockyer risked saying. 'Nazma might have been looking to have fun.'

'Yeah, but they're trying to make her sound like some slutty man-eater, guv! And letting themselves right off the hook in the process. It just . . . it's not fair, when she's not here to tell us what really happened.'

'I agree with you,' Lockyer said. 'And I'm sure Birch's relationship with Nazma went further than he's admitting to. Whether it went as far as her getting pregnant, I don't know. He did seem surprised to hear about that.'

'Yeah, well, he's a liar.'

'But not a very good one. And Nazma's friends describe her as loyal – loyal to Chapman in particular.'

'But the baby *couldn't* have been his, guv. He'd been firing blanks for years.'

'The baby not being Chapman's doesn't automatically make it Rhys Birch's.'

'Someone *else*'s? Who?'

'I don't know, Gem. But there were plenty of other men at Avebury that summer, and we need to keep open minds.'

She fell into a brooding silence as he pulled back out onto the M4, heading west.

'This one's getting to you, isn't it?' he asked gently.

Broad looked down at her hands, unclenching them. 'A bit,' she admitted. 'It just seems to me like Nazma was lied to a lot – by the man she was seeing, and maybe by the new man she thought she'd met. And neither of them claims to have realized she just . . . *vanished*, that autumn. And I don't think I believe either of them. *Something* was going on that Nazma didn't feel able to tell her best mate about. Whether that was being pregnant or something more, I don't know. And when she went to a family member for help she was turned away. And I just think . . . I keep thinking how *alone* she must have felt. And none of them "gave her a second thought" when she dropped off the face of the planet.'

'She's got us, now, Gem,' Lockyer said. 'We're not going to let it go.'

'I know, guv. But we're most likely about two decades too late.'

He knew she was probably right about that. 'Well, I can think of someone who might be more willing to speak to us about Rhys Birch's relationship with Nazma than he was,' he said.

'Who?'

'His first wife. Let's track her down.'

12

Day 10, Wednesday

Giannis Andino was a huge man with bloodhound eyes and a nose ruined either by rosacea or alcohol, or both. His black hair was defiantly resisting the incoming grey, and he spoke to them from the brightly lit terrace of a coastal home. Water sparkled tantalizingly in the background, and Lockyer realized how long it had been since he'd seen the sea.

'Hello, hello!' Andino bellowed at his computer screen. 'You want to talk about the woman I saw? The people I saw? In Marlborough, yes?'

'Yes, please, Mr Andino. We appreciate that it was some time ago, now,' Broad said.

'Long time ago, yes,' the big man said. 'Many years. Why now? Something changes?'

'Further evidence has come to light, yes, sir,' she said. 'It's possible that what you witnessed was related to a crime after all. Can you describe what you saw?'

'Man and woman, crossing the street near my van, going from back of high street to the car park. In a bit of trouble – that's what I thought. She's in a bit of trouble.'

'What made you think that, Mr Andino?'

'Please, I am Giannis. The woman is not walking well. Holding herself, you know? Crouching. She keeps stumbling. The man is holding her under her arms to keep her up.'

'And that's what made you think she must be drunk?'

'No, no. *Police* say that to me, when I speak to them. They say, "Do you think she was drunk?" And I say, "Yes, maybe." But at first – the first thing I tell them – is that I think she is in pain, you know? She is sick. Stomach hurting. The way she is hunched forwards, yes?'

Broad flicked a quick glance at Lockyer. 'Can you remember anything about their appearance? Like, how old they were? Or what they were wearing?'

'No, no. It was dark. A lot of people around, queuing at my van. I think he is much taller than her, but maybe this is because of how she is walking, yes? I see she has very dark hair, quite long. Shiny shoes. Man is wearing a dark coat. He has brown hair, bit messy. I don't see his face, not enough to remember him. When young girl is in the paper, gone missing, I telephone at once to the police.'

'So you were suspicious enough of what you'd seen to connect it to reports of a woman's disappearance?'

'Yes.' Andino gave a solemn nod. 'I feel bad. I think, I should have gone to see she is okay, yes? But it was busy-busy, a lot of people wanting food. Maybe he is only helping her. She is ill, and he is helping her. And it was only a short moment. Then they are gone. But this girl, she turns up, she is in London, no problem.'

'Did you feel relieved?'

The big man spread his fingers expressively. 'Yes, and also no. I think, Okay, it was not her I saw. It was someone else.'

'But that didn't reassure you?'

'No, because . . . the woman I see is in trouble. I know this in my gut.' He laid one hand on his mighty paunch. 'I *hope* I am wrong. Maybe it *was* too much booze, like me, or she got sick from the fairground rides.'

'It could have been,' Lockyer said. 'Thank you for speaking to us, Mr An— Giannis. Is there anything else you can tell us, at all?'

He shook his grizzled head. 'Now, I *act*. If I see something like this again, I *do* something. I think perhaps I miss the chance to help this woman.'

Lockyer waited until the screen was blank before speaking. 'Sounds like he knows what he saw,' he said.

'Yeah.'

He tapped the photo of Nazma that Jonathan Tate had taken at the Marlborough Mop. 'She was wearing gold trainers that night. Those could be the "shiny shoes" Andino remembers.'

Broad nodded solemnly. 'One time, when we were playing rounders at school, I got whacked in the stomach. Really hard. God, it hurt – it winded me. I couldn't stand up straight, no matter how hard I wanted to style it out. I *couldn't*. Not for about ten minutes. It was horrible.'

'There's also the possibility that something was happening with the baby,' Lockyer said.

'You mean a miscarriage?' Broad said.

He nodded. 'I've also seen cases where pregnant women have been deliberately punched in the stomach. As an attack on the foetus as much as the mother.'

Broad recoiled. 'That's atrocious.'

'People can be.'

She grabbed the mouse and clicked a few times, bringing up Darren Mason's file. In his juvenile mug shot he looked both belligerent and frightened, his cheeks peppered with acne. His hair had been longer and scruffier back then, brushed forwards like one of the Gallagher brothers from Oasis, back in the day.

'Darren's not that tall,' she said. 'But Nazma was only five foot two. If she was bent over, he'd look a lot taller than her. His hair was long enough back then, and the right colour to match Andino's description.'

'As was Rhys Birch's,' Lockyer pointed out. 'And Edward Chapman's, for that matter.'

'Chapman has an alibi. And he didn't know she was pregnant,' Broad pointed out. 'Nazma would hardly have told him, if he couldn't have been the father.'

'No, I suppose not.'

'Plus, Darren Mason is far more the type to resort to violence than the other two, don't you think?'

'Possibly.'

'We could get Darren in?' Broad said. 'Push him on a few

things – like Inez's meds? And the mysterious boxes that disappeared?'

Lockyer leant back in his chair and stared out at the cold white sky. 'I don't think we've got enough on him, Gem. Definitely not enough for an arrest, and I very much doubt he'd come in voluntarily.'

'I could try him?'

'Knock yourself out.' He checked his watch. 'I'd better update the DSU.'

He was reluctant to, since they still had no real idea who might have wanted to harm Nazma. Detective Superintendent Considine liked to see a clear direction of travel. They needed a breakthrough to pull it all into sharper focus but, with cold cases even more than with live ones, it was possible simply to hit a dead end. To run out of things to check, people to speak to, evidence to find.

The threat of that happening stalked Lockyer every day.

He thought again of Hari and Liz Kirmani, worn down by the corrosive agony of not knowing. Of all the many murder victims whose killers still hadn't been identified. Felt himself tensing, his jaw clenching, at the idea of Nazma becoming – of her *being* – one more of them. He re-heard his own words of a moment before: *He knows what he saw.*

'Gem, were the Kirmanis ever shown the footage of Nazma from Islington nick? Or the picture?'

'Don't know, guv. They must have been, surely.'

'They never mentioned it, and we never asked. But wouldn't *they* know whether or not it's her? It might look like her to us, or to any stranger, but to her parents?'

'Want me to call them and check?'

'I'll do it.'

But before he could, his mobile phone rang. He hesitated before answering.

'Hedy, what's up? I'm at work.'

It sounded like she was in a car, but she no longer fitted comfortably behind the ridiculous square wheel of her vintage Austin. There was a lot of background noise, and her breathing was ragged down the line.

'The baby,' she said shakily.

Lockyer's heart jerked hard in his chest. 'It's . . . *now*? Are you in labour? Where are you?'

'No, no!' she whispered hoarsely. 'No, Matt . . . I'm in a taxi . . .'

'Hedy, what's going on?' With a cold rush, he thought she might be leaving.

'The baby's stopped moving. This morning.'

'What?'

'It's stopped moving. I – I knew something wasn't right as soon as I woke up, but I thought it was just asleep. But I've done my stretches and had hot tea. I've played some music, and – and I've tried massage. But . . . it's not *moving*, Matt! Not for hours.'

'Okay. Okay.' His thoughts had scattered like startled birds. 'It's probably fine, but you need to get to the hospital—'

'Why do you think I'm in a fucking taxi?' she hissed.

'Right. Good.'

He heard her snatched breaths – the edge of panic, instantly contagious.

'This is the part where you say you'll be right there, Matt,' she said. 'Where you say "I'm coming."'

'I'm coming, Hedy.'

She rang off, and Lockyer stared stupidly at his phone for a few seconds.

'Guv?' Broad said. 'Everything okay?'

He looked across at her. 'No. No, I don't think so.'

'Sounds like you need to go and be with Hedy?'

'Yeah.' He swallowed. 'Yeah.'

Lockyer had spent a lot of time at Salisbury District Hospital over the summer, sitting with his mother while she fought the extreme immune response to Covid that had almost killed her. Still, it took him longer than it should have to find the maternity unit. But, then, he hadn't been to it before – or to any of the check-ups or classes. A combination of Covid and Hedy had kept him away, and now he felt utterly clueless. Useless, in fact. He was directed to the Day Assessment Unit, where he joined a handful of other men and one prospective grandma in the waiting room.

He wasn't allowed beyond that point, to whichever room Hedy was in. Hedy and the baby. *His* baby.

Lockyer had already stopped trying to think of things he might say to comfort her if something was very wrong. There would be nothing to say. No way to make it better for *either* of them. So he focused on feeling impatient, and angry at his own helplessness. It was better than simply sitting in fear, with the dawning realization that all the time he'd been wrestling with the way he'd got into his present situation, quietly, all unobserved, he'd come to love his unborn child.

He watched the seconds tick by on the white plastic clock on the wall. Went repeatedly to the water dispenser to fill a paper cone and wet his dry throat. He tried to phone Hedy, and texted, but got no response. Paced the corridor for a while, until he was told to go back and sit in the waiting room. Covid rules. Two hours passed during which he was viscerally reminded, if he'd needed to be, of the agony of waiting, dreading, and not knowing.

'Matt?' Hedy called to him from the doorway. She was in a wheelchair, being pushed along by a nurse. Hands resting on the bump. He lurched to his feet. 'It's okay. We're okay,' she said.

A rush of oxygen hit his lungs. 'Okay,' he said.

'Is this your ride home?' the nurse said, smiling behind her visor.

'Yes. This is my partner, Matt.'

'All right then. I'll leave you here,' the nurse said. 'Good to meet you, Matt. This one's to rest, okay? Feet up, chill out. Give Baby an easy ride. Got it?'

Hedy shot him a black look.

'Got it,' he said.

'Pop the chair back into Reception once you've got her out to the car,' she said.

But as soon as they'd gone round the corner, Hedy made him stop so she could walk.

'Hedy—'

'Honestly, the doctor said it was fine. I'm just not to go out jogging or anything. Like I could.'

Lockyer moved the wheelchair out of the way then turned to face her, taking a gentle hold of her shoulders. 'Tell me.'

Her face was pinched with worry and fatigue. 'It's fine. The baby's heartbeat is fine. It's getting plenty of oxygen, even when I move, and there's no sign of an infection.'

'So why the change?'

She shrugged. 'Just having a lazy day. Or getting so fat they're wedged in there, and it's much harder for them to move.' Her face gave the little flicker it did when she was feeling something he couldn't. 'Here.' She grabbed his hands, held them to her middle, and he felt a faint thump. Fist or foot, difficult to say.

He caught his breath. It was the most reassuring time he'd ever been punched.

When he looked up, Hedy was watching him with a crooked smile.

'It really *wasn't* just a ploy to find out how you feel about the baby,' she said. 'But I guess now I know.'

He nodded. 'You and me both.'

She pulled his head closer to hers, touching their foreheads together. 'Let's go,' she said. 'I hate hospitals.'

13

Day 11, Thursday

Sheer exhaustion knocked them both out early, and Lockyer slept straight through until eight the next morning, when Hedy got up to go to the bathroom. He scrambled out of bed, disoriented. He couldn't remember the last time he'd slept so soundly. He was dressing clumsily when Hedy returned.

'What's the rush?'

'I'm late.'

'No, you're not. You're just used to going to work before most people are even up.'

She wasn't completely wrong.

'Everything okay in there?' he said, nodding at her mid-section.

She nodded. 'All good. Having a yawn and a stretch.' She sat on the edge of the bed, in a shaft of cool lemon sunshine, and reached out a hand to him. 'Come back to bed.'

'Sorry, Hedy, I really can't. I've got to—'

'Five minutes. *One* minute then . . . Come *on*, Matt. It won't be just you and me for much longer. Pretty soon we'll be looking back wistfully at all the times we got up when we could've stayed in bed.' She gave him a piercing look. 'I do know what it's going to be like, you know. I've seen the TV shows. I'm going to end up banging on about how your job is more important than me and the baby, and you're going to claim it's not true even while you bolt out of the door, gripped by the misconception that only *you* can solve the case you're working on . . .'

'Ouch,' he said. But he really *didn't* want to have to drop it all and take paternity leave, when it felt as though they were getting somewhere. When he was *determined* to get somewhere.

Hedy sighed. 'Look, I'm fully prepared to be the bitter, eye-rolling other half of an over-zealous detective. But you'll have to give in sometimes, so you might as well practise now, before sleep deprivation turns me into a complete psycho.'

'Well, when you put it like that,' he said, unbuttoning the shirt he'd been halfway through doing up.

In the car, a thought occurred to him that might have done days before if he hadn't been so preoccupied. He pulled over, and dialled Kevin's number. His oldest friend. They'd gone shoulder to shoulder through school from the age of five, and only that long-ingrained loyalty, those shared roots, had kept their friendship alive when Lockyer had left to go to university, and then into the police. Kevin had stayed in the village of his birth, caught in the web of minor organized crime that his father made his business.

'Matt,' Kevin said, as he picked up. 'You good? Had a baby, have you?'

'No, not yet. All okay there?'

'Same old, same old. What can I do you for?'

'Just wanted to ask whether the name Darren Mason rings any bells with you?'

'Dunno. Should it?'

'He's someone I've come across on a case. Based over in Avebury Trusloe.'

Kevin paused. 'Oh, right. You mean he might be someone in my old man's line of work?'

'That's what I'm wondering. Any chance you could ask around a bit? On the QT?'

Kevin laughed briefly. 'What am I – your snout, now?'

'No more than I'm your tame copper.'

'Right, right. But you put your neck on the line for me, so now it's payback time?'

'Never said anything of the sort, Kev.'

'Good. Because you did put your job on the line for me, Matt, and you know I'll never forget it. But if I start asking questions about the wrong people, it's *literally* my neck on the line. Plus me bollocks, kneecaps, the lot. Right?'

'I'm not asking you to put yourself in danger. Just . . . if you hear anything.'

Kevin sighed through his teeth. 'What sort of work are we talking about here?'

'Prescription drugs. Handling stolen goods. Maybe more.'

'Right. Funny – you've been on at me for decades to step away from all that shit. Now you want me to jump right in.'

'If I thought for one second you'd managed to step away from it all, I wouldn't ask.'

'Thanks for the vote of confidence, mate.'

'Come on, Kev. We'll name the baby after you.'

'Liar. Nobody'd do that to a kid these days.'

When Lockyer reached their cramped office, he was surprised not to find Broad in it. It was after nine. He thought back, remembering just one other time she'd been late to work – she'd been cycling in along the towpath and got a puncture. He tried calling her, but it went straight to voicemail.

On his desk, he found a short note she'd left, giving contact details for Rhys Birch's ex-wife, Laura Miller. Laura had remarried and was living in Winchester, where she was the deputy head of a private girls' school. *Happy to talk to us either mornings before 10 or after 4 p.m.* Lockyer was about to dial the number when Broad came hurrying in, face flushed. Her hair was bedraggled and her shirt buttons done up wrong, but the look she gave him begged him not to ask. With a tremendous effort of will, he didn't.

She swallowed, catching her breath. 'Everything all right, guv? With the baby, I mean?'

'Yes. False alarm. Strict orders for Hedy to take it easy.'

'Okay, great. Thank goodness for that.'

Broad struggled out of her coat and pushed up her sleeves, then seemed to change her mind and pulled them back down. Not before Lockyer had caught sight of scattered bruises on her forearms. Finger-sized. She sat down abruptly

and pulled in her chair, tucking stray curls of her pale hair
behind her ears.

Lockyer couldn't help it. 'Gem, are you ... There's no
trouble, or anything?'

'No, no.' She couldn't meet his eye. 'All good.'

'Right. Well, I was just about to call Laura Miller, but it
can wait while you get a coffee.'

'I'm fine. Let's just—'

'Get a coffee, Gem. Catch your breath.'

She sat for a moment, staring down at her keyboard.
Lockyer noticed her hands shaking. Adrenaline? Shock?
Surely she'd never tolerate any *physical* bullying from Pete –
or anyone? Broad was the opposite of aggressive, but she
was getting better at standing up for herself. Frustrated,
Lockyer felt the impulse to force the truth out of her. Then
he recognized how very male his last two thoughts had
been: that anyone ought to be able to defend themselves in
a physically abusive situation, and that force was right there
in his toolkit, if there was something he wanted to know. A
recent joke about him being available if Broad ever needed
someone kneecapped was suddenly no longer funny. But
then she looked up with a quick smile, and went to fetch
a coffee.

Accepting defeat, Lockyer sent a Teams link to Laura
Miller.

She had a short, chic haircut, rose-gold jewellery, and
was dressed in an elegant grey suit. She looked the precise
opposite of the deputy head Lockyer remembered from his
own schooldays.

'Mrs Miller, thank you for talking to us at such short notice,' Lockyer said, once they'd introduced themselves.

'Not at all. Very intrigued to hear how I can help.' She had an efficient way of speaking, but it wasn't unfriendly.

'We're currently reviewing an investigation that took place in October 1999, and we're interested in any involvement Rhys Birch may have had.'

At the mention of him, the corners of Laura's mouth tweaked downwards. 'That's quite some time ago.'

'Yes, we appreciate that.'

'Is this about the girl at Trusloe Hall? That was around the time, if I remember correctly?'

'That's right, yes. We think your husband may have been involved with a young woman called Nazma Kirmani, who went missing that year.'

Laura blinked. 'She went *missing*? I . . . Well, look, my ex-husband is a worm, but I don't believe he'd actually harm anybody.'

'You'd be surprised how often we hear that,' Lockyer said. 'And how often it turns out to be wrong.'

'You're not suggesting he *killed* her?'

'No. We're not. We'd just like a better idea of him, and his relationship with Miss Kirmani.'

'A better idea of him? Well, he's a spineless egomaniac who lets his genitals make most of his decisions. Does that help to clarify things?'

'You think they were sleeping together?' Lockyer asked.

'I know they were.' She raised her eyebrows. 'Well, I strongly suspect as much. They were certainly *involved*, or whatever you want to call it. And that rarely stopped at kissing and love notes, with Rhys.'

'He'd been unfaithful to you before?'

'Yes. Before we were married. He swore it was just cold feet, and wouldn't happen again, et cetera. Silly me. Perhaps the affair with this girl in 1999 was because Freddie was on the way – our first child. If I'd quizzed him, I expect that would've been his excuse.'

'But you didn't quiz him?'

'No, Inspector. I didn't see the point. Sadly, learning to tell when someone's lying to you doesn't mean they'll start telling you the truth.'

'What made you suspect he was having an affair with Nazma?'

She sighed. 'All the usual things. An uptick in his mood, sudden bunches of flowers, and other little presents – seriously. Frowning at his phone every time it pinged if I was in the room. Smiling at it when he thought I wasn't looking.' Her voice dripped resignation. 'Really, he was about as subtle as a brick.'

'And you never confronted him about it?' Broad said.

'I might have done, if it had carried on after Freddie was born, but it didn't.'

'You're certain?'

'I heard him break up with her. He thought I was at yoga, but I'd felt dizzy so I'd come back early.'

'It was over the phone? Can you remember when that was, Mrs Miller?' Lockyer said.

'Only a week or two before I went into labour. So, late

September that year.' She sighed again. 'That's when I discovered he'd been lying to her, too.'

'How so?'

'I eavesdropped, naturally. I heard him call her Nazma –
that was how I found out her name. It sounded like she
was asking to come and stay with him. Of course, he was
pretty panicky about that, came out with a string of feeble
excuses, but I guess she persisted because in the end he had
to 'fess up. "I'm married, we're about to have a baby, it's just
not possible," that sort of thing. She must have been pretty
upset because he spent a while trying to be nice, but I could
hear him getting impatient, and I – I actually felt a bit sorry
for her. He told her it had just been a summer thing, not
real life, and that he thought she'd understood that. That
whatever mess she'd got herself into, it wasn't his problem.'

Laura's face settled into flat lines of disgust at the memory.
'Now I hear it back, he was clearly an utter shit to her. At
the time, I was so bloody pregnant I was just relieved to hear
he wasn't going to leave me on my own with a newborn to
look after.'

'You're sure about what you heard?' Lockyer asked. 'That
Nazma was asking for help?'

'I'm sure. That's how I knew it was really over – no
woman, however smitten, would've taken him back after
a brush-off like that.'

'But you couldn't get any sense of what the mess she was
in might have been?'

'No. Sorry. She must have hung up on him in the end
because he stopped talking mid-sentence, and that was

that. Our marriage lasted about another two years. Then Rhys started sleeping with an extra in another show he was working on, and I hit my limit. The scales fell from my eyes, and all that. I was pregnant that time too,' she reflected, 'but less scared, I suppose. I realized I had no respect left for him, let alone any love. I'd have quite happily never set eyes on him again, if he hadn't been Freddie and India's father.'

'Can you remember anything else he said to Nazma? Did you ever see any messages on his phone?'

'No, sorry. He was very careful. There was one time I managed to . . . take a look – and I'm not proud of it. But, in any case, he'd deleted all but the most mundane things.'

'And you weren't aware that Nazma Kirmani had gone missing? Your husband never said anything about it?'

'No. Not a word.'

'Did you notice any strange behaviour on his part, in the weeks after the phone call you overheard?'

'No. Not at all. If anything, he seemed happier. Probably relieved to have got away with it – the affair, I mean.'

'Can you remember whether he was at home on the night of October second?'

'October the second, twenty-one years ago? No, sorry, I haven't a clue.'

'When was Freddie born, Mrs Miller?' Broad asked.

'October the nineteenth. Rhys was back and forth with work right up until I went into labour, but he stayed at home with us for several weeks afterwards.'

'So he could've been away for work on the second?'

'He *could*. But I really don't know.'

'Thank you, Mrs Miller,' Lockyer said. 'If you remember anything else about that time, please get back in touch with us.'

'That was you asking for an alibi for Rhys, wasn't it?' she said, as though only just realizing. 'For the night she disappeared. My God, do you seriously think he could have *done* something to her?'

'He had a lot to lose, Mrs Miller. Nazma may have threatened to tell you about the affair. Perhaps he didn't think you'd forgive him a second time.'

'But he's not . . . Look, Rhys is many things but, primarily, he's an emotionally stunted coward. If she'd been pressuring him, he's more likely to have made a tearful display of contrition to *me*, rather than kill *her*.'

'In my experience there's just no telling what a person might do if they feel threatened,' Lockyer said. 'But, at this point, we have no evidence that Rhys was involved in Nazma's disappearance. And I would be very grateful if you didn't mention this conversation to him.'

She widened her eyes. 'Believe me, I won't.'

They ended the call.

'Well, he's a proper scumbag, as suspected,' Broad said. 'Do we think he's a killer?'

'I think Laura's right about him being a coward, and that might be reason enough for him to kill. People do, to keep things they're ashamed of from coming to light.'

'I don't know, guv.' Broad sounded sceptical. 'Like you said, he'd already had one fling and been forgiven.'

'A repeat offence would have been far more damaging,

though, don't you think? And what if the "mess" Rhys was denying any involvement in was her pregnancy? If he *was* the father, perhaps Nazma couldn't let him walk away quite as easily as all that.'

'If she was packing that bag for a trip to London, and planning to have a termination, maybe Rhys gave her the cash to help. To pay for a hotel, or something.' Broad thought for a moment. 'Maybe he was *pressuring* her to get rid of the baby.'

'So why kill her?'

'She changed her mind? Was going to keep the kid, and go after him for child support? There's a fast track to a finished marriage, right there.'

'Perhaps,' Lockyer said. 'So ... what? Nazma tells him some of that over the phone? He travels down to Wiltshire, picks her up at the Mop – or basically snatches her. Maybe he just wants to talk to her. Maybe he plans to take her up to London and make sure she gets the termination. But it goes wrong. She doesn't cooperate. Ends up dead.'

'And he goes back to Trusloe Hall to get her bag, and make it look like she just ran away?'

'Right. He'd have her wallet, and he lives in London, not that far from Islington. He could have found someone willing to pose as her, and put us off the scent.'

'If we can get some link to him from the boot print in the barn, it might be enough, right?' Broad said. 'Since the shoot was over, and he wasn't supposed to be there any more.'

Lockyer made a face. 'We can hope.'

'And with what Laura Miller just told us, we can get him in for questioning, right?'

'Absolutely,' Lockyer said. 'I want to hear his excuse for lying to us.'

An emotionally stunted coward. Lockyer recalled Laura Miller's description of the man sitting in front of them, on the other side of a Perspex screen fixed along the middle of the table, in one of their dingy interview rooms. Rhys Birch had declined legal counsel, claiming to have nothing to hide, but he couldn't sit still. He'd made a point of leaning back in the chair, spreading his knees and folding his arms, in a show of nonchalant forbearance. But he fidgeted constantly, his expression wavering between anger, scorn and fear, as he shot repeated glances at the voice recorder. Lockyer supposed it must be stressful for a habitual liar to know there'd be a permanent record of whatever they said.

'You seem anxious, Mr Birch,' he said.

'Well, I'm not. I just don't know why you've dragged me here when I've done nothing wrong.'

'We don't like being lied to. Particularly when it involves a missing person.'

'I haven't lied,' Birch said, but Lockyer could see him weighing up how much they might have found out.

'You *were* in a relationship with Nazma Kirmani in the summer of 1999.'

Birch spread his hands on the table and studied his own neat fingernails for a long moment. Then he looked up. 'I want to be very clear about this,' he said earnestly. 'It was just a fling – barely even that. I was totally up front with Naz about being married. I said I couldn't get involved. She said that was fine, she was with Chapman. It was supposed to be a bit of fun, for both of us. You know what it's like.'

'What what's like?' Broad asked coldly.

'When you meet someone you just click with but, yeah, the timing's all off, and you tell yourself nothing can happen. But that only seems to make it harder to resist.'

Broad didn't blink. 'Forbidden fruit. Grass is always greener, that kind of thing.'

'Well, yeah – but not the way you're making it sound.'

'How am I making it sound, Mr Birch?'

'Like – like there was no *thought* involved. No consideration.'

'Consideration for Nazma Kirmani, you mean? Or consideration for your wife?'

'Both,' he said crossly. 'And on her part, for Chapman.'

'So, you claim you told her you were married,' Broad asked. 'Did you tell her you had a baby on the way?'

Again, Birch eyed her as though trying to figure out what she already knew.

'I didn't go into detail.' He folded his arms, leaning back again. 'In any case, I'm pretty sure I'm not legally required to divulge my sexual history to the police.'

'You are when it affects what could well be a murder inquiry,' Lockyer said. 'Why did you lie to us about the relationship?'

'Why do you think?' Birch shot back.

'You were ashamed of your behaviour?' Broad said.

Birch glowered at her.

'Where were you on the night of October second, 1999?' Lockyer said.

Birch gave a cynical little laugh. 'Are you serious? You expect me to be able to answer that off the top of my head? It was over twenty years ago, for God's sake.'

'Did you travel to Marlborough that night?'

'No.'

'Did you meet up with Nazma?'

'No'

'Did you take Nazma to London with you? Or anywhere else?'

'*No!* I didn't see her again after the shoot wrapped in September. That was the end of it.'

'Who ended it?' Lockyer asked.

'Nobody. We just . . . agreed.' Birch's eyes slid away to one side, and he meshed his fingers, tapping his thumbs together a couple of times. It was the most blatant tell Lockyer had ever seen.

'So Nazma never asked you to help her with anything? She never asked to come and visit you at home?'

Birch stared at him, his eyes widening. 'How the—'

'Just tell us the truth, Mr Birch,' Lockyer cut in. 'It may not be something you make a habit of, but give it a go.'

'Fuck's sake,' he muttered. 'Okay, so she rang me a week or two after the shoot ended. She wanted to come and see me. I had to be firm that it was over. That I was . . . married.'

'Oh? So you *hadn't* been up front with her about that?'

No reply.

'How did she take it?'

'How do you think?'

'Well, I don't know. The way you've described it, it was barely a relationship, and she knew all along that you were already attached.'

'Yeah, well, I guess she felt . . . I guess she'd fallen for me more than I realized. Thought maybe we could both break up with our partners and get together.'

'Did she ask you to do that?' Lockyer said.

Birch frowned, thinking back, 'Well, no, actually. She just said she needed a place to stay for a while. But it was obvious she was hoping to carry things on.'

'Maybe she just needed a place to stay for a while,' Broad said.

'Maybe. Whatever.'

'Did she say why?' Lockyer asked.

Birch shrugged. 'I can't remember. Maybe something was going on with that bloke of hers. I don't know. Or the Trusloe Hall lot – she'd made friends with the mad woman that lived there. She was always telling me this thing or that thing Mrs de Whatever had said or done. To be honest, I didn't pay much attention.'

'Did Nazma tell you she was pregnant?'

'No.'

'That seems unlikely to me, Mr Birch,' Lockyer said.

'Well, I don't give a shit if it seems unlikely. She *didn't*.'

'I'd expect a young woman to inform her lover if she'd accidentally fallen pregnant.'

'Yep.' He nodded. 'Except there's no way the kid was mine. That's probably what stopped her.'

'Whatever precautions are taken—' Lockyer started to say.

'Well, that's what I've been trying to tell you,' Birch cut in. 'Naz and I never had sex.'

It was Lockyer's turn to be surprised. This didn't fit with the vanity he'd ascribed to the man, the tendency to brag. Nor was he showing any of his tell-tale twitches. In fact, he looked almost grudging about confessing it.

Birch shot him a cynical little smile. 'That's a bit of a spanner in the works, isn't it?'

'You never had sex?' Lockyer said.

'We never had sex.'

'Why not?'

'Because Nazma was still young enough to believe in love, and being faithful, and all that sort of thing. She said it would be *wrong* while she was still with Chapman. Said she couldn't be unfaithful to him, which was a joke.'

'Why was it a joke?'

'Well, we'd done just about everything else. But apparently an actual shag was a step too far. Like, as long as she kept her knickers on, none of it counted as cheating. She still went white as a sheet when I suggested we tell Chapman about it.'

'Why did you want to do that?' Broad said.

'I didn't. I was just pointing out to her that she'd already crossed the line. So she might as well . . . you know . . . go the whole hog.'

'How kind of you,' Broad said. 'I'm sure she was grateful for the clarification.'

'What's your problem with me? *Hm?*' Birch asked Broad directly. 'Is this a "sisterhood" thing? Because Naz was every bit as responsible for what we did as I was.'

Broad's stare was flatly hostile. 'If you hadn't lied to her about your situation, she might've thought twice.'

'Did it wind you up?' Lockyer asked. 'Must have been frustrating.'

'It was,' Birch said. 'But some women like to tease. It's a power trip. No wonder they end up—'

'No wonder they end up *what?*' Broad asked.

'Getting dumped.'

'Oh? So if she'd put out you'd have carried on seeing her after your son was born?'

Birch clenched his teeth. 'That's not what I said.' He drew in a deep breath, leaning back again. 'Look, I was twenty years younger then, all right? I suppose I was a bit of a lad, at times. Naz wouldn't sleep with me, and it . . . stung. Dented my ego, or however you want to put it. So we broke up. She rang a while later and wanted to come and stay, so I told her no way. That's the whole of it. That's the truth.'

Again, none of his tells. Lockyer wondered if Birch was finally being honest, or whether he was, in fact, very good at lying. Good enough to play them, to fake all those guilty signals, in order to be able to drop them when it really mattered. Then he remembered something else Laura Miller had said: *He was about a subtle as a brick.*

'I need you to think back, Mr Birch,' Lockyer said. '*Why*

did Nazma ask to come and stay with you? What had happened? Was she in some kind of trouble?'

Birch hitched his shoulders. But he took a moment to consider it. 'I honestly don't know. I think she did give a vague reason, but I can't remember what it was. I was more worried about getting her off the phone before my wife came home. And *keeping* her off it.'

Lockyer reached across to shut off the recording.

'Interview terminated at two thirty-three p.m.'

Lockyer could guess Broad's thoughts on what they'd been told, but he asked anyway, as they climbed back up to their office.

'I think he's a barefaced liar,' she said.

'I agree. But I believed him about not having sex with Nazma.'

'Seriously?'

'Why would he say it, if it wasn't true? He's a peacock. It hardly suits his image that he failed to seduce her.'

'Gets him off the hook for getting her pregnant, though, doesn't it?' Broad said. 'For having a motive to get rid of her – and the baby.'

'It does. And I'm not ruling him out, Gem. I just got the impression he'd stopped lying, by the end.'

'Well, that wasn't the impression *I* got.'

'No?' Lockyer said, nettled by her hostility. '*Is* this a sisterhood thing, Gem? I mean, do you just not like him because he's a philandering pig?'

She flinched. 'Seems a pretty good reason to me, guv.'

'Agreed. But it's not like you to make your personal feelings about a suspect so obvious.'

For a second she looked furious – such an unusual expression for her that Lockyer recoiled. But then it stalled, and her cheeks roared with colour, and he instantly regretted his tone.

'Look, Gem, I get it—'

She turned and headed back down the stairs. ''Scuse me, guv. I just need to . . . go to the . . .'

She was quiet when she returned to the office a little while later, but showed no signs of upset beyond an unwillingness to hold Lockyer's gaze for more than a second or two. Towards the end of the afternoon, she took a call.

'Mr Kirmani, thanks so much for calling me back.' She glanced across at Lockyer. 'I'm just going to put you on speakerphone so that DI Lockyer can join our conversation, if that's okay?'

She put him on hold for a second.

'Guv, I sent them the still from the Islington nick footage yesterday, after you had to rush off to the hospital.'

With a start, Lockyer realized it had vanished from his head, chased out by the sudden stress, the spasm of fear, of the baby going still. He'd dropped the ball, and for a second considered trying to bluff his way out of it.

'Christ. I totally forgot,' he said instead.

'Understandable,' Broad said generously.

'Not good enough,' he countered. 'Had they seen it before?'

She shook her head. Lockyer nodded at her to restart the call.

'Mr Kirmani, we can both hear you now,' she said.

'All right,' came the old man's soft voice. 'This picture . . . Why was this picture not shown to us before now?'

'I don't know, Mr Kirmani,' Lockyer confessed. 'It can only have been an oversight on the part of the original investigation, for which I apologize.'

They heard his breathing on the line, quiet but none too steady.

'If we had been shown this . . .' he said. 'We are her *family*!'

Lockyer felt a creeping sense of dread, unsure if he wanted to hear that the girl at Islington police station had or hadn't been Nazma. The former might mean she was alive and well somewhere – a faint, barely there hope, and a bombshell for her family. The latter, that she was almost certainly dead. Killed by someone clever enough to misdirect the investigation, and allow her murder to slip right through the net.

'I have looked and looked because I *want* this to be her,' Mr Kirmani said. 'I want to think that, for some reason, she ran away and left us. Even if that means I did not know my own daughter. Even if that means my child could not come to me when she was in danger. Better a wound like that than what I fear to be the truth.'

'Is it her?' Lockyer asked.

'No. It is not.'

Broad pressed her lips into a thin line, and Lockyer clenched his fists on the desktop.

'You're certain?'

'You think I could mistake her? My own daughter? No. I could not mistake her. This girl is not my Nazma. She is too broad – her shoulders, her waist – and the chin is different. Also, the earrings she is wearing. Nazma was scared of needles and all things like that. She did not have her ears pierced.'

'I see.' Lockyer looked across at Broad. 'They could be clip-on—'

Liz Kirmani appeared on the call. 'Come on, now, nobody wears clip-on earrings any more, and Naz never wore *any* earrings. It was one of those things – a way she liked to be different from other girls.'

'This is not our Nazma,' Hari Kirmani stressed. 'And if we had been shown this image twenty-one years ago we could have told you. We could have said, "You need to keep investigating. She is still missing."'

'Mr and Mrs Kirmani, I am so sorry,' Lockyer said. 'I . . .' But he couldn't think what else to say, and the silence hung on the line like a frozen heartbeat.

'You find her, please,' Hari Kirmani said. 'It is not too late, even if she is dead. You find her now.'

He rang off, and Lockyer's promise to do so died on his lips. He leant back in his chair, ran his hands down over his face. Broad took a big breath and let it out slowly. 'I know, Gem,' he said.

'I can't believe they've never been shown it before. I mean, why in God's name not?'

'She'd been positively IDed. The SIO must have thought that was good enough.'

'Well, they ought to have been shown. It's something to ask DS Brodzki, perhaps.' Broad's clipped tone betrayed her frustration.

Lockyer shook his head. 'She's been helping us. And the investigation was manipulated – by somebody thinking very clearly.' He paused. 'Perhaps somebody who'd done this kind of thing before.'

Broad looked across at him. 'I thought we'd discounted the serial-killer theory? That this *wasn't* an opportunist stranger snatch?'

Lockyer nodded. 'But just because Nazma knew her killer it doesn't mean it was the first time they'd killed.'

He was speculating, but as he spoke Lockyer felt a chill. The sensation of having caught a glimpse at something truly horrifying, lurking beneath the surface of the everyday world.

14

Day 12, Friday

Lockyer was wide awake in the small hours, but he didn't go out walking. In slow motion, he laid his hands on the baby bump instead. Waited a good while, until he felt that squirm of movement in response. Hedy mumbled in her sleep and shifted her hips. Reassured, Lockyer took his hands away, but he still didn't sleep. He just lay there, with the unfamiliar sensation of his *child* being beside him. It had been there for weeks, of course, but since the scare – since the possibility of something going wrong had forced its way into his consciousness – he'd felt a whole new awareness of it. *His* child, almost ready to come out into the world. A whole new person.

And just as new was the knowledge that he'd do *anything* to protect them. Including lying awake in the night, not escaping to walk, in case something were to happen that his presence might prevent.

*

Broad was on time into the station in the morning, tidy and composed.

'What's that, guv?' she said, indicating the file he was reading through.

'Inquest transcript for Mimi Draper,' he said. 'One of Chapman's ex-girlfriends. It just came through. Antigone Chapman was a witness.'

Broad raised her eyebrows. '*Antigone?* Why?'

'She owned the club where Mimi was working as a receptionist. It was a Dempsey Grace private members club. Ever heard of them?'

'Yeah, I have. Not that I've ever been to one. My cousin wanted to have her wedding at one, but it was six figures just to stick a marquee on the lawn. You know the sort of place – used to be a stately home. All raked gravel, drinks on silver trays, and bushes cut into fancy shapes.'

'Topiary.'

'Yeah, that. The one my cousin wanted even had a maze.'

'Well, I took a look at the Dempsey Grace website. Turns out Antigone Chapman was born Antigone Christabel Dempsey Grace. Her great-grandfather opened his first private members club in London in 1922, and it took off from there.'

'Right, so I guess it's no mystery what paid for that lush house of theirs,' Broad said.

'And perhaps that's how Chapman met Mimi – at the club. I can't imagine they'd have moved in similar circles, otherwise.'

'How come Antigone had to be at the inquest?'

'Because she'd just fired Mimi for misconduct. She was required to testify about that, and about Mimi's behaviour at work.'

'What was the misconduct?'

'Criminal damage, though no charges were brought. She defaced a client's car. Smashed the headlights and wing mirrors, and scratched the word "Prick" into the paintwork. They caught it all on the security cameras.'

'And I bet it was a posh car,' Broad said, not seeming to make the connection.

'Well, we could always ask Edward Chapman,' Lockyer said.

'You mean . . .?'

'Unless she was splitting up with someone else at the same time as she was splitting from Chapman, then, yeah, I reckon it was his car.'

'So Chapman's named in the inquest?'

'No. Somehow they managed to keep his name out of it. The police simply stated that Mimi's former partner had been ruled out of any involvement.'

One makes the messes, the other endeavours to clear them up, just as Antigone had said to him.

'It must've been as embarrassing for her as it was for him, I guess,' Broad said. 'Especially since it was at the club, if they knew people there. Husband knocking off the young receptionist. Not a good look.'

'Definitely not,' Lockyer agreed. 'And Antigone Chapman seems the sort of person who's *very* good at keeping up appearances.' He turned his chair to the window. Outside, a brisk wind was snatching the last mottled leaves from the ash trees. 'There's something else,' he said. 'Mimi Draper was around ten weeks pregnant when she took her own life.'

'Shit,' Broad said. She thought about that for a moment. 'Was this before or after Chapman had the snip?'

'After,' Lockyer said. 'Mimi died in 'ninety-three. Chapman's vasectomy – according to him – was in 1990.'

'So . . . Mimi had another boyfriend?'

'Or, at least, she had sex with someone else.'

Broad nodded. 'Bit of a coincidence, isn't it? Two of Chapman's girlfriends getting pregnant by men other than him, and then, well, something happening to them.'

'It is,' Lockyer said. 'How reliable is a vasectomy, anyway?'

Broad did a quick search. 'Almost a hundred per cent,' she said. 'Other than abstinence, it's considered the safest method of contraception.'

Their eyes met for a fraction of a second, and Broad coloured faintly.

'I think we should look closer at the Chapmans,' Lockyer said. 'Antigone in particular.'

Broad's reply was cut off by Lockyer's phone ringing. It was the desk sergeant, to say that someone wanted to see him.

'His ears must have been burning,' Lockyer said, as he stood up. 'Chapman's downstairs. Wants to talk to me about something.'

'Shall I sit in, guv?' Broad asked.

Lockyer shook his head. 'I'll record it. You make a start

on Antigone. Find out exactly where she was on the night of October second, 1999.'

Edward Chapman was in the reception area of the station, wearing brown cords and a checked flannel shirt beneath a knitted gilet. Hair swept back from his forehead, he was standing with an easy slouch, hands in his pockets, as he studied the posters on the notice board.

'Mr Chapman,' Lockyer announced, and Chapman turned with a brisk smile. 'Would a phone call not have done?'

'Oh! Well, I thought since you'd been out to us, it would be within the rules for me to come here. I rather fancied an outing. Cabin fever, you understand.'

'Your cabin is quite a bit nicer than most people's.'

'True enough,' Chapman said. 'We're very lucky. Am I in trouble? I've remembered something, you see. Something about that summer.'

'Then you'd better come through.'

Lockyer led him into an interview room, and Chapman immediately looked apprehensive.

'I hadn't realized it would be so formal,' he said.

'If what you have to tell me proves materially important to the investigation, I'd rather have a proper record of it,' Lockyer said. He set up a new recording, prefacing it as a voluntary interview before introducing himself and inviting Chapman to do the same.

'So you are still investigating?' Chapman said. 'I mean . . . you really *do* think something might have happened to Nazma?'

'Yes, I'm afraid so,' Lockyer said. 'And I mean to find out what, exactly.'

Chapman nodded sadly. 'Well, I hope to God you're wrong, but if you aren't, I'm glad you're looking for her, Inspector. And I'm very curious to know what sparked your reinvestigation.'

Lockyer studied him, weighing up how much to say. 'Items belonging to Nazma were found in the River Kennet recently.'

Chapman's forehead laddered. 'In the *river*?'

'What was it you wanted to tell me, Mr Chapman?'

'Did you find the man in the photograph you showed me? The one you were looking for?'

'We did, yes.'

'Who was he?'

'I'm afraid I can't discuss that, Mr Chapman.'

'No, of course. It was only that . . . if he *was* involved with Nazma . . . But I suppose, at this point, I am merely being nosy.' He cleared his throat diffidently. 'You see, after we spoke the last time, I started to really rack my brain about that summer. Who was there, what had gone on. I even dug out my old photographs and had a look through – though I'm afraid I didn't find anything particularly interesting. Mostly pictures of archaeological finds, and of my staff at work, which I'd taken for our own publicity purposes.'

'I'd be interested to see them, if you wouldn't mind,' Lockyer said.

Chapman looked mildly surprised. 'Yes, of course. I'll send them on – though, as I say, there's really nothing out of the ordinary on them. But I *did* remember something about Nazma.'

'Go on.'

'Well, I saw her having an argument with a man up at Inez's pile. I think it was that young chap Inez euphemistically calls her nephew. I was coming from the avenue to check in at the cist site, and I saw them by that old barn where they'd been camping. Looked like an ordinary conversation at first, but then – I remember this quite clearly – he grabbed her arm. Here.' Chapman grabbed his own upper arm tightly. 'Like this. Quite abruptly. Naz threw her arm to get him off, then went into the house.'

'And you've just remembered this now?'

'Well, yes, because, you see, it got subsumed by what happened next. I went over to the cist, and I'd been there for perhaps ten minutes before I realized Nazma still hadn't come back from the house. I went to look for her, and as I got to the door she came storming out, with tears in her eyes and one hand holding her face.' Again, Chapman mimed the pose. 'I made her stop and tell me what had happened. She said it was nothing, but it was obviously *not* nothing, so I asked again. She said it was just a misunderstanding. Inez had got upset, but it was nothing to worry about. And I could quite believe it – Inez was always very . . . changeable. Moody. The drink, you understand.'

'Is that all?' Lockyer said, disappointed.

'Almost. When Nazma took her hand down from her face, her cheek was very red. I know a handprint when I see one.'

'Someone had hit her?'

Chapman nodded. 'I'm certain of it. And if I'd thought for one second it was the so-called nephew, believe me, I'd have had words about it.'

'So you think it was Inez?'

'I do.'

'What do you think the "misunderstanding" was about?' Lockyer asked.

'I only wish I knew, but Nazma simply refused to go into it. I tried Inez instead, later in the day. Went in to check that all was serene, and found her working on one of her truly awful rook paintings. She wouldn't say any more than Nazma. In fact, she didn't seem to have a clue what I was on about. But, then, I've always wondered about that.'

'About what, Mr Chapman?'

'About how *convenient* her haziness can be at times.'

That struck a chord with Lockyer. He'd thought the same himself.

'Can you remember exactly when this was?' he asked.

'I'm afraid I can't, and I *have* tried. All I've got to go on is the progress of the cist excavation, as far as I can recall it. Which would make it perhaps late August or early September. What I can't fathom is why on earth Nazma wouldn't just talk to me about whatever had caused the spat. She'd always brought her troubles to me in the past – not that there were many – and I'd always done my best to resolve them.'

Lockyer sat in silence for a while, thinking about Nazma not wanting to tell Chapman whatever this had been. About Nazma's flirtation with Rhys Birch. Her unexpected pregnancy, which – if Birch was to be believed – indicated the involvement of a third party. A third man. For the first time, he caught himself wondering if that third man had been Darren Mason.

'Mr Chapman, was your wife visiting Trusloe Hall that day?'

Chapman blinked. 'My *wife*?'

'Yes. She told us she went to visit Inez a couple of times during the dig and, on one occasion, met Nazma there.'

'Tiggy . . . Tiggy *met* Nazma?' Chapman blanched. 'You mean, she *knew*?'

Lockyer watched him closely. 'So she tells us.'

Chapman looked a bit lost for a moment. He swallowed a couple of times. 'I . . . I hadn't realized.'

'Was she there *that* day, can you recall? Could she have been the one who hit Nazma?'

'Oh, no. No, I'm sure not,' Chapman said. 'She's been trying to persuade Inez to sell her the house, you see, on and off for years. The board want to open a new club in the Marlborough area, and Tiggy thought it'd be a win-win situation – freedom, and a lump sum of cash, for Inez, and a bargain for Dempsey Grace.' He swallowed again, gathering himself. 'Inez has been having none of it, of course. She's as tight as a hermit crab in there. We even came up with a scheme whereby she could remain in a cottage in the grounds for the rest of her days – one of the barns could be converted for her, or something like that. But no dice. In any case, Tiggy wasn't there that day.'

'You're sure?'

A solemn nod. 'If she had been, I wouldn't have gone anywhere near Nazma.'

'Ah, no. Of course not,' Lockyer replied sardonically.

'Let he who is without sin cast the first stone, Inspector. I'm not proud of my behaviour. But aren't we all merely struggling to find those rare moments of joy in life while we can?'

'Can there ever be real joy, when it comes at another's expense?'

'Ah! You're something of a philosopher, Inspector?'

'Not really,' Lockyer said, irritated by the man's grandiosity. 'In any case, your wife appears to have forgiven you.'

'I'm a lucky man, Inspector. I met Tiggy at one of the lowest points in my life, and she raised me up. In so many ways. I owe her a very great deal – not least for her unwavering loyalty towards me.'

'What kind of low point?'

'Christ, every kind. I was jilted, would you believe? A girl I'd met at university. Lara Chamberlain. I was quite besotted with her and, at that age, I couldn't see past her beauty to the selfishness beneath. Oxford's full of that type. She was very much one of the in-crowd, and I'd put up with endless ribbing from her friends about my being a scholarship boy, son of a shopkeeper. But I thought she loved me, and I thought I loved her.'

'What happened?'

'She left me at the altar, no less. Ran off with her ex, who was old money, naturally. There I was, buttonhole wilting, Mother in her new hat.'

'That must have been embarrassing.'

'Oh, yes.' Chapman leant forwards. 'And I can tell from your tone that you've no *idea* what it's like to be publicly humiliated in that way. A man would have to be made of very stern stuff to simply brush it off. I honestly thought the world had ended, for a time. It was the blackest feeling. And Mother didn't speak to me for months. Couldn't forgive the shame of it.'

'I've heard that your mother was a difficult woman.'

'Difficult? She was vicious. She ought never to have been allowed to raise a child.' He leant back with a sigh. 'Still, I loved her. Children have no choice, do they? And I can see now that I had a lucky escape. Lara married the fellow she ran off with, but it soon ended. She was a model for a while, then a groupie. Took a lot of drugs in the eighties and died young. Whereas *I* found Tiggy.'

'How did you meet?'

'In London. At the opening of an exhibition – Francis Bacon.'

'I didn't have you down as an art lover.'

'Art? No, not especially. But I was forever trying to improve myself.' He paused to reflect. 'I was quite possibly still trying to please my mother, though she'd passed away by then. It's easier to see these things in retrospect, isn't it? A pity, really, that she died when she did. She'd have been over the moon with dear Tiggy.' A wry little smile. 'Very much the *right sort*.'

'Meaning old money?'

'Antigone is a thoroughbred in ways that go beyond wealth, Inspector.'

'Perhaps worthy of being treated with respect, then,' Lockyer said. 'It's a bit of a coincidence you coming in this morning, actually, Mr Chapman.'

'How so?'

'We'd just been reading about another of your girlfriends. Or your *petites folies*, as I believe your wife terms them. Mimi Draper.'

'*Mimi?*' Chapman exclaimed. He stared at Lockyer for some moments, lips parted in shock. '*Petites folies?* Is that really what Tiggy said to you?' he asked.

Lockyer nodded.

'But . . . no, that's not right. "Little madnesses"? No, no.' Chapman hung his head. 'That's unkind.'

'Would you tell me about Mimi?'

'Tiggy was *very* angry with me about it. And rightly so. It was very foolish of me to get involved with poor Mimi. I didn't know until it was too late, you see.'

'Know what?'

'How deeply troubled she was.' He looked up, eyes stark. 'She'd had a *terrible* time in her childhood. Abused most despicably by her stepfather.' He shook his head. 'The sort to cause lifelong aftershocks. She'd gone off the rails as a result, crashed out of school. Alcohol, drug-taking, prom-iscuity. But I didn't know *any* of this to begin with – only afterwards. Her abuser had made her pregnant, you see. She'd had to have an abortion at the age of fourteen, the poor, poor girl.'

He sighed heavily. 'She told me none of this, to begin with. Such a pretty girl. She got a job on the front desk at one of the clubs, and that was where I met her. And the very first time I saw that smile of hers . . . Well, I knew I was in trouble. But nowhere near as much trouble as poor Mimi. She had profound issues with attachment. She fell so deeply in what she *thought* was love with me that it drove her to distraction.' He glanced up. 'I can see from your face that you blame me. That you find *me* despicable. And, when it comes to Mimi, I fear you might be right.'

'What happened?'

'I had to break it off. As kindly as I could, but still – she went off like a landmine. She'd told my wife about us, you see, claiming I was going to divorce Tiggy and marry her. Then she started coming to the house, creating such a rumpus that she'd wake the girls. Threatening to hurt herself. I – I had to be firm with her. Cut all contact.'

'Is that when she vandalized your car?'

'No. In fact, that incident was a week or so *before* I finally brought the shutters down. Believe me, I do know how self-serving that sounds, but I truly thought it would be the best way to help her get over it all and . . . move on.'

'But instead she took her own life,' Lockyer said.

Chapman nodded. 'She did. *Mea culpa*. I had *no* idea how vulnerable she was until it was too late. But I wasn't the start of her troubles. I really wasn't.'

'Mimi was in the early stages of pregnancy when she died. Was it yours?'

'No.' Chapman rubbed at his eyes with a thumb and forefinger for a moment. 'Perhaps another boyfriend, or a fling, I don't know.'

'Are you certain you weren't the father? As I understand it, vasectomies *can* fail, even if it's rare,' Lockyer said.

'They can, especially in the early days,' Chapman said. 'When Mimi told me she was pregnant I went to get tested, just to be sure. There were no viable sperm in my sample. So for that part of the tragedy, at least, I was not responsible. Of course, when I explained to Mimi that the child couldn't be mine, she flew at me, red in tooth and claw. But the fact was undeniable.'

'How is it your wife was required to speak at the inquest, as Mimi's employer, and you weren't, as her lover?'

'My wife can be very persuasive when she puts her mind to it, Inspector. And she has friends in high places. Given that I'd broken with Mimi several weeks prior to her death, and could prove I wasn't the father of her child, my name was kept out of it.'

'Discretion being the better part of valour,' Lockyer said flatly.

Chapman lifted his chin. 'I make no claim to valour, Inspector. Not when it comes to poor Mimi. But had I known the effect our relationship would have on her, I would never have commenced it.'

'How many other *petites folies* have there been, Mr Chapman?' At this, Lockyer saw that flicker of irritation again.

'I really don't see how that's relevant.'

'But there have been more.'

'There *had* been, before Mimi. But not afterwards. It took Tiggy a very long time to forgive me. We were badly shaken.

If our daughters hadn't been so young, I think it might have spelt the end. I made up my mind to do better. To be a better husband, a better father. And I was, for several years.'

'Until you met Nazma Kirmani,' Lockyer said.

'Yes. Until I met Nazma. She stole my heart before I had time to second-guess the wisdom of it.'

Chapman leant forward again, fixing his eyes on Lockyer's through the Perspex. A look full of longing. 'Because I did love her, you see. I *loved* Nazma. And the idea that something terrible might have happened to her has been like the steady tightening of a vice, ever since you told me.'

Afterwards, out of curiosity, Lockyer ran a quick search for Lara Chamberlain, the woman who'd left Chapman at the altar. He found a few fashion shots going back to the late seventies, and some grainy paparazzi images of her on the arm of a famously leathery rock star. She barely came up to his shoulder, her glittery dress hanging from a fragile frame, and hollow eyes staring out of an elfin face. The only other result was an episode of a TV show called *Ghostfinder General*, featuring the West London mansion where model and It-girl Lara Chamberlain had died of what was thought to be an accidental overdose. Her spirit was rumoured to walk the halls, trailing the perfume Calandre behind her.

It was hard to imagine that troubled waif and Antigone Chapman occupying the same space.

'So, do you think this was the spat between Darren and Naz that Inez also told us about?' Broad said, when she'd listened to the recording of Chapman's interview.

Lockyer shrugged. 'Could be. Could be another time altogether, though when I think back, Inez did imply that something had been going on between Nazma and Darren.'

'Did she?'

'Obliquely. She said she thought Darren had put Nazma's nose out of joint, and in the next breath that, actually, Nazma had been going out with Chapman. That says to me that she thought the thing with Darren might've been a lovers' tiff.'

'Maybe.' Broad frowned, thinking back. 'So, who do you think hit Nazma? If we accept that it wasn't the day she inadvertently met Antigone?'

'Given the circumstances, I think Chapman really would have made sure he knew where his wife was, if she was in the habit of intermittently appearing at Trusloe Hall. And I think it's far more likely that Inez hit Nazma than that Darren did.'

'Really?'

'If Darren had got angry enough to hit her, it would have left more than a red handprint.'

'Yeah, maybe.'

Broad got up and went to the whiteboard, where pictures of the people in Nazma's life that summer were pinned: Antigone and Edward Chapman, Inez de Redvers and Darren Mason, all with arrows pointing to at least one of the others as well as to Nazma; Rhys Birch off to one side, with Ingrid Roach and Jonathan Tate, her fellow archaeologists. An arrow from Ingrid to Chapman, along which Broad had written *In love with*. Alongside Nazma's picture she'd written:

Sought help from Alina Shah and Rhys Birch. Re pregnancy? Termination? Possible criminal activity at Trusloe Hall? In one corner, with no photo, was the name Philippa Harmon.

'So, Nazma was involved enough with Birch for him to give her his T-shirt, and for her to think he might let her come and stay for a while,' Broad said, tapping Birch's photo. 'But if we believe that they never slept together – which I'm not at all convinced about – who fathered her child? Darren Mason?'

She sounded profoundly sceptical, but Lockyer spread his hands. 'It's at least possible. He was more or less her age; from a completely different background, yes, but that can be attractive.'

'You mean that whole "bad boy" thing.'

'Right.'

He followed Broad's lead, and studied the pictures for a moment. 'We could ask Inez. It shouldn't be too hard to trip her up, if we talk about it as though we already know.'

Broad looked uneasy. 'Is that ethical, guv?'

'I don't care, if it gets us nearer to the truth. She knows more than she's saying, Gem. Whether she *knows* she knows is another matter.'

'Shouldn't we tread carefully, though? Given her mental state?'

'Yes. And the longer we can leave her in situ rather than bringing her in, the better.'

'Bring her *in*?'

'The prescription drugs. Handling stolen goods.'

'But if that *is* what's going on, then she's just being cuck-ooed. Darren's using her.'

'Maybe, but maybe not,' Lockyer said.

'He could be our killer,' Broad insisted.

'We've no compelling evidence of that yet – or for any of them. So let's focus on getting some.' He thought for a second. 'What I can't work out is *why* Nazma would get involved with either Rhys Birch or Darren Mason. Her friends say she was still loyal to Chapman. Still very much with him.'

'Well, it wouldn't have been easy, would it?' Broad said. 'If she'd fallen out of love with him . . . It's a big thing to have to admit to yourself, especially if you thought they were the one, I imagine. Plus, he was her boss, and she loved working with Brittonic. Maybe she thought she'd have to leave, if she and Chapman broke up – and she was probably right. So she'd have been looking at a *major* upheaval.'

'She was only ever on placement with Brittonic.'

'But still.' Broad turned back to Nazma's smiling photo-graph, speaking quietly, as if directly to the vanished girl. 'Flirting with other people, even starting something with another person, can just be a way to . . . force the situation to a head. You know? A way to effect change, when you're not quite sure how to do it.'

'You mean, she didn't have the guts to leave Chapman so she started behaving in a way that might make him do it for her?' Lockyer said. 'Not very grown-up.'

'No,' Broad said tersely. 'But not everyone is, guv. And it can be frightening. For lesser mortals than yourself, of course.'

'"For lesser—"?'

'Sorry. I didn't mean . . .' She took a breath. 'I just some-times think you don't really get . . .' She glanced across at him. 'Look, you know the numbers, guv. Two women are killed *every week* in the UK by a current or an ex partner. Stuff like that makes you second-guess yourself. It makes you scared.'

Lockyer let that sink in. He thought of the bruises he'd seen on her arms. 'You're right, Gem. Sorry. Liz Kirmani did say to me that Naz was a people-pleaser. That she didn't like to upset anyone. So that wouldn't have made it any easier for her.'

'She was young, Chapman was older and in a position of authority. She quite possibly had *no idea* how to leave him. Maybe she'd thought Rhys Birch was someone she could turn to – even just as a friend – but he let her down. Her cousin let her down. For whatever reason, she felt she needed to run away. But it turned out she had nowhere to run to.'

'And we're going to find out who she was running from, I promise,' he said, then ploughed on before he could change his mind: 'And if you *ever* need that kind of help, Gem, I – I hope you know you could come to me.'

'Thanks.' She went back to her desk and moved some papers around, cleared her throat. 'By the way, guv, Finan-cial have sent back some preliminary stuff on the Chapmans. The headline is, Antigone's got Edward by the short and curlies.'

'Oh?'

'Yeah. It's all in her name – the house, the business, the cars, the credit cards. She's from old money, as we know, but he came into the marriage with more or less nothing, in spite of going to Oxford and all the rest of it. Brittonic ticks along fine, but if they were reliant on his income alone, they'd be living in a place more like mine than theirs. And I *bet* she got a pre-nup.'

'What makes you say that?' Lockyer said.

'Just from having met her. Far too business-minded to put half her assets on the line, I reckon, however much she loves Edward.'

Lockyer was inclined to agree with that.

'Chapman has a history of starting up companies that fail. Going right back into the 1970s, in London. The first was a radio rental shop – whatever that is. He's been through various specialist finance ventures, including arranging loans for yachts, and some dodgy-looking filmmaking investment scheme. He's also imported wine, olive oil and Ibérico charcuterie.'

'Trying to get rich off the rich,' Lockyer observed. 'Like Ingrid Roach said, archaeology never made anyone a millionaire.'

'Right. Plus, there's a portfolio of rental properties he's built up over the years. There I was picturing him as an honest scholar, mud under his nails and all that, but he's always been trying to climb the greasy pole. Hit the jackpot when he married into the Dempsey Graces.'

'And all those other companies folded?'

'Like dominos. All except the rental places. He still has . . .' she quickly checked '. . . twenty-seven properties on the books of a company called Farview Property Management, all mortgaged but bringing in more than enough to finance the debt – although I would have expected the turnover to be higher on that number of places.'

'So, there's nothing to prevent Antigone divorcing him, even if there isn't a pre-nup,' Lockyer said.

'No. She'll never not be rich. There are family trusts she's attached to that Edward can't touch. And guess who else won't ever not be rich?'

Lockyer waited.

'Inez. Darren was just a *bit* out when he said she didn't have two pennies to rub together – she's got nearly seventeen and a half million quid accruing interest in a high-yield account. Her father's legacy.'

Lockyer whistled. 'Nice.'

'Yeah. Except she hasn't made a withdrawal in at least thirty years. Not one. Whatever her reason for letting that house sink into the ground, it's not for want of cash.'

'No,' he said. 'She's *choosing* to let it rot. Well. Keep digging, Gem. It might be a blind alley, but I have the feeling we're not going to know what we're looking for until we find it. Did you get anywhere with Pippa Harmon?'

'No, guv. Difficult, when we still don't have a photo of her. I've run her name through Missing Persons, and all the usual databases, with all the possible variations of her date of birth. Nothing comes up. I'm still waiting to hear back from the Netherlands.'

'Well, if she deliberately vanished, it sounds like she did as good a job of it as Nazma Kirmani.'

Broad gave him a look. 'And if she didn't, somebody found a very good hiding place. For both of them.'

15

Later in the day, the authorization to access Inez de Redvers's medical records came through. She'd been referred onto treatment programmes for alcohol dependency on three separate occasions during the 1990s, though whether she'd actually attended the courses, or completed them, wasn't noted. She'd first been prescribed diazepam in November 1999; it had been reviewed and reissued twice before March 2000, but not after that. The GP's notes stated that Inez had been back three times to request more, but had been refused due to concerns about dependency. She'd been referred for yet more counselling. There was no mention of a hospital visit for her injured ankle, or any follow-up treatment. In fact, she hadn't seen a doctor at all since May 2000.

'Didn't need to, did she?' Broad said. 'Darren's been getting the benzos for her – if that's even what's in those blister packs. Because it could be any old rubbish.'

'The dates aren't what I expected to see,' Lockyer said. 'I thought her use of diazepam would tie in with Pippa's exit, not Nazma's.'

'Inez was still drinking in the summer of 'ninety-nine,' Broad said. 'Maybe she stopped, then needed something to replace it.'

'Perhaps. Or maybe something happened at the time Nazma disappeared that was even worse than Pippa leaving.'

Lockyer suddenly remembered the painting of Inez's that had so troubled him, ostensibly of the cist burial: *The Hollow Grave*. A dark pit, just waiting to be filled. *It seemed so ghastly suddenly*, Inez had said. *I haven't been near it since*. He thought of the painting that looked like a face, with black holes for eyes. The skin prickled at the back of his neck.

'Let's go back to Inez,' he said. 'I think we need to push her harder. She may well be a victim in all this, but we don't know that for sure, and we never will if we keep letting her wave our questions away as though she doesn't speak English.'

It had been raining steadily since sunrise. Damp sharpened the chill inside Trusloe Hall, and strengthened the reek of mould. The sound of dripping water came from a dozen different places. There was the usual charade of Inez offering tea, and inviting them to sit by the fire. She wasn't wearing her turban this time, and rattails of iron grey hair lay pasted to her skull. The tremor in her hands was worse than ever.

'Inez,' Lockyer began, 'you mentioned to us before that you remembered Nazma being very upset one day, here at the house. A witness has come forward to say that they saw her leaving here in tears on one particular occasion, and that they think she'd been slapped around the face. Can you tell us anything about that?'

Inez blinked owlishly, her hands fluttering up from her lap. 'Slapped? You mean somebody *struck* her?'

'That's what I mean, yes.' Lockyer stared deep into Inez's restless eyes.

'Well! That can't be right,' she said. 'Who on *earth* would want to hit her? She was such a sweet, sunny thing.'

'Was something going on between Nazma and Darren Mason? Were they seeing each other? Romantically, I mean?'

'Darren and Nazma? I don't *think* so . . .' Inez's gaze drifted off into a far corner of the room. Lockyer might have taken it as a tell, except that her gaze roamed constantly, her focus coming and going. 'He was too young for her, surely? Still a boy. No, no – she was carrying on with that rather smooth chap. Yes, that's right – poor Tiggy's husband.'

'Why "poor" Tiggy?'

'Antigone Chapman – haven't you met her? Betrayed again! I did think it was rather naughty of Nazma to pinch someone else's husband. Then again, all's fair in love and war. And Tiggy made a mistake in marrying that man in the first place – I remember thinking so at the wedding. Altogether *too* charming. And far too good at pretending to be something he isn't.'

'You mean . . . wealthy? From good stock?' Broad said.

'I mean husband material,' Inez said. 'How on earth she didn't spot him for a philanderer is beyond me. But, then, love is blind, if you'll excuse yet another cliché.' She reflected on that for a moment. 'Tiggy was never a *pretty* girl, you see,' she went on. 'Her nickname at school was "Penny Plain" . . . Children are so unkind. She turns herself out *beautifully* – always has – but no amount of grooming can hide that unfortunate bone structure. Her mother was really rather cruel about it, and it left her very insecure, I believe, when it came to men.'

'Given her pedigree, I can't imagine she was short of offers,' Lockyer said.

'Offers – plenty. Genuine admirers? Fewer of those.'

'But Edward Chapman was one of them?'

'Possibly, or simply a very accomplished flatterer. Difficult to say. It all happened very fast – the wedding, I mean. Tiggy was starry-eyed over him.'

'Did Nazma ever talk to you about ending her relationship with Edward Chapman?' Lockyer asked.

'Ending it? No. She rarely spoke about him at all – it was weeks before I found out it was going on.'

'She never spoke to you about having to go away? Perhaps about . . . being in trouble of some kind?' Lockyer was careful not to feed her the information that Nazma had been pregnant. 'Did she ask for your help?'

'Help? With what?'

'With anything. For example. Did she ask to borrow any money?'

'Ask for *money*? Heavens, no.'

'It seems that she'd packed a going-away bag, you see. Perhaps she kept it hidden in here, with you, rather than out in the barn?'

'Why on earth should she hide a going-away bag?' Inez arched her pencilled eyebrows. 'She loved it here. Never wanted to leave.'

'We're not sure,' Lockyer said. 'And it seems she never took it anywhere, in the end. We think it was thrown into the river. Here, at Trusloe Hall.'

Inez nodded at him with every appearance of paying close attention, but her eyes had a vacancy that Lockyer no longer entirely trusted.

'Into the river, you say?' she murmured. 'How very peculiar.'

'Yes, it is peculiar,' he said. 'And I don't think it was her that discarded it. Did you ever see anyone throw anything into the water?'

'She,' Inez said.

'She what, Inez?'

'You do not think it was *she who* discarded it.'

Lockyer waited.

'Well, I'm sure I never saw anything of the sort,' Inez said. 'But it was rather a long time ago.'

'How did you come to hear about Nazma's relationship with Edward Chapman?'

'Now that I *do* remember because – oh, what a scene! Frightful. Tiggy came for tea one day – trying yet again to persuade me to sell her this house – and I made the error of introducing her to Nazma. It was a wholly innocent mistake, I assure you, but there was no way to undo it.'

'What happened?'

'Well! Nazma looked as though I'd poured cold water all over her, and Tiggy would have turned the poor girl to stone if she'd been able to. Really, I did feel awful. Nazma endeavoured to make a swift exit, but Tiggy's never been one to back away. She said a few very unkind things until Nazma finally bolted, the poor child. I thought it all rather unnecessary, but then, he isn't *my* husband.'

'What did she say?'

'Tiggy? Oh – the sort of thing you might expect. "So, you're the latest little fool" and "You can't imagine you're the first," that sort of thing. She mentioned some poor girl who'd hurled herself down some stairs when Edward broke up with her, and that she hoped Nazma wouldn't do the same, since the inquests were a crashing bore. Heavens, she really was in a cold fury!'

'Inez, did Antigone hit Nazma?' Broad asked.

'No. I don't think so.' Inez gazed at her as though from far away. 'At least, I didn't *see* her do so. That I recall.'

'When Nazma ran out, did Tiggy follow her?'

Inez gave a funny little toss of her head. Her hair didn't move. 'I honestly can't remember. I think not. It was all very well within these four walls, but Tiggy wouldn't have gone in for the public airing of dirty laundry.'

'How well do you know Edward Chapman?' Lockyer asked.

'Not overly. He came along with Tiggy a few times, in the early days. But not for years, now. Not very interesting for him, I suppose, listening to us reminisce about our school-days.'

'Have you never been tempted to let Antigone buy this place?' Broad ventured. 'Edward Chapman told us they'd offered to build you your own cottage in the grounds. It might be nice, mightn't it, to have somewhere neat and tidy – and warm?'

'Oh, my dear girl, *no!* She wants to turn it into a *health spa.*' Inez's tone spoke loudly of the desecration this would be. 'I can feel my father spinning in his grave at the very *suggestion.*' She gave a little laugh, which died strangely on her lips.

'Inez,' Lockyer said. 'We need to ask you about your medication.'

Her underwater gaze lit upon him briefly, then moved on. 'Yes?'

'Your pills. The diazepam.'

'Well! Is it . . . is it any of your business, really? The doctor prescribed them for me. They help with my nerves.'

'The doctor did prescribe them, yes,' Lockyer said, 'but that was a long time ago. More than twenty years ago, in fact.'

Inez said nothing. She fiddled with the frayed edge of her robe for a moment. Beneath it, Lockyer caught a glimpse of filthy jogging bottoms.

'Who gets you the pills, Inez?' Lockyer asked. No reply. 'You told us Darren brings them for you. Do you know where he gets them?'

'He's *such* a helpful boy. He collects them from the pharmacy for me.'

'In order for him to collect them from a pharmacy, you'd have to have been prescribed them by a doctor. And you haven't been, Inez. So where do they come from?'

She gave no sign of having heard him speak. It was as blatant a use of a strategic *no comment* as Lockyer had ever seen.

At length she murmured: 'Where *has* Jenny got to?'

'Inez, you are aware that obtaining drugs like these without a prescription is a criminal offence?' he said.

Again, Inez ignored him. She shot a tremulous smile in Broad's direction. 'Do you never wear your hair loose, my dear? It's *such* a pretty colour.'

'Inez—'

'But it's nobody's *business*, is it?' Inez cut Lockyer off, suddenly slapping the flats of her hands down on her knees.

'We're police officers, Inez. I'm afraid it very much *is* our business,' he said.

'We're just concerned, that's all,' Broad said, laying a soothing hand on Inez's arm. 'If you aren't sure where Darren's been getting your pills, there's no telling what might be in them. It could be very dangerous.'

'But I really *do* need them for my nerves,' Inez hissed at her, with such sudden vehemence that Broad flinched back.

'I understand that. But—'

'It's simply none of your business,' she snapped, fumbling for her walking stick and struggling to her feet.

Broad shot Lockyer a desperate look as they also stood. 'Inez, I'm worried about you,' she said. 'Does Darren often store stuff here? Like those boxes we saw in the big room where you do your painting? Do you know what was in them?'

Inez looked down at the gnarled toenails poking out of her rancid surgical boot. 'It was very good of you to call, but I really must be getting on,' she said. It was the first time she'd asked them to leave, and Broad looked crestfallen.

'We only want to help you, Inez,' she said.

Inez tottered towards the door, making a wordless whimpering sound under her breath.

Broad followed. 'We think Darren might be—' she began again.

With a sudden cry Inez turned, swinging her stick in a wide arc that missed Broad's nose by millimetres and crashed into an ornate standard lamp, shattering the bulb and sending the whole thing toppling onto a heap of old curtains. Inez stared at Broad, her eyes snapping but bewildered.

Broad spread her hands, ready to dodge out of the way of any further strikes. Inez stood panting for a moment. Then her face filled with chagrin. She lowered the stick and leant heavily on it, her spine sagging to one side. 'Why must you *persecute* the poor boy? It . . . it's my *nerves*, don't you see?' she whispered. 'I . . . And Pippa? What of her? You said you'd find her!'

'I said I'd try, and I am. We are,' Broad said. 'But, so far, I've not found any trace of her, not in the UK. I'm checking in the Netherlands, but it'll take—'

'The *Netherlands*? She'd *never* go back there!' Inez cried. 'Oh, it's hopeless. Hopeless!'

'Inez—'

'Leave it, Gem,' Lockyer said, as Inez stumped off along the corridor. 'Let her calm down. I think she's told us plenty for now.'

'But, guv—'

'If that stick had connected with your head we'd be on our way to A and E right now. Come on.'

Reluctantly, she followed him back across the spongy floorboards to the door.

Outside, Lockyer saw movement at the far end of the house and turned to see Darren Mason coming out of the old vaulted kitchen, stooping low, trying to stay out of sight. It was terrible timing – for him. He glanced over his shoulder, clocked them, and halted with an almost comical display of exasperation. Head back, hands curling into fists.

'Mr Mason,' Lockyer called, 'might we have a quick word?'

Darren folded his arms, making no move to approach, so Lockyer and Broad picked their way through the sodden nettles to reach him. He was wearing a coat this time, but the rain had plastered his short hair to his forehead in dark spikes, like sharks' teeth.

'Yeah? What?' he said, as they reached him.

'What were you up to in there?' Lockyer said.

'I wasn't "up to" anything. I just put some milk in the fridge, a couple of ping meals.'

'You didn't want to stop in and say hello to Inez?'

'Heard you two in there, didn't I? Didn't want to intrude.'

'Right. Are you supplying Inez with knock-off prescription medication?'

Darren clenched his jaw. 'No. I'm not.'

'I'm not sure I believe you.'

'Not much I can do about that.' He turned and began to walk away.

'We can have this conversation at the station, if you'd prefer?' Lockyer said.

'You're gonna arrest me? What for?'

'Obstruction.'

'You're pathetic, mate,' Darren said. He gestured at the house behind him. 'She'd have been dead years ago if I didn't help her.'

'She could well be dead the next time she takes one of the pills you get for her, Mr Mason.'

He glowered. 'Nothing to do with me.'

'That's not what Inez says.'

'Yeah, well, she's batshit.'

'Actually, I'm starting to think she isn't half as vague as she makes out.'

'Believe me, she is. I came in the other day with some bog roll and that, and couldn't find her. Spent ages looking, and I found her curled up in the big fireplace in the dining room, under an old rug, shaking like a leaf. Said her dad was in one of his moods and was going to thrash her.' He looked away across the ruined garden. 'It was fucking . . . *pathetic*.'

'I believe you care about her, Darren. I really do,' Lockyer said. 'But illegal meds aren't the answer.'

'Better than the drink. And they're the only thing that keeps her off it.' He shot Lockyer a glare. 'Wherever she gets them, she'd most likely be dead by now without them.'

'Has she ever taken anything else that you know of?'

'Hardly going to tell you, am I?'

'She's just as protective of you, you know,' Lockyer said. 'Nearly took my constable's head off with her walking stick just now, when we started asking questions about you.'

Darren's eyes darted to Broad, then back to Lockyer. 'What questions?'

'Is that normal? Has she been violent before?'

'She— No. She loses her shit at times, that's all. It's not . . . She's not trying to hurt anyone. She just loses it sometimes. That's why she needs the pills.'

'The pills might well be causing her confusion, and the erratic behaviour,' Broad said.

Darren shook his head. 'Nah. She's been like that ever since I've known her.'

'When we first spoke, you said she started taking the diazepam after Pippa disappeared. According to her medical records, it was actually after Nazma Kirmani disappeared.'

'No, it— Well, yeah. Could've been, I suppose. I can't remember. She drank a lot after Pippa, so maybe that's right.'

'Tell us about Nazma Kirmani, Darren.'

'What about her? I don't know nothing about her.'

'We know that's not true. You argued with her – two different people have told us that. Someone also thinks Nazma was hit around the face here at the house, at some point. Was that you?'

'No, it fucking wasn't! I never laid a hand on her!'

'So, what did happen?'

'*Nothing*, all right?' His pale face writhed with anger, but Lockyer saw fear underneath it. 'She was just like you – going on at me for the state Inez was in, like it was *my* fucking fault!'

'That's all? She didn't work out what you were up to, and threaten to report you?' Broad said.

'What are you on about?'

'Stolen goods, Darren. Maybe drug-dealing as well. Using Trusloe Hall as your stash house is what we're on about,' she said.

Darren shook his head with a cynical grimace. 'You're pissing up the wrong lamppost, the pair of you.'

'Are we? You've got previous for drug-dealing, assault, and burglary.'

'Yeah, from about a thousand fucking years ago. I told you, I'm not into any of that any more. And it was only a bit of skunk.' He waved one arm behind him. 'Search the place. Let me know if you find any stolen goods.'

A thought occurred to Lockyer. 'Have you ever stolen anything *from* Inez?'

Darren blinked.

'I bet the house is full of valuable things, if you're willing to dig for them,' Lockyer went on. 'Antiques, paintings, maybe jewellery. And Inez would never know, would she? Easy money. I expect it's *years* since she set eyes on most of her possessions.'

'You wouldn't catch me digging in there,' Darren muttered. 'Not without a hazmat suit.'

'That wasn't quite a denial, Darren.'

Darren glared at him in silence.

'What did you argue with Nazma Kirmani about?'

'I've already *told* you! About Inez. About her drinking and the state of the place.'

Lockyer could believe it. He knew from Liz that Nazma had been the type to take action when she saw injustice. Perhaps even if it put her at risk of harm.

'Did you ever attack Nazma?' he asked.

'No,' Darren ground out. 'I never attacked her.'

'Did you ever sleep with her?'

Another startled blink. 'Which is it, mate? Am I knocking her around or shagging her?'

'No reason it couldn't be both.'

'Well, it's neither. She had a go at me for not looking after Inez. I told her it was none of her fucking business. End of.'

'Did you ever take anything from Nazma? Or perhaps find something she'd left in Inez's possession?'

'Now I really don't have a clue what you're on about.'

'A bag of Nazma's personal possessions, including valuables, was thrown into the River Kennet – from here, we believe. At the bottom of the field.'

'If you say so.'

'You never saw a bag like this?' Broad opened a picture of the Nike duffel bag on her phone and showed it to him.

'*Everyone*'s got a bag like that. But, no, I never saw it.' He thought for a second. 'And if I did I'd hardly chuck it in the river with the goods still in it, would I? If someone nicked that off her you should be asking the history lot, not me. The ones kipping in the barn. Ask that miserable cow who used to follow Nazma around like a bad smell.'

'A woman? Who?'

'Funnily enough, I never got a proper introduction,' Darren said. 'Big ox of a thing. She was one of the more senior ones, I think. Inez had me sweeping the barn and emptying the bins and all that shit, and twice I went in and found her rummaging through people's stuff.'

'How do you know it wasn't her stuff?'

'The way she dropped it like it was hot when I caught her. Looking daggers at me. Had the nerve to ask me what I thought *I* was doing in there.'

'You saw her taking things?'

'No. I don't know – maybe not. Just . . . going through stuff. Looking in people's bags, and under the beds, and that.'

'Would you recognize this woman if you saw her again?'

'Yeah, maybe.'

Lockyer pulled up the group shot of the Brittonic team in front of the marquee at the end of the excavation, Edward with his hand on Naz's shoulder, Inez stately in her chair.

'Is she in this picture?' he asked, showing it to Darren.

Darren squinted down at it, zooming in and scrolling left to right. His nails were bitten right down to the quick, the first two fingers stained yellow with nicotine. 'Yeah. That's her. Back row, second from the left.' He handed the phone back. 'Now just leave me alone, will you?'

Lockyer let Darren stomp off through the wet under-growth, and wiped the rain from his phone screen as he zoomed in on the image. Back row, second from the left. Squinting in the sunshine, hands clasped awkwardly behind her back, furrowed knees and sturdy calves.

'Who is it, guv?' Broad asked.

He handed her the phone.

'That's Ingrid Roach,' she said.

Lockyer nodded. 'And what do we know about Ingrid Roach?'

'That she had feelings for Edward Chapman. And wasn't exactly a fan of Nazma.'

Lockyer thought back to what Jonathan Tate had said about Ingrid: . . . *trying to manifest the end of Naz's relationship with Edward . . . as though Naz was the only barrier to him being with her instead.*

'Tate said Ingrid couldn't *stand* Naz,' Lockyer said. 'I took it as a flippant remark, but maybe it went deeper than we thought.'

'And another thing, guv,' Broad said. 'Look at her hair. It was short back then. Giannis Andino saw a tall figure – a man – with scruffy brown hair. But isn't Ingrid tall and well-built enough to be mistaken for a man?'

'Across a busy car park, in the dark? Definitely,' Lockyer said. 'Remind me where she's living now?'

'Didcot.'

'Maybe it's time we paid her a proper visit.' Lockyer looked at his watch. 'It's too late to get over there now. I'll go in the morning.'

'I'll come with you, guv. If you want.'

'Take your weekend, Gem. We're not going to get any overtime on this.'

'I don't mind,' she said quickly. 'I want to hear what she's got to say. Can I bring Merry, though? He'll be good as gold, I promise.'

'Merry? Won't he be bored in the car?'

'No way. Loves a drive.'

Lockyer didn't have to try too hard to think of a reason why Broad might prefer to work her weekend rather than be at home with Pete, and in the quiet few minutes that followed, yet another opportunity to say something useful passed him by. His silence on the matter was starting to feel like a chokehold he didn't know how to break.

'We've still not discussed Inez de Redvers attacking you just then,' he said, as they made their way back to the car.

'I wouldn't call it an *attack*—'

'She lashed out, with a weapon. And if her aim had been better, you could've been seriously injured. So what *would* you call it?'

'A brief . . . loss of control,' Broad said.

'I'm not sure that's any better. She clearly has highly volatile responses to certain things, and given her history of abuse, it's hardly surprising. But she's proven herself capable of violence when she feels threatened. Agreed?'

'I suppose so, guv.'

'So what if she felt threatened by Nazma, for some reason? Or by Pippa?'

'*Pippa?*'

'If you're terrified of being abandoned, then someone announcing that they're leaving is *absolutely* a threat. A violent threat, psychologically speaking.'

'I don't believe Inez has any idea where Pippa is,' Broad said.

'And Nazma?'

'I don't know. *Maybe*, if it was an accident, or something?'

'It's difficult to *accidentally* hide a violent crime – and a body – so well that no trace of either is ever found,' Lockyer said.

'Not in that house,' Broad countered. 'And Darren might know a few good places.'

She gave him a startled look. She'd been arguing *against* Inez's involvement, but had somehow offered up a very plausible sequence of events instead.

Back at the station, they found a slim man in his thirties waiting for them in the foyer. Broad clearly recognized him.

'Mr Kirmani?' she said, and he leapt to his feet.

'Hi. Yeah,' he said. Rattling with pent-up energy.

'Guv, this is Andrew Kirmani. Nazma's brother.'

'Pleasure to meet you,' Lockyer said.

'Thanks. You're the guy in charge? Can I talk to you?'

'Sure. Come through.'

Lockyer took him into a soft interview room – more sofas and friendly posters than dented plaster and sweaty chairs – but Andrew couldn't relax. He sat forwards, hands clasped, left leg jiggling. He was fairer skinned than Nazma, but with the same mahogany eyes and dark hair.

'What can I do for you, Mr Kirmani?' Lockyer said.

'I spoke to my parents,' he said. 'They told me about the woman in London. The one you thought was Naz, back in 1999. The one who isn't her. Why weren't we shown it at the time?' His voice was tense, accusatory.

'Oversight,' Lockyer said. There was no point trying to sugar-coat it.

'You mean, they should have done, but they didn't?'

'If I'd been running the investigation, you would have

been shown the image. But whoever was in charge back then was satisfied with the identification.'

Andrew shook his head fiercely. 'So it was just a cock-up? My parents have been killing themselves these past twenty years because of a *cock-up*?'

There was nothing Lockyer could usefully reply to that. 'Would you tell me about your sister?' he said.

Andrew got up, folded his arms. Sat down again. There were tears in his eyes. Anyone supposing that the stress and pain of Nazma's disappearance was in the past needed only to look at him.

'Mum says you think she was pregnant.'

'We do, yes. You mentioned to DC Broad that that wasn't something you'd have expected her to confide in you about?'

'I was *fourteen*. Of course she wouldn't.'

'But you were close?'

'Yeah. She looked out for me. Never took the piss, even when I was being an idiot. She never called me her *half*-brother. Never made anything out of us having different mums.'

'Sounds like she was great to have as a sister.'

He nodded. Wiped his eyes angrily.

'I used to bump heads with Dad a bit. I always messed about at school, didn't work hard enough, got into trouble. *Why can't you be more like your sister?* You know? Mum used to hate it when he said that. I'd get sent to my room, and instead of gloating or anything like that, Naz'd come and sit with me. She'd smuggle me in a Mars bar if I hadn't been allowed dessert, and ask me what I was going to be when I grew up. This was when I was, like, eight or nine, and she was already doing her A levels. I'd say something like film star, or Premier League footballer, and instead of laughing and saying I had no chance, she'd ask me what team, what position, would I play for England as well.'

Andrew smiled. Just for a second.

'Everything changed for ever when she disappeared. *Everything*. It was like . . . we were broken. We fell apart. And I've got on. I've grown up, got married. I'm a father now. But I . . . I don't think any of us has been truly happy since then. My wife calls it my cold spot. Says she can always tell when the sun hasn't reached it, some days.'

'I can't imagine how hard it's been,' Lockyer said. 'But I hope I can do something about it now.'

Andrew fixed Lockyer with a hungry stare. 'Do you know who did it? I know you won't tell us until you've got proof, or whatever, but do you *think* you know?'

'Not yet.'

His disappointment was almost palpable, as was the returning tide of his anger.

'But I think we're close,' Lockyer said. 'Getting closer.' He knew he shouldn't make promises, however tempting it was. Not when he didn't know if he could keep them.

'You *think* you're getting closer?' Andrew echoed. He swallowed, and got up to leave. 'That's not much, is it?'

'I *will* find the person responsible.' The words were out before Lockyer could stop them.

Something in his tone made the younger man pause. They exchanged a long look, then Andrew nodded, once, and left without a word.

16

Day 13, Saturday

Ingrid Roach lived in a black and white 1950s chalet bungalow in the remnants of a village being swallowed by Didcot. An electric doorbell played the Westminster Quarters in a shrill tone that set Lockyer's teeth on edge.

Ingrid opened the door with an expression of mild affront. Her grey hair was tied back in a low ponytail, and she wore no make-up. Her face might have had a kind of weathered magnificence if it hadn't been for those small, cold eyes. The lines around them were of appraisal rather than laughter; her whole demeanour that of someone assured of being let down by the shortcomings of other people.

'Miss Roach,' Lockyer said. 'I'm Detective Ins—'

'Yes, we met. I'm rather surprised to find you've travelled all the way here, since a video call worked perfectly well the last time. Isn't there a lockdown going on?'

'We do prefer to talk to key witnesses in person.'

Ingrid raised her eyebrows. 'I don't see how I can possibly be a "key witness" when I hardly knew the girl.'

'May we come in?'

'No, I'd rather you didn't. I've managed not to contract the virus yet, and I'd prefer to keep it that way.' She squinted up at the sky, which was the colour of chicken bones. 'I'll get a coat, and join you outside. If you go back onto the driveway, at least our feet will stay dry.'

Lockyer and Broad made their way back to where Ingrid's car was parked.

'She's definitely tall enough to have towered over Nazma,' Broad said quietly. 'Especially if Nazma was hunched over.'

'I agree, but let's not get too carried away. It's a big jump from being jealous of a love rival to wiping them off the face of the Earth.'

'People have killed for less,' Broad said.

At the sight of Broad approaching, Merry propped his front feet on the back window of Lockyer's car and grinned out at her, tail wagging hopefully. Ingrid emerged from the house wearing long boots and a Barbour coat.

'Is that your dog, Inspector?' she said.

'No, he's mine,' Broad said.

'Well, do let him have a run. He can't get out of the garden, once this gate is shut.'

'Are you sure?'

'I used to have cairns,' Ingrid said, with a brisk smile.

'Okay, great, thank you.'

Released, Merry sniffed Ingrid's fingers and boots thoroughly, before running off to check the perimeter.

'Sweet little chap,' Ingrid said, with a noticeable thaw. Lockyer suspected it wouldn't last long. She thrust her hands deep into her pockets. 'Well, out with it,' she said. 'What do you want to know?'

'I'd like to hear – truthfully – about your relationship with Nazma Kirmani and Edward Chapman in 1999.'

'I've already told you.'

'I don't think you've been completely honest with us.'

'I can assure you I have.'

'Witnesses have told us otherwise. They've told us you were devoted to Chapman, and couldn't stand Nazma.'

'Ha!' she burst out. 'That's a *bit* strong, I must say.'

'When we last spoke you suggested that Chapman and Nazma weren't even in a relationship.'

'They weren't. Not a proper one.'

'How would you define a "proper" relationship?' Broad asked.

'One in which you can be open and honest with each other, and the rest of the world, for a start. Not one built on lust and deceit.'

'You described Nazma as "low-hanging fruit".'

'Sounds about right.'

'Do you still have romantic feelings for Edward Chapman, Miss Roach?'

'No,' she said, with exaggerated patience.

'Did you in 1999?'

'No. We were good friends and colleagues. He was married – still is, as far as I'm aware – to a very successful woman. I felt it was rather undignified of him to fool around with a girl half his age – and an employee, to boot.'

'You thought it ought to end?'

'I thought it should never have started.'

'Did you take any steps to hasten its end, Miss Roach?'

'Take any steps? What on earth do you mean?'

'I mean, did you seek ways to sabotage their relationship?'

'Really, you're giving it all ridiculously *theatrical* over-tones, Inspector. No. I didn't involve myself at all. Edward was never so tactless as to seek my opinion on it, and I was certainly never rude enough to offer one – he was my employer too, don't forget. And I never had any sisterly chats with Nazma, either, if that's what you're wondering.'

'We have a witness who says they saw you going through Nazma's belongings in the barn at Trusloe Hall.'

Ingrid's ice-blue stare was unblinking. 'Well, they're lying,' she said. 'I did no such thing.'

'Why would they?'

'Haven't a clue. You're the detective, aren't you? Probably trying to deflect your attention away from themselves.'

'So you never went through Nazma's things? Or followed her around – spied on her?'

'That's preposterous.'

'You've already told us you noticed her flirtation with a younger man on the dig. That's something not even her closest friend at Brittonic had spotted. So you must have been watching her pretty closely.'

A mottling of pink had appeared at the base of Ingrid's neck, but her self-possession never wavered.

'The girl simply wasn't very subtle about it,' she said.

'In which case, do you think Chapman knew?'

Ingrid didn't answer at once. 'Something *was* going on with that other man, then?' she said. 'Nazma was unfaithful to Edward?'

'According to you they weren't in a proper relationship, so you can hardly call it cheating,' Lockyer said levelly.

'Maybe not. But it only goes to show that I was right about her – she wasn't a serious person. Very immature.'

'Miss Roach, did you tell Chapman what you'd seen? Did you tell him Nazma had been getting close to somebody else?'

'No,' she said firmly. The mottled flush deepened a fraction, and Lockyer's gut told him she was lying. 'I don't go in for gossip, Inspector. And there was really no need for me to interfere. It would have played itself out in due course. It always did, with Edward. He loved – loves – his wife very much, in spite of his lapses.'

Even with her schoolmistress delivery, Ingrid's tone was resonant with admiration. As though she couldn't help herself, when it came to Chapman. Frustrated, Lockyer realized they weren't going to get anything from her. Not without material evidence. He made a final stab at surprising her.

'Miss Roach, a bag containing personal items belonging to Nazma was thrown into the river at Trusloe Hall. Do you know anything about that?'

'I do not.'

'Did you find the bag in the barn, perhaps hidden among her other things? It contained clothes, her passport, and some money.'

'No.'

'We think she was planning to travel somewhere.'

'Seems a safe assumption.'

'You didn't find it and tell Chapman about it? Or the other man Nazma had befriended? You didn't throw it into the river to prevent her leaving?'

'No, no and no,' she said coolly. 'Why on earth would I? Now, I really have nothing further to add, Inspector. It sounds to me as though you're clutching at straws.' She turned her flinty eyes to Broad. 'I hope you brought some poo-bags with you. Your dog has made a mess over there, by the cotoneaster.'

With that she went back inside.

They stopped at a roadside café on the way back. A bacon roll and coffee for Broad, scrambled eggs and tea for Lockyer, and a handful of gravy bones from a jar on the counter for Merry, who parked his backside on Lockyer's left shoe and settled down for a nap.

'He likes you,' Broad said. 'He won't sit on just anyone's shoes, you know.'

'I'm honoured.'

'You should be. He's very discerning.' She smiled around a bite of her roll. 'So, Ingrid's lying, right?'

'Yep. I'm just not sure yet what she's lying about.'

'She's a big, strong woman. She'd have had no trouble overpowering Nazma.'

'I thought you were more for Darren Mason being our perp?'

'I am. I'm just trying to keep an open mind.' She took

a gulp of coffee. 'I hadn't thought of it that way, before – about the bag, I mean. That whoever threw it in the river might have done it to stop Nazma going anywhere.'

'Me neither,' Lockyer said. 'Not that it would've prevented her going anywhere full stop. She still had her wallet, and presumably a credit card. But as a symbolic gesture, if nothing else – ditching her passport and all the rest of it. So I suppose the question is, who wouldn't have wanted her to leave?'

'Edward Chapman?' Broad said. 'If Ingrid did tell him about Rhys Birch – or he found out some other way. I expect Ingrid would've been thrilled at the possibility of Naz running off with a new bloke.'

'I agree.' Lockyer thought for a moment. 'As to how Chapman might have reacted to that news . . .' he shrugged '. . . it might actually have been a complete bonus for him. Clean break, and he gets away without any drama this time.'

'Not realizing that his wife already knows about Nazma,' Broad said. 'Funny how Ingrid actually seems to like Antigone – or at least to respect her – when she was after Edward for herself.'

'Being in love with someone isn't the same as wanting them for yourself,' Lockyer said. 'Perhaps she feels Antigone has rights as Chapman's wife that Nazma didn't have. Plus, Antigone and Ingrid are cut from more or less the same cloth, wouldn't you say? Apart from the wealth gap.'

'Yeah. Kind of.'

Lockyer finished his tea. 'Something to keep in mind is that Antigone told Nazma about Mimi Draper, that day at Trusloe Hall. That's what Inez said. She told Nazma she wasn't the first, and that another of Chapman's girlfriends had thrown herself down some stairs. Which, indirectly, told Nazma that the marriage had survived it, and would most likely survive her, too.'

'I hadn't thought of that,' Broad said. 'Do you think that might be the point at which Nazma started making plans to leave?'

'Well, it can't have been fun to hear. Emma Billingham told us she sensed Nazma cooling on Chapman, don't forget. And Alina Shah remembered her saying something about things not being what she'd thought,' Lockyer said. 'I wish we could get a clear timeline for everything that was said and seen and done that summer, but it's going to be pretty impossible. I *can* think of someone else who might not have wanted Nazma to leave, though.'

Broad gave a small sigh. 'Inez?'

'If Ingrid had the opportunity to snoop through Nazma's things and find her escape bag, then Inez absolutely did too. She might have developed stronger feelings for Nazma than she's letting on – and it's obvious she liked her very much. Perhaps she'd been hoping Nazma might stick around.'

'But she would have known Nazma was straight,' Broad said.

'We can't assume that, just because Nazma had been seeing a man,' Lockyer said.

'No, you're right.'

'And she clearly wasn't someone worried about an age gap in a relationship. Perhaps things had gone further between the two of them than anyone realized.'

Broad nodded thoughtfully. 'Rhys Birch is still in the running, right?' she ventured. 'Maybe Nazma wasn't taking no for an answer about going to see him, and going public.'

'In which case I can imagine a row, maybe even him killing her. But if he chucked the bag in the river it wasn't to prevent her leaving. It was to make it look as though she had. To hide evidence of his involvement.'

'Which might also be why *Darren* chucked it,' Broad said.

Lockyer turned to watch the busy pavement outside the café. An elderly couple walked by, arm in arm, their clothes decades out of date. He tried to picture himself and Hedy like that in forty years' time. He had no idea if they'd make it work. If they'd stay together, until death parted them. It seemed unlikely. 'Still too many maybes,' he said, bringing himself back to the present. 'We need to rule some of these people *out*, as much as in.'

'We could look at everyone's alibis for the night of October second again? Try and pinpoint the sketchiest ones?'

'Worth a try,' Lockyer said. 'What did you get from Antigone Chapman?'

'She was at a charity do, like Chapman said. Something her Trust puts on every year. She said hundreds of people could confirm that she was there all evening.'

'Did she give you any actual names?'

Broad shook her head.

'She's a very determined woman,' Lockyer said. 'And I don't believe for one second she's as immune to losing her temper as she makes out.'

'She can go on the list of people who might have chucked the escape bag just to make it look like Nazma had left of her own accord, I guess,' Broad said.

'Oh, they're all on *that* bloody list,' Lockyer said. 'As long as they knew about the bag in the first place.'

Broad nodded ruefully. 'What you up to the rest of the weekend, guv?'

'Finishing the baby's room. Still no name,' he added, before she could ask. 'Might see if I can talk to my mate Kevin – I asked him to keep his ear to the ground for any intel on Darren Mason.'

Broad nodded, but didn't ask. She had a rough idea of the kind of family Kevin came from.

'How about you?' Lockyer asked.

'Oh, I dunno,' she said. 'Might take Merry to the dog field with our hour of exercise time. Otherwise it's housework and the supermarket. All the fun stuff, while Pete polishes his wretched car for the fourth time this week.'

'Very *Peter and Jane*,' Lockyer said.

'Who?'

'They were reading books, back in the dawn of time when I was a kid,' Lockyer said. Broad usually jumped at any chance to make fun of his age. 'You know the kind of thing – Jane helps Mummy make a cake, Peter goes fishing with Daddy.'

'Oh, right.' Her gaze slid off to one side. 'I get it. All a bit gender unreconstructed.'

'I was only teasing, Gem.'

'I know.' She gave a brittle sort of smile, and avoided eye contact until they were back in the car and she could stare out at the road instead.

At home, Lockyer found Hedy wrapped up in jumpers and scarves, walking a slow circuit of the muddy garden.

'Don't tell me I might slip, or that I should be resting,' she said. 'If I don't get some fresh air, I'm going to lose my mind. I had to come out while it wasn't pissing down.'

Lockyer looked around at the drab ground and the dripping, lifeless trees beyond. Hedy had been living in France before coming back to him, by the sea near La Rochelle, with boats and shops and cafés.

'Fancy a change of scenery?' he said.

She looked up with such longing that it stung him.

'What about lockdown?' she said.

'We're allowed to travel five miles for exercise, remember? Nobody's going to pick on a pregnant woman. And, besides, there aren't going to be many people around on a day like today.'

They manoeuvred her into the car, and he drove them north to Seend; pulled up at the side of the road and led her a short way along the backs of some grand houses to a bench looking out over a drop in the land. The view stretched for miles across marshy farmland, where swollen streams and flood water shone the colour of beaten steel. Distant stands of beech, regal solitary oaks. Hedy shaded her eyes and stared into the horizon, where the ridge of Salisbury Plain suddenly reared up, climbing over a hundred metres. A pair of buzzards were circling, almost too high to see; gulls flew more chaotically lower down. It was the landscape of Lockyer's birth. He felt himself unwind.

'Don't you ever think of moving somewhere else?' Hedy said.

Lockyer's heart sank. 'Not really, no.'

She looked across at him, eyes searching his face. 'There are crimes to solve all over the place, you know. And houses that need renovating. With gardens that even get the sun, sometimes.'

'Sunlight only makes the weeds grow.' He took a deep breath. 'My family's here, Hedy. I couldn't leave them.'

'They've got Jody to help them, now. They seem to be getting along fine.'

'Maybe. But I'm the only son they've got left.'

'That's it, isn't it?' she murmured. 'Because you blame yourself, of course.'

Lockyer waited, and was glad when she didn't tell him he shouldn't feel guilty, or bound to stay because Chris was gone. She'd lost her sister to illness and her best friend to a hit-and-run, both in childhood. She understood survivor's guilt, and the corrosive power of the eternal what-if.

'They'd understand, you know,' she said instead. 'I may not know them that well, but I do know that all they want is for you to be happy.'

'I am happy.'

'Are you?' It wasn't asked accusingly or angrily. She merely wanted to know.

'I think so,' Lockyer said.

Hedy made a face. 'Hm. I think being happy might be like being in love. If you only *think* you are, you probably aren't.'

'I'm not so sure. I've always thought it's probably something you doubt until you know you *aren't* happy.'

'You mean, you don't know what you've got till it's gone?'

'Right. This might actually be me at my most buoyant,' he said, smiling wryly.

'God help us.' She sighed. 'But then, me too, perhaps. Now that I'm out, and it's all behind me, I keep waiting to feel the way I did at the age of twenty-two, before it all happened. Before I lost everything. But I'm never going to, of course. I'm a different person now.'

'Not a bad thing, necessarily,' Lockyer said.

Hedy found his hand and wove her fingers into his, staring into the horizon again. Lockyer fought the urge to ask if she could be happy, staying in Wiltshire. Living with him in his small house, not twenty miles from where she'd been born. She had her payout from the government for the fourteen years she'd been imprisoned. She could go anywhere, do anything. He didn't ask if she needed to be far away – to travel, to go where nobody knew her – because he was a coward. He didn't want to know the answer. If she needed to go, he didn't know what they'd do. Because he needed to stay.

She shivered. 'Think the pub down by the canal would do us a bag of chips to take away?'

'I think there's a very good chance.'

'What is it, a mile? Barely even that. Let's walk.'

'Hedy—'

'Slowly. Downhill. I'll be fine. Please.'

'Okay. But you're not walking back up. I'll come and get the car.'

'Deal.'

Lockyer got no answer when he rang Kevin's phone that evening, but a short while later his old friend rang back. Hedy was asleep in front of the fire, so Lockyer got up and took the call in the kitchen.

'All right?' Kevin's voice was marred by the buffeting sound of the outdoors.

'Hope I didn't call at the wrong time,' Lockyer said.

'Nah, 's okay. Just don't want the kids hearing. They've got big ears and even bigger gobs.'

'Right.'

'I've thought of a brilliant name for the baby.'

'I'm afraid to ask,' Lockyer said.

'No, no, seriously. Heard it on TV the other night: Skylar.'

'Skylar? What if it's a boy?'

'It's a girl. I can feel it in my bones. You'll see I'm right. So, what do you think?'

'I'm not sure it's going to pass the "nothing made up, nothing foreign" test.'

'God, you can be a boring sod at times. It's not *foreign*. And all names were made up, at some point.'

'It sounds American.'

'Ask Hedy, bet she loves it.'

'Bet she doesn't, but I'll ask her.'

'Good. Right. I did what you asked. Put out a couple of

feelers on your mate Darren Mason. Found out a few things.'

'Great. Thank you.'

'You know I'm not going on record with any of this, right?' Kevin said. 'And I'm not going to be making a habit of it, either.'

'Understood.'

'He's small-time really. More of a gofer than a player, but I hear he's a safe middleman if you need a warehouse.'

'Drugs? Weapons?'

'No, no, none of that. Not that I've heard. Just stuff that's a bit warm. Fallen off the back of a lorry, sort of thing. He used to deal, party drugs mostly, but he's been trying to go a bit straighter.'

'Only trying?'

'Yeah, well. In the blood, isn't it?' Kevin said ruefully. 'You might know his old man. Doug Smallbone.'

'Douglas *Smallbone* is Darren Mason's father?'

Smallbone was the kind of local underworld figure well known to the police. Caught now and then for the small stuff, but suspected of being involved in far worse. Arrested many times, with never quite enough evidence to make a charge stick. He ostensibly ran a sawmill and timber yard on the edge of Savernake Forest, south-east of Marlborough. A yard that had been raided repeatedly, over the years, with nothing more incriminating than some unregistered workers ever found.

'Yeah,' Kevin said. 'Darren took his mum's name – can hardly blame him for that. He lived with her, growing up, but for a while he was shaping up to be a right chip off the old block. He was a rough little sod when he was younger. Hard to break those kinds of habits, I guess, but he's giving it a go. Got married, popped out a couple of kids.'

There was a pause as they acknowledged that Kevin could have been talking about himself. His own career path.

'"Rough little sod" like someone you'd have steered clear of, say, twenty years ago?'

'I don't know, do I? I'm not bloody clairvoyant.' Kevin sniffed. 'But I do know I wouldn't want anything to do with *any* of Doug's lads. You heard what happened to Benny Taft?'

Lockyer had. Benny had been a small-time drug-dealer, found the year before in a landfill site near Swindon, naked, with his hands cable-tied behind his back and his skull smashed in. 'That was Smallbone?' he said.

'*Lloyd* Smallbone, the eldest of Doug's boys,' Kevin said. 'Nobody's exactly sure what Benny did to piss him off, but whatever it was he won't do it again.'

'I think I get the picture.'

''Cept no one's saying Darren's as bad as all that. But you can't change your DNA, I guess. Whether he's taken a step back from his old man or not, if Darren wanted harm done to you, chances are it'd get done, pretty damn quick. And that's why I'm not going to be asking anyone anything else about him, right?'

'Right. Don't. Thanks, Kev. That helps a lot.'

'Watch your step, Matt. Doug Smallbone's got something missing in his head. He's got no fear of the police – or anything else.'

They ended the call there. Now that he knew about it,

Lockyer thought he could see a family resemblance between Darren Mason and Doug Smallbone, in the thick lips and low forehead. Which didn't necessarily make Darren a killer. Lockyer was not at all convinced that the man he'd met – the man who delivered loo roll and teabags to Inez de Redvers – would kill a young woman just because she'd threatened to shop him for fencing stolen goods or for prescription fraud. He seemed far more likely simply to lie low until Nazma had moved on.

But Darren being Doug Smallbone's son did mean one thing: if he ever found himself with a corpse on his hands – whether that person had died by accident, or by the hand of someone to whom he was loyal – he'd know *exactly* where to go to make the problem disappear.

17

Day 15, Monday

Broad's eyes widened when Lockyer told her about the connection between Darren Mason and Douglas Smallbone.
They'd got straight to work, no chit-chat about how they'd
spent the remainder of their weekends.

'That changes things, right?' she said.

'It does. But having a dodgy dad doesn't make Darren a
murderer.'

'Doug Smallbone is more than just dodgy, guv.' She
thought for a second. 'Can we go and see him? Go to Smallbone's yard, I mean?'

Lockyer smiled. 'And say what? "Did you dispose of the
body of a young woman your son had killed twenty years
ago?" I'm pretty sure I know what he'd say.'

'Yeah. All right. Maybe not yet.'

'It's just another thing to keep in mind,' Lockyer said.

'Can I put it on the board?'

'That one of our suspects has links to organized crime? Definitely.'

Broad printed out a grainy image of Smallbone, stuck it up alongside Darren's juvenile mug shot and drew an arrow between the two.

'I've finished looking through the Chapmans' financial stuff,' she said, sitting down.

'Anything interesting?'

'Well, Antigone paid herself a salary and dividends totalling around seven hundred grand last year.'

'Not too shabby.'

'I literally don't know what I'd do with that much money,' Broad said. 'I might go berserk.'

'Don't worry. Wiltshire Constabulary's never going to spring a shock like that on you.'

'Ha – too right. Her personal wealth, in shares and whatnot, is well into the millions, so I don't suppose Edward Chapman feels he has to try too hard with his own businesses. Remember I said the property rental company didn't make as much as I'd have thought? It's because some of the places haven't even got tenants. They're just sitting empty. Why would he do that?'

Lockyer shrugged. 'There are all sorts of standards a place has to meet before it can be rented out. If those houses aren't in a fit state for whatever reason – like they need a full rewire or something like that – then perhaps he doesn't want to invest the money. Or can't be bothered to sort it. They'll still accrue value if he just leaves them empty.'

'That's so wrong,' Broad muttered. 'I bet there are plenty of people who'd love to move in.'

'You're right, Gem. But there's not a lot we can do about it.'

'A bit of a theme on this case, guv.'

'Well, our job is to find out what happened to Nazma Kirmani. And it feels like we're getting closer.' He *did* think he could see shapes in the fog of Nazma's final summer. Furtive movement, as though dark things, long undisturbed, had heard them coming.

'About an inch at a time,' Broad said sombrely.

Lockyer glanced at her, but she kept her eyes on her screen. He was usually the one throwing his hands in the air, grinding his teeth at their lack of progress, while she reassured him that they *would* succeed. And, quite often, she then turned up the one piece of information that prompted him to connect the dots. But a spark was missing this time. He knew he had to do something about it, but he still had no idea what.

'We're looking at alibis, right?' he said. 'Let's start with the Chapmans.' He got up, reaching for his coat.

Broad looked surprised. 'What – you want to go down there again? We could just set up a call?'

'We could, but I want to see them in action. And I want Antigone to have to be polite to us again. It's so much fun to watch.'

Now, finally, Broad smiled.

In fact, Antigone Chapman barely bothered being polite for a third time. She didn't offer them coffee, but sat opposite them in the conservatory with barely concealed dislike. Outside, the garden was bathed in pale sunshine, casting crisp shadows from the box hedging of the parterre. Edward Chapman seemed restless. He was managing to do a fair impression of a man sitting casually, happy to talk, but Lockyer wasn't convinced. There was tension around his eyes and mouth, and in the unnatural set of his shoulders. Lockyer wondered whether he and Antigone had perhaps discussed the fact that she had not only known about Nazma far sooner than Chapman had thought, but had *met* her, and told her a few home truths.

'We appreciate you speaking to us again,' Locker said.

'I can't think what else you expect us to add,' Antigone said tersely.

'We're asking everyone who was involved with Nazma that summer to provide firm evidence of their whereabouts on the night of October second that year,' Broad said.

'*Involved* with her?' Antigone repeated coldly. She flicked a glance at her husband, who studiously didn't meet her eye. 'You can't imagine that *I* fall into that camp?'

Broad coloured ever so slightly. 'Not the best word, perhaps,' she said. 'I only meant people who had dealings with her. Got to know her.'

'I didn't get to know her.'

'No,' Lockyer broke in. 'But you certainly had dealings with her.'

Antigone held his eye for a long moment. 'You can't go relying too heavily on anything Inez tells you.'

'We've been hearing that a lot, lately,' he said.

'Well. Perhaps you ought to listen.'

'Are you refusing to provide a verifiable alibi for the evening in question?' Broad said, surprising Lockyer with her forthrightness.

Antigone regarded her coolly. 'No, Constable. I'm not.' She got up and left the room, and a moment later they heard her footsteps on the stairs.

Edward Chapman shot them a cringing smile. 'She's awfully cross with me about all this,' he said.

Lockyer nodded. 'I was getting that impression.'

'Far better for her not to have known about Nazma at all, I suppose,' Broad said icily.

'Well, I understand your disapproval, but yes. Far better.'

'We've been talking to Ingrid Roach,' Lockyer said. 'It seems she was keeping a close watch on Nazma that summer. Perhaps with an eye to discouraging your relationship.'

Chapman grunted. 'I wouldn't be surprised.'

'No?'

'She always carried bit of a torch for me, ever since our Oxford days. Well, for me *and* Antigone, truth be told. Rather more like the crushes you have at school, for a teacher or an older boy or girl. Something more like idolization than lust.'

'Did she tell you anything about Nazma that summer?'

'Oh, yes. There was a steady drip of covertly nasty remarks, dressed up as concern. I never paid any attention.'

'What kind of remark?'

'Oh, that she was far too young, bound to let me down eventually, and wasn't Tiggy simply marvellous in whatever her latest endeavour had been? That sort of thing.'

'Did she ever tell you Nazma had met somebody new? Or that she was planning to leave?'

'No.' Chapman's face showed consternation. 'You think she was?'

'The items of hers we found in the river seem to suggest so.'

'Oh.' A beat. 'With the man in the photograph you showed me?'

Lockyer didn't reply.

'Well, Ingrid never said anything to me about it – and I think she *would* have done, if she'd known for sure. She'd probably have been delighted, after all.'

'Perhaps,' Lockyer agreed. 'How far do you think Ingrid's idolization of you went? Was it . . . an obsession?'

'An *obsession*? Well, I rather doubt it. I mean, still waters may run deep, but I never got the impression Ingrid had any such depths. Without wishing to be unkind. She's a good scholar, and we go back a long way. But we never socialized beyond work functions, once she'd joined Brittonic. And I barely hear from her these days.'

'I see,' Lockyer said. 'Can anybody confirm that you were here throughout the evening Nazma went missing? Your daughters, perhaps?'

'I'm afraid I put them to bed at eight, as per usual, and they were both good sleepers. We never heard a peep from them after lights out, unless there was a bad dream or something like that. I ate the supper Tiggy had left for me, drank one or two glasses of wine and watched something on the box – couldn't tell you what. Probably dozed off myself, if truth be told.'

'You didn't leave at any point?'

'I'll admit to many failings, Inspector Lockyer, but not to being a neglectful father. I would *never* have left the children alone.'

'And what time did your wife return home?'

'A little after midnight, I believe.'

'And she drove herself?'

'She did. Tiggy never drinks at Trust functions – admirable restraint. I've seen her make a glass of champagne last three hours.'

'You mentioned that you had a nanny at that time. Did she live in?'

'Yes – in the annex. But it was her night off.'

Broad consulted her notebook. 'According to DVLA records, three cars were registered to this address in 1999. A silver Mercedes SLK?'

'My wife's car,' Chapman confirmed.

'A green Range Rover?'

'Mine. Sadly more in the garage than out of it – as it was that week. I'd had to cadge a lift home from Avebury.'

'Who with?'

'I haven't a—' He thought for a moment. 'No, wait – I remember. A chap from Shaftesbury Museum, who'd been visiting the dig.'

'Can you tell us his name?'

'Minchin. Cliff? No – Clive. But I'm afraid you'll struggle to check on that. The poor chap died about five years ago. Cancer, I believe.'

'That's a shame,' Lockyer said.

'It is. Especially for his family. But we've used the same garage for years, just up the road – Cooper's. They might have a record of the Range Rover being in with them then. I sold it shortly afterwards. It was just too unreliable. Brand new the year before, but it was a lemon.'

Broad took down the name of the garage. 'And also a blue VW Polo?' she said.

'That was the nanny car. But, as I said, it was her night off, so she'd gone out in it.'

'Do you know where she went?'

'Haven't a clue. Into Warminster to flirt with the Royal Dragoons, most likely. She'd made friends with the Tuckwells' stable girl, who was a proper little minx. Led our Greta astray somewhat – not that she seemed reluctant to be led.'

'Greta . . .?' Broad asked.

Chapman puffed his lips. 'Now you're asking. Besel? Besser? Something like that. German girl, from somewhere near Munich, I think. We went through about seven au pairs in all. They only ever stayed a year or two before getting homesick. Or heading up to London for a bit more excitement.'

'I don't suppose you have contact details for Greta?' Broad said, with faint hope.

'No, sorry. One of the girls might. I could ask them, if you like? They keep in touch with some of them on Facebook, I think.'

'If you wouldn't mind giving us your daughters' contact details, we can ask them directly,' Lockyer said.

A flicker of annoyance from Chapman. 'Very well. But don't you think you're taking this a bit far? I had nothing whatsoever to do with whatever happened to Nazma. I wish I knew something helpful to tell you, but I really don't.'

'It will be helpful to be able to verify your non-involvement,' Lockyer said. 'Yours and your wife's.'

Chapman eased back a fraction. 'Yes, of course.'

As if summoned, Antigone returned with a glossy brochure in her hand.

'Tiggy, darling, what was that German au pair's surname? Greta what, can you remember?'

She replied without looking at him. 'Bessler. Why?'

'Are the girls still in touch with her at all?'

'Haven't a clue, but I rather doubt it. She used to make them cry with horrible stories about trolls that came to eat unruly children.' Antigone looked at Lockyer and Broad with the first softening since they'd arrived. 'Our girls were always sensitive, and highly imaginative. They took things like that to heart. Greta was something of a blunt tool, as I recall.'

'Do *you* have contact details for Greta?' Broad asked.

'Heavens, no.' She handed Lockyer the brochure then sat down. 'But here you go – the Trust's yearbook for 1999. If you turn to page thirteen, you'll see a photo from the Auction of Promises I hosted that night, at our club at Anstey House. There are any number of people who can vouch for my presence there from seven in the evening until its conclusion, shortly before midnight.'

In the picture, Antigone was wearing a jade green dress

that made her look like an architectural feature. Her hair was swept into a chignon, and diamonds sparkled in her ears. The unfortunate bone structure Inez had mentioned was evident, but she looked regal in her finery.

'I'm surprised you drove yourself in an outfit like that,' Lockyer said.

'I got dressed there, of course.' Antigone stood back up, and, as though he'd been sent a subliminal message, Chapman did the same. 'Will that be satisfactory?' she said.

'For now, yes. If we can just have those additional contact details – the garage, the other people at the charity function, and your daughters,' Lockyer said.

'I refuse to give out our daughters' contact details,' Antigone said coldly.

'We can find them for ourselves. It would just be far quicker if you told us.'

'I don't see that you ought to be contacting them at all. They're bound to want to know why, and at that point you would be grossly invading our privacy,' she said. 'I'll ask them if they keep in touch with Greta Bessler, and I'll thank you to wait to hear from me. My husband will find you the other things you've asked for, and see you out.' She stalked away to some other part of the large house.

'If I could borrow those photographs you mentioned, as well?' Lockyer added.

Chapman did as he was told. 'You must understand why she wouldn't want any of this to reach our daughters' ears, Inspector?' he said, sounding defeated, as he led them to the door at last.

'We believe a young woman was murdered, Mr Chapman,' Lockyer said. 'A woman you claim to have cared about. So I'm sure you'll understand why we need to ask questions. We'll be as discreet as we can about your affair, but that really isn't our main concern.'

'No, of course.' He stood out on the doorstep, his expression subtly sad. 'How awful to hear that word used in relation to Nazma,' he murmured. '"Murdered". How *terrible*.'

He watched as Lockyer and Broad got back into Lockyer's old Volvo and pulled away, tyres crunching slowly on the perfectly raked gravel.

'Are you just a little bit tempted to put your foot down and leave a dirty great set of skid marks?' Broad said.

'More than a little,' Lockyer said, as he crept decorously to the gate.

They'd gone about a quarter of a mile down the narrow lane when a small dark car came speeding the other way, so close that Lockyer had to swerve into the hedge. He cursed at the sound of twigs squealing on paintwork. The sun was in his eyes, but he glanced angrily at the other driver as he sped past and, with a jolt, turned as the car disappeared around the corner.

'Shit,' he muttered.

'That looked like . . .' Broad said, also turning.

'It looked *very* much like Darren Mason,' Lockyer said. 'Now, why on earth would he be down here, on his way to the Chapmans' house?'

He put his foot down and lurched the car out of the

hedge, but was forced to drive some distance before he found a gateway wide enough to turn around in.

'Shit,' he muttered again, hurrying back the way they'd come. Broad clung on to the grab handle, saying nothing. They had little chance of catching up with the smaller car, and when they got back to the Chapmans' place it was nowhere to be seen.

'Maybe it wasn't him,' Broad said.

Lockyer shook his head. 'We both saw him. Maybe he saw us too, and changed his mind about stopping.'

'It could be innocent – maybe Darren had a message from Inez, or something?'

'Maybe. But if it was innocent he'd be in there now, delivering the message.'

Lockyer took out his phone and dialled the Chapmans' number. Antigone answered on the tenth ring.

'Yes?'

'Mrs Chapman, this is DI Lockyer. Have you heard from Darren Mason lately? You or your husband?'

'Who? Oh – you mean Inez's pet gorilla? No, why on earth would we?'

'Because we just saw him. Heading in your direction.'

'Well, I have no idea why he should think to come here. And, in any case, he hasn't. As I'm sure you're aware, given that I can see you're parked right outside. Good day, Inspector.'

She rang off, and they sat watching from the lay-by for another minute or so, surrounded by steam from the exhaust. Lockyer was certain she was lying, but there was nothing to do but turn for home.

'Let's check the traffic cameras,' he said. 'Make sure it *was* Darren.'

Back at the station, Broad requested an automatic number-plate recognition – ANPR – search for Darren's car, and set to work tracing the names Chapman had given them: Cooper's Garage – the owner confirmed that Chapman's car had been in for repairs; the other members of the board of trustees who'd been at the charity function with Antigone; and Greta Bessler.

'Great. Another low-priority overseas search,' she muttered, turning up nothing on the UK databases. 'Are we really going to wait to hear from Antigone about any contact their daughters might still have with Greta, guv?'

'Nope. Get on to them, Gem. No need to say exactly what it's about, but if the Chapmans end up fielding questions, that's their problem.'

Lockyer flicked through Chapman's photographs of the dig in 1999, which were mostly of trenches and finds, just as he'd said. Given that they'd come from his camera, there were a surprising number of Chapman himself, standing beside excavated stones: back straight, arms folded. One had been taken at an exhibition about the archaeology of Avebury. Banners of prominent men who'd dug there in the past hung in a row, from John Merewether to Alexander Keiller, and Edward Chapman had positioned himself at the end of the row, wearing a self-satisfied smile. The next in line.

Wondering whether Edward's mother Shirley would

HOLLOW GRAVE | 314

have been impressed, Lockyer threw down the pictures and went back over the alibis Darren Mason, Inez de Redvers, Rhys Birch and Ingrid Roach had given. The headline was that nobody had any idea where they'd been that night. They'd only been able to say where they *hadn't* been. Not at the Marlborough Mop. Not anywhere near Nazma Kirmani. Probably at home; definitely elsewhere. The problem was, if anyone asked Lockyer where he'd been on any given date twenty years ago, chances were he'd have no clue, either. Other than on the night of Chris's murder, that was: *that* was branded into his memory. He'd been hiking on Dartmoor. He'd chosen to be alone, rather than go out with his younger brother, so he'd completely failed to prevent what had happened. Not something he'd ever be able to forget.

For those for whom it'd been an ordinary, unremarkable night, however, it was entirely reasonable for them to have forgotten it altogether. Lockyer went back to their notes on the Chapmans. Was it more suspicious, then, that they *had* been able to give alibis, rather than that they hadn't? Or was the twenty-year gap just a convenient excuse for somebody else? Somebody who was lying to them. A smiling face on his desk caught his eye: Mimi Draper. Then his phone rang, and he scrambled to answer when he saw the forensic laboratory's number.

'DI Lockyer? This is Dr Clare Warren, at Cellmark.'

'Hello, Dr Warren.'

'I've been working on a twenty-one-year-old soil sample, collected from a boot print. Yours, I believe?'

'Yes, great. What have you got for me?'

'Well, something quite exciting, actually,' she said. '*Blastenia coralliza*, to be exact. Also known as the coral firedot lichen.'

'Right . . .?'

'It's very rare, Inspector. In fact, it's only ever been found at five sites in the UK. It's picky – it needs a well-lit veteran oak tree to grow on, and very clean air. I'll put all the details in my report, so you can learn about it at your leisure.'

'Can you tell me where those five sites are?' Lockyer asked.

'One place in the far south of Wiltshire, on the edge of the New Forest. Two places in Wales, and one at the northern tip of Herefordshire. But, given where your sample was collected, I'd say it's site five you're going to be most interested in. Savernake Forest.'

'Savernake?' Lockyer echoed. His pulse jumped.

'Yes. It's on the far side of Marlborough.'

'I know it, yes.'

'Well, I can't give Savernake as the definitive location these spores were collected into the boot print, but it'd be something of a coincidence if not. Quite remarkable, really – there's a good chance the coral firedot is now extinct, you see. But twenty years ago, it would have been there.'

'That is *very* interesting. Thank you, Dr Warren. Anything else in the sample I should know about?'

'Nothing as exciting as the lichen spores, no. There'll be a full breakdown of pollen species and soil composition in my report.'

'Thank you. Sincerely.' Lockyer hung up the phone and got to his feet.

'Something we can use?' Broad said hopefully.

'You bet. Grab your coat.'

'Where are we going?'

'To bring Darren Mason in for questioning.'

18

Darren wasn't happy about it. His wife came out with their baby on her shoulder, her face pale and thunderous, but Darren agreed, grudgingly, to go with them. The navy-blue VW Golf was on the driveway. Lockyer put one hand on the bonnet: there was no heat in it, but it had probably had enough time to cool down.

Darren sat in stony silence as they splashed along the rain-drenched road, under a granite sky peppered with rooks. The sight of them made Lockyer think of Inez's unsettling paintings, with their threats of burial, their dizzying drops. The indistinct black pits reminiscent of empty eyes. *Blood everywhere*, she'd said. Who knew what or when she'd been thinking of?

Darren was allowed time alone with the duty solicitor before they started the recorded interview and Lockyer formally cautioned him. 'Mr Mason, is it all right to call you Darren?'

'Whatever.'

'Have you ever been to Savernake Forest, Darren?'

Darren blinked nervously, peering up at Lockyer from beneath glowering brows. 'What?'

'Savernake Forest. It's about seven square miles of ancient woodland to the south-east of Marlborough. Ever been there?'

He took a long time to answer. 'Yeah. My old man lives there. As I reckon you already know.'

'Your father is Douglas Smallbone. Is that correct?'

'You know it is. Why you asking?'

'When did you last see him?'

'I dunno. Ages back. Before the virus.'

'Oh, right. You've been adhering to the lockdown measures, have you?'

Darren looked down at his thick fingers and bitten nails. 'I never saw him much, anyway.'

'Why's that?'

'Come off it,' he snapped. 'You know why.'

'He's a known criminal, yes. But he *is* your father.'

'Yeah, well, he's never been much fun to be around. And he was a right twat to my mum, so there you go. We're not exactly close.'

'Surely there's *some* family loyalty there? Between you, your dad, your brothers—'

'*Half*-brothers,' Darren interrupted.

'Half-brothers, then.'

'Why are you asking about them?' Darren said. 'I've got nothing to say about any of them. I try not to have anything to do with them.'

'You can't choose your family, I suppose.'

Darren grunted in reply, then said: 'If they've done something – if that's what this is about – you're wasting your time. There's fuck-all I can tell you.'

'We're more interested in what they might have done *for* you,' Lockyer said.

Darren looked up again, forehead creasing, and Lockyer tried to read him. Whether he was calculating – trying to work out how much they knew – or simply puzzled and anxious.

Broad cleared her throat. 'At the time Nazma Kirmani disappeared, on the second of October, 1999, police forensics officers recovered soil from a boot print found close to Miss Kirmani's bunk in the barn at Trusloe Hall,' she said. 'Analysis of that soil shows that it's highly likely to have come from Savernake Forest.'

'So what?'

'Did you leave that boot print, Darren?'

'No.'

'Had you been to your father's place earlier that night?'

'No.'

'Where were you that night?'

'I've no sodding clue. At home, most likely.'

'Not much of an alibi, is it, Darren?'

'Yeah? Well, where the hell were *you* that night?' he fired back at her. 'Bet you don't know, either.'

'I don't, but that's because I was about three years old. Did your father or your half-brothers come to see you at Trusloe Hall that night? Maybe to help you with something?'

'Come to see me?' His face twisted in disgust. 'No. They didn't.'

'How can you be sure, if you can't remember where you were?'

'I'd remember that, for fuck's sake! They've never been to Inez's place – they don't even know about it. Or about her.' He sank lower in the plastic chair. 'I've made sure of that.'

Lockyer stepped back in. 'I'd like to put a scenario to you, Darren. We know you're very fond of Inez de Redvers. We know you've got a nice little set-up there – you get her the diazepam, and you get to store stolen goods there whenever you need to. You've also got a ready supply of antiques to sell, in lean times—'

'I never—'

Lockyer talked over him. 'We know Inez made friends with Nazma. We know you and Nazma argued more than once. I suspect Nazma found out what you were up to, and tried to warn Inez. I suspect Nazma was causing trouble for you both, and I suspect she came to harm as a result of it. We know that Inez can be violent when she's frightened or angry. Perhaps she simply didn't want Nazma to leave. Or perhaps Nazma was threatening to go to the police.' Lockyer watched Darren carefully. 'Did you follow her to Marlborough that night, Darren?'

'What? No. This is all complete—'

'Did you pick her up there, and take her back to Trusloe Hall? Maybe threaten her, try to scare her into keeping quiet?'

'No.'

'I suspect there was a fight. I suspect Nazma never left

Trusloe Hall that night – at least, not alive. And that you either took her to Smallbone's yard to dispose of, or called your dad or one of your brothers to come to Trusloe and help you get rid of the body.'

Darren's face contorted. 'This is bullshit.'

'I think *you* left that boot print, when you went to retrieve Nazma's escape bag. Inez'd had ample time and opportunity to discover that bag – you both had. Clever to get rid of it, and help the police think she'd run away of her own accord. Not so clever to just chuck it in the river, though. If you'd burnt it, or buried it with her, we might never have found it. So perhaps that was Inez. If she was drunk at the time, then you'd hardly expect her to come up with a brilliant plan. Who was the girl at Islington police station?'

'What? Who?'

'Friend of a friend, sent up to London with Nazma's handbag, pretending to be her?'

'DI Lockyer,' the duty solicitor broke in, 'what evidence do you have to support any of this?'

Lockyer ignored him. 'Well, Darren? What do you think of that scenario?'

'I think it's *bullshit*.'

'That boot print is a concrete link to *you*, Darren.'

'It's a concrete link to somebody who'd been to Savernake Forest,' the solicitor pointed out. 'As I understand it, the forest has many public footpaths. It could be pure coincidence—'

'I don't believe in coincidences,' Lockyer said, still only looking at Darren.

'Better start believing in them,' Darren muttered. "'Cause it was nothing to do with me.'

'You were nineteen at the time. I've heard someone who knew you back then describe you as a "rough little sod". Not somebody you'd want to cross.'

'Who said that?'

'Do you think it's a fair description, Darren?'

'No.'

'No? You're squeaky clean, are you?'

Darren snorted. 'I try to be. These days. Look, I wasn't always, all right? You know that. Maybe I have ... done some shit—'

'Mr Mason, I recommend—' the solicitor began, but Darren waved him off.

'But I swear to God I never touched that girl. I never went to Marlborough, never picked her up, never hurt her ... or helped anyone else do anything to her. Okay?'

Lockyer noted the slight glitch halfway through that final declaration. He stared hard at Darren, who was picking at the ruins of his thumbnails. He was scared, that much was obvious: the anger was a front. Scared of being caught, or of being wrongly accused? Impossible to say.

'Why did you go to see Edward and Antigone Chapman this morning?'

Darren swallowed. 'What?'

'We saw you, Darren, so don't lie to us. Constable Broad and I both saw you, earlier today, driving your car not two hundred metres from the house of Edward and Antigone Chapman. Chapman being Nazma Kirmani's former boss and lover, his wife Antigone being an old friend of Inez de Redvers and, in the past, a regular visitor to Trusloe Hall.'

Darren was shaking his head. 'It wasn't me.'

'It wasn't you?'

'No.'

'It was another man looking very like you, driving a car that looked very like yours.'

'Must've been,' he muttered.

'That would be another big coincidence. They seem to be stacking up around you, Darren.'

'Did you by any chance note the registration number of the car you saw, Inspector?' the solicitor asked.

'No. But we've requested the ANPR data from traffic cameras in the area. So I'm sure we'll be able to prove it *was* you, Darren.'

'It's hardly a crime, even if my client *was* driving his car in the area,' the solicitor said.

'What were you doing there?' Lockyer pushed. 'How well do you know them?'

'I know her a bit – Tiggy, from her coming to see Inez. We're not *mates*, though, and I've never been to her house. You think they'd associate with the likes of *me*?'

'Not willingly, no. But I don't think you'd have any trouble getting their address from Inez de Redvers. So, why did you go to see them?'

'I never. I don't know them, all right? If they're saying I went there then they're fucking lying.'

'Did you see my client at the address in question,

Inspector?' the solicitor asked. 'Have the people you mentioned suggested that my client visited them?'

Again, Lockyer ignored the man. 'You can see why we might think you had something to do with all this, can't you, Darren?'

'Maybe,' he said miserably, and it jarred Lockyer, somehow – that single, sullen word. 'But you're wrong.'

'I could arrest you for the illegal supply of prescription medication. I expect your prints are all over the many empty packets lying around Trusloe Hall.'

Darren simply shook his head. 'Not me.'

'Pull the other one,' Broad muttered.

Lockyer sat back with a quiet sigh. Even though a lot of what they had was circumstantial, or uncorroborated, it amounted to a body of evidence against the man sitting in front of them. He was obviously lying to them, and though Lockyer wasn't sure of the complete picture, he was sure they were on the right track.

'Are we finished, Inspector?' the solicitor asked.

'For now,' Lockyer said. 'While we continue our enquiries. But if I get ANPR evidence putting you within five miles of the Chapmans' address earlier today, Darren, I'll be arresting you.'

He looked up, alarmed. 'For what?'

'Obstructing a murder inquiry. Interview terminated at four forty-seven p.m.' Lockyer turned off the recording. 'Don't go far, Darren. I'm sure we'll be seeing you soon.'

*

'We need to search Smallbone's place,' Broad said, when they got back to their office. She hit the light switch with more force than was necessary, turning the wan grey daylight a wan yellow instead. 'And Trusloe Hall.'

Lockyer took a deep breath. Black, empty eyes: bottomless pits that threatened to swallow you whole. Were Inez's paintings an attempt to tell the world what she knew? What she'd seen – or even what she'd done?

'I'll tell you a great place to bury a body,' he said. 'In a prehistoric cist that's already been excavated, documented and found to be empty. Nobody's ever going to dig that up again.'

'And if she's not there, she's down the well. Bet you anything,' Broad said.

'So why do we need to search Smallbone's yard?'

'Darren either went there, or one of his family came from there to Trusloe. Maybe they hid other evidence at the yard. Like her handbag – once they'd used it to present the fake Nazma in Islington. Has Darren got any sisters? Female cousins? If so, they could easily have dressed her up with make-up and the right clothes.'

'But the wrong earrings.' Lockyer picked up a pen, tapped his desk in thought. 'When Darren said he kept away from his family, and that they didn't know about Trusloe Hall, it had the ring of truth to it.'

'Okay, guv, but even if that's the case, the boot print still ties Darren into it all. Maybe he went to see them a few days before. Who knows?' She shrugged. 'It doesn't matter. We know he's lying about the pills. We know he lied about how involved he was with Nazma that summer. We know he went to her bunk in the barn at around the time she disappeared, most likely to retrieve and get rid of her escape bag.'

'Why would he go down to see the Chapmans?'

'No idea,' she admitted. 'Maybe it *wasn't* him we saw.'

'It was him,' Lockyer said. '*This* is what's bothering me, Gem – it's that we're not seeing the full picture.'

'Well, finding Nazma's body at Trusloe Hall will give us a *big* piece of it.'

Which was basically what Lockyer said to DSU Considine, as he tried to persuade her they had enough to warrant a search.

'It doesn't feel all that concrete to me, Matt,' she said, via a video link.

'I can't claim there's nothing speculative about this search request, but I believe there are grounds.' He didn't mention Inez's paintings. *The Hollow Grave*, the empty eyes, the rooks. The possibility of a confession being hidden in them. That would definitely be a piece of speculation too far for Considine. 'Inez de Redvers is very unstable, and has been for a long time,' he said. 'Darren Mason was – and probably still is – involved in criminal activity at Trusloe Hall. He also has family ties to organized crime. The forensic link to Savernake isn't bulletproof, but it'd be a hell of a coincidence if that boot print *wasn't* left by Darren, or some associate of his.'

Considine, sitting with her arms folded, drummed her fingers as she thought about it.

'Trusloe Hall is a shambles,' Lockyer went on. 'There's a

well in the old kitchen a hundred feet deep, and a filled-in archaeological site in the garden. A collapsed barn, and four storeys of near-derelict house, full to the rafters with crap. And it wasn't searched when Nazma disappeared – none of it.'

At this, his boss raised her eyebrows.

Lockyer took a breath. 'Inez de Redvers took a swipe at DC Broad with her walking stick. Could've broken her jaw, if she hadn't missed.'

'She *attacked* Gemma?'

'Yes. Gem had been pushing her about Darren's criminal activities, and about the prescription drugs.'

'Well, in that case, leave it with me.' Considine unfolded her arms and sat forward. 'I'll get you that warrant.'

'Thank you, ma'am.'

It was dark by the time he turned into the track that led to his cottage, spraying muddy water up from the deep ruts. Then the sweep of the headlights picked out the shape of a person, standing to one side. Startled, Lockyer hit the brakes, peering out past the regular swipe of the wipers, thinking for a second it could be Mrs Musprat. That she'd started to wander. Then the figure stepped closer, and he got a better look.

It was Jason McNeil.

Lockyer opened the window. 'Jase?'

Rain had slicked the younger man's face; his short dreadlocks hung heavy over his forehead. 'Yeah. Hi. It's me.'

'What are you doing here? Is everything okay?'

'I think . . . maybe not.' He was uneasy. Almost shaky.

'Okay,' Lockyer said. 'Well . . . come inside, get dry. Tell me what's going on.'

'I'm not sure I can.' Jason made a strange gesture with one hand, alongside his head. 'Bad day. I'm not great company.'

Lockyer hesitated. 'Well, get in the car, at least,' he said.

'I'll get the seat wet.'

'It'll dry out. Don't tell me you *walked* here?'

It was an easy enough route, straight across the Plain along old chalk tracks. But it was twelve miles. Then Lockyer remembered that when Jason had run away from his old life in Swindon, as a teenager, he'd walked for days before washing up at Old Hat Farm.

Jason shook his head. 'I came on the bike. It's back there.' He indicated the dark trees beside the track.

'Get in, Jase.'

Lockyer shut off the engine as Jason climbed in. The metallic patter of rain filled the silence, and Lockyer waited as the faintly animal smell of wet hair and clothes filled the old Volvo.

'My brother died at the end of a knife. Same as yours,' Jason said at last.

'Yes. I know,' Lockyer said.

'Right,' Jason said flatly. 'You found out all about me, I guess. When you thought I was a murderer.'

'Sorry, Jase. I had to.'

''S okay. I get it.' His head twitched, scattering drops of rain from the ends of his hair. 'I ran away from all that. All that shit they were involved in – that *I* was involved in, practically from birth, you know? The gangs and the feuds. Drugs. Turf wars. People getting shanked for not showing *respect*.'

'I can't imagine what growing up around all that must've been like,' Lockyer said carefully.

'Nah, you can't.' Jason's breathing was deep and quick. He was just about calm on the outside, but something else was going on within. 'I just . . . ran away. Saw something one night, when I was out with them and there was a rumble, and something in my head said: *Run*. It was like I . . . hit a limit. I didn't even think about it. And for a long time after I couldn't even remember that night. I just kept going, until I got to Old Hat Farm. And then I waited. Shitting myself, thinking Benjamin would find out where I was – him and my cousins. That they'd come and get me, and make me go back. I loved Ben but . . .' Jason trailed off. 'Funny how kids are, isn't it? That you can love someone so much, even when you know they're bad. That they're doing you harm.'

'Have you been back in touch with your family since everything that happened this summer?' Lockyer asked.

'A little. Just with Mum. But she tells me stuff. She tells me not much has changed – Benjamin dying made no difference. Made it worse, if anything. Tit for tat, an eye for an eye. Kids the age of fifteen, sixteen, bleeding to death in fucking McDonald's.' He tsked, rolling his head.

'Have you . . . got information about something that's happened in Swindon, Jase? Is that what this is?'

Jason stared out at the rain-spattered windscreen, his eyes focused on nothing.

'What you did took incredible courage,' Lockyer said. 'It's hard to say that without sounding patronizing, but I mean it. I meet plenty of people born into families where crime is a first resort, not a last resort, and most of them never manage to turn things around. Get past that history, and the trauma of it. Build a completely different life.'

'Didn't feel like courage. Felt like cowardice,' Jason murmured.

'Well, it wasn't. No one I met while I was investigating Holly's death had a bad word to say about you, Jase. And you never hurt anyone – not even when you were grief-stricken and barely thinking straight.'

'Yeah, I'm a real hero.' A quick, sad smile. 'If . . . if I did know something, what would you do?'

'You mean, if you told me about a crime?' Lockyer said. 'I'd have to report it.'

'And it would be investigated? People arrested?'

'It would be investigated, yes. Whether anyone was arrested or not would depend. There'd have to be good supporting evidence.'

For perhaps a minute there was no sound but the rain.

'Are we talking about something that's happened recently?' Lockyer asked.

'A while back.' Jason looked across at him. 'But that doesn't make it any less, right? You and me, we both know that. Time doesn't heal. Not when things don't feel *finished*. That shit won't go away.'

'No,' Lockyer said. 'It won't.'

Jason nodded, looking away again. 'And you'd have to report it? Get all your copper mates on it?'

'Isn't that why you're telling me whatever this is, Jase? Because I'm police?'

A fluid shrug of one shoulder.

''Cept now I'm here the words don't want to come out. Can't get them back once I've said them, can I?'

'No.' Lockyer chose his next words carefully. 'You've moved on, Jase. You've left that life behind. Maybe . . . don't revisit it. Not if you don't have to. Unless . . . Is it your mum? Is she in any danger?'

'No. Other than the danger of more heartache, perhaps. But no one would touch her.'

'I spoke to her, you know, to confirm your alibi for the day Lee Geary died. It wasn't a long conversation, but she told me you were different from the others. She was glad you'd got away. That you weren't involved in any of it any more.'

'So don't be involved? That's what you're saying?'

'Maybe. Yes.'

Jason absorbed that for a moment. 'Feels like I still am, though,' he said, in the end. 'Feels like I always will be, if I don't finish things properly.'

But a second later he opened the car door and went back out into the rain.

19

Day 16, Tuesday

Inez de Redvers looked mystified when she was handed the search warrant. She didn't read it. It hung limply in her trembling hand, and her eyes widened as the trio of uni-formed officers filed in, quietly businesslike. One carried a case of inspection camera equipment.

'Shall I sit with you while they get on?' Broad said to her. 'I've brought you a coffee – the one you liked last time. And some doughnuts.'

'How very kind,' Inez murmured.

'Come on, then. You can tell me some more about the protest camps you used to stay at.'

'Yes, all right.' Inez took Broad's arm, and allowed herself to be led away.

Lockyer waited until they were in the drawing room, with the door closed, before turning to the other officers. 'For God's sake, be careful. Right now you're standing in one of the *least* dangerous and cluttered parts of this building. The floors upstairs are rotten. If you're in any doubt at all, stay out, and we'll send the cadaver dog up when he's finished outside. Perhaps you two should stick together – I know it'll take longer, but at least someone will know if you hit trouble. Start in the basement.' He turned to the officer with the camera equipment, a young man whose eyes shone with purpose behind his visor. 'You're with me.'

'Right, boss.'

Lockyer led the way to the leaky, beautifully vaulted room where Inez's paintings were growing mildew. Her portrait of Pippa was still facing the room, and the amber eyes seemed to watch as they made their way over to the well. Lockyer felt his heart beating harder in anticipation. The well exhaled cold, damp air. A black tunnel, straight down into the earth. The young officer leant over to peer in, and Lockyer yanked him back.

'Seriously,' he said. 'Do *not* fall in there.'

Swallowing, the officer knelt down and began to unpack the equipment. It was the same sort used for drain inspections: a camera about the size of a pen torch, on a long lead, connected to a screen that relayed the footage in real time.

'Is that going to be long enough?' Lockyer asked.

'Got fifty metres, boss.'

Lockyer nodded. 'That ought to do it.'

He crouched beside the screen as the operator began to feed the camera into the well, saw old brickwork, furred with algae. A few small ferns were growing near the top, but they soon gave up as the camera went deeper. There were spiders, and the odd snail. Then, from about ten metres down, nothing at all. Lockyer watched intently. At twenty metres there was a glint from below: a reflection of the camera's light.

'Still got water down there,' the operator said.

'Is this thing waterproof? Can we drop it right through the water to the bottom?'

'Yep, no problem.'

In the end, they didn't need to. The bottom of the well was rocky, with puddles of silty water just an inch or two deep. It didn't appear to be flowing. The well might once have tapped into an underground stream, but it had changed course since then. Lockyer felt a rush of disappointment. The operator fed the camera right to the bottom, and rotated it slowly. They saw flint, chalk and broken pottery, an old tin can, and a corroded Dinky toy – a lorry, still with chips of yellow paint and the remains of lettering.

'Weetabix, if I'm not mistaken,' the operator said. 'Might be worth a bob or two to a collector.'

Lockyer grunted, then saw a flash of something white, close up to the camera. He jerked forwards. 'Go back! That looked like bone.'

The operator obeyed, his face intent. 'That's bone all right, boss,' he said.

A skull with eye sockets that seemed far too big for it, yellow teeth at the front, and a delicate string of vertebrae behind it. It looked like a rabbit.

'Hope that wasn't someone's pet,' the operator said. They both sat back on their heels, the tension dissipating. There was no way out of the bottom of the well, no way human remains could have washed away. Nowhere for them to hide.

'It was worth a look. Thanks . . .?'

'PC Mathers, boss.'

'Thanks, Mathers. Get packed up, then come and give us a hand with the rest of the house.'

Lockyer went outside next, down from the overgrown terrace and over the choppy lawn, to the field where a dog handler was surveying the cist burial. The cadaver dog was a tan and white springer spaniel called Delta. She was running sweeps to and fro across the site, tongue lolling, nose down.

'Anything?' Lockyer asked her handler, a female officer, who shook her head.

'Sorry. I've run her three times. She's not finding anything.'

As if to confirm this, Delta returned to sit at her handler's feet, panting, and got a tennis ball as a reward.

'What's her success rate, generally?' Lockyer asked.

'Cadaver dogs? Generally about ninety-five per cent,' the woman told him. 'But Delta has never got it wrong.'

'Seriously? Not once?'

'Not once. Not yet.'

'If the person we're looking for is down there, they might have been there for twenty-one years. Would that make it harder for her?'

'Potentially, yes. But last year she found a bloke who'd been missing for twenty-*seven* years. Nothing left but his skull and a few leg bones. And earlier this year, she detected skeletonized remains twenty-five feet beneath the surface of a reservoir.'

'That's amazing,' Lockyer said.

'She is,' the woman said proudly. 'If there was a body down there, Inspector, she'd have told me.'

He nodded grimly, sensing dark clouds of failure massing on the horizon. 'Have you got time to sweep the rest of the grounds? And the collapsed barn, over that way?'

She nodded. 'You've got us all morning, so we'll search wherever you like.'

Lockyer went back into the house. From the drawing room, where Inez had her nest, he heard a laugh.

'And, do you know, he never did find out . . .' Inez said, then lowered her voice, so Lockyer didn't hear what came next. He made his way to the stairwell. From the basement came sounds of sneezing and movement.

'Anything?' he called.

'Mould, boss,' came the rueful reply. 'Never seen anything like it.'

'Anything else?'

'Not yet. Except there's wine down here that's probably worth a mint.'

'Keep looking. Anything that looks like it might have belonged to a young woman, and particularly any mobile phones. Be *thorough*.'

Lockyer looked up the stairs. He ought to follow his own advice and not go up alone – or perhaps not at all. Delta was far less likely to go crashing through a rotten floor than his fourteen stone. He moved the mouldering boar's head out of the way and tested the first step. It creaked, but didn't give.

Gingerly, kicking aside bags of who knew what, he made his way up to the first floor.

A long central corridor mirrored the one downstairs, dimly lit with borrowed light from the rooms that opened off it, and the stairs carried on up to the servants' quarters in the attic. Lockyer went through the nearest door. It took him a moment to realize he was in a bathroom. The only obvious sign of it – the bathtub itself – was overflowing with clothes and magazines; the rest of the fixtures were completely buried. Rotten shreds of pink silk hung from the walls.

Lockyer moved a few things aside as he made his way further into the room: he needed a team of twenty to search the place, not four. He ground his teeth in frustration. Four was what they had, and they'd have to make do. The cadaver dog would be useful, when she finished outside, but she wouldn't spot Nazma's mobile phone or her blue shoulder bag.

Lockyer found a stack of brand-new washing-up bowls, still with their labels attached. A mink stole and matching hat. A collection of antique OS maps. There was no rhyme or reason to any of it. Just chaos. He saw with increasing clarity that it was the work of a woman with profound mental-health issues.

After about ten minutes he uncovered the toilet, and immediately wished he hadn't.

Abandoning the bathroom, Lockyer picked his way along the corridor. He took a look into each of the rooms: more of the same. Only one room was slightly more accessible – there was a pathway to and from a huge four-poster bed, from the bed to a wardrobe, and also to one of the sash windows. One of the lower panes of the window had smashed at some point, leaving shards of glass on the carpet and a swathe of mould down the wall and curtains. Not far away he spotted the hole in the floor he had seen from below. The hole Inez said she'd made one day, nearly falling through.

The skeleton of a rook lay on the windowsill, in a halo of black feathers.

Treading very carefully, and hoping his weight wouldn't be the final straw, Lockyer crossed to the end of the bed. It had been Inez's room, he realized, perhaps the room she'd shared with Pippa, once upon a time. A rumpled duvet and bedspread were thrown back on the bed; the dents from two heads remained in the pillows. The sight of them made Lockyer's skin prickle with unease. One day, for whatever reason, both women had stopped sleeping in this room. He swept his eyes around the mess. Large pieces of furniture rose like islands from a sea of clothes and books and papers. A French armoire hung open, paused in the act of vomiting its contents onto the carpet.

Lockyer's gaze moved past it. Then went back.

Something had caught his eye in the heap of clothes in front of the wardrobe, just the other side of the hole in the floor. One small note of order in the surrounding cacophony. He struggled to locate it again, but there it was: the patterned sleeve of a blouse that was laid out straight rather than scrunched up. The long leg of some blue jeans, also lying neatly along the floor. The prickle on his skin became an electric charge. He followed the sleeve to the cuff, and saw finger bones. A skeletal hand. And there, all but buried in fabric: a chin, a jaw bone. Teeth bared; no lips or gums. A few scraps of hair that he'd taken for a wig at first glance.

However she'd died, the woman had been lying there for a very long time.

The floor creaked ominously. Lockyer backed away, and went downstairs. He opened the door to the drawing room in silence. Broad turned to look at him, Inez too, her eyes wide. She was on her feet, her walking stick gripped with white knuckles. 'I heard sounds upstairs,' she said tremulously. 'It isn't safe up there!'

'I've been up to your room, Inez,' he said.

'It . . . it isn't *safe*!' she gasped, and as she stared at him, her face drained. 'You've found her,' she whispered.

'Guv?' Broad said.

'You've found her,' Inez repeated. 'Haven't you?'

'Yes,' Lockyer said.

Inez swayed, then her legs went out from under her and she collapsed back onto the couch. 'Oh, thank God,' she murmured. 'Thank God.'

'Found who, guv?' Broad said. '*Nazma?*'

'*Is* it Nazma, Inez?' Lockyer said.

As they took Inez into custody, Darren Mason came hurrying over. His expression at seeing Inez outside, limp and compliant, was one of frank astonishment.

'What the hell is this?' he said. 'Where are you taking her?'

'Back to the station to answer a few questions,' Lockyer said.

'You can't just drag her out of there like this! She'll—You'll frighten her! You can't seriously think she did anything to that girl?'

Lockyer closed the car door securely and turned to him. Watched closely. 'We've just found a body in there. Upstairs, in Inez's old bedroom.'

For a second, a look of pure panic flitted across Darren's face. But then he let it settle into its habitual, distrustful scowl. 'Bullshit. There's no body in there.'

'You're claiming you knew nothing about it?'

'I – I don't . . . You're not serious?'

'I'm completely serious.'

Darren stared at him, apparently speechless. Or being careful to give nothing away.

'There'll be officers here for the next few days while a full forensic search is carried out. I suggest you keep away, Darren. You know where I am, if you've got anything you want to tell us.'

Darren spoke up as Lockyer turned to go. 'What about Inez? You can't keep her banged up for no reason, so where's she going to go?'

'*If* we release her, I'll call you. Perhaps you might be able to put her up for a few days?' Lockyer said. To his slight surprise, Darren nodded readily enough.

The search team didn't have to worry about leaving a mess at Trusloe Hall, at least. Delta's handler took her dog all over the premises, finding plenty of dead rats, mice and birds, but no other human remains. Lockyer could hardly sit still while they waited for an ID on the body, but Inez was too distressed to tell them, so he had no choice but to hang on for the pathologist's call.

'Dental records are a match to Philippa Harmon,' she told him on the phone, at the end of the day.

Lockyer sat down abruptly, disappointment crashing through him. A wall of frustration. He'd thought they'd found Nazma Kirmani. He gave Broad a tiny shake of the head, and watched her deflate, too.

'Right. Thank you. How did she die?'

'Not sure yet, and I might never be able to tell you, given how little of her is left. I'll start the PM first thing tomorrow. You're welcome to observe, if you wish.'

'Yep. I'll do that.'

Broad was subdued as they went down to talk to Inez.

'So, Pippa did get buried under an avalanche of junk, just like I said at the start,' she said.

Lockyer stopped her outside the interview room. 'Look, the fact that we haven't found Nazma doesn't mean that Inez and Darren weren't involved in her disappearance,' he said. 'Right at the start of this case we talked about the possibility of finding a serial killer. Well, what if we have?'

'What – *Inez*?'

'I'm willing to bet she killed Pippa because Pippa was going to leave. Maybe she did the same to Nazma. Maybe she's done the same to others, in the past.'

Broad stared into the middle distance as that sank in.

'Ready?' Lockyer said. She nodded without a word.

Since Inez hadn't yet been charged with anything, and her clothes weren't needed for forensics, she'd been allowed to stay in them: jogging bottoms with one leg scissored off above the rancid orthopaedic boot, a hairy pink jumper, a tiger-print satin wrap, turquoise earrings, and one of her turbans. Sitting next to her, her legal brief was a grey sparrow beside a shambolic tropical bird. A pungent reek of body odour and unwashed clothes was already filling the room. Lockyer suspected the plastic boot was the main source of the problem.

He started the recording. 'Interview at five thirty p.m. on Tuesday, the seventeenth of November. Present in the room are Detective Inspector Matthew Lockyer . . .'

'Detective Constable Gemma Broad . . .'

'Sarah Cramer, duty solicitor.'

'Oh! Should I say my name?'

'Yes, your full name, please,' Broad said.

'Inez Gabriella Cora Linley de Redvers.'

Inez's tremors were so bad that her head bobbed slightly at the end of her neck. She looked terrified and confused. A frail, mentally impaired, long-term drug addict. Lockyer hardened his heart to it. Whether it was genuine or not, they couldn't let her distress prevent them from establishing the truth. 'May I address you as Inez?' he asked.

'Of course you may.'

'I would like to postpone this interview until my client has undergone a full medical and psychological assessment,'

Sarah Cramer said. 'I am not at all convinced that she's well enough to answer your questions.'

'We'll keep this short,' Lockyer said. 'And I completely agree that Inez should be seen by a doctor. To get rid of that ankle brace, if for no other reason.'

The solicitor gave a curt nod, perhaps unconsciously leaning away from the source of the stink.

'Inez, you've been arrested on suspicion of the murder of Philippa Harmon, in the early part of the year 1999, for concealing a body and for preventing a lawful burial.'

'Oh, no, no! I didn't *kill* her,' Inez gasped. 'I swear it, on my very soul!'

'But you did know she was dead?' Broad said. 'You knew she was up in that room, all this time.'

Inez nodded, then shook her head: 'No, I— That is to say . . . I rather thought it was all some terrible *dream* I'd had . . . The rooks, you see. How she hated them! Battering at the glass like they were possessed by demons! That's what she said. She couldn't stand them another minute. Or . . . or . . . *me*.' Her face drooped sorrowfully. 'I was like a leech, she said. A weight around her neck. Oh! She could say such unkind things, when she lost her temper.'

'She intended to leave you,' Lockyer said, for clarity.

'Yes. She went upstairs to pack some things. I . . . I thought it best just to let her calm down – her storms blew them-selves out, quite often. But the rooks . . . the rooks, you see.'

'What about the rooks?' Lockyer asked.

Inez simply stared at him with haunted eyes.

'You didn't go upstairs with Pippa? You didn't try to persuade her to stay?'

'No. I think . . . no. I stayed downstairs. Oh, *Pippa!*'

'For how long?'

'I – I'm afraid I really can't remember. It was . . .' She trailed into silence. 'So in the end, you see, she left,' she said, in a small voice. 'Left, and never even came in to say goodbye to me. I thought that was *very* hard of her. She knew how much I loved her!'

'But she *didn't* leave, Inez,' Lockyer reminded her. 'Philippa died, upstairs in the bedroom. How did she die?'

'*Oh* . . .' Inez breathed, tears flooding her eyes. 'Oh, my poor, *poor* Pippa . . .'

'How did she die?'

'She . . . I don't know! I really don't know.'

'She said hurtful things. Did you lose your temper, Inez? Did you lash out? Or push her?'

'No! I would *never* hurt her!'

Inez collapsed into sobs, fighting for breath, and the solicitor shot Lockyer a hard look. 'I really think we need to stop,' she said.

'Soon. You knew where Pippa was all this time, Inez,' he said. 'You kept asking us to find her, when you knew all we needed to do was go upstairs. And you made it very clear that it was unsafe for us to do so.'

'Oh, but it *is*. The floors, you see . . . treacherous.'

'So it wasn't because you didn't want us to find Pippa's body?'

'Her body?' Inez seemed confused again.

'You knew she was up there, didn't you?'

It took a moment for Inez to get control of her voice. 'I – I need my pills,' she said. 'Please. I must have them!'

'We'll get you something as soon as you've answered our questions,' Lockyer said, ignoring the anxious look Broad aimed at him. 'How did you know where she was, Inez?'

'The – the rooks! I *heard* them,' she whispered.

'What do you mean? The rooks told you?'

'I heard them upstairs! They'd smashed the glass – they'd got in! And Pippa . . . poor *Pippa*! She always said they were evil!'

Lockyer thought of the painting he'd seen – the gaping black holes that had looked like eyes. A terrible idea occurred to him. 'Inez, are you saying that rooks got in and were pecking at Pippa?'

Silence followed his words. Lockyer felt the horrified stares of all three women in the room. Tears rolled down Inez's sunken cheeks. '*Wicked* creatures,' she whispered. 'To do such a thing!'

'What did you do next, Inez?' Lockyer could guess at the answer: she ran. Put her foot through the floor in the process. Tried very hard to blank out what she'd seen.

'I'm afraid I – I don't remember. I think I must have been very upset.'

Her gaze pleaded with him, though for what, he couldn't guess. Perhaps forgiveness, or for him to tell her that she *had* dreamt it all.

'Anyone would have been upset,' Broad said gently.

'Did Darren know what had happened?' Lockyer said. 'Did he see Pippa – did you ask for his help, at all?'

'For his help? No, I . . . It wasn't safe for anyone to go up there. I told him—' She broke off, making a high keening sound in her throat. 'She always *hated* those birds.' Her voice was strangled. 'Please, I need my pills. I'm not well. I can't . . . I simply can't *bear* it, you see . . .'

'Interview suspended at five forty-four p.m.' Lockyer stopped the recording. 'We're going to get a doctor in to see you now, Inez. Is that all right?'

Still weeping, she nodded, and let Broad walk her slowly back to the custody suite.

They told the doctor about Inez's history of alcoholism and long-term diazepam use. He promptly requested a transfer to Salisbury District Hospital, finding that she was acutely dehydrated, her kidneys were swollen, and she was suffering from severe cellulitis on her leg – a painful skin infection, most likely caused by prolonged use of the orthopaedic boot. Meekly, Inez allowed herself to be strapped into a wheelchair, beneath a red fleece blanket. She chatted to the paramedics while they loaded her up and took her away, as though they were off on some everyday outing. As though she'd managed to forget, yet again, what she'd seen the last time she'd gone up to her bedroom.

'I don't think she killed her, guv,' Broad said, as they returned to their desks. 'Do you?'

'I'm not so sure,' Lockyer said. 'She's clearly capable of wiping things from her mind. Things she doesn't want to remember. We'll hopefully know more tomorrow, after the PM. But we need to brace ourselves for it to be inconclusive.'

'And if it is?'

'Then we'll have to grill Inez again, once she's fit – and much harder than we did today. If we can't get a confession, and the pathologist can't rule out natural causes, I doubt the CPS will pursue it.'

'Pippa *could* just have tripped in all that mess – especially if she was in a rage, and hurrying. Fallen and hit her head on something.'

'Let's wait for the PM report,' Lockyer said. 'Until then, we keep on with alibis for the night Nazma disappeared. And I'm going to make some calls, make sure any relatives Pippa had get to hear that we've found her.'

20

Day 17, Wednesday

Hedy was already awake when Lockyer opened his eyes.

'Richard,' she said.

Lockyer shook his head. 'Kev says it's a girl. Says he has a sixth sense about these things.'

'Rubbish,' Hedy said firmly. 'I think it's a boy.'

'He thinks we should call her Skylar.'

'Well, we're not going to.'

'What about Cora?'

'I thought you didn't want anything posh?'

'Is it posh?' Lockyer thought of the string of names Inez had given in her interview, where he'd heard it and thought it pretty. 'I suppose it is.'

'What does today hold?' Hedy asked.

'Bones,' Lockyer said.

Her eyes darkened, and he didn't elaborate.

He'd arranged to pick up Broad first thing, on his way to the post-mortem, to save her driving the wrong way into the station first. But when he turned onto the block paving of the small modern house she shared with Pete, there was no sign of life. She usually came out as soon as he pulled up – some instinct seemed to make her want to keep his interaction with her boyfriend to a bare minimum. Lockyer did try to conceal his antipathy towards the younger man, but he possibly didn't do a very good job.

He got out and looked up. Thought he saw a quick furtive movement in one of the upstairs windows. Pete had been working from home since the first lockdown, and both of their cars were on the driveway. Lockyer rang the bell, and waited. Then he knocked. Stepped back and looked up at the windows again. No movement this time, and no sounds from inside. He wondered if Broad had forgotten the plan, and was on her way into the station on her bike. But the sky was low and ominous, so it seemed unlikely. He went back to his car, dialling her mobile, but it went straight to voicemail. Tried it again, pointlessly. He didn't have a landline number for her – he wasn't sure she had one. He sent a WhatsApp: *Gem, need to get going. Have you gone in? If so no prob. See you after.* He added: *Hope all is well?* Pressed send, and waited for the double tick to show it'd been delivered. Only one tick appeared.

Resisting the urge to go back and take a closer look through one of the windows, Lockyer set off for the forensic mortuary at Flax Bourton, south-west of Bristol. But it was strange of Broad not to answer her phone, or to let the battery die. Strange of her to forget a plan.

There was an uneasy feeling in his gut. He tried to ignore it.

At the mortuary he got into his PPE, and signed himself in. He'd met the pathologist, Dr Middleton, several times before. She was calm and very competent, and gave him a nod when he appeared at the viewing window. With lockdown measures back in place, he wasn't allowed into the cutting room with her. Philippa Harmon's bones were laid out on one of the metal tables, and Lockyer saw at once that she hadn't been a large woman. Roughly the same height and build as Nazma Kirmani.

'About five foot three,' Dr Middleton said, when he asked. 'Slightly built. If you wouldn't mind, Inspector, I'd like to finish my examination. You can ask any questions afterwards.'

Lockyer watched her perform a close inspection of Pippa's remains, making a few comments into a digital voice recorder as she did so. The bones didn't seem to have much to tell her.

'Historical fracture of the lateral malleolus of the left ankle, well healed,' she said at one point.

Lockyer stared at the empty eye sockets, the smooth brow and grinning white teeth of the skull. Pippa had had sharply pointed canines, and a gap between her front incisors. He pictured the vivid amber eyes almost glaring out of Inez's portrait of her. Tried not to picture the rooks that had got into the bedroom through the broken window, and what had probably become of those eyes. It wouldn't have taken the birds long to find her: carrion eaters would smell a corpse a long time before any human could.

'Right, Inspector Lockyer,' Dr Middleton said, breaking into his dark imaginings. 'Ask away.'

'Cause of death?'

'Hard to be definitive,' she said, making his heart sink again. 'The hyoid bone is intact, so it's less likely – though not impossible – that she was choked or strangled. There is a minor hairline fracture to the left temple area. She could have been struck, or fallen and hit it.'

'Can't you normally tell the difference?'

'If there was a brain to look at, then yes. But not with an empty skull. I did notice from the crime-scene photos that one of the dresser drawers near where she was found was open. And in all that mess, I wouldn't be surprised if she'd stumbled, gone down and hit her head on the way. Tell whoever's processing the scene to look closely at that drawer, and at any other hard edges in the room. They may well find blood, perhaps a fragment of skin or a hair.'

'So the head wound killed her?'

'It's *possible*, but I'd be surprised. As I say, the fracture is very small. It's likely to have knocked her unconscious, per-haps for several hours. She'd probably have had concussion, but it doesn't look like a fatal blow to me.'

'Care to take a guess at what *did* kill her?'

'I've never been a fan of guessing, Inspector.' Middleton glanced back at the body, at the cap of mummified skin and hair still clinging to the skull. 'Do you know when she died?'

'Not precisely, but we think it was in the early weeks of 1999.'

'Winter, then.' Dr Middleton nodded. 'Was the room heated?'

'I very much doubt it.'

'Given that some of her skin and organs have mummified rather than decomposing, I'd say she had a chance to get cold and to dry right out before the weather then got warmer. If she knocked herself unconscious, and the room was unheated, it's entirely possible that she died of hypothermia.'

'Really? Indoors?' Even as he said it, Lockyer thought of the broken window. The clinging chill of Trusloe Hall.

'Absolutely,' Middleton said. 'She was petite. If she didn't have much body fat, it wouldn't have taken that long. If the room was, say, ten degrees Celsius, or colder, she could've died within a couple of hours.'

'I see. So if her partner had gone up in search of her, and found her sooner . . .?'

'Oh, she could have been saved. Most likely.'

'Christ,' Lockyer muttered.

'Tragic,' Dr Middleton agreed. 'If you're going to have to point that out to the partner in question, then rather you than me.'

'Thanks. But if she was hit over the head and left to die, it's still murder,' Lockyer said. 'Nothing else you can tell from the body?'

She gave a shrug. 'No signs of disease, no other injuries, except a childhood broken ankle. Signs of post-mortem predation in places, perhaps by rodents. I think finding forensic evidence on whatever gave her the wound will be your best bet – I'm not going to be able to match the fracture to any-thing. It just isn't pronounced enough.'

'Okay. Thank you, Dr Middleton.'

'It's fine to call me Robin,' she said.

'All right. Robin . . . that's a really nice name,' he said.

She smiled. 'Thanks. I'll let my parents know.'

'My girlfriend's expecting,' Lockyer said. 'We can't decide on a name.'

'Ah.' The tiniest hint of a let-down in her voice. 'I see. Congratulations.'

'Thanks. I'm . . . Matt's fine, by the way.'

'Right you are, Matt,' she said, already turning away.

Outside, Lockyer dialled Broad again. It still went straight to voicemail, and his WhatsApp still hadn't landed. *Nothing conclusive of events from Pippa's PM*, he wrote, in a new mes-sage. *All good?* He hit send and watched it not be delivered again. Felt a flash of impatience, bordering on irritation. He wanted to know where she was and what she was playing at, vanishing when she was supposed to be at work. But then he checked himself. Anger arising from fear – it was something Broad had pointed out to him. Particularly in men.

He got back into the car and set off for her place, faster than he should, his unease growing all the while. All the signs he'd spotted that something wasn't right, all the chances he'd had to intervene, to say something, that he'd let go by because he'd felt awkward about it. He drove with such fixed intensity that he almost ran a red light. Swerved onto the block paving again and went straight to the door. Thumped it hard with his fist. Again and again.

He kept it up with dogged determination until Pete finally opened it. His face was red and unshaven, his eyes shadowed. He looked as if he'd slept in his clothes. Lockyer hesitated, suddenly thinking there could have been a death in the family, or something like that.

'What do you want?' Pete said.

'Gemma didn't turn up for work today. And her phone's off.'

'Yeah. So?'

'So, where is she, Pete?'

'Thought you were her boss, not her dad.'

'Where the hell is she? What's happened?'

'Nothing's happened, she's just ... not well. Taking a duvet day,' Pete said sullenly. He kept hold of the door, and Lockyer was tempted to barge through it. They stared at one another, then heard a thump from upstairs that sounded very like a fist or a foot against a door, and Merry barking from further away. Maybe out in the garden. Pete's face tightened, and Lockyer did a quick calculation of how much taller and fitter he was than the younger man before shoving past him.

'*Oi!* For fuck's sake, you can't just come in here—' Pete broke off. He didn't follow Lockyer up the stairs.

'Gem? Are you up there?' Lockyer called, as he climbed. He thought he heard a muffled sound from behind one of the doors, and saw that it was bolted from the outside. A quick glance around the hallway told him that *all* the doors had bolts fitted to the outside. He didn't waste time wondering why anyone would do that, just started unlocking them.

It didn't take long to find her, standing in a guest bedroom with her hair a wild mess and her cheeks streaked with tears. At the sight of him she gasped, her face crumpling in dismay. She dropped her head into her hands, and Lockyer saw angry red marks around her wrists. The shock of the whole situation silenced them both for a moment.

'Gem,' he said at last. 'What the hell— Are you okay?'

'Yep,' she said, still behind her hands. 'I'm fine.'

'Come off it,' he said, fighting to be calm.

The front door slammed, and from outside they heard Pete's car starting, the engine gunning as he pulled away at speed. Broad sagged in relief.

'What the hell's going on?' Lockyer demanded. 'Did he . . . has he . . . hit you?'

'Not really,' she said, finally lowering her hands but still unable to meet his eye. She looked so miserable that it stabbed at him. 'Can we please not talk about it right this moment? I need to go and let Merry out of the shed.'

'Why is he locked in the shed? Why are *you* locked in the spare room?'

Broad swayed. She shut her eyes for a moment. 'Can we please not talk about it, guv?'

Lockyer bit back all his questions. He would ask them, but it didn't have to be now. The silence rang.

He cleared his throat. 'Want a lift to work?'

She nodded, wiping her face with her hands. 'I just need to . . . tidy up.'

'Take your time.'

'I'll just get Merry . . .' she mumbled, heading down the stairs.

Lockyer waited in the hallway as Broad got changed, and Merry bolted some food and bounced around, hyper-excited at being released. She found her phone in the kitchen, and switched it on to a slew of pings as all the stalled messages landed.

'I need to call the dog-sitter. See if she can take Merry for the rest of the day,' she said.

'Bring him with you,' Lockyer said, as much to cheer her up as anything. 'Considine's not in today.'

'Okay. Thanks. But he needs a walk—'

'Then let's take him for one now. I can catch you up on Pippa's PM just as well on foot as at the station.'

Still subdued, Broad nodded.

They walked to the end of the road, where a stile led into a field and previous dog-walkers had trampled the footpath to mud. Broad let Merry off the lead and he charged away, running sweeps along the hedgerows, gathering dirt.

'He'll make a mess of your car, guv,' Broad said, sounding a bit more like herself. As though her dog being locked up had been the most upsetting part of it all.

'He can try,' Lockyer said. 'I haven't cleaned the inside for about a decade.'

Broad smiled faintly.

Taking a chance that it would be easier to talk while they were walking, rather than face to face, Lockyer said, 'So . . . want to tell me what that was all about?'

She sighed. 'Not really, guv.'

'Were you in there all night?'

A reluctant nod.

'It looks as though we ought to be talking to Pete about assault and unlawful imprisonment. I've seen the bruises you've been getting lately, Gem.'

'I – I don't think he meant to—'

'Please don't defend him. I might blow a fuse if you do.'

She took a deep breath. 'I slept with someone else,' she said. Then put her face into her hands again, slowing to a standstill. 'Oh, *God*.'

Lockyer was stunned. It was about a million miles from what he'd expected her to say next.

'Oh. Right. Who?'

'Hardly matters *who*, does it?' she said, sniffing.

'No. Fair point,' Lockyer said. 'That's what started the row? Pete found out about it?'

'No, I – I told him. Weeks ago. He said he forgave me but . . .'

'But he hasn't.'

'I didn't *want* him to forgive me!' she said, with sudden vehemence. 'Oh, *God*. I've made such a massive balls-up of it all. Now he just keeps going on and on about us having a baby. About how that'll prove my commitment.'

'Prove your—' Lockyer cut himself off. 'You know that's not a good reason to have a baby, right?' It sounded far more like control. A way to keep her close to home.

'I know. I've tried telling him that. He says . . . he says it's hardly surprising he can't trust me any more.'

'Trust is – a separate issue. Trying to fix a relationship with a child is—'

'I know.'

They walked on in silence for a while, watching Merry chase a passing collie, having the time of his life. Lockyer thought back to something Broad had said about Nazma: that flirting or sleeping with somebody else could be a way to force a situation to a head. A way to end a relationship when you didn't know how to leave.

'Gem, if you want to break up with Pete you should just do it,' he said.

Broad looked away. 'You make it sound easy,' she said quietly. 'But it's not.'

He tried to understand. 'You've been together a long time. It'll be hard to unpick your lives, and start again, I get that. But if you're not happy, then isn't it better to just . . . rip the plaster off? Get it over with?'

'You *don't* get it, guv,' she corrected him sadly. 'Sorry, but you don't.'

He chose not to argue. 'Do you need a place to stay?'

'No, thanks. I'll be all right.'

'You're not going back there?' The words were out before he could hold them.

'I'll be all right, guv,' she said again.

'If Pete— If he . . .' Lockyer didn't bother to finish the sentence. They both knew he was actually powerless. Only Broad had any say in what happened next. 'I don't care what the row was about,' he said instead. 'What Pete did was completely wrong. Locking you in, preventing you going to work. Mistreating your dog. And if he restrained you, or handled you in any way that left bruises, that's assault. You know it is.'

'Yes.'

'It can't happen again.'

'What should I do? Taser him?'

'It's not funny, Gem.'

'I'm not laughing, guv.'

Lockyer thought of Philippa Harmon, storming upstairs to leave and ending up dead instead. Pecked by rooks, gnawed by rats.

'From observational experience only,' he said carefully, 'relationships rarely get any better once they've reached the point you're at.'

Her silence was bleak. She folded her arms against the cold, or perhaps against her own situation, then whistled for Merry, who by then was a brown and white speck in the distance.

'I thought you were going to tell me about Pippa's PM,' she said.

They went back to work, having reached an uneasy, unspoken agreement to pause the discussion. Lockyer toyed with the idea of paying Pete a visit in private, dismissing it because it felt disrespectful to Broad. But he would keep asking, he decided. He would keep checking in with her. And if she was ever prevented from leaving the house again, he'd arrest Pete himself.

In the afternoon the initial forensic report on Inez's

bedroom came in. Traces of blood and hair had been found, not on the open drawer Dr Middleton had spotted but on a front corner of the huge wardrobe. The samples had gone for testing, but nobody was in much doubt they'd be a match to Pippa.

'Well, I guess there's no question of Inez picking up the wardrobe and hitting her with it,' Broad said, sounding relieved.

'No, but she could have pushed her. That would still be murder, even if she hadn't meant to hurt her,' Lockyer said.

'Isn't it far more likely that she just tripped over the mess?' Broad said.

'Luckily for Inez, I think the CPS will agree with you.'

Broad nodded. 'You don't *really* think she meant to kill Pippa, do you, guv?'

'I don't know. On balance, probably not, but I'd be far happier if we'd managed to prove it, one way or the other. Because as things stand, if we're not clear what happened to Pippa, we're no clearer on what happened to Nazma, either.'

'Perhaps we never were.'

'You mean perhaps there's no connection between the two deaths?' Lockyer said. He got up, went to the whiteboard and tapped the photo of dried mud from the boot tread found near Nazma's bunk. 'This print puts Darren Mason next to Nazma's bunk the night she disappeared.'

'Does it, though?'

'Didn't we both decide it was too much of a coincidence, otherwise?' Lockyer said.

'I mean, yeah, it's Darren's boot print. But he could've

just been snooping around, right? Maybe looking for stuff to nick.'

'There's no way he found her escape bag and got rid of it without keeping the cash.'

'Agreed.'

'So you're saying it *wasn't* Darren?'

'No, guv. I'm just saying if it *was* him, we're going to have to find some other way to prove it.'

'Right,' Lockyer said. 'Any thoughts on what that other way might be?'

She looked apologetic. 'No.'

Lockyer flung himself back into his chair. Swivelled it to and fro. 'If Darren *was* the man in Marlborough, who snatched Nazma and brought her back to Trusloe Hall for some reason, and if Nazma then died at Trusloe Hall, she isn't there now. Agreed?'

'Agreed.'

'So maybe he took her straight to Savernake. Disposed of her there. Left the boot print when he got back and Inez told him about the escape bag – he or she having the idea of getting rid of it to make it look as though Nazma had simply bolted.'

'Or maybe Inez wasn't involved at all,' Broad said.

'Inez had a better motive to kill her than Darren – or, rather, a more convincing propensity. Darren wasn't even sourcing diazepam for Inez at that point, remember?'

'But he probably *was* nicking stuff from the house. And maybe getting up to other things we don't know of, but that *Nazma* found out about.'

'Okay. Agreed.' Lockyer stared at the board again, where he'd put up a map with red pins stuck into the key places: Trusloe Hall and the two dig sites; Marlborough, where Nazma was last seen; the spot along the River Kennet where her bag was found; Savernake Forest. 'Nazma isn't at Trusloe Hall, and she isn't in Marlborough. She's either way off this map, in London or beyond, or . . .' he pointed '. . . she's here.'

'Savernake,' Broad said. 'I'm pretty sure we won't get sign-off for a search of that size.'

'Course not.'

Lockyer went back to twisting his chair, trying to pick his way towards a next move, a way to advance the investigation when everything they tried seemed to lead to more maybes and nothing concrete. Nazma smiled her sweet smile at him from the whiteboard. He thought of Pippa's empty eyes, her grinning teeth. *Signs of post-mortem predation.* The glint of the silver locket around Nazma's neck, in every image of her they had. She'd been wearing it the night she'd gone missing; it was there in the photograph taken at the Marlborough Mop.

'Why take off her necklace?' he murmured, half to himself.

'What was that, guv?'

'Why take off Nazma's necklace – and it was *taken* off, not torn off – put it in her escape bag and chuck it in the river? Why do that?'

'In case it helped to identify her?'

'They'd have used DNA, even back then. And if people didn't know that, they knew about dental records. Right? So why take it off her?'

'I don't know,' Broad admitted. 'Couldn't have been for a trophy, since they didn't keep it.'

An email landed, snapping Lockyer to attention. It was the ANPR data, showing that Darren's VW Golf had passed through a traffic camera heading south on the A350 near Warminster at ten thirty-two a.m. on Monday, and north again at ten fifty-seven. Either side of their sighting of him near the Chapmans' house in Kingston Deverill, and very much in the area.

'Want to get him in, like you said, guv?' Broad said, with a trace of her old eagerness in spite of the blue smudges under her eyes.

'Let's hold off,' he said. 'He'll just deny everything again. Make up some bullshit about going for a drive. We know where he is – he's got a wife and a new baby. I doubt he's going to do a runner.'

'There really *could* be an innocent explanation, I suppose,' Broad said.

Lockyer shook his head. 'If there was, he'd have given it.'

'Okay, not innocent, but unrelated to this case.'

'Maybe.'

'I've spoken to Mr Stone Roses again. Rhys Birch. Told him to go away and remember where he was working on the second of that October, and come back with some way to prove it. I'll wait and see what he comes up with.'

Lockyer grunted his approval.

'So, what's next, guv?'

He spread his hands. 'Well, we can't take a search team to Savernake. But we can go ourselves.'

'Door to door?' She sounded sceptical.

'Door to door, Gem. Shoe leather. Like in days of yore.' He glanced at the window. 'But it'll be dark in an hour, so it'll have to be tomorrow.'

Lockyer felt wrong heading home at the end of the day, knowing – or, rather, not knowing – what Broad was going to face when she walked through her own front door. He'd always hated bullies, of every kind, and he counted in that group any man who'd ever used physical or psychological intimidation towards a woman. He remembered seeing his little brother get bullied at school, and longed for the simplicity of those days, when he would just wade in and meet violence with violence. Bloody noses and broken teeth. The primal pleasure of dishing out instant, unambiguous retribution. Things got a lot more complicated in adulthood. Even more so when you joined the police.

'There's nothing else you can do,' Hedy told him, once he'd given a brief sketch of the problem, mentioning no names. 'Not if your friend has declined your help.'

She sat down beside him on the sofa, and he looped one arm around her shoulders, still a little self-consciously, the gesture not yet so well worn as to be taken for granted. 'I know,' he said. 'I just don't ever want it to be another of my what-ifs.'

'You think she might be in real danger from him?'

'He manhandled her into a room and locked her in overnight.' Lockyer shook his head slowly. 'It'll only go in one direction from there, right? You see it so many times, in my job – a single punch thrown in a fight. A shove during an argument. Someone ends up hurt, or dead.'

Like Pippa Harmon, perhaps.

Hedy frowned. 'Locking her in – that's about control,' she said. 'Keeping her where he wants her. Curtailing her freedom.'

Lockyer felt a slight prickle. A faint echo of things he and Broad had discussed, as they'd speculated on the fate of Nazma Kirmani.

'He's always seemed a bit that way to me,' he said. 'The boyfriend. Checking up on her, tracking her phone, that sort of thing.'

'I guess you just have to trust her, if she's told you she'll handle it,' Hedy said quietly. 'And trust that she'll ask for help when she really needs it.'

'What if she can't?'

'You can't fix it for her,' Hedy said. 'If you go wading in when she's asked you not to, she won't trust you with it again.'

'Have you ever . . .' Too late, Lockyer changed his mind about asking. He ploughed on. 'Have you ever misbehaved as a way of ending a relationship?'

'No,' she said neutrally. 'But I didn't really have any serious boyfriends before Aaron.'

Aaron, who'd lied to her, deliberately conned her. Left her bankrupt and at breaking point.

'Sabotaging a relationship would never have been my style, in any case,' she went on. 'But if you'd been with someone since you were young, and if they'd been slowly oppressing you all of that time ... I don't think you can underestimate the sheer effort of guts and – and *will* it'd take to break away.' She shook her head. 'The sad fact is that, for a lot of women, leaving an abusive relationship is the single most dangerous thing they'll ever do.'

Lockyer stared at her, profoundly troubled by the statement.

They changed the subject, put *The Now Show* on the radio, batted some baby names back and forth. But Lockyer kept circling back through thoughts of Nazma Kirmani, and Philippa Harmon, and Gemma Broad. The parallels kept drawing themselves, and the unease that had lodged in his gut since that morning remained.

Hedy was also distracted. As they got ready for bed, she paused in the act of brushing her hair.

'Aaron didn't break me because of what he took, Matt,' she said. 'It wasn't because he'd been a bully, and it wasn't even because he'd made me love him.' She swallowed. 'It was because he'd made me believe that he loved *me*. That was how he did it. I trusted in him. Completely.'

She stared at him with a naked expression, and he understood what she was trying to tell him. How hard it was, now, for her to trust him. What guts it had taken for her to come back at all.

21

Day 18, Thursday

A glittering, sun-drenched morning. Early frost had melted into sparkling droplets on every leaf, twig and gutter. Broad arrived at the station on time, her face serious but not puffy. She was brisk and businesslike and, remembering what Hedy had said the night before, Lockyer chose not to push.

They drove for half an hour to the eastern side of Savernake Forest, where a scattering of farms and dwellings, including Douglas Smallbone's yard, sat at the edge of the ancient wood. Lockyer parked the car in a muddy lay-by, at a point where the lane closed to traffic and became a private track. They walked over to the gates of the yard, taking a good look before going in. Huge piles of tree trunks lay ready to be milled. There was a vast metal shed, and various smaller ones. Several pick-up trucks were parked, and the sound of machinery came from somewhere out of sight.

'Are we really going to just go in and *ask* him?' Broad said.

'Yep,' Lockyer said. 'I'm going to pretend we're unaware

of any connection between Nazma and Darren, or Small-bone – only to Savernake. Let's just . . . get a feel for him. Watch him when I ask about Nazma. He's a pro, so he's unlikely to give anything away, but watch anyway.'

Broad nodded, using her cuff to blot a drip from the end of her nose. They crossed the yard towards the main shed, and stepped into a space smelling powerfully of wood sap and machine oil. There was a rough and ready office cubicle at one end, but nobody inside it. They headed towards a far corner instead, where two men were feeding logs into a hydraulic splitter. Both wore thick padded shirts, filthy jeans, and safety boots.

'Excuse me,' Lockyer said loudly.

'Shouldn't be over here,' one of the men yelled above the din. 'The office is back that way.'

They showed their ID.

'DI Lockyer, Wiltshire Police. This is DC Broad. Could we have a word, please?'

The two men exchanged a look.

'Could you turn off the machine, please,' Lockyer shouted.

There was a deliberate pause. Then the second man drove his knee into the kill switch and lifted his visor. They were both young, still in their twenties.

'Thank you,' Lockyer said.

'What's this about?' said the first man, who had a bristling blond beard and watchful eyes.

'We're investigating the disappearance of a young woman who went missing in October 1999.'

'*1999?*' the blond man echoed incredulously.

'Yes. Our investigation has found a link to Savernake Forest, so we're going door to door, asking if anyone remembers her, or saw anything unusual at the time. Her name was Nazma Kirmani.'

Broad brought out Nazma's graduation photograph, but neither of the men so much as glanced at it.

'Do you recognize her at all?' Lockyer said.

The men shook their heads.

'Could you look closely, please? Any information at all might help us find out what happened to her.'

They did as they were asked, but then the blond man nodded at his colleague. 'Ricky wasn't even *born* in 1999, and I was five years old. Sorry, mate, can't help you.'

'Fair enough. Have you ever heard the name Nazma Kirmani?'

More head shaking. Always with that watchfulness, that default setting of silence.

'How long have you worked here?' Lockyer said.

'Him about a year,' said the spokesman. 'Me more like six. This is my uncle's place.'

'Oh, you're a Smallbone?'

'Yeah.' He glowered, as though even this was too much to have admitted.

'Could we take your names, please?' Broad chipped in. 'Just so we can keep track of who we've spoken to.'

'Ross Smallbone. This is Ricky Stanton.'

'Does Ricky not speak at all?' Lockyer asked.

'Not much,' Ross replied, unsmiling.

'Is your uncle around? We'd like to talk to him, or anyone else who might have been working here in 1999.'

Ross pulled off his headgear and gloves. 'Wait here.'

Without Ross to speak for him, Ricky wouldn't make eye contact. He sniffed loudly. There was a tense silence.

Lockyer had only ever seen Doug Smallbone's mug shot. In the flesh, as he came towards them, he was shorter than Lockyer had imagined, but barrel-chested. Somewhere in his early sixties, his hair and face were becoming grizzled, but his eyes glinted keenly in a face entirely devoid of warmth. Broad rocked slightly, perhaps fighting the urge to step back. The man's aggression was overt.

Lockyer didn't waver. 'Mr Smallbone?' No response. 'I'm DI Lockyer, and this is DC Broad. We're investigating the disappearance of a woman named Nazma Kirmani.' He showed Smallbone the photo. 'Do you recognize her at all?'

Smallbone gave the picture a brief glance. 'No.'

'Are you sure? Please look again. She disappeared from Marlborough on the night of October second, 1999, and we—'

'I don't need to look again, I don't know her.'

Smallbone stared up at Lockyer with cold hostility. Lockyer did his best to meet his eyes with a level non-reaction. He'd met the type before. Career criminals who felt about the police the way most people feel about cockroaches. Cockroaches that could give a painful bite.

'Were you in operation here in 1999?' he asked.

'Since 'seventy-seven.'

'Do you remember where you were on the second of October 1999?'

'No.'

'Do you remember seeing anything unusual around that time? Any unfamiliar vehicles or people acting suspiciously?' Lockyer already knew he wasn't going to get anywhere, he was just wasting a little of the man's time. Smallbone knew it, too. He took a breath, swelling his chest, then turned and walked away.

'Ross, see the filth off the premises,' he called over his shoulder.

With a tight little smile, Ross ushered them back the way they'd come. He stood in the doorway, watching, until they were clear of the gates.

Broad let out an explosive breath. 'Well! He was rude.'

Lockyer couldn't help smiling. 'Doug Smallbone was *rude*? There's the understatement of the year. He'd break our legs for the fun of it, if he thought he could get away with it.'

'I'm not sure we achieved a lot, there, guv.'

'Well, we let Smallbone know that we're looking for Nazma. If he *was* involved – or he knows that Darren was – it might cause a ripple; a trip-up of some kind, best-case scenario.' He took in Broad's sceptical expression. 'And, besides, I was curious to meet him. We'll get him for something, one day.'

'I hope so.'

They walked further along the lane to a row of three ter-raced cottages, their front lawns sodden with dew. Squinting in the low sun, they knocked at each of the doors, intro-duced themselves and asked their questions. It soon became a patter, because they got the same answers every time.

Nobody knew the name Nazma Kirmani, or recognized her picture, or could think of anything they might have seen at the time she disappeared. After the cottages there was a farm, with a series of converted barns: same answers again.

Lockyer consulted the map on his phone. 'There's a couple more places up ahead,' he said, nodding to where the lane got muddy and signs warned of a dead end. It led them into the woods, where the light flickered through a filigree of bare branches; a mulch of dead leaves was soft underfoot. In spite of their mission, Lockyer felt himself relax. There'd always been something about trees.

'So, this lichen in the soil sample, it only grows on the right kind of old oak tree,' Broad said. 'Did the scientist narrow it down to any particular part of the forest?'

'No. I suppose anyone walking past the right tree could've picked it up. But Smallbone's does all the forestry for the Savernake Trust, so if the oak in question had been cut down and milled, the lichen could even have been present on the yard.'

'Right,' Broad said. 'And I don't suppose the Trust keeps a record of stuff like that, either.'

'Of trees felled twenty years ago? No. Not likely.'

They came to another small house, reminiscent of a gate-house to a grand estate, and got no answer at the door. The windows were bare and Lockyer peered in, seeing a scatter of fallen debris in front of the fireplace, and a dune of dead insects along the windowsill. 'Empty,' he said. 'Has been for a while, by the look of it.'

'I hate empty houses,' Broad said. 'And not just because

there are so many people with nowhere to live. There's just something creepy about them.'

'Make a note of this one. If someone was living here in 1999 we could try to find them.'

'Guv,' she said, stopping just short of a sigh.

They could be wasting their time, Lockyer was prepared to admit. But the fact was that they didn't know what they were looking for, so the only way to find it was to search until they did – or until Considine called them off, which was perhaps more likely. He hated the thought. Remembered what Jason had said, the rainy night he'd come to see him: *Time doesn't heal. Not when things don't feel finished.* Hari and Liz Kirmani *needed* to know what had happened to their daughter. They needed to understand, and to believe that they weren't somehow to blame. That she hadn't simply walked out and left them. He remembered what he'd said to her brother, Andrew: *I will find the person responsible.* There was no way he could put aside the search, no way he'd let the dark thing he'd glimpsed slink away again, out of reach.

The last house at the end of the lane was small and Victorian, with scalloped fascia boards, and smoke rising from crown chimney pots.

'At least someone's in,' Broad said. 'Warren Cottage,' she read, from the sign on the front gate, and frowned.

'What?'

'No, nothing. Just . . . *déjà vu.*'

'We've not been going *that* long,' Lockyer said, and she smiled fleetingly, leading the way up the path. Trees surrounded the cottage and its garden, far taller than the chimneys.

Broad cleared her throat as she rapped her knuckles on the door, then delivered their spiel to the woman who answered. She looked to be nearing forty, with dark hair, a small, pinched face, and hunched shoulders. She didn't look well. Pink eyes, chapped lips, and a darting way of looking past them that seemed hyper-vigilant. Lockyer wondered if she was somehow connected to the Smallbone family, and lived permanently on edge as a result. Or if it was just Covid anxiety.

'Could I ask your name, please?' Broad asked sweetly, as if trying to put her at her ease.

'Christina Reeves,' she said, pulling the sleeves of her cardigan down over her hands.

'And can you tell us how long you've lived here?'

Christina's face twitched. 'Um, a while. Yeah.' She nodded. 'Quite a while now.'

'Were you living here in 1999, Ms Reeves?'

She nodded, her fingers going up to fiddle with her necklace, pulling the pendant back and forth on its chain with a faint rasping noise.

'Okay,' Broad said. 'This is a picture of the young woman I mentioned, Nazma Kirmani. Does she look familiar? Or do you perhaps recognize the name?'

A shake of the head. Hesitantly, Christina took the photo and held it close to her face. In need of glasses, perhaps. 'Is she dead?' she asked.

'We don't know,' Broad said. 'But we're trying to find her. Do you recognize her at all?'

'No. Sorry.'

'Do you remember seeing anything unusual around that time? Even if it doesn't seem important, it could be.'

As Broad said this a girl of about six ran up behind Christina, threw her arms around her legs, and peeped out at them from behind her hip.

'Oh, hello,' Broad said. 'And what's your name?'

The little girl smiled, but buried her face in her mum's jeans rather than answering.

'This is Angel,' Christina said, dropping her necklace to put her hand on the child's head. The pendant caught Lockyer's eye: a horizontal figure of eight, the symbol of infinity.

'That's a lovely name,' Broad said. 'Is it just the two of you, living here?'

Angel shook her head, and muttered, 'Olly.'

'My son, Oliver. He's only three. He's upstairs having his nap.'

She made no mention of the children's father, and Lockyer thought of a possible third reason for her nervousness: a broken relationship, a messy divorce. Maybe a custody battle.

'Well, we won't take up any more of your time,' Broad said. 'I'm going to give you my card, and if you think of anything, or if you ever need any help, please just give me a call.'

Me, Broad said, not *us*. Talking woman to woman, Lockyer surmised. Perhaps recognizing something in Christina.

'Thanks,' the woman said meekly. 'Sorry. I – I hope you find her.'

She shut the door, and Broad shot Lockyer a tight look that told him exactly what she thought: that here was someone living in a state of chronic fear. Someone else they were powerless to assist.

Back in the car, they checked the map again, then drove in the other direction to the last few houses still within striking distance of Smallbone's yard. No one had heard of Nazma, or had anything to say, other than one woman, who checked both ways along the lane before hissing: 'It'll be that miserable sod at the sawmill, bet you anything. He's a right dodgy bastard – you lot ought to do something about him.'

After that, they set off to find some lunch.

Edward Chapman looked slightly sheepish when Lockyer finally got him on screen, and asked again about Darren Mason.

'Well ... as far as I'm *aware*, he's never been here,' he said. 'But perhaps you'd better speak to my wife.'

He disappeared, and Antigone came on, her face so rigid that Lockyer suspected it might be her version of embarrassment.

'In actual fact, I *have* had cause to speak to Darren, on occasion, over the years,' she said. 'He keeps an eye on poor old Inez, you know.'

'We do know. He actually seems to care about her,' Lockyer said.

'Precisely.'

'So why would he drive down to see you? What did he want to say that he couldn't say over the phone?'

She gave a small sigh, looking off to one side. 'I haven't a clue – he *didn't* come here last Monday, so I've no idea what he was doing in the area. Perhaps he simply wanted an outing – I gather that those people who haven't had a terrible year have had a profoundly boring one.'

Lockyer's impatience flared. 'Well, Darren denies any association with you, so I know there's something I'm not being told. And I will keep on until I find out what it is.'

She tutted. 'Very *well*, Inspector. I thought he might be able to help me with something.'

'With what?'

'He cares for Inez, just as you say, and he sees that selling Trusloe Hall would be by far the best thing she could do, both for the house and for herself.'

'Selling it to *you*, you mean, to turn into a club.'

'Well, yes. Just so.'

'And for a song, no doubt. How very selfless of you.'

'I assure you, the sum I've been offering is more than fair, given the dilapidation. And Darren agrees.'

Lockyer took a beat. 'He agrees because he'll be getting a cut. Is that it?'

Antigone said nothing.

'So, you're basically paying the person your old friend – a vulnerable woman – most trusts and relies upon to pressure her into selling the home she loves.'

'Actually, I genuinely believe she *hates* the place. That's why she lets it rot. She stays because she can see no other way, not because she loves it. How could she? It's packed to the rafters with unhappy memories.'

HOLLOW GRAVE | 378

On that point, Lockyer was prepared to admit that Antigone might be right.

'How much are you paying him?' he asked.

'I really don't see how that's relevant. Or any of your business.'

'Why would seeing us nearby make Darren change his mind about coming to see you?'

'I have no idea. You'd have to ask him. There was certainly no arrangement for us to meet that day. But there's nothing illegal, or even immoral, about paying a finder's fee in a property transaction.'

'Well, you keep telling yourself that, if it helps. "Poor old Inez" might see it differently.'

'Spare me the disapprobation, Inspector. Inez ought to be in safe, warm accommodation, where she can be looked after. Selling that house is quite obviously her best course of action, and I can't imagine *anyone* could argue to the contrary.'

Lockyer cut the call angrily, because it was hard to disagree with her. It was only the cool, high-handed way she was going about it that put his back up. To his surprise, he also found himself slightly disappointed in Darren. As if Inez's insistence that he was a rough diamond, good at heart, had been stealthily convincing him.

Broad, who'd heard every word, turned her chair towards him. 'Poor Inez,' she said.

'Yeah. But Antigone has a point,' Lockyer said. 'The situation can't go on much longer. Remember what Darren said when we first went to see him?'

'He thought we'd found her dead.'

'And it's only a matter of time. That house would be a health hazard for a robust person, let alone someone with Inez's vulnerabilities.'

'I know,' Broad said. 'The thought of her tucked up in a nice clean hospital bed since we arrested her has been ... a relief.'

'Must be a load off Darren's mind, too. Perhaps they'll keep her in for a while, or at least until her addiction's under control.'

'So why would Darren swerve when he saw us, then deny everything?'

'Because he probably feels as guilty as sin for taking money to bully Inez.'

'Wouldn't that make him, like, a decent person?' Broad ventured.

Lockyer shrugged. 'He still took the money. So perhaps he's the sort of person who does the wrong thing for the right reasons.'

'Like helping to conceal a crime, for someone he cared about,' Broad said neutrally.

'Yeah,' Lockyer said flatly, not missing the obvious parallel to himself.

At the end of the day Broad stayed at her desk when Lockyer got up and shrugged on his coat. The sun had set and the windows were black, showing them their own wan reflections.

'Not heading off, Gem?' he said.

'I'm going to keep digging on Rhys Birch,' she said. 'He fits the description of the man in the car park with Nazma, and he does have motive. He emailed me his alibi earlier, thought I might see if I can blow it out of the water.'

The last thing Lockyer wanted to do was discourage initiative, but his gut was telling him Rhys Birch hadn't had enough at stake to kill Nazma. 'All right,' he said. 'But you know we're not going get overtime on this, right?'

'It's okay, I don't mind.'

He shoved his phone into his pocket. What to say, when it was obvious she just didn't want to go home? 'I could come back with you. If you wanted,' he said.

Broad looked up, colour rushing to her face. 'Why?'

'Just to . . . I don't know. Remind him what you do for a living. Remind him that you have friends who can do more to back you up than just . . . shoot him a dirty look. I could—'

'*No.*'

It was as close as she'd ever come to raising her voice to him. She dropped her head. Sat rigid. Then, in a more normal tone: 'Thanks, guv. But it really wouldn't help.' She took a breath. 'He thinks it's you.'

'It's me what?'

'You that I . . . slept with.'

Lockyer was startled silent for a moment. 'Oh. But that's ridiculous – I mean, it's not *ridiculous*, but I'm your boss. And twice your age.'

'Yeah. Well. That's what he thinks,' she said. 'And it doesn't matter how many times I tell him it wasn't because I won't tell him who it *was*, so . . .'

Lockyer didn't know what else to say. The silence hung awkwardly between them. 'I just . . . I'm here to help, if I can,' he said quietly.

'Work helps. Talking about it doesn't.'

A straightforward declaration that Lockyer completely understood. 'Don't stay too late. You're no use to me burnt out.'

'Night, guv.'

22

Day 19, Friday

Broad looked weary when she got to the office, just a few minutes after Lockyer. He wondered what time she'd eventually gone home. Or if she even had.

'Rhys Birch's alibi stacks up,' she said, sounding flat.

'Oh?'

'Yeah. He was working on the pilot for a comedy-crime series called *Hot Coppers* the night Nazma disappeared. They were filming on location in Bath – well within striking distance of Marlborough, which was exciting for about five seconds.'

'*Hot Coppers*? Sounds crap.'

'It was never picked up. The pilot aired in the autumn of 2000 and sank without trace. But I managed to get hold of some others on the crew, and it turns out the night of Saturday, October the second was the wrap party. They all went clubbing in Bath – two of them remember Birch being there until the small hours.'

'Right. Well, at least we can rule him out. Any joy tracing the Chapmans' au pair from 1999?'

'No. Both of their daughters have come back to me saying they didn't particularly like Greta and didn't stay in touch. I can try to find her on social media, but it'll be an uphill struggle.'

'Right.' Lockyer ran a hand along his jaw, gripping it hard. One by one, things that had seemed like leads were falling apart in their hands. Fizzling out. They needed a breakthrough – *another* one, since they hadn't managed to capitalize on the forensic link to Savernake Forest. But he didn't know where to look for it, and impatience was starting to crowd in on him.

'Where are you going, guv?' Broad asked, as he got back to his feet.

'Trusloe Hall. They're wrapping up the search there today.'

'Have they found anything else?'

'Not that I've been told. But we'll see.'

Albeit gingerly, the search team had been through every inch of Trusloe Hall to be sure that nothing of Nazma Kirmani's was hidden anywhere. They were spending the final morning trying to put things back more or less as they'd found them, but it was impossible: they were leaving it far tidier. Lockyer showed his ID to the officer at the perimeter, then made his way to the vaulted room with the empty well and Inez's dark, oppressive paintings. He gazed again at the one that looked like empty eyes, and the many featuring a malevolent chaos of rooks. *The Hollow Grave*, where the ground threatened to swallow the viewer without trace, which had convinced Lockyer, for a while, that Nazma was buried in the cist like the ancient ancestor before her.

The senior SOCO appeared at his elbow. 'We found this, sir. Thought it might be of interest.'

'Thanks,' Lockyer said, taking a heavy, damp photo album.

He opened it carefully, the pages parting with a tearing sound. Inez in her teens, standing with a man Lockyer assumed was her father, on the front steps of Trusloe Hall. Inez with people Lockyer had no hope of identifying. Smiling, intimate pictures of young women – Inez's various girlfriends, perhaps. And then, instantly recognizable from the portrait Inez had shown them: Philippa Harmon, wearing a white shirt tucked into black leather trousers, her auburn hair cut into a geometric bob, and those arresting amber eyes. Lockyer stared at her for a long time. She'd died in her early forties. So much life left to lose. Lockyer was still no clearer in his own mind whether or not Inez might have played a more active role in her death than she was willing to admit, even to herself.

He thought again of Inez's father, who'd drowned in his bath. According to Antigone, Inez had found his body. But had she done more than that? He'd been an abusive bully, scathing of his daughter's sexuality. If he was old, and unwell, it wouldn't have been hard for her to lift his legs, and keep his head under until it was over. Repeat killers didn't always target strangers to serve some twisted need. They sometimes attacked the ones they loved, and the ones who hurt them, because they knew no other way to cope.

He copied the picture of Pippa onto his phone. At least

they could put a face to the skull now pinned to their white-board.

Outside, as the crime-scene tape was taken down and rolled up, Lockyer spotted Darren Mason hovering near the front gates, his hands stuffed into his pockets. Their eyes met, and when Darren didn't turn to leave, Lockyer went over.

'They done snooping, then?' Darren said, squinting against the sifting drizzle.

'Yes.'

'Find anything that shouldn't be there, did you?'

'Other than the corpse of Philippa Harmon, no.'

Darren flinched, shook his head. 'Still can't believe that.'

'You really didn't know?'

'No, for fuck's sake. Inez told me just now, in the hospital.' He made an exasperated sound. 'Look, I'll put my hands up to lifting a few things over the years. Course, if you try and nick me for it I'll deny everything, but I did it. Some fancy candlesticks, some of her old man's snuff box collection. A painting that was just chucked in the basement – it was only some bloke on a horse, but I got over a grand for it. I stopped all that years ago, and even when I was at it I'd *never*'ve gone into Inez's bedroom.'

'Was it around the time Pippa supposedly left that Inez started sleeping downstairs?'

'Yeah, I suppose. Because she'd hurt her ankle, she said, putting her foot through the floor up there.'

Lockyer blinked. 'She's been wearing that ankle boot for *twenty years*?'

'Yeah. She started saying it wasn't safe to go upstairs, but any idiot could see that.'

'So, we know that upsetting events have extreme and long-lasting effects on Inez's behaviour,' Lockyer said. 'She drank more after Pippa "left", but she didn't develop her reliance on diazepam until after Nazma also "left". What happened that time, Darren? What upset her so badly?'

'I don't know. Just ... her going off, I guess. Leaving so soon after Pippa had—' Darren cut himself off, remembering that Pippa hadn't "left", and that perhaps Nazma hadn't, either. He swallowed. 'Inez really liked her. Nazma. She was the happiest she'd been since Pippa went, that summer.'

'And you really don't know what happened to Nazma?'

'How many times do I have to say it? I've *no sodding idea* what happened to her. On my life. All that stuff about my old man.' He shook his head heavily. 'If you think I'd go to him with something like that, you're mental. If you think I'd want him anywhere *near*— He'd have me for life, you get it? He'd *own* me.'

Lockyer saw the truth of this in Darren's troubled eyes.

'Someone who'd been to Savernake Forest was also in the barn, by Nazma's bunk, on the night she disappeared.'

'Yeah, I know how that looks – and I know you'd love to pin this on a Smallbone. But it *wasn't me*.'

Lockyer chose not to press the issue, for now. 'We know it *was* you driving down to the Chapmans' house the other day. Traffic cameras picked you up.'

Darren's shoulders sagged.

'And we know Antigone Chapman's paying you to persuade Inez to sell the house to her.'

'Fuck's sake,' Darren muttered.

'Not very nephew-y of you, Darren.'

He set his jaw defiantly. 'She needs to get out of that place before it kills her. I've been trying to convince her for years. Then one day Mrs Chapman collars me and offers to pay me for it.' A shrug. 'I was hardly going to turn it down, was I?'

'Apparently not. How much is she paying you?'

'Fifty grand,' he said, some of his defensive hostility returning.

'Tidy sum. Why were you going down there the other day?'

'Inez gave me the nod. Right before you carted her off she said she'd sell up. Mrs Chapman said I'd only get paid when her signature was on the contract, but we need the money – or an advance on *some* of it, at least. Nicky's boss fired her the second the pandemic started, the miserable twat. My work's dried right up, and with the new baby and everything . . .'

'But Antigone wouldn't pay up?'

'She said the terms of the agreement were clear. I went down to try and persuade her. I mean, Christ, what's a few grand to the likes of her? She probably carries that much around in her handbag.'

'So why did you leg it when you saw us?'

'Dunno.' He sniffed, looking down at his feet. 'Habit, I guess. I feel bad about it. About taking the money to . . . gang up on Inez.'

Lockyer shook his head. 'You should've been up front with me about it, Darren.'

'Whatever.' Darren turned to go. 'You going to nick me, then? For pinching stuff from the house?'

Lockyer shrugged. 'Probably not. Bigger fish to fry. But I will have you for the diazepam, if you continue to supply Inez. She's in the system now, and they'll help her with it. But you need to help her, too.'

Darren stared at him a moment longer, then turned and was gone.

Back at the station, Broad was slumped at her desk scrolling through endless search results for Greta Bessler.

Lockyer put a cup of tea beside her before collapsing into his own chair.

'Thanks, guv.' She sighed.

'Greta may well have got married, of course, and changed her name,' Lockyer said.

Broad's face fell even further. 'Now you point that out?' she said. 'Nothing of interest from the search at Trusloe?'

'A photo of Pippa for our whiteboard, but that's it. I did have a chat with Darren, though.'

'What was he doing there?'

'Just lurking. Curious about the search, I think. I asked him about the money Antigone Chapman's paying him. He admits to the deal, but he's not happy about it. They're up against it, him and his missus.'

'That's no excuse to take bribes to bully an old lady out of her home,' Broad said.

'Well, I don't think it's as black and white as that, but I take your point. And I think Darren does, too.'

'You're going off him as a suspect, aren't you?'

'I'm going off him as a killer. As for the disposal of a body on behalf of someone else . . . not sure.'

'So, what next?'

'Let's go and talk to the someone else.'

Lockyer had expected to find Inez in one of the elderly care units at Salisbury District Hospital, but reminded himself that she was only sixty-eight. She was actually on an endocrinology ward, and when he first looked he couldn't see her, and thought the nurse had got it wrong. But there she was in one of the beds, all but unrecognizable without her smudged make-up and outlandish clothes. She'd clearly been assisted to a thorough wash, and tendrils of clean hair were now draped over her shoulders. A drip was attached to one arm. She had her eyes closed and headphones on, and beneath the sheet, her toes were tapping.

'Hello, Inez,' Broad said. When there was no response, she touched Inez's forearm.

'Oh! Hello!' Inez cried, far louder than was necessary.

Smiling, Broad pointed to her ear, and Inez lifted off the headset. 'How *are* you, my dear? I'd say you look a little tired,' she said.

'I'm fine, thank you,' Broad said. 'More to the point, how are *you*?'

'Really rather good, actually,' she said. 'They *are* lovely here – nothing's too much trouble for them. They bring me meals, and cups of tea, and I can listen to music all day without a care in the world!'

Broad smiled. 'That's great, Inez. How's your leg?'

'Wretched sore, but it's something of a relief to have it out of that cast. They sent me for an X-ray, and, do you know, there's not a single thing wrong with my ankle? Other than this skin condition.'

'Well, that's great news too.'

Inez flapped the arm with the drip. 'I'm on some substance or other for it, and apparently my kidneys are rather dicky, so they're doing something about that while they're at it. But I've slept, Constable Broad! I've slept and slept. It's been *marvellous*.'

With rising optimism, Lockyer realized that Inez was more lucid than at any time they'd seen her before. Scrubbed bare, her face actually looked younger, in spite of being deathly pale, and out of the gloomy half-dark of Trusloe Hall he saw hints of green in her eyes.

'I'm glad to hear you're feeling better, Inez,' he said, and she turned to him with that same subtle cooling as always. He knew by now that it wasn't personal, that she had a preference for women that most likely had less to do with her sexuality than it did with past experiences. 'I've just been having a chat with your Darren.'

'He came to see me. Poor boy – he has an absolute *horror* of hospitals.'

'He mentioned to me that you'd decided to sell Trusloe Hall to Antigone Chapman.'

Inez looked startled. 'Well, I don't know what on earth

has given him *that* impression. He will keep asking, but I keep telling him it's *my* house, and she shan't have it.'

Lockyer and Broad exchanged a quick look. 'You're sure you didn't suggest that you might be willing to—' Broad said, but Inez cut her off.

'Absolutely not. It isn't really Tiggy's fault, it's the way she was brought up, but I never could stand to be badgered.'

'Right, okay,' Broad said. 'Darren must have got the wrong end of the stick.'

'I don't know how. I've been perfectly clear.'

Which meant, if Inez had it right, that Darren had lied. To Antigone, and also to Lockyer. A desperate attempt to get his hands on the money, perhaps, and he could always claim that Inez had changed her mind at a later date. Which was doubtless why Antigone wanted ink on paper before she handed over a penny.

'Would it be all right to ask you a few more questions?' Lockyer said.

Inez's face fell. 'About Pippa?' She gave a sad little sigh. 'It's like some dreadful dream. I know you won't believe me, but I genuinely didn't know she was ... Somehow I'd ... forgotten it. I drank, you see. I drank far too much, back then.'

'But you did see her, after she'd died,' Lockyer said, watching closely.

'Yes,' she whispered. 'Yes. It was *awful*.'

'We think she fell, and hit her head on the side of the wardrobe,' Lockyer said. 'Do you have any idea how that could have happened?'

'No.'

'You didn't argue? Perhaps get into a struggle?'

A solemn shake of her head. 'We argued, but that was why she went upstairs. It was *before*, not afterwards.'

'You're certain of that? There couldn't be more to it that you aren't quite remembering?'

Inez's eyes flooded. 'I don't *know* – how *can* I know, if I can't recall? But I would *never* have wanted to hurt her!'

'It's all right, Inez,' Broad soothed her. 'I'm sure it was an accident.'

Lockyer suppressed a flare of irritation. Inez was a tragic figure, and clearly vulnerable, but they were investigating a murder. Potentially more than one. Reluctantly, he decided to let it go, for now.

'What about Nazma Kirmani?' he said. 'Do you remember anything else about her, at all?'

Inez raised her watery eyes to meet his. 'But I'm sure I've told you all of it. The poor girl was getting very het up – first Antigone went for her that day, then she had a bit of a set-to with Darren. I never did get to the bottom of that. Unless it was about the baby, of course,' she mused. 'I suppose it *could* have been . . . though I rather doubt it.'

Lockyer felt the skin between his shoulder blades tighten. 'Tell me more about that, Inez,' he said evenly. 'Nazma told you she was expecting?'

'She did. Rather unwillingly – I don't think she wanted *anyone* to know, since she hadn't decided whether or not to keep it. But I found her in the barn one day, you see, weeping buckets, and out it all came. I gave her a hug, and told her she could talk to me if she ever wanted to. I'd been pregnant, in the past, and had an abortion.'

'That must have been difficult,' Broad said.

'Oh, yes. Very. But there was never any question of my keeping it, given how it'd come into being – I was raped, you see. It was while I was at college in London. Some fellow whose name I never even knew had his way with me at a party, while I was in no fit state. I think he might have put something into my drink.' She gave a little shrug. 'Men can be such *beasts*.'

'Oh, *Inez*,' Broad breathed.

'And then there's such a stigma attached to what one must do afterwards . . . I told poor Nazma there was no shame in it. If you're unhappy about mothering the child, for *whatever* reason, it's entirely correct not to go ahead.'

'Did Nazma tell you who the child's father was?' Lockyer asked, holding his breath for the answer.

'Well, Edward, of course, Tiggy's husband. They were an item, you know. Rather naughty of both of them – him particularly. It was supposed to be very hush-hush.'

Lockyer deflated. 'Inez, it couldn't have been Edward Chapman's baby. He'd had . . . a procedure, after his daughters were born. He wasn't able to father any more children.'

'Well, *yes*, that's why she was so upset. He'd told her it was all taken care of, and there couldn't be any accidents. But he'd lied.'

Lockyer let that sink in. 'We thought Nazma had perhaps found a new boyfriend that summer,' he said carefully.

'No, no, absolutely not. She was devoted to Edward – far more so than he deserved, in my opinion. She swore to me that she hadn't been to bed with anyone else since she'd met him.' She arched her eyebrows. 'The baby was his, and she'd been lied to. And left to deal with the consequences.'

Lockyer's heart was thudding. The dark thing in the shadows moved, trying to hide, but he was closing in. Broad was staring at Inez in shock.

Lockyer took a breath. 'Inez, had Nazma told Edward she was pregnant?'

'She . . .' A small frown. 'I'm not sure. I think not. I suppose that would have been *my* next question, but we were interrupted. That brutish archaeologist woman – Irene? Inga?'

'Ingrid? Ingrid Roach?'

'That's the one. She came bustling in to fetch some piece of kit or other, and made a snippy remark about falling behind with the schedule, so poor Nazma hauled herself up by her bootstraps and went back to work.'

'Did you get the chance to talk to her about it again?' Broad asked.

'I tried, but she really had no wish to discuss it. She swore me to secrecy – needlessly, I was quick to reassure her. She told me she'd decided what to do, and that she'd be all right . . .' Inez trailed into silence. 'How desperately sad, if she wasn't all right, after all.'

'Yes,' Lockyer said.

Inez gave a little sigh. 'Well, I had a root around a few hiding places and put together a little money for her, just to help. Though I had to insist she take it.'

Lockyer nodded. The hundred and seventy pounds in cash that had been in Nazma's escape bag. Broad reached down and took the sick woman's hand.

'Inez, would you like to report the rape?'

'Report it? My dear, it was a hundred years ago.'

'It's never too late, not these days. Whoever attacked you ought to face justice, don't you think?'

'Oh, undoubtedly, but I wouldn't know where to start. I didn't know his name, and I wouldn't know him now if I passed him in the street.' A shiver ran through her, and she added, quietly, 'Although, perhaps I would.' She patted Broad's hand. 'It's very kind of you to mind, but I think it's best forgotten about.'

They left Inez soon afterwards, once Broad had been down to the shop to buy her chocolate digestives, apple juice and a book to read. Back in the car, they sat in silence for a moment or two.

'So maybe Rhys Birch *was* telling the truth about them not sleeping together,' Broad said. 'And it can happen, right? Vasectomies can fail.'

'They can,' Lockyer agreed. 'Chapman said he got himself checked out after Mimi Draper fell pregnant, and that he was still sterile. That was in 1993.'

'Six years before he met Nazma. Is that long enough for something to have gone wrong with it?'

'I'm no expert, but I imagine so. That's not what's bothering me.'

'What, then?'

'Why was Nazma hiding in the barn in floods of tears, and telling Inez she'd been lied to? Why would she assume that, rather than that it'd been an accident? Why not go and tell the man she was so devoted to, even if her feelings *were* cooling? Why keep quiet, pack an escape bag and plan to run away to London?'

'Because she was scared of him,' Broad said quietly.

It was the only logical answer.

Lockyer nodded slowly. 'Let's go and ask him.'

23

This time, Lockyer pulled onto the driveway of the Chapmans' immaculate house with a swerve that sent the gravel flying. Broad shot him a small smile as she climbed out.

Chapman opened the door, and Lockyer saw that flicker of irritation again, just for a second before he managed to replace it with his affable, self-effacing smile. For the first time, Lockyer found himself wondering if there was more to it than impatience at being disturbed. If that flicker was the tip of an iceberg, a glimpse of something far bigger, and far darker, going on inside the man.

'Officers,' he said, amiably enough. 'Really, you're beginning to make a mockery of the whole concept of the lockdown. Could we not have spoken online?'

'We'll stay outside, if you like,' Lockyer said.

Something in his tone seemed to alert Chapman. He glanced over his shoulder, then said, 'Well, hold on. I'll fetch a coat and join you.'

He returned moments later. 'Probably best we're out

here, anyway,' he said. 'Tiggy's got some of her people in for coffee – strictly for work purposes. How can I help you, Inspector?'

'When was your fertility last checked, Mr Chapman?'

'I *beg* your pardon?' He gave a quick laugh.

'Your fertility. You told me you had it tested after what happened with Mimi Draper. Have you had it tested since?'

'Well, no. Why on earth do you ask?'

'I thought you might have done, given that vasectomies *can* fail.'

'I've had no cause to be concerned about that. My wife is— Well, I've had no cause to be concerned. Really, this line of questioning is incredibly intrusive, and I think I'd prefer not to discuss it.'

'Nazma believed that you were the father of her child.'

There were a couple of seconds of silence before Chapman replied. 'I honestly can't imagine how you've managed to construe that, Inspector, but, if it's true, I assure you she was mistaken.'

'She told a friend, and she was quite clear. And very upset, by all accounts. She *hadn't* slept with anyone else. The baby was yours, and she felt that you must have lied to her about your fertility.'

'*Lied* to her?' Chapman looked aghast. 'About something like that? I – I'm appalled she would think that. That I would deliberately mislead her . . .'

'But you hadn't been checked since 1993. So it's possible, isn't it, that your vasectomy had failed and you *could* father a child?'

'Well, it's *possible*, but after almost ten years I believe the odds are *vanishingly* small.'

'Would you be prepared to provide a sample, to be tested?'

'Really, this is becoming ridiculous, Inspector. No. I think Nazma must have been fooling herself – or perhaps endeavouring to hoodwink whichever friend she told. Perhaps she simply didn't want to admit that she'd been unfaithful to me, because if she *hadn't*, surely she'd have come straight to me, and told me what had happened? She knew I wouldn't have been angry with her.'

'Why should you be angry?' Broad said. 'It takes two people to get pregnant.'

Chapman gave her a quizzical look. 'Well, precisely.'

'But she didn't come and talk to you about the pregnancy? You had no knowledge of it?'

'As I already told you, no, I did not.' Chapman rocked back on his heels, hands in his pockets. 'I suspect that young man in the photograph you showed me is the more likely culprit.'

'We've spoken to him. He denies having had a sexual affair with Nazma.'

'Well, I'm sure it suits him no end to do so.' Chapman gave a solemn nod, as though reaching a conclusion. 'If I had accidentally got Nazma pregnant, and she genuinely hadn't strayed, then she would have come to me, and we'd have talked about it. And, no, it wouldn't have been convenient, but if she'd wanted to keep the child, she'd have had my full support. And likewise had she chosen to abort. But she didn't come to me, and I didn't know about it. And the only explanation for that is that the child was *not* mine, and she knew it.' He sighed. 'It sounds as though she'd got herself into a bit of a pickle. I only wish she'd been more *open* with me about it all.'

Lockyer let the silence hang. Their eyes met, and for another split second Lockyer saw that glint again, that trace of hostility, and something else – something almost like amusement. Gone so quickly he wasn't sure if he'd imagined it.

'Well,' Chapman said, 'I wish you happy hunting, Inspector.'

He went back inside, and his parting comment hit Lockyer like the shock of cold water. He stood blinking as the wind stung his eyes. Beside him, Broad found a tissue and blew her nose.

'You all right, guv?' she said, as they finally turned to go back to the car. Lockyer looked round at the beautiful house, the shreds of smoke whipping from its chimney pots. Everything so clean and perfect, not even any cobwebs at the corners of the windows.

'It's him,' he said.

'What?'

'It's Chapman. I *know* it is.'

'How?'

'God – we've been so blind! You said it yourself, Gem – days ago. Every week in this country, at least two women are killed by a current or an ex-partner. And Hedy said something else the other night: that leaving an abusive partner is the single most dangerous thing some women will ever do.'

'How did that ever come up in conversation?' Broad asked.

Lockyer didn't reply. He got into the car, and a second later, she followed.

'No one's ever said *anything* about Chapman being abusive,' she said, at length. 'Wouldn't Nazma have told her family? Her friends – her flatmate?'

'Have you told any of yours how Pete's been treating you?' Lockyer asked. 'Would *I* know, if I hadn't seen it first hand?'

Broad stared out at the hedgerow. 'No.'

'No,' Lockyer echoed gently.

'But he's not that type, is he? *Tiggy* wears the trousers – she's got the money and, as far as I can tell, she calls all the shots.'

'And isn't that just the *perfect* camouflage? He puts up with the emasculation because it gives him free rein elsewhere. No one suspects him. He can take it out on a young woman like Nazma – kind, impressionable, quick to trust.' A people-pleaser, as Liz Kirmani had described her. Susceptible, then, to persuasion.

'Antigone puts her husband's infidelity down to his mother being cold,' Lockyer went on. 'But what if that's only one piece of the picture?'

'What picture?'

'The picture of what turns a man into a murderer.'

Broad was quiet for a moment. Then: 'But if Nazma didn't tell anyone any of this, and even Inez didn't think she'd told Chapman she was pregnant, how are we ever going to *know*?' she said.

Lockyer started the car. 'I don't know. But we're going to have to find a way.'

'You can't be sure about this, though? About him?' Broad said. 'We really haven't got anything new on him.'

Lockyer checked his own sudden certainty. Chapman's carefully concealed moments of anger or scorn. The hint of amusement just then. The beautifully maintained portrayal of a hen-pecked husband. The way he'd come to the station to tell tales about Darren Mason, and probe for information on the direction of the investigation. Endeavouring to steer it.

'It's him,' he said again. 'And it's *all* about control. His alibi for the night she disappeared . . . we've basically been taking his word for it that he wouldn't have left his daughters by themselves. *Shit*.' He thumped one hand against the steering wheel in sudden fury.

'Yeah, but he also didn't have access to a car,' Broad said.

'But we've only got *his* word that the au pair was out all night in the nanny car – maybe she got home early. Maybe he was sleeping with her, too, and pressured her into covering for him – who knows? But it's the leakiest alibi of the lot!'

'Okay, it is, but a leaky alibi doesn't prove he did anything to Nazma. Or that he had a motive to.'

Lockyer pulled the car away abruptly. More strewn gravel. 'Well, we'd better bloody well find proof, Gem. We'd better go back through every last thing we've got with a fine-tooth comb. Because he did it. He killed her.'

It was getting dark by the time they got back to the station, and as they turned into the car park Lockyer caught a glimpse of a familiar figure, heading away down the street. Hands shoved into his pockets, shoulders hunched against the weather. Lockyer hit the brakes, leant out of the car.

'Jase!' he called. 'Jason!'

The wind snatched at his voice, and the figure didn't turn. Lockyer almost went after him, but changed his mind. The decision to confess to whatever was troubling him had to come from Jason, after all. Lockyer was already wondering if he'd been wrong to suggest that silence was golden, that it would be better for Jason to stay out of whatever it was. It simply wasn't his call. He got back into the car, and pulled forwards to park. Only as they both climbed out did he notice that Broad was radiating nervous tension.

'What's up?' he asked.

'Nothing. Was that Jason McNeil?'

'Yeah, it was.'

'What do you think he wanted? Why would he come here?'

'I don't know. He pitched up at my place on Monday night, too. Seemed like he wanted to tell me something, but in the end he changed his mind.'

'Tell you what?'

'Like I said, I don't know. He mentioned his brother – how he died. Something that had happened with his family in the past. I sort of suggested he should keep his mouth shut, but maybe I was wrong.'

Broad gave a short sigh and pinched the bridge of her nose. A gesture of profound stress.

'What is it?' Lockyer asked.

'Nothing. He ... uh ... I thought he might have been looking for me.'

'Why?'

She looked at him across the roof of the car, face lit on one side by the station lights.

'I ... went to see him a couple of times, at Old Hat Farm. After everything that happened this summer. I don't know. I felt bad for him, I guess.'

'I did, too. It's not every day you find out the people you love are murderers.'

'That wasn't it, exactly. I ... liked him.'

'Yeah, me too.'

Broad made an exasperated sound, and gave Lockyer such a significant stare that it dawned on him what she might be trying to say. 'Oh. Right.' He was disproportionately shocked. 'So, he's the one you ...?'

She gave a quick nod, and even in the low light he saw her cheeks flare. It ought not to have come as such a surprise. He'd noticed the chemistry between them, the subtle flirting, even while they'd still been working the case. He'd also noticed the way it had put his back up, ever so slightly. Made him feel oddly possessive of her – a feeling he'd done a careful job of quashing.

'Please don't tell anyone,' she said.

'Gem – as if I would.'

'No, I know. It's just ... *ugh*. It's all such a *mess*.'

'So, do you think you and Jase might ...?'

'No. I don't know. I really, seriously, need to just forget about it, for now.'

He thought back. 'And then I drove you over there a couple of weeks back. Talk about putting my foot in it. Sorry.'

'Please, *please*, forget about it.'

'All right.'

They carried on inside without speaking, and spent a while standing in front of their whiteboard. Lockyer grabbed a marker pen and drew a red circle around Edward Chapman. Affable, charming, subservient to his wife. But also a serial womanizer, and perhaps a predator. A wolf in sheep's clothing.

'So . . . why?' Broad said.

'Why kill her? I can think of two reasons. First, he thinks the baby isn't his. Takes it as proof Nazma has been unfaithful to him, and is planning to leave, and punishes her for it.'

'Okay. And the second?'

'He knows the baby *is* his, and they fall out about it. She's angry with him for lying to her about his fertility, as she sees it. Maybe he demands she gets rid of it, but she decides to keep it – and that's why she was planning on running away. Either way, it's about *control*.'

'It usually is, when a man is violent to his partner,' Broad said quietly.

'Right,' Lockyer said. 'He might not have meant to kill her. It could have been a row that got out of hand.'

'So we're saying he left his kids home alone—'

'Or with the au pair, if she *was* there.'

'Okay. Either way, he leaves late in the evening, drives to

Marlborough, and stalks the Trusloe Hall group until he can get Nazma alone. Frog-marches her to his car, and . . . what? Takes her where? Kills her how?'

'I don't know yet,' Lockyer said.

'Both versions depend entirely on one thing we also don't know,' Broad pointed out. 'If the baby was the flashpoint, and Nazma planned to leave because of it, then Chapman must have known about both. Nazma didn't tell him, as far as we can tell – and she definitely wouldn't have bothered packing a secret escape bag if she planned on telling him she was going. So, how did he find out?'

Lockyer stared at the board: everyone they'd looked at, everything they'd been told. 'I have a strong suspicion,' he said. 'But it'll have to wait till the morning.'

'Well, I'll come too, whatever it is,' Broad said at once, and he didn't bother to argue.

'You staying late again tonight?' he asked.

A shrug. 'Sure.'

'All right. I'll stay, too.'

'Shouldn't you get home to Hedy, and the bump?'

He hesitated, then shook his head. 'We're close, Gem. I can feel it.'

'All right. So, what do you want me to look at?'

'Everything. Go back to the finances, but focus on *Edward* Chapman this time. Look for . . . I don't know. Anything strange around the time Nazma disappeared. Or anything at all relating to a fertility clinic, something like that, because I bet you anything the Chapmans don't use the NHS.'

'Right, guv.'

He started doing the same – re-reading all his notes, all the things they'd been told, all the pictures they'd been sent.

Edward Chapman, trying desperately to climb the social ladder, to please his overbearing mother. Laughed at, derided, abandoned at the altar. *I felt as though the world had ended.* Nazma at the Marlborough Mop, with her guarded smile and the little blue bag they'd never found, wearing the necklace that they *had* found. That still bothered him – why either she or her killer had taken it off and put it in her bag. Nazma's silence, to her friends, her family, about what had actually been going on in her relationship that summer – about her pregnancy. She'd told her cousin Alina because she'd had to, and she'd told Inez because she'd been caught off guard. He wished he'd known what her decision about the baby had been. Because perhaps, even if she'd wanted to keep it, she *hadn't* wanted to stay with Chapman and be tied to him for ever by the child. As he'd said to Broad before, and come to fully appreciate: that was a lifelong bond. Whether you wanted it or not.

I always wanted more than two, Chapman had told them. *I wanted four, five, six, a whole gaggle in fact . . .*

'He killed the child, too,' he murmured.

'What was that, guv?'

'When he killed Nazma, he killed the baby too.'

'Right. So, that ties in with her refusing to have an abortion, right? And him trying to force the issue.'

'Except he loves children. Said he would've liked to have more.'

Broad shrugged. 'Could've been lying. Or he meant more

kids with his *wife*, not illegitimate babies with a girl half his age.'

'Yep, I take your point. Perhaps keeping up appearances – and keeping his wife – was more important to him than another child.'

'You don't sound convinced.'

'I'm not.'

'Well, you did say her death could have been an accident. Unintentional.'

'Yes. But I'm thinking about what Giannis Andino said. "I think she's in pain. Stomach hurting."'

They exchanged a long look. 'Something might have been going wrong with the baby, we thought,' Broad said. 'Or she'd been *deliberately* punched in the stomach.'

Lockyer gave a slow nod. The very idea made him feel sick. He clenched his teeth, assailed by the memory of small hands and feet pushing out from Hedy's belly to meet his touch.

'You got anything?' he said eventually.

'No. Well, one thing that might be interesting.'

'Tell me.'

'Just looking at Chapman's latest bank transactions. Earlier this month, on the fourteenth, he withdrew twenty-five thousand pounds in cash from an account at Lloyds in Warminster.'

Lockyer blinked. 'Twenty-five *grand*?'

'Yep. I didn't even know you could *do* that.'

'I expect he had to give them notice for such a large amount.'

'Well, anyway, he got it. That was on the Saturday. And on the Monday—'

'We headed Darren Mason off as he was about to pay them a call.'

'Right.' Broad sat back in thought for a moment. 'Maybe Edward decided to do the decent thing by Darren, and give him an advance on some of the money Tiggy'd promised? Even though she'd said no?'

'Maybe.' Lockyer frowned. 'But that would mean buying into Chapman's whole "friendly pushover" act, which I no longer do.'

'Or a coincidence. Chapman paid someone in cash as a VAT dodge? For something totally unrelated.'

'Except there's no such thing as a coincidence, right? But I seriously doubt Darren will tell us any different – or that he'll have paid the money into his bank account—'

'He hasn't. I checked that, too,' Broad said. 'He's *way* overdrawn.'

'All right. Note it as something to ask when we next speak to either of them. But I want something *concrete* before we do.'

They worked past eight, until Broad's stomach growled audibly and they called it a day. Walked out of the station with all the unspoken things about what Broad was going home to driving a wedge between them.

'Call me if you need me,' was all Lockyer said, as they parted. Broad's reply was a non-committal nod.

At home, Hedy was curled up under a rug on the sofa. Her

face, though still gaunt, looked younger and more peaceful in sleep. The dark fringe of lashes along her eyelids, the straight, resolute line of her nose. Lockyer sat down beside her as softly as he could. She'd been reading – the book was on the floor where it'd dropped. She had no friends who could come and see her, no family in the country. The quiet in the cottage was total, and Lockyer felt a pang of guilt. How solitary her days must be, while he was out and busy, wrapped up in his own desire to find Nazma, to get justice for her.

And he'd told her she'd get used to not having a TV. Like a sanctimonious arsehole.

He couldn't resist putting his hand on the bump. Waiting to feel that reassuring movement, and the almost unreal notion of a person related to him being on the other side of her taut skin. Not yet breathing but alive; hearing, feeling, waiting.

Something about Nazma's case clicked into place in his mind. The powerlessness he'd been feeling; the control a woman had over a baby, before it was born; his love for, and instinct to protect, his unborn child. *I can go, if you want,* Hedy had said, more than once. *You needn't see either of us again.* It was as much a threat as an offer.

Lockyer stiffened, moving away, and Hedy opened her eyes.

'Oh, good, you're back. I'm ravenous.'

She looked at him with the slight befuddlement of the newly woken, wholly trusting, just for that moment, and Lockyer relaxed. She hadn't meant it as a threat: she'd merely been signposting a clear exit. Probably as much for her own peace of mind as his.

'You shouldn't have waited.'

'I didn't. But I'm ravenous again,' she said. 'What's up? You look like you've seen a ghost.'

'I just realized something. About the case . . .'

'Oh. Right.' She sat up with a yawn. 'Well, if you need to go—'

'It can wait until the morning.'

'No, really—'

'It can wait. What do you fancy? You name it, I'll cook it.'

'Hmm, I would like a full spread of Mexican street food, please. Tacos, pulled pork, pickled chillies, empanadas, the lot.'

'Right,' Lockyer said. 'How about cheese on toast with hot sauce?'

'Bingo.'

24

Day 20, Saturday

They pulled up outside Ingrid Roach's mock-Tudor bungalow at half past nine in the morning. Rain was pouring steadily from a gunmetal sky.

'I realized last night we might've been getting it wrong about Nazma's pregnancy,' Lockyer said, as they pulled up.

'Oh? How so?'

'We've been assuming Chapman would have wanted Nazma to have an abortion, but maybe he didn't. Maybe he wanted to keep the baby. As a way of keeping *her*.'

Broad tilted her head. 'Then he's hardly likely to kill her, is he?'

'Could have been an accident – just like Pippa. And if Nazma was determined *not* to have the baby, that might have been *very* hard for him to bear. It could have started a fight that escalated.'

Broad didn't look convinced. 'Well. Let's get wet.'

There was no immediate answer to their knock, but

Ingrid's car was on the driveway and an upstairs light was on. So Lockyer kept thumping until she appeared in the window beside the door, twitching a voile curtain aside. She was dressed but it looked like a hurried job, and her hair was hanging loose. She opened the window a crack.

'It's *Saturday*, Inspector,' she said pointedly.

'Yes, it is,' he replied. 'We have a few more questions to ask you.'

'Well, they'll have to wait. This really isn't a convenient—'

'Would it be convenient for you to come back to the station with us – in Devizes – and talk there?'

She bridled. 'Don't be ridiculous. You've no grounds whatsoever to take me anywhere.'

'I very much do, if I decide that you're impeding my investigation, Miss Roach. So which is it to be?'

Ingrid stood back and folded her arms, leaving the window open. 'Well, I'm not inviting you in, and I'm damned if I'm coming out in this weather. So you'll have to get wet.'

'That's fine, we won't dissolve,' he said. 'How much did you tell Edward Chapman, Miss Roach?'

She rolled her eyes. 'This again? Really?'

'This time I want the truth.'

'I already told you—'

'I said the *truth!*'

His sudden shout silenced Ingrid, though her expression went quickly from shock to outrage. She reached for the window latch. 'I simply will *not* be spoken to that—'

'If you shut that window I will arrest you for obstruction. Don't try me, Miss Roach. I mean every word, and I am sick to death of being fobbed off. It's possible that your interference had serious consequences. So, you will talk to us, here or under caution at the station, and if you keep lying to me it *will* have consequences. Am I making myself clear?'

Ingrid looked furious, but also rattled. She pressed her lips together, which Lockyer took for acquiescence.

'You told Chapman you'd seen Nazma flirting with another man on the dig at Trusloe Hall.'

'Yes, but he really didn't pay any—'

'You went through Nazma's things in the barn, and found her escape bag.'

A single curt nod.

'You told Chapman what you'd found.'

'No. Not until— I thought she was going to just *go*, you see. And I was perfectly happy to let her.'

'But she didn't. She stuck it out until the end of the excavation. And one day you walked in on her in the barn, talking to Inez de Redvers. Nazma was very upset. She'd found out she was pregnant. How long did you loiter outside before interrupting them, Miss Roach?'

More silence.

'How much of their conversation did you hear?'

She drew herself up. 'All of it.'

'And how soon did you tell Chapman?'

Ingrid faltered, one eyelid fluttering slightly.

'You did tell him,' Lockyer said. 'Was that when you told him about the bag she'd packed as well?'

'I was just . . . I was so *disappointed* in him. To have been so careless! His poor wife, having to find that out . . . A *bastard child*, for heaven's sake.' She shut her eyes in disgust. 'I heard what that girl said – that Edward oughtn't to have been able to father a child. She was playing the innocent, of course, but I'd *seen* her with that other man, and I thought Edward ought to know.'

'So you went and told him,' Broad said, her voice scathing.

'He had a *right* to know! The girl was making a fool of him. I've no doubt she'd have carried on the lie, and – and *fleeced* the poor man until the child, that *other* man's child, turned eighteen.'

'What exactly did you tell him, Miss Roach?' Lockyer said.

She glared at him furiously. 'It was twenty years ago. You can hardly expect me to remember word for word.'

'*Try.*'

'I said . . . I said I thought I ought to warn him about it all, as a friend. She'd been planning to run off with her new boyfriend, and I told him he ought to just let her go, and not let her claim the baby was his. She had him over a barrel, after all – she could threaten to tell Antigone about their affair whenever she liked.'

'All things you had merely supposed, which had no basis in fact.'

'I know what I saw. And what I overheard—'

'No. You *don't*.' Lockyer struggled to contain his anger. 'How did Chapman take the news?'

'How do you think?'

'In your own words.'

'He was very upset. He actually went a little pale, as I recall. Speechless for a few moments. I felt desperately sorry for him, but at the same time – as I said to him – he was far better off without her. She was a shallow, selfish girl.'

Ingrid's self-righteousness was back. She lifted her chin defiantly, only to be met with such stony expressions from both Lockyer and Broad that she faltered again. 'He had a right to know!'

'Don't go pretending you had anyone's interests at heart but your own, Miss Roach,' Lockyer said. 'You invaded Nazma's privacy, extrapolated wildly, then told malicious tales. And it's very possible that in doing so you incited a serious crime.'

It was Ingrid's turn to go pale.

'Is there anything else you feel we ought to know? I recommend you tell us now, because if I have to come back again I won't be in such a lenient mood. Did you pass on *any* other information to Chapman, or to anyone else? Did you speak to Nazma at all – perhaps to advise her to move on sooner rather than later?'

'I never spoke to her.' Ingrid was subdued now. 'You don't seriously think . . .?'

Faced again with their silent stares, she didn't finish the question.

As they turned to go, Lockyer added: 'Don't even think about contacting the Chapmans to tell them about this conversation, Miss Roach, whatever spin you think you can put on it. Seriously.'

Lockyer watched Edward Chapman through the interview-room observation window. He was sitting with his legs crossed, hands clasped on his knee, just as he did at home. He didn't look nervous, or put out, or in any way interested in his dingy surroundings. Lockyer was more convinced than ever that it was an act.

He glanced at Broad beside him, seeing the doubt on her face. Chapman didn't look like a killer, with his claret-coloured jumper and navy-blue cords, his swept-back hair and handsome, benevolent face. He'd already proved himself a liar, but Lockyer wondered if they'd brought him in too soon. He wished they'd been able to find something concrete, something to give them more ammunition. Focusing, he led the way in and started the recording.

'Mr Chapman, you're being interviewed under caution in relation to the disappearance of Nazma Kirmani in 1999, and have declined legal counsel. Is this correct?'

'Quite correct, yes. I have nothing to hide. In fact, I'm not completely sure why I'm here.'

'You're here because you've been lying to us, Mr Chapman.'

'I don't believe I have.'

'You told us you had no idea Nazma was pregnant at the time of her disappearance. That was a lie. You told us you had no idea Nazma was planning to leave. That was another lie. You told us you didn't know anything about Nazma seeing anyone else in the summer of 1999. There's a third.'

Chapman's face showed nothing but mild confusion.

'We know that Ingrid Roach told you all of those things,' Lockyer said.

'*Ingrid?* You can't honestly think I'd pay any attention to anything she said. She'd have told me Nazma had three husbands and two heads if she'd thought it would break us up. She'd said similar poisonous things about other girlfriends of mine, in the past. I told her again what I'd told her before: that she ought to mind her own business, and that gossiping is a profoundly unattractive habit.'

'Why do you think she'd make up something like that?'

'Because she isn't terribly subtle, and she's inexplicably possessive of me. We had the merest hint of a fling about a century ago, but back then she simply would not keep her nose out. I'm not sure if she was in love with me or wanted to be my sister. Or perhaps it was my *wife* she worshipped. Who knows? I only know I'd be a fool to take her word on *anything* relating to my private life.'

'She told you that she'd overheard Nazma talking about her pregnancy, and it had no impact on you whatsoever? I find that hard to believe.'

'Well, I'll admit that I did ask Naz about it. Indirectly.'

'How do you ask someone "indirectly" whether or not they're pregnant?'

'I said I'd heard a rumour, and wasn't it funny, given that people didn't know I'd had a vasectomy? She laughed. Assured me there was nothing in it at all.'

'Really?'

'Yes, really, Inspector.' Chapman raised his eyebrows. 'And I believed her. Ingrid was – and doubtless *remains* – a thoroughly unreliable source.'

'Why didn't you tell us any of this when we first asked you about the possibility of Nazma having been pregnant?'

'Well, for the exact reasons I just set out, Inspector.'

'We believe Nazma planned to travel to London to have a termination. How did you feel about that?'

'You mean how *would* I have felt, had the child existed, and been mine?' The ghost of a shrug. 'I'd have felt rather sad, I imagine.'

'That's all? Such lukewarm affection for your newest child.'

The tiniest flicker crossed Chapman's face, gone before Lockyer could read it.

'Well, change the adverb to "very" then, if it suits you better,' Chapman said. '*Very* sad. But I'd have understood. I wasn't planning to leave Antigone, and Nazma had her career to think about. Raising a child almost single-handedly could only have set it back.'

'You wouldn't have helped?'

'I would, of course. Financially. And I'd have continued to see them as much as I could. But it wouldn't have been love's young dream, and I'm sure Nazma would have understood that. But this is pure speculation, Inspector. Nazma told me she wasn't expecting, and even had she been, the child couldn't have been mine.'

'And yet you aren't prepared to prove that you remain infertile.'

'I simply feel no need to. It strikes me as being singularly irrelevant when Nazma had been seeing somebody else, and when I had nothing to do with her running away.'

'Oh? I thought you paid no attention to anything Ingrid told you, which would include the – inaccurate – report that Nazma had been unfaithful to you?'

Chapman's gaze remained entirely dispassionate.

'I merely meant to say that if the tale about there being a baby on the way *was* true, then perhaps the rest of it was, too. I find that far more plausible than that one of my *vas deferens* reattached itself of its own accord. And I'm surprised to hear that you do not.'

'Were you having an affair with your au pair, Greta Bessler?'

Chapman laughed. 'I'm sorry – forgive me, but what on *earth* can have given you that idea? And just how much energy do you suppose I have, man?'

'Another young girl, away from home, lonely and in need of friends. Perhaps it was straightforward enough.'

Chapman sighed. 'And this would be to debunk my alibi for the night Nazma ran away, I suppose? Well, sorry to disappoint you, Inspector, but no, I didn't seduce my children's nanny. There's a revolting expression that nevertheless springs to mind in this instance – that one ought never to mess where one sleeps.'

His calm was impenetrable. They only had Ingrid's word against his. Lockyer fought to keep his frustration from showing. There was no point threatening to get a court order to take intimate biometrics from him – they didn't have enough evidence, and Chapman knew it. And in any case, his being fertile again now didn't prove that he'd been fertile in 1999. All Lockyer had was his instinct about the man, and that wasn't going to get him an arrest.

Chapman cleared his throat diffidently. 'I do understand, you know.'

'What do you understand, Mr Chapman?' Lockyer said.

'How puzzling it is that Nazma's bag should turn up now. How odd it is that, wherever she went, she didn't take it with her. But the fact remains that she clearly *did* plan to leave, and she made good on that plan. She presented herself in London, to reassure the police that she was well. It serves no purpose for me to speculate as to why she left so precipitously, but I can't help feeling that you're . . .'

'I'm what?'

'Jumping at shadows, Inspector.'

'Nazma's family say the woman who presented herself at Islington police station *wasn't* their daughter.'

'I'm sure they're *desperate* to believe it wasn't her,' Chapman said sadly. He leant forwards, resting his hands on the desk. 'It's been hardest on them by far, of course. But who on earth was it, then? Which is the more likely scenario? That the young woman who looked like Nazma, and had documents proving her identity, *was* in fact Nazma, or that some imposter nobody has seen before or since was sent in her stead?'

They had no choice but to release Chapman without charge. Antigone, who'd been waiting in the car park, drove him away with a face like thunder, and Lockyer supposed his own expression wasn't any better as he watched them go. He had a scrambling feeling in his gut. Fear of having to let Chapman go for good. Of having to give up and move on.

'Guv?' Broad appeared at his elbow. 'Coming back up?'

He watched until the silver Range Rover was fully out of

sight, then gave a silent nod. Considine was calling when they reached the office, but Lockyer didn't answer. He went to stand in front of the whiteboard, hands in fists at his sides. 'We can't let him get away with it, Gem.'

'We just . . . We haven't got enough.'

'Then we need to look again!' he snapped.

'Look where?' she fired back. 'I don't want to contradict you, guv, but what if Chapman's right? It looks weird that her bag was in the river, but we still don't know *why* it was. We've been guessing all along. I mean, maybe she legged it that way, for some reason, and dropped it by accident. Or maybe whoever picked her up in Marlborough was *helping* her, and they'd been to fetch it.'

'And accidentally dropped it into the river?' Lockyer asked scathingly.

'It's *possible*,' she insisted. 'It'll be what a defence counsel will say. Or the CPS – or most likely the DSU, before we've even got that far.'

'Fuck's sake,' Lockyer muttered. She was right.

'We've convinced ourselves that this was a snatch and kill. But maybe the reason we can't prove it is because there *isn't* proof,' Broad said. 'Because it – it never happened. Nazma planned to leave, and she left.'

Lockyer threw himself into his chair, and pushed impatiently at the papers on his desk. Always messy, compared to Broad's orderly workspace. He tried to make himself consider her words, but they were impossible to swallow. *I wish you happy hunting*, Chapman had said. *She talked about him less, and smiled less when she did*, Nazma's flatmate, Emma

Billingham, had said, right back at the start. *Because she was scared of him*, Broad had said, only recently. *She said things weren't what she'd thought*, Alina Shah had told him. Surely, this was the slow dawning that the man Nazma had loved was not who he pretended to be? *Far too good at pretending to be something he isn't*, Inez had said.

'Why would you pack an escape bag, and have it ready?' he said.

Broad took a deep breath. 'Guv?'

'If you were planning to leave, why would you do it in secret?'

'Because you expect someone will try and stop you,' she said.

'Yes. And not try with words – not try to persuade you to stay. *Make* you.'

He moved more papers, turning up a photo of a smiling young woman with exuberant blonde curls and slightly crooked teeth. Mimi Draper. He stared into her eyes and wondered what she might have been able to tell them about Edward Chapman, had she been alive. Had she survived the end of her relationship with him.

Then he saw it.

He sat up abruptly, scrabbling for the picture and looking closer. He was right. It was tiny, but the resolution was good and the silver was catching the light.

'Mimi Draper is wearing the same necklace Christina Reeves was,' he said, lurching up and handing Broad the picture.

'What?'

'Christina Reeves, at Warren Cottage in Savernake. Remember? She was wearing the exact same necklace. The infinity symbol, on a silver chain. She kept fiddling with it – tugging it around.'

'Are you sure, guv?'

'One hundred per cent.' His heart was thudding. 'That links Mimi Draper to Christina. And Christina links us to Savernake Forest. Gem? What's wrong?'

The colour had drained from Broad's face, and she'd put one hand over her mouth.

'Are you feeling sick?'

She shook her head. 'Oh, God,' she murmured, turning to her computer and clicking through a few tabs until she found the right one. Scrolling down. When she found what she was looking for, her hand went back to her mouth, aghast. 'Oh, my *God*. I'm – I'm so sorry . . .'

'What is it?'

'It doesn't say Savernake Forest, you see. It's just a Marlborough address, so I . . . didn't . . .'

'*What* is?'

'Warren Cottage.'

'Christina's place?'

'It belongs to Farview Property Management. Edward Chapman's company. It's one of his empty houses.' She looked at him tearfully. 'Except it's not empty. I'm so, *so* sorry. The name rang a bell when we were there but I didn't connect it . . .' She hung her head. 'I just missed it. I can't believe I missed it.'

She sounded so crushed that Lockyer's flare of indignation

was immediately smothered by the urge to console her. Awkwardly, he put a hand on her shoulder. 'It's okay, Gem. Really. It's no big deal.'

'It *is* a big deal. I should've spotted it.'

'You've spotted it now, so stop beating yourself up and get your coat.'

Lockyer forced himself not to speed. Huge puddles at the sides of the road dragged at the wheels as he ploughed through them. It was early afternoon but seemed to be getting dark already, the sun smothered behind thick layers of cloud. They drove in silence. Broad was still pale, her eyes glassy and staring. She'd been distracted – but not without good reason. Lockyer dropped the ball now and then for the very same reason; they were only human. Later, he'd say all this to her. Right then his whole focus was on the road, on getting them to Savernake Forest as fast as he safely could.

'You take the lead, Gem,' he said, as they pulled up outside the Victorian cottage at the edge of the woods. 'This is going to need a light touch.'

Christina opened the door and flinched at the sight of them. A faint twitch of her face and body, as though she'd hoped never to see them again and would have liked nothing more than to shut the door. Her wariness bordered on fear.

'Hello, Christina,' Broad said. 'Sorry to bother you again. Could we come in for a minute, please? We'd just like to ask a couple more questions, and it's cats and dogs out here.'

Christina hesitated, then stood back to let them in.

Inside, the cottage was warm and plainly furnished. She

led them through to the sitting room, where the little girl, Angel, was watching *Peppa Pig* on TV, and a small boy was building shapes with Lego Duplo. A fire was burning in the grate, and along the mantelpiece were photographs of other, older, children. Christina gestured them towards the sofa, and perched herself on the edge of an armchair.

'What's this about?' she said quietly.

'We understand that you rent this cottage. Is that correct?' Broad said.

Christina nodded.

'Do you mind me asking how much rent you pay?'

'I . . . uh . . .' Christina swallowed. 'I'd have to check.'

'Of course. Do you know the landlord much at all?'

Her eyes flicked from Broad to Lockyer, then down at her lap, where she ran her nails over the fabric of her jeans. 'I – I've met him. Once or twice.'

'We believe his name is Edward Chapman. Is that right?'

She looked at them, clearly trying to guess what they were driving at. Eventually, she gave a noncommittal sort of nod. Broad shot Lockyer a look. It was going to be hard work.

'That's a pretty necklace,' she said brightly, as though just noticing it. The infinity symbol on its silver chain, glinting at the base of Christina's throat. 'Was it a gift?'

At the mention of it, Christina looked down again. She started to shake. 'It's an . . . um . . . eternity necklace,' she said, so quietly that the TV almost drowned her out.

Broad leant towards her and spoke in a low voice. 'We can help you, Christina. We can protect you. If you want to leave, there are places you could go, safe places, for you and the kids.'

Christina looked at her with hopeless, frightened eyes. 'I *can't*,' she whispered. 'You can't *leave* him. He won't let you.'

Lockyer looked at the little boy, concentrating so earnestly on his building blocks. Blue eyes, with a backward sweep to his forehead. 'Edward Chapman is the father of your children,' he said. 'Isn't he, Christina?'

Christina gazed across at giggling Angel, and earnest Oliver. Picked up her pendant and slid it to and fro. Her lips moved a little, but she said nothing.

'Christina, please listen,' Lockyer said. 'We really can help you, but we need you to talk to us. Do you know anything about Nazma Kirmani? Did he ever . . . bring her here? Do you know what happened to her?'

An expression of pure fear crossed her face. 'I need you to go,' she said. 'I – I can't talk to you. I don't know anything.'

'Christina—'

She stood up. 'Please. I need you to *go*.'

Lockyer stood as well. Tried not to tower over her. 'Okay. But please tell me just one thing, and then we'll leave you alone. Did Edward Chapman give you that necklace?'

She didn't respond at once. Lockyer wasn't sure she was going to. Then, eventually: a single, shaky nod.

They hurried back to the car, where the rain was sliding down the windscreen in a solid curtain.

'Do you really think those are his kids, guv?' Broad was obviously shocked.

'I do.'

'What about his vasectomy?'

'What proof do we have that he ever had one? We never even got Antigone to back it up – she was out of the room when he told us. I think he lied to us about it, just like he lied to Nazma and to Mimi Draper. And probably to Christina, at least at first.'

'Jesus. I mean, I know he said he wanted more kids, but that's mad—'

'It's not about the children, Gem. It's about the mothers.' Lockyer was thinking fast. 'How many empty properties are on Farview's books?' he asked.

'I'd have to check. But it's about twelve, I think.'

'Twelve? Jesus Christ.'

'You don't think . . .' Broad stalled as the implications sank in. 'You don't think he's got a girlfriend in *every one* of those?'

'I don't know. But we need to check. And I think "girlfriend" might be a gentle euphemism for the situation they're in. Because those *are* his kids in there – I'd bet my life on it.'

'*Shit.*'

'You said just the other day that Nazma's necklace couldn't have been taken as a trophy, since whoever it was didn't keep it. But what if it was about making her wear that eternity necklace instead?'

'Like . . . *tagging* her?'

'Exactly like tagging her.'

She swallowed. 'That's horrible.'

'He gets them pregnant so they can't leave him,' Lockyer murmured. He could barely imagine how Nazma must have felt when she realized that. No wonder she'd planned to escape without telling him. 'We're bringing him in. We can link him to Savernake now, and I want him in custody while we check his other properties.'

'Is it *enough*, though, guv?' Broad sounded worried. 'Isn't he just going to throw his hands up and confess to having a mistress at Warren Cottage? He could've picked up that lichen on his boots just by going to visit her, right? By going for a walk near Warren Cottage.'

'And then depositing it right by Nazma's bunk?'

'But we – we can't *prove* the print was made that same night. Or why.'

She was right, but Lockyer didn't want to hear it. 'I want him in custody. We can arrest him with reasonable grounds, and push him till he lets something slip.'

'And if he doesn't let anything slip?'

'Then hopefully Christina will. Or someone else in one of his "empty" properties. But we're bringing him in, Gem. I'm *not* letting that bastard get away.'

With that he swung the car around, and put his foot down.

This time it was Antigone Chapman who opened the door, with a sigh of displeasure.

'Mrs Chapman. We're here to see your husband,' Lockyer said.

'Again? It's only a couple of hours since you last saw him.'

'Certain things have come to light that we need to talk to him about. Is he here?'

'No. He had to pop out, but he'll be back soon.' She ran her eyes over their streaming coats, their sodden shoes. 'You'll have to go around the back, to the conservatory.'

They did as she asked, and Antigone made a show of unlocking the glass doors unhurriedly, while they got even wetter, before letting them in.

'Where is he?' Lockyer snapped.

Antigone sighed again. 'Just up the road, with a neighbour. Their Aga is forever going out, and Edward has a knack for getting it going again. I'm sure he won't be long.'

'When did he leave?'

'About an hour ago, I suppose. Perhaps a little longer.' She frowned briefly. 'I expect they've given him a glass of wine for his efforts. If you want to take your coats off, I could hang them to dry while you wait.'

'No, thank you,' Lockyer said.

They remained standing there, and Antigone's expression drifted gradually from bemusement to affront, then into discomfort. She clasped her hands together, rubbing one thumb into the opposite palm.

'What is it that's "come to light", Inspector?' she asked at last.

'I'm afraid I can't discuss that with you, Mrs Chapman,' Lockyer said.

'He won't have done it, you know. Whatever you think he might be mixed up in.' She left a gap that Lockyer didn't fill, then said: 'Is this something to do with Savernake Forest?'

Lockyer was jolted. 'What makes you say that?'

'I spoke to Darren yesterday. He told me about your search of Trusloe Hall, with sniffer dogs and all sorts, and you finding Pippa buried in all the mess, dead as a doornail. And that you suspected him, but only because of his family in Savernake. I think he was trying to reassure me that it was all groundless, in case I were to pull out of our deal.' She looked troubled. '*Do* you suspect him?'

Neither Lockyer nor Broad replied.

'But, in any case, you can't imagine *Edward* is involved?' she went on.

'Not in that, perhaps,' Lockyer said.

'Then in what? I know he's always had a slightly . . . slipshod approach to his finances. Is that it? I'm sure it won't be anything *sinister*, Inspector. Edward simply isn't the type.'

'Your husband recently withdrew twenty-five thousand pounds in cash from one of his bank accounts. Do you have any idea what that was for?'

'No. I do not.' Antigone swallowed. 'That *is* it, then? Some sort of . . . dodgy deal?'

Lockyer studied her closely, picking up a trace of hope, a trace of relief, in her question. 'No,' he said. 'That's not it.'

The silence hung.

'He's a weak man, Inspector, but he isn't a bad man.' Antigone's defiance was losing steam.

Lockyer gave her a hard look. 'I think you might be wrong about that, Mrs Chapman.'

'Perhaps I'll give him a quick call. Hurry him up,' she said.

'Stay where you are, please,' Lockyer said, and she halted, more from surprise than obedience.

'Really—'

'Did he take the car?'

'Yes. Not very green-spirited for such a short trip, but in this filthy weather . . .' she said.

'Would you normally expect him to be gone this long?'

'Well, no. But, as I said, they've probably offered him—'

'They rang, did they? The neighbours?'

'Yes, of course they rang. They're forever ringing to—'

'Did you speak to them?'

'No. Edward answered the phone.'

'Has anyone else called since then?'

'No. I don't see what—'

'Stay here. Where's the phone, please?'

Antigone looked bewildered. 'It's on the table in the hall— Oh, do please take off your shoes!'

Lockyer ignored her, striding across the plush carpet to pick up the phone. He dialled 1471 and listened for a few seconds. Then slammed the receiver down.

'Gem! Let's go!'

She hurried over to him, Antigone right behind her.

'It was an 01672 number,' Lockyer said. 'That's Marlborough.'

'*Marlborough?*' Antigone echoed. 'That can't be right. I'm going to call Edward and—'

'*No!*' Lockyer's barked command pulled her up short. She stared, her face stripped of its usual composure, its usual disapproval, and oddly blank as a result. 'Do *not* call him, Mrs Chapman. I mean it.'

'But why on earth not?'

'Did you tell your husband we were looking at Savernake Forest? Did you tell *him* we'd been using a cadaver dog?'

'Well, I . . . Yes, I suppose I did. Not that we've talked much about that girl—'

'Stay here, Mrs Chapman. We'll be in touch soon. And if I find out you've called your husband, I will arrest you for assisting an offender. Do I make myself clear?'

'I really don't understand any of this.'

'Just wait here, and don't call him. Don't call anyone.'

They retraced their steps, Lockyer squinting past the flailing wipers and the dazzling headlights of the oncoming traffic. He hit one puddle so hard that the steering wheel bucked and wrenched in his grip, and for a sickening moment he had to fight for control. Broad grabbed the door handle with a gasp, and Lockyer forced himself to slow down.

'Sorry, Gem,' he muttered. 'I want him to be there when we arrive.'

'Christina must have called him right after we left,' Broad said.

'We spooked her. Shouldn't have expected her to trust us, just like that. To turn on him after all these years. She was obviously terrified.'

'Should I call for some back-up?'

'No. Hold off until we know what's going on there.'

'Don't you think she could be in danger?'

Lockyer didn't answer at once. If he was right about Chapman, and why he'd gone straight there when Christina called, she was in very real danger.

'All right – call it in. See if uniform can do a welfare check. Tell them to observe but *not* to intervene, unless the situation immediately warrants it.'

He focused on the road while Broad got on the phone, hoping they'd beat the responders there. He didn't want *anything* tipping Chapman off. He wanted to catch him in the act – and he had a fair idea what that act might be. His pulse was jumping, and the thought that Antigone might ignore his threat and call him, the thought that they might get there to find him gone, was excruciating.

It was fully dark when they reached Warren Cottage again, the rain unrelenting. Lockyer tried turning off the headlights for their final approach, but he couldn't see a thing. He pulled up a good way back along the lane instead, and grabbed a torch from the glove box.

'Ready?' he said, and Broad gave a terse nod. 'If it gets violent, keep back. If he is who I think he is, he's a killer.'

'If he gets violent I'll kick him where it hurts,' she said grimly.

'Yeah. Or that.'

There was no sign of a squad car as they reached the cottage, but Chapman's car was parked right outside. Lights were on inside the house, but the curtains were closed.

'What's the plan, guv?' Broad asked quietly.

'Hold on here. Shout if you see anything. I'm going to check at the back.'

He made his way round to a garden overarched by dripping branches. There was a sagging wooden shed, and a plastic washing line with pegs dotted along it. A foot gate led through into the forest, and Angel's pink bicycle was leaning against the back wall of the house. The kitchen window was bare. Carefully, Lockyer peered in. Through the door into the living room he saw Christina, sitting on the edge of the sofa. She was shredding a paper tissue in her hands, her face streaked with tears, but she appeared unharmed. There was no sign of the children, or of anyone else. He waited a full minute in case Chapman appeared, then returned to the front door.

They knocked. Christina didn't respond.

'Christina?' Broad called through the letterbox. 'It's DC Broad again. I'd just like to see if you're okay.' She waited a few beats. 'Could you open the door, please, Christina?'

'Come on,' Lockyer said, leading the way to the back door.

As he'd suspected, it wasn't locked. Christina jumped up as they let themselves in, her face slack with fear.

'You can't just come in here!' she cried. 'You *can't*!'

'Where is he, Christina?' Lockyer said. 'Where's Chapman?'

'He's – he's not here. I don't know who you mean . . .'

'Look, I know you're frightened, but I need you to trust us. Please. Is he upstairs?'

A tremulous shake of her head.

'Then where? We know he's here somewhere – his car's outside.'

'He isn't,' Christina whispered. 'He was but he – he went again.'

'On foot? Where?'

Tears dropped down over her cheeks. She flicked her eyes towards the back of the cottage.

'He went out the back? No, we'd have seen him as we— Wait, you mean into the forest?'

'Will I . . . will you take the children away from me?' she asked. 'He always said you would, if I . . . if I ever said anything.'

'He lied to you, Christina,' Lockyer said. 'Stay with her, Gem, and chase that back-up. I'm going after Chapman.'

He grabbed the poker from beside the fire and ran out of the door, through the garden gate and into the waterlogged blackness of the forest.

Lockyer's night vision was good, but this darkness was more like a physical substance than a simple lack of light. The narrow beam of his torch jerked ahead of him as he ran a few metres almost blind. He made himself stop, think. Turned the light to the ground instead, and picked out water-filled footprints, fresh enough that the rain hadn't blurred them out. He followed them at a steadier pace, sliding on moss and squelching mud. At least the rain meant that Chapman wouldn't hear him coming – its constant roar drowned out everything else. He strained his eyes as the footprints led him about two hundred metres into the trees. Then, up ahead, he saw a pinprick of light between the trunks.

He turned off his own torch and carried on, careful not to give himself away as he drew closer to the edge of a small clearing, at the centre of which stood a gnarled oak tree, raising its dead, bare branches into the night sky. A figure was digging beside it; stamping a spade into the saturated soil. Lockyer could hear his ragged breathing even over the rain. He'd propped his torch against the tree trunk to free his hands, and a plastic sheet was rolled up on the ground beside him.

'So, this is where you buried her,' Lockyer called.

Chapman's head jerked towards him, grimacing as he tried to see, ribs heaving like bellows. The rain had slicked his hair down over his forehead. He was no longer handsome.

'Inspector,' he gasped. 'Tenacious bastard, aren't you?'

'Usually.'

'Don't come any closer. I have a gun.'

'Let's see it, then,' Lockyer said.

Chapman took a firm grip of the spade, and gave a mocking grin. 'Ah, well. There you have me,' he said.

'No. Guns aren't your style, are they?' Lockyer said. 'Young women, all of them petite – just like Lara Chamberlain. I expect you like to use your bare hands on them. Does it make you feel like a man?'

Slowly, Lockyer went closer.

'I can still cave your head in with this shovel, if I have to,' Chapman said.

'Come off it,' Lockyer said. 'What good will that do? It's over.'

'*Over?* Who the *hell* are you to say so? And I imagine I'd find it enormously satisfying.' He hefted the spade. 'One might as well be hanged for a sheep as a lamb, after all.'

Lockyer was close enough now to see the hole Chapman had been digging. And, in the edge of the torch beam, a scrap of rotten, colourless carpet. His stomach twisted at the sight. All this time. While texts had been sent from her phone, while a woman had pretended to be her in London, while her family had hoped against hope: she'd been here, all that time.

'Were you planning on moving her?' he said.

'It seemed wise to, since you'd found Christina, and some link to Savernake,' Chapman said. 'And I've been hearing all about your bloody sniffer dogs that can find a body at the bottom of the sea.'

'Where were you going to take her?'

'I hadn't quite decided. All a bit on the hoof, to be honest. But there are other places.'

'Your other empty properties, you mean?'

Chapman's face writhed, and Lockyer knew he'd landed a blow. 'We have officers heading to each of them as we speak,' he lied. 'Perhaps some really are empty, but perhaps some have residents who'll be relieved to talk to us. And they will *all* be searched.'

'Ha!' Chapman grinned again. 'Tenacious *bastard* . . . Come on, then! Come and get me. Let's see if you can – my spade versus your . . . What *is* that? A fire iron? Good grief, all a bit Mickey Mouse, isn't it?'

Lockyer shrugged. 'I've already got you,' he said calmly, even though his pulse was ticking in his throat. 'I only need to stop you getting away. Back-up is coming, so if you feel like making a run for it, now's your chance. Not that you'll get very far.'

Chapman was up to his ankles in mud and still gasping for breath. His face was a snarl, and Lockyer saw that he wasn't remotely ashamed to have been caught – or at all frightened. He was *furious*. As if on cue, a flicker of blue lights came through the trees way off to Lockyer's right, and he heard snatches of raised voices coming up behind him. Chapman heard them too, and lurched forwards with a strangled roar, teeth bared, swinging the spade high over his shoulder to strike.

A split-second calculation. Lockyer dropped the poker, took two strides forwards, one step to the side, and swung his fist hard into Chapman's face. The wet crunch of his nose was intensely satisfying, even as pain shot through his own hand. Chapman collapsed to his knees with a groan, and Lockyer wrenched the spade from his hands.

'Edward Chapman, I'm arresting you on suspicion of the murder of Nazma Kirmani on or around the second of October 1999. You do not have to say anything, but it may harm your defence if you do not mention when questioned something which you later rely on in court. Anything you do say may be given in evidence. Do you understand?'

Chapman made a revolting hawking noise.

'Sit tight,' Lockyer said coldly. 'One of the lads might know some first aid.'

25

Day 22, Monday

Nazma Kirmani's post-mortem examination took place first thing in the morning. Lockyer and Broad made sure they were there on time to observe. Laid out on the steel table, her skeleton looked almost childlike: narrow shoulders and hips, tiny hands and feet. The time she'd spent in the fertile ground of Savernake Forest had robbed her of almost everything but her bones; no flesh or hair remained, just the stained remnants of her plastic watch and gold trainers, and a necklace, darkly tarnished. The symbol for infinity on a silver chain. There was no trace of the baby that had died with her. Those bones had been too fragile to endure.

Dr Middleton was definitive on the cause of death.

'Her hyoid bone is broken in three places,' she said, her voice tinny over the intercom into the observation room.

'Strangled?' Lockyer said.

She nodded. 'With some force. Her neck must have been severely compressed to cause an injury like this.'

He thought of Chapman's tanned arms in the episode of *Dig Britain*, the long-fingered hands and hard, sinewy muscles. Felt that deep fury again. When he glanced at Broad her face showed a different emotion: some strange mix of sorrow, guilt and fear.

'Okay, Gem?'

She glanced at him. 'Yep. I mean, no. But yep.'

'Yeah. I know what you mean.'

Edward Chapman had been stripped of his clothes and personal belongings, and put into a custody-suite tracksuit. He wore it as though it were very much beneath him, but besides that slight discomfort, and his bruised and swollen face, he seemed at ease. His nose had been straightened, and was splinted with a criss-cross of plaster. His eyes were bloodshot, and had crimson rings beneath them. Lockyer tried to remain measured as they went in to interview him, but it wasn't easy. There was nothing whatsoever to justify what this man had done to Nazma Kirmani. No mitigation of any kind. He'd simply killed her because it had suited him, perhaps because she'd defied him. And he showed no signs of remorse whatsoever.

Chapman didn't fidget as Broad ran through the preliminaries for the recording. Legs crossed, hands resting on one knee, as always. He'd appointed his own solicitor, but they neither spoke nor looked at one another.

'Tell me about the night of the Marlborough Mop, on October second, 1999,' Lockyer said. 'Constable Broad has managed to track down your au pair's friend, Katie Goodwin, who was working as a stable girl for your neighbours, the Tuckwells, at the time. She confirms that she was with Greta that night, but that *she* always drove them when they went out. She didn't trust Greta to remember to drive on the left. So we know the nanny car was at your disposal.'

'Indeed it was.'

'And you *did* leave your children unattended that night.'

'Sadly, it was necessary. But they were sound asleep. I'm certain they never knew anything about it.'

'You went to Marlborough.'

'I did. I knew a group of them were going, including Nazma. I also knew how crowded Marlborough would be. It's very easy to disappear in a crowd.'

'And to make someone disappear.'

'Well, quite.'

'Talk us through what happened.'

'I think you have the gist of it already. Nazma left the others to relieve herself. I followed her, and tried to talk to her. But . . .' he shook his head sadly '. . . she'd uncovered a stubborn streak in herself that I don't think either of us had been aware of before then.'

'That *you* hadn't, perhaps. Did you believe what Ingrid had told you? That she'd met somebody else?'

'Oh, she admitted to that readily enough, but she swore it'd been merely a flirtation, nothing physical.'

'But you didn't believe her?' Broad said.

'I very much *did* believe her, in fact.'

Broad blinked. 'But then why did you . . .?'

'Why did I kill her? You can say it, Constable. None of us will shatter,' he said, with faint amusement.

Broad simply stared at him.

Chapman gave a slight sigh. 'She just *would not* see things my way. My girls stay with me – it's about *loyalty*, you see. They stay with me, and raise the children, and in return they are looked after. They never have to work a day in their lives. Nazma said she'd decided to leave me. Just like that. She refused to *consider* keeping the baby.' That flicker of suppressed anger crossed his face. 'I'm afraid I simply couldn't allow it.'

Lockyer felt a vague tug of unease. Something to do with the anger he'd felt when he'd found out Hedy was pregnant, and was keeping the child. No discussion. That feeling of impotence, and how he'd resented it. It shamed him, now. He fundamentally refused to have *any* common ground with the man sitting in front of him.

'She wasn't *your* girl,' he pointed out. 'And it's not about loyalty. It's about control. You tie them down with children. You make them dependent on you.'

'Well, I see little point in arguing with you about it, Inspector. I doubt you'll ever see it my way.'

'You're right. I won't.' Lockyer took a breath, keeping his temper on a tight rein. 'Why did she plan to run, when she found out she was pregnant? Why didn't she just come and tell you?'

'I've wondered about that, too. But she was intuitive, and perhaps I'd been a bit heavy-handed with certain things, that summer. I'd had to insist she stop taking her birth-control pills, you see. I'd told her how bad for her they were, and that she didn't need to poison herself with them while she was with me. She was stubborn about it, but eventually agreed. Then I found out she was still taking them, in secret. We had a bit of a row about that.'

'How much of a row?' Broad asked. 'Did you hit her?'

'Well, no, but perhaps I gave the impression that I might. That was an error. One always achieved a great deal more with the carrot than the stick, with Nazma.'

'But she stopped taking it?'

Chapman nodded.

'So when she fell pregnant, she probably guessed you'd done it on purpose,' Broad said.

'That would be my surmise. An *accidental* pregnancy is always preferable. It's the perfect fait accompli, and eliminates so much tedious deliberation. Women have all sorts of instincts that kick in. Well, usually.'

Lockyer waited for Broad to follow up on this, but when he glanced at her she'd gone ashen.

'Nazma wouldn't agree to have the baby,' he said. 'You marched her to the car in Marlborough. Then what?'

'We drove for a while. It was all rather fraught, but she wouldn't change her mind. And I'd been so patient with her – so understanding when she would insist on wearing that relic of her mother around her neck, rather than the pendant I'd given her. I'll admit I was rather angry by then. For all her tears and her pleading, *she* had caused the situation, you see. If she'd only done as she was supposed to, everything would have been fine.'

'You mean, you'd have installed her as a brood mare in one of your properties, while you moved on to the next young woman.'

He looked rueful. 'I knew I was taking a risk with her, right from the start. She had friends, and close family. That often complicates things. But I simply couldn't resist those dimples.'

Broad was looking at Chapman as though she might either throw up or attack him. Perhaps both. Lockyer knew exactly how she felt.

'Tell me what happened,' he said.

'I drove her to Savernake. Pulled up in a quiet spot. And I gave her another chance to . . . well, to do the right thing. To do as she was told.' He leant forwards slightly. 'But nothing I said would change her mind, and she didn't even have the sense to lie to me about it. So, I lost my temper.'

'How did she die?' Lockyer asked.

'With my hands around her neck.'

'Because she stood up to you.'

'Because she'd proved herself a disappointment. Both wilful and ungrateful.'

'*Ungrateful?*' Broad choked out.

Lockyer shot her a warning look. 'What happened next?'

'I buried her, as you know.'

'She was wrapped in a carpet. Where did that come from?'

'Warren Cottage, of course. The sitting-room rug. Christina helped me.'

'I imagine that has helped Christina to stay "loyal" to you ever since.'

'Oh, yes. Very motivational, I'm sure. But she's always been a good girl, that one. Knows when she's well off. Pregnant at the drop of a hat.'

'Then what? Once you'd buried Nazma?'

'I went back to Trusloe Hall. Ingrid had told me about her escape bag. It was too good an opportunity to miss – she'd been planning to run away, so why not let everyone think she had?' An easy shrug. 'I'd already made her text those garish friends of hers, to say she was taking a taxi home from the Mop. And I had her phone, so I could send a few more messages to allay suspicion.' He paused to reflect. 'I do wish I'd kept that escape bag, though. Or disposed of it more thoroughly. If I had, I dare say you and I would never have met, Inspector.'

'Why didn't you?'

'Oh, that lump Darren turned up. Saw me in the barn. I should have confronted him, but it had been a long night and, like a fool, I let him rattle me. So I headed off, and threw the bag into the river.' A small sigh. 'He's been blackmailing me, you know. You ought to haul him up for that.'

'Darren Mason's been blackmailing you? For how long?'

'Only since you turned up and started asking about Nazma. I suppose he finally put two and two together about my being there that night. Not the sharpest, but he got there in the end. A one-off payment, he said. But it never is, is it?'

Lockyer said nothing.

'I might have had to resolve the situation differently, eventually,' Chapman added. 'If he'd made a habit of it.'

'Lucky for Darren that we've caught you, then.'

This was met with a stony silence, and Lockyer saw that, for all his composure, Chapman didn't want to be reminded that it was all over. His unfettered life of lies, abuse and control. 'Tell me about Mimi Draper,' he said.

At this Chapman lifted his eyebrows, and said nothing.

'Come now, Mr Chapman,' Lockyer said. 'As you said yourself, you may as well be hanged for a sheep as a lamb.'

'Ha! I suppose you're right.' Chapman glanced at his brief, who gave him a subtle nod. 'Mimi was another mistake. I had no idea how unstable she was.'

'Was her baby yours?'

'Oh, yes. At least, I think so. I'm fairly sure she *had* been unfaithful to me, you see. But, in any case, she wouldn't stop drinking, and taking all sorts of things. Drugs. She was harming the baby, you understand – deliberately harming it. Oh, it was *vile*.'

'And her death?'

'Entirely necessary, I fear.'

'You pushed her down that stairwell?'

Chapman's stare was steady. 'I did, and I don't even think she minded, particularly. Barely a murmur as she fell.'

'What about Lara Chamberlain's "accidental" overdose? Was she your first?'

'Lara?' He raised his eyebrows. 'No. I'd have quite liked the chance, it's true, but she did that to herself.'

'And you never actually had a vasectomy.'

'Oh, I did. I tried to get out of it, but Tiggy was adamant – practically marched me to the clinic. So I went ahead and had the procedure. The final trophy in her cabinet: my balls.' He smiled. 'It really was unbearable. I felt like half a man. It was reversed about six months later, up in London.'

'How did you manage to conceal that from your wife?'

'With ease, and a little careful management. Tiggy has never been particularly interested in sex.'

'DC Broad has identified twelve apparently empty properties on the books of your company, Farview Property Management. One of them is a maisonette on Liverpool Road, in Islington.' It was a stone's throw from Alina Shah's place near Barnard Park. Lockyer had been so close to it when he'd gone to talk to her. 'A woman by the name of Carmen Perera lives there. She's of Sri Lankan heritage. She wears one of your necklaces, too.'

A young Asian woman of similar age and build to Nazma, from an entirely different country, with an entirely different face. It hadn't mattered. They'd looked the same to Police Sergeant Keith Wheeler.

'Now, you're not to trouble Carmen with any of this, Inspector,' Chapman said seriously. 'She was simply doing as I'd asked. I want to make that very clear.'

'Oh, we won't be bringing any charges against her. But she *was* the woman who posed as Nazma, wasn't she? After you'd given her Nazma's handbag and wallet.'

In the still from the CCTV: the flash of a silver necklace at the girl's throat.

'And she did an admirable job.' Chapman actually sounded proud.

Lockyer took a moment. He wanted nothing more than to

crack Chapman's façade. To be able to infuriate him again, even if he couldn't frighten or shame him.

'She was very happy when we told her you'd been arrested,' he said.

'Was she indeed.'

'Oh, yes. Burst into tears by all accounts. She kept thanking the officers who'd given her the news. Over and over again.'

'Well, Inspector, perhaps you ought to go and meet her so that she can thank you in person,' he said coldly.

'Do you know I might just do that?' Lockyer said.

'How many other bodies are we going to find?' Broad cut in. Chapman turned his bloodshot gaze on her, and it became curiously empty. She was young, she was female. There was a flicker of derision in his eyes, and Lockyer wanted to re-break his nose for him.

'I really have no idea how many you'll find.'

'How many have you *killed*?'

Chapman didn't answer at once. 'It has never been about killing them,' he said eventually.

'No,' Lockyer said. 'It's been about keeping them. A collection. A harem of women too frightened to leave you. Is your ego really that fragile, Mr Chapman? Has it made up for being abandoned by your father, and ditched by Lara Chamberlain?'

'I wouldn't expect you to understand.'

'And if any of them ever had the nerve to try to leave, you made sure they'd only do it once.' *You can't leave him.* 'How many children have you fathered, Mr Chapman?'

At this, Chapman looked proud. 'Forty-two, at the last count.'

'I doubt you'll see any of them ever again.'

'Well, that hardly matters.'

'No. They were only ever a means to an end, weren't they?' Lockyer shook his head. 'You're right, Mr Chapman, I don't understand, I'm very glad to say.'

Once Chapman had been led away Broad all but bolted from the room. Lockyer gave her a moment before following, and found her leaning against the front wall with her head tipped back, letting the cold wind blow into her face. Breathing slowly.

'You okay?' he asked. 'I was worried about you in—'

'I'm *fine*,' she snapped. 'Sorry. It's just . . . that man. Being in the same room as him . . .' She shuddered. 'I mean, he's . . . evil. Properly *evil*.'

'Yeah. He is.' Lockyer leant on the wall alongside her. 'But we got him, Gem. He can't hurt anyone else ever again.'

'Those women . . . the ones who are still alive, and the families of the ones who aren't, they'll hurt for the rest of their lives.'

She was right. There was no way around it. 'But at least they'll know he's hurting too.'

'*Can* you hurt someone like that?' she said. 'He's not normal. Doesn't seem like he feels *anything*.'

'Not for other people, no. But for himself? You bet he does – and I don't think it's hit home yet that it's all over. That the rest of his life is going to be *properly* shit.'

'Well, I wish I could be around to witness the moment it does.'

'We might have to make do with knowing that it will. Sooner or later.'

She nodded slowly. 'He's not what I thought a serial killer would be like.'

'He's got good camouflage,' Lockyer said. 'They often have. That's how they get away with it. The odd one looks like a monster, but most don't. And they don't write riddles, or leave clues. There's no *artistry*. They're just . . . mundanely awful people, killing for sexual gratification, or to make up for one inadequacy or another.'

Broad rolled her head towards him with a desolate look in her eyes.

'They're also very rare,' he added.

'How many never get caught, do you think?' she said. 'How many are so well camouflaged that they keep on killing, and getting away with it, all their lives?'

There would be some, perhaps many, though even one was too many.

'Not this one, Gem,' he said. 'We caught this one. Hang on to that.'

At the far side of the car park, Lockyer spotted a silver Range Rover with the silhouette of someone at the wheel. He left Broad and went over. Antigone Chapman was in the driver's seat, still buckled in. She was staring straight ahead, and flinched when Lockyer knocked on the window.

'Mrs Chapman,' he said, when she lowered it. 'Your

husband is going to be staying in custody for now.' For ever, if Lockyer had anything to do with it.

'So I gather,' she said.

'Did you want to see him?'

'Is that allowed?'

'It can certainly be arranged, if you want.'

She swallowed. 'I'm not sure I do.'

Thinking back through his conversations with her, Lockyer realized something.

'Your husband wasn't mentioned at Mimi Draper's inquest,' he said. 'And he wasn't named in any of the press releases about her death. We'd never have found out about her if you hadn't mentioned her to me.'

Antigone flicked her harried eyes at him, then away.

'Have you . . . had suspicions about your husband, Mrs Chapman?'

'Are you mad? *No.* Of course not.'

'Then why tell me about Mimi?'

'I just . . . I thought you'd find out. I wanted to explain that it – it wasn't Edward's fault.'

'You were his alibi for the night Mimi died, right? You lied.'

She shook her head wordlessly, but tears were brimming in her eyes and Lockyer saw guilt there. Guilt, fear, indecision. A stubborn refusal to acknowledge something so shameful. His anger flared again. 'You could have saved a lot of people a lot of pain and suffering, Mrs Chapman. You could have saved *lives*.'

'I didn't *know*! I still – I don't *believe* it! He'd never—' The statement ran out of steam.

'I think you know full well that he would. And that he has – killed, that is.'

Another flinch, and after a long pause, she said: 'I remembered ... When you started asking about Greta, I remembered that her friend always used to pick her up for their nights out.'

'But you said nothing?'

'What could I have said? Edward is my *husband*—' She broke off to stifle a sob. 'Our children ... our girls *adore* him. Oh, *God*! How am I ever going to explain this to them?'

It was on the tip of Lockyer's tongue to tell her about the other forty children Edward claimed to have fathered. And that he'd killed at least two of them – Nazma's and Mimi's. But he stopped himself. She'd learn it all, in time, and anger was no excuse for cruelty.

'Have you been frightened of him, Antigone?'

She wiped her nose. 'Frightened of him? Don't be ridiculous. Edward *loves* me – he's always loved me ...'

She trailed off, her gaze turning inwards as she struggled to frame what she was just now finding out. Lockyer remembered something Hedy had said to him, about how Aaron, her ex, had got away with his lies and his scheming. *He'd made me believe that he loved me. That's how he did it. I trusted in him. Completely.* A level of trust that could blind you.

He left Antigone alone with the cold, hard truths she was going to have to live with for the rest of her days. Collected Broad and went back up to their office. When he looked out again several hours later, the Range Rover was still there, Antigone still at the wheel.

Lockyer went alone to Darren Mason's house in Avebury Trusloe. Darren opened the door warily.

'Could I have a quick word?' Lockyer said.

With a resigned nod, Darren led Lockyer away from the door to stand by the garage.

'I need you to come in and make a statement about what you saw in the barn at Trusloe Hall on the night of October second, 1999.'

'What?' Darren said, unconvincingly. 'I don't know what . . .' The words faded into a defeated sort of silence.

'Tell me what you saw there that night.'

'Edward Chapman. I saw him.'

'Right. What was he doing?'

'I dunno. He was going through stuff by the bunks. I saw his torch flashing about from outside, and I knew all of the history lot still kipping there had gone to the Mop. So I went to look.'

'And what happened?'

'When he saw me he legged it. He'd been looking at a bag – like, going through it – but when I showed up he just grabbed it and ran for the other door.'

'What did you do?'

A shrug. 'I watched him go. Made sure he was off the premises. Didn't think nothing of it until you turned up and said you'd found that girl's bag in the river.'

'And instead of coming forward and telling us what you'd

seen – which would've saved us a *lot* of time and effort – you decided to blackmail Chapman.'

Darren looked cagey. 'Yeah. Well. Sorry,' he muttered. 'We needed the money. I mean, we really *needed* it.' His shoulders sagged. 'I suppose we'll have to give it back now, won't we? Are you arresting me? *Fuck!* Nicky's going to kill me – she said this would happen.' He dragged one hand down over his face. 'And I've been straight for bloody *years*.'

His despair was obvious. Lockyer looked at him, and saw the years of hard-scrabble and endeavour, some of it legal, some of it not. A man who'd been dealt a shitty hand in life, and had been doing his best with it ever since. Not always succeeding, but trying.

'You've still got the money?' he said.

Darren looked up. 'Yeah. Apart from a few hundred quid. We needed some things for the baby. Topped up the electric. Trip to the supermarket.'

'You've kept it as cash, and not paid it in anywhere? Anyone seen you with it? Have you told anyone?'

'Told anyone? Are you nuts?'

'Not Inez? Antigone Chapman?'

'No.'

'Nobody but you, your wife and Edward Chapman know about it?'

A nod, and a tentative flicker of hope in Darren's eyes.

'Well, Chapman's facing multiple criminal charges. He's got a lot going on right now, and so have we. I doubt anyone will remind him to press charges against you, and I might forget that you just confirmed his allegation. In all the excitement. As long as you come in and make that state-ment, of course.'

'Are you . . . are you messing with me?'

Lockyer sniffed. 'Nope.'

Darren stared at him, his face a picture of suspicion and relief.

Lockyer handed him Broad's card. 'My DC is really keen to hear how Inez is getting on, and to help, if she can. I'd let her, if I were you.'

Darren put the card in his pocket. 'Thanks,' he said, as Lockyer turned to go.

When Lockyer got home, Hedy wasn't in the house. He went through to the kitchen, and saw her out in the garden. Bundled up, walking her slow laps in the dark, her breath making clouds. Moving carefully, her back clearly painful. *Our bodies do the hard part, and are never the same again – and our brains even more so*, Jody had said. And she was right, of course. That really was just the way it was, so women having the casting vote was simply the natural order of things. Edward Chapman sat at the extreme end of any attempt to pervert that natural order, and Lockyer wanted no part of it. His resentment vanished. There ought to have been full disclosure, yes. There ought to be transparency; but, ultimately, here was a situation in which he couldn't expect to have control. *Get on board, or don't*, Jody had said. And he knew then that he was.

26

Day 24, Wednesday

Mid-morning, Lockyer took a call from one of the MCIT officers who'd taken over the investigation into Edward Chapman. Early the previous day, ground-penetrating radar had revealed the location of a burial in the back garden of another of Chapman's 'empty' properties, in Reading, where a woman called Dina Moyes lived with her three children. Wearing a silver infinity symbol around her neck. The body had been exhumed, and dental records had found a match: Tommy Archer, who'd disappeared in 1989, at the age of twenty-one. Lockyer pulled up her misper file. Found a picture of a skinny, dark-haired girl, holding a red rosette and grinning at the camera from the back of a grey pony. Squinting in the golden sunshine of a stolen youth. A vanished life.

He wondered if she'd tried to run away from Chapman, if she'd refused to bend to his will, like Nazma. Early indications were that Tommy had no next of kin. No remaining family. No home for news of her to be delivered to.

Something about that squeezed Lockyer's heart. She'd had two brothers, but both had died without knowing their sister's fate. There was nobody left to remember what her laugh had sounded like, or the name of her grey pony.

The searches would continue, at every location linked to Edward Chapman, until all hope of finding any others was extinguished. But there would be others. Lockyer was certain of it.

Later, DSU Considine appeared in their doorway, keeping a safe distance.

'This one's going to make a big splash,' she said, from behind her visor. 'And it won't be you two doing the press conferences, or making the headlines.' She gave them each a direct look. 'But *we* all know who caught Chapman. God knows how much longer he'd have carried on if you hadn't lifted the rock he was hiding under.' She left a beat for emphasis. 'Bloody good work, the pair of you.'

'Thank you, ma'am,' Lockyer said, as Broad turned pink.

'Thanks, boss,' she muttered shyly.

With a nod, Considine left them to it.

They exchanged an awkward glance, neither of them comfortable with praise, then went back to their paperwork.

'I forgot to tell you, guv – good news,' Broad said. 'Darren Mason rang me. Inez has agreed to go into sheltered accommodation.'

'Really?'

'Yep. Apparently, she's been having such a lovely time in hospital, with the nurses to keep her company, that she got a whole lot more receptive to the idea. So Darren showed her the brochure of some insanely expensive place near Salisbury – state-of-the-art, blah blah blah – and she can't wait to go and take the tour. She'll have her own apartment, but there's a communal lounge and dining room if she wants company. And staff always on hand. *And* an arts and crafts room.'

Lockyer smiled. 'Sounds perfect. I'm glad.'

'Darren said she doesn't even want to go back to Trusloe Hall. Like, ever. It's going on the market, on the condition that it's sold to a family and not to a chain of leisure clubs.' Broad shrugged a shoulder. 'I think she was only holding on there until we'd found Pippa.'

Lockyer thought about that. 'You could well be right.'

'Oh, and one other thing.' Broad's cheeks blazed. 'I've . . . um . . . moved. Me and Merry. I've stuck the new address on your desk – it's on that Post-it note.'

Lockyer was struck dumb for a moment. 'Oh. Right.' He felt a surge of jubilation, and wondered whether it would be appropriate to congratulate her. He decided not. 'What brought that on?'

Her face tightened. 'You mean apart from all the blindingly obvious stuff?'

Lockyer said nothing.

She took a deep breath, eyes down. 'It was something Chapman said. That thing about engineering an "accidental" pregnancy – about it being a good way to get what he wanted.'

Looking back, Lockyer remembered how pale Broad had gone at the time.

'Right,' he said, not understanding.

'It's just ... You know Pete's been going on about us having a baby?'

'You've mentioned it, yes.'

She hesitated. 'He ... We were having an argument a couple of weeks back, and he ... flushed my pills. You know, *the* pill. I mean, it was blatant. He wasn't sneaky about it. But the ... the intention was the same.' She shook her head. 'Then hearing that evil *bastard* say he'd done something so similar ... That was the final straw, I guess.'

'This far and no further,' Lockyer murmured. 'Are you okay? I can't imagine Pete took it lying down?'

'Actually, guv, he literally did. Didn't get up off the sofa when I came down with my bags. Didn't say a word. Wouldn't even look at me.'

'I guess he knew it was coming.'

She gave a small nod. 'I think we've both known it for ages. And, yes, I am okay. I didn't think I would be, but I am. In fact, I'm *great*.'

'A load off your mind. I imagine.'

'Yes.'

She glanced up, looking exhausted but calm, and Lockyer had a powerful urge to hug her. Instead he cleared his throat, and went back to the paperwork.

In spite of the lockdown, Liz Kirmani invited them in and made them all a cup of tea. Her face was lighter, less tense. Andrew was also there to hear what Lockyer had to say, and sat between his parents on the sofa, clasping his mother's hand tightly. Once they were ready, Lockyer talked them through what had happened to Nazma on the night of October the second, and why. Hari Kirmani sat up straight, his hands braced against his knees, staring at Lockyer with an intensity that bordered on hunger. As though the out-come might turn out to be something other than the one they all knew.

When he'd finished speaking, Lockyer gave them time to take it in, and decide what they wanted to ask.

Hari Kirmani drew in a long, heavy breath. 'So ... it would not have mattered if the police had searched high and low the very next day. Perhaps they would have found her sooner ... but not alive.'

'No,' Lockyer said softly.

'But if they had searched as you have searched, we would have known all of this twenty-one years ago. We would not have had to suffer, as we have suffered.'

'Possibly. But her killer did a very good job of misdirecting the police, Mr Kirmani. They – and the people Nazma was with that night – believed she'd gone to London of her own accord. At which point there was little they could do.'

'If they had listened to us, they would have known it was not true,' he protested quietly.

'Yes. You're right. I'm so sorry, Mr and Mrs Kirmani, Andrew.'

'What will happen to him now? What'll happen to that bastard?' Andrew couldn't bring himself to say Chapman's name.

'He'll go before the magistrate tomorrow morning, and

be remanded in custody until his trial date. And I doubt that he'll ever be released.'

'Good,' Andrew said.

'And there are ... others?' Liz asked. 'Other girls he's killed?'

'Two more that we know about. There may well be more. We'll keep looking, until we're sure.'

'Good,' Hari said sombrely. 'Their families must be told. Even if it is so very terrible to hear.'

Andrew was shaking. 'Why didn't she just *talk* to us about what was going on? If she'd come home instead of going to Marlborough that night ... If she'd come home and we'd *talked* about it ...'

Broad cleared her throat quietly. 'Abusive partners are very good at separating people from their families and friends. Nazma trusted Chapman, and he'd made her keep their relationship a secret. He'd convinced her to hide it from you, and that would have made it very hard for her to confide in you when things started to go wrong. I don't think ... Nazma probably didn't understand the danger she was in. She obviously believed she could handle it herself, and end the relationship. She *can't* have known who Chapman really was, or what he was capable of. And if she had, I'm *sure* she would have come to you.'

Fighting not to cry, Andrew nodded. Liz squeezed his hands tightly.

'Then it was ill luck,' Hari said quietly. 'Ill luck that she was interested in archaeology, and wanted to study it. Ill luck that, of all the work placements she could find, it was with him. With that man. Ill luck that he should . . . choose her.'

'It was the most terrible bad luck,' Lockyer said softly.

Tears made silver tracks down the old man's face. 'When can we bury her?'

'Soon. I'll find out from the coroner when she can be released to you, and let you know.'

'I am finding it very hard to thank you,' Hari said. 'The words won't come – perhaps it is too soon to be grateful for anything. But I do know what you have done. You two have brought Nazma home to us, and ended the pain of not knowing. And one day, I am sure, I will be grateful.'

'We don't need to be thanked, Mr Kirmani,' Lockyer said. 'But I hope you can forgive us – forgive the police – for taking so long to find her.'

Mr Kirmani blotted his face with a handkerchief and looked Lockyer in the eye. 'Perhaps, in time, that too will come,' he said.

Outside, Broad heaved a sigh. There was nothing to say. The relief of knowing, and the satisfaction of justice, could only ever be bittersweet if the loved one was still gone. If they were never coming home. Lockyer pulled in at a pub on the way back to Devizes, and they went in for something to eat.

'At least now they have answers, I guess,' Broad said eventually.

Lockyer nodded. 'It's like something Jase said to me recently. Time can't heal if things don't feel finished.'

At the mention of Jason McNeil, Broad stiffened, and

Lockyer kicked himself for putting his foot in it again. She reached for a chip and dipped it in ketchup. Ate it in thoughtful silence.

'You never heard back from Jase about whatever it was he wanted to tell you?' she said.

'No,' Lockyer said. 'I've been wondering about going to see him. Sounded like it could have been something big, so maybe I was wrong to tell him to leave it.'

'Maybe, maybe not,' Broad said. 'Sometimes it's better to let sleeping dogs lie.'

'That's true. The last time someone wanted to confess something to me, it was a body buried out in the woods,' Lockyer said. Attempting to start joking with her about his shambolic handling of Iris Musprat's dark past, earlier that year.

Broad pulled a face. 'Too soon,' she said. Then fell serious. 'You don't think Jase was involved in anything *that* bad?'

'I don't know. But his family was mixed up in some pretty serious shit. His brother died in a knife attack, too, don't forget.'

Broad eyed him carefully. 'Yeah. I remember.'

Lockyer frowned, remembering something else Jason had said the night he'd come to Lockyer's place: *I just . . . ran away. Saw something one night, when I was out with them all, and there was a rumble, and something in my head said: Run.*

'What is it, guv?'

He shook his head. 'Nothing. Eat up, we'd better make tracks.'

But Lockyer was distracted by lingering doubts all

afternoon, thinking about the things Jason had said that rainy night he'd come to visit. The way he'd reacted when they'd discussed Chris the time before – the how and when of his death. Leaving abruptly, with his cup of tea barely touched. You never knew with Jason. His synaesthesia, and the things he'd been through, made his reactions unpredictable at times. Still, Lockyer couldn't quieten his sudden unease. He remembered how reluctant Jason had been to have his DNA and fingerprints taken during the Holly Gilbert case that summer. In the end, nothing had flagged up on the system. But perhaps Jason had *expected* something to flag up . . .

Eventually, Lockyer gave up trying to ignore the thread he'd started to pull. He opened the file from the investigation into Holly's death, and found the transcripts of their interviews with Jason McNeil. Read through until he found a section that made his stomach clench.

DI LOCKYER: *We were concerned you might have gone on the run.*

RESPONSE: *I'm done running.*

DI LOCKYER: *Have you got something to tell us?*

RESPONSE: *No. I – I just meant, that's how I got to Old Hat Farm in the first place. Running away.*

DC BROAD: *How did you find it?*

RESPONSE: *I walked.*

DC BROAD: *From Swindon?*

RESPONSE: *No, we were in Chippenham the night I decided to go.*

Lockyer was still staring at the screen when his mobile rang. So fixated that he didn't hear it.

'Guv,' Broad said eventually, as it cut off and immediately started ringing again.

'Hm? Oh.' He saw Hedy's number on the screen and fumbled to pick it up. 'Hedy? You okay?'

'I think so,' she said breathlessly. 'I'm in a taxi, again. Going to hospital.'

Lockyer went cold. 'What's happened? Is it the baby? Is something wrong?'

'Well, yes, it is the baby. But I don't think there's anything wrong, it's just . . . on its way.'

Lockyer's mind went blank.

'Matt? Are you still there?'

'It's coming? But it's not due for another two weeks.'

'Well, I guess it misread the schedule,' she said. 'So . . . think you might like to pop along to the hospital?'

'Yes. Christ. Yes. I'm on my way.' He rang off.

'Want me to drive you?' Broad said. 'You look a bit . . . distracted, guv.'

He was standing stock still by his desk, temporarily paralysed by the shock of it. A few more hours might pass, but then he would be a father. For the rest of his life. Nerves surged up into his throat. He felt sick.

'No. I'm good,' he lied. 'I'll be fine. But thanks, Gem.'

27

Day 26, Friday

Lockyer hadn't been allowed to see Hedy when he'd first arrived at the hospital. He'd had to sit and wait for her WhatsApp updates, so he had some warning when she was finally taken into the delivery room, where he was permitted to join her. By that time she'd been drenched in sweat and full of fear, eyes unfocused, so consumed by what was going on inside her body that she'd seemed barely to register his presence. But the final stages of labour had progressed quickly, without a hitch, and then they had a daughter. Small, pink, angry, perfect.

'And what's this little one's name?' asked the midwife, in the scant moments Lockyer was allowed to stay with them before they were to be taken onto the neonatal ward. Lockyer and Hedy exchanged a look. Her expression was raw, open, full of love – for their child, but also for him. It was the first time Lockyer had been certain of what she felt.

'We don't know,' she said.

'Tommy,' Lockyer said.

'Tommy?' Hedy echoed.

'Short for Thomasina? Or Tamsin?' the midwife said.

'No. Just Tommy,' Lockyer said.

Hedy considered it for a moment, looking down at the scrunched-up face in the crook of her arm. 'I think you're right,' she said. 'Hello, Tommy.'

'Can I hold her? Before they whisk you away?' Lockyer said.

'Sure.' Hedy didn't sound at all sure, and the transfer of the baby into Lockyer's arms was done with extreme care.

So small, so light. It beggared belief that all the various bits and bobs a human needed to survive could fit into such a tiny body. Lockyer marvelled at it, as a wave of love and terror rushed through him – an all new understanding that here was a person to whom he must never, *ever* allow harm to come. 'When we went to Seend, and I said that I might be at my most happy, I was wrong,' he said. 'But now I am.'

Hedy smiled. Unguardedly.

'Right, we'd better shift you, I'm afraid. Got people queuing up out there,' the midwife said.

'Come back and get us first thing tomorrow,' Hedy instructed.

'Best to wait until the doctors are happy to discharge you, then give him a ring,' the midwife suggested, but Hedy shook her head.

'We're not staying here a *second* longer than we have to. I want to take her home.'

Lockyer sat in a public area for a while afterwards,

gathering his wits. *Home*, she'd said. Meaning his place. Their place.

Lockyer brought his small family home in the dying days of November, and a series of long, ecstatic video calls began, with both sets of new grandparents and the few friends Hedy still had after her long stay in prison. On the second of December the lockdown would end and they'd all be able to visit, but nobody seemed willing to wait.

During one long conversation Hedy was having with his mother, Lockyer got a call from Jody.

'Thought I'd see how you were doing, since everyone's so busy frothing over the kid,' she said, with a subtle roll of her eyes. 'You good? Not lost your shit, yet?'

'Not yet. Probably will, at some point,' he said.

'Mad, isn't it? One minute there's just a weirdly swollen-up woman, the next there's a whole new person in the room.'

'It is properly bizarre.'

'Yeah, well, don't worry. You'll soon be too knackered to wonder about it. Or about anything else.'

'That's reassuring.'

'Happy to help.' She smiled facetiously, holding the phone close so that her face filled the screen. Deep brown eyes, and the no-nonsense set of her mouth. 'Tommy's a good name. I was worried the Duchess was going to opt for something puke-inducingly twee.'

'Well, I'm glad you approve. Actually, I came up with it.'

'Yeah?'

'I happened to hear it, and liked it.' He wondered whether to say more. 'There was— The killer we've just caught . . . One of his victims was a girl called Tommy Archer. I saw her picture. She looked like a good kid, full of beans. No family, though. It took us so long to find her that there was nobody left to remember her.'

Jody's eyes gleamed. She blinked. 'Shit, Matt,' she said. 'I mean, yeah. That's lovely. I wouldn't tell her, though. Hedy. She's going to get her heart broken at least twice a day for the rest of her life. No need to start with that.'

'Yeah. Maybe you're right.'

Jody rubbed her eyes furiously for a moment. 'Course I'm right. But you were right about something, too.'

'I'm stunned. What was it?'

'I should've told Danny's dad. Should've given him the chance to know his kid.'

Lockyer wasn't sure what to say, and Jody sighed, suddenly sounding so sad that he was taken aback. 'Jody, are you—'

'Yep. Congratulations, Matt. To you both. I hope . . . I hope you'll be really happy together.'

She cut the call.

Lockyer did a supermarket run as the light was failing, piling the trolley with alien things from the mother-and-baby aisle, and with food that would be quick and easy to prepare. When he got back to the house the frost was setting. His breath clouded in the still air, and the puddles along the driveway all had thin crusts of ice. Lockyer peered in through the living-room window and saw Iris Musprat sitting on his sofa, Tommy cradled in her arms and Hedy hovering beside her. The old lady was wearing a helpless sort of expression, and Lockyer realized it might be the first time he'd ever seen her smile. He watched in silence for a second, then went back to unpack the car.

Movement in the darkness caught his eye.

Someone was approaching up the track, silently, on foot. Lockyer's pulse jumped, but then the figure stepped into the light and he recognized Jason McNeil. His moment of relief was quickly replaced by unease. He put down the plastic bags he'd been holding. Closed the boot of the car. Jason stopped about six feet away, and stood watching him. Anxiety sang from every line of his face. He was underdressed for the cold, and shivering. Lockyer waited.

'Your lady's had the baby?' Jason said, seeing the big bag of nappies by Lockyer's feet.

He nodded. 'A daughter. Tommy.'

'I'm happy for you, man,' Jason said. His face shifted, as though struggling with something inside. 'I wouldn't have come if I'd— I'll . . . I'll go.' He turned to leave.

'Jason, wait!' Lockyer said. His mouth had gone dry. 'You were there that night. Weren't you? That's what you've been trying to tell me. You were in Chippenham the night my brother died.'

Jason gave a single unsteady nod.

Lockyer's head rang with a hollow sound. 'Did you see what happened?'

Another nod.

ACKNOWLEDGEMENTS

My sincere thanks to Police Constable Charlotte Sartin and Police Sergeant William Monk, of Wiltshire Police, for being willing to answer my questions, discuss their work, and plug my work in the very highest circles . . .

As ever, I am so grateful to Jane Wood, Florence Hare and the whole team at Quercus Books for their passion, skill and dedication. DI Lockyer could not be in better hands! Huge thanks to my agent, Mark Lucas, for bringing all his wisdom and insight to bear in getting the very best from my books; and to brilliant fellow authors, Kate Riordan, Mimi Hall, Vanessa de Haan and Hannah Richell, for being supportive, suitably cynical, and endlessly inspiring.

Last but never least, thank you, James, for all that you do.